MOST LIKELY
TO SUCCEED

John Dos Passos'
Contemporary Chronicles

Chosen Country

Three Soldiers

Manhattan Transfer

U.S.A.
The 42nd Parallel
Nineteen Nineteen
The Big Money

Most Likely to Succeed

District of Columbia
Adventures of a Young Man
Number One
The Grand Design

The Great Days

Midcentury

MOST LIKELY TO SUCCEED

John Dos Passos

HOUGHTON MIFFLIN COMPANY BOSTON
The Riverside Press Cambridge
1966

First Printing   c

Copyright © 1954 by John Dos Passos
All rights reserved including the right to
reproduce this book or parts thereof in any form
Library of Congress Catalog Card Number: 66-17513

This book was first published in 1954 by
Prentice-Hall, Inc. Portions of it had previously
appeared in *Esquire* magazine.

Printed in the United States of America

CONTENTS

MOROCCO

It was quiet and airy in the drawingroom of Suite A. Through the window came the salt Atlantic reek and the crunch of broken water as the great hull slid through the swells westward. Jed, tipping back the chair to look in her eyes as he talked, could feel the rumble of turbines from the engineroom in the deck under his feet. Her light head jiggled in the trepidation of the liner's twentyseven knots. Her eyes were dark blue between her dark lashes, or were they violet? They sat staring at each other.

"If we ever did get to know each other," she was saying, biting each word off with her little sharp teeth, "you'd know I hated bad grammar."

"Ain't is perfectly good grammar. Shakespeare said ain't. Do you want me to prove it to you? . . . Now as for the fingernails," he went on with his most schoolboy smile, "what can you expect from a steerage passenger?"

"Go on with the story." She crossed her legs, took out a cigarette and tapped it on her striped cigarettecase.

"There I was flat as a flounder in Tangier of all places,

3

when the cable came Adolph Baum was ready to back a new play . . . Wait till I tell you about Tangier . . . Tangier in this year of grace 1926 . . . So I said to myself I'll cable 'em for an advance to see if they are serious. Quick as a flash there came a cable back with five hundred dollars on the Crédit Lyonnais. I jumped into the mail plane and started home . . . Golly that was a cold ride." Jed threw his head back and laughed until the tears came to his eyes. She was looking at him as if she didn't know whether to laugh or not. "You'd laugh too if you knew what a flop my last play was; *Flight from the Sun;* I don't suppose you saw it."

She shook her head. "I was in Santa Barbara last winter."

"Flight from the boxoffice was more like it . . ." he got to laughing so the chair started to topple over backwards. He made an upward jump like a fish and landed on his feet with the chair in his hand. "That's one of my best tricks," he was bowing in various directions.

"Legs aren't long enough," she said. He winced visibly. "And please don't make so much noise. You aren't supposed to be here." She had begun to titter behind her cigarette.

"Merely a waif from the steerage . . . It's an experience I thought I needed."

"It's not that. It's that young women traveling alone aren't supposed to entertain strange men," she was saying in a voice he identified as her mother's chaperone voice.

"I promise you I won't be strange long."

His voice sounded almost too boyish.

She let her lips soften into a very small smile: "How on earth did you get to know Adolph Baum?"

He walked over to the table under the mirror where a champagne bottle stretched its gilt neck out of its whitemetal pail. As he leaned over her to fill her glass, his eyes followed the tan down her smooth cheek past the slender shaded curve

4

of her neck until it disappeared in the dark of the V of her plain ivorycolored eveningdress . . . Tanned all over; that kind of a girl, he told himself. Antibes, probably. His golden girl; would it be too bromidic to call her that? . . . A flush of high spirits mounted to his head quite separate from the bubbles of the Widow Clicquot.

"To tell the truth," he said and poured a fizzy splash into his own glass, "I don't know him from Adam . . . He's obviously an intelligent man even if he is a millionaire . . . He must have seen *Flight* and liked it so he's now backing this outfit to produce a new one." He raised his glass, looked her smirking in the eye, and clicked his heels: "I give you Adolph Baum." He plunked himself down on the couch beside her. "The joke is," he said exploding with laughter again, "that I've got a play all ready . . . I had it all fixed up to go across the mountains and interview Abd-el-Krim but I wrote a play about him instead. I'd sworn off plays, see . . . Broadway, the interests, commercialism . . . I'd decided I wouldn't try to buck Broadway any more, I'd be a foreign correspondent. But what did I do in Tangier when I got broke? I sat down and wrote a play, and then comes this bombshell from Adolph Baum and buying my play sight unseen for this new organization, The Craftsman's Theatre . . . Of course I should have taken a look at Abd-el-Krim but it would have meant riding a mule for days across those damned mountains. I don't like mules and mules don't like me . . . What was the use? I had my plot and my characters, even the stage-set, more atmosphere than I could use. I don't believe too much in atmosphere. And I was tired, emotionally tired, see? A man gets tired bucking the interests. That's what I've been doing all my life, bucking the commercial interests."

His eyes sought out hers and found them. He felt his eyes had a hurt look; she was softening; he sighed.

"It's been a strenuous summer. First this damn play flopped. Mind you it was an artistic success, or Adolph Baum wouldn't have been so crazy about it. All the critics said so . . . And then I kept waking up and finding myself in bed with some woman. There was a Spanish girl in Tlemcen who wore her hair a little like yours. She said she used camomile but she was only a common prostitute."

"Aren't you a little bit too frank for a stranger?"

"But I don't want to be a stranger. My name as I said before is J. E. D. Morris. People call me Jed."

She opened her eyes wide for once: "I've seen that name. I saw it on a billboard."

"See, I'm no stranger. What's yours?"

"Jane Marlowe . . . Never mind my husband's name."

"I'll call you Marlowe, that's a golden name. Jane's too much like June. June's my wife's name."

"An adulterer, eh?"

"Consummate . . ." He stared hard in her face and started laughing again. She couldn't help laughing too, just a little bit. "No but I'm getting a divorce." His voice had an explanatory whine. "Last spring everything went to hell in a hack."

"I just got a divorce myself . . . I'm not telling you my ex's name. You'll find it on the passenger list."

"The story is I'm going to marry a girl named Felicia . . See, I believe in complete honesty between the sexes."

He tried to snuggle up to her on the couch. She drew herself up into her dress.

"It started out to be such a dull crossing." She yawned and stretched a little. "The captain insisted I sit at his table."

He went back to the champagne bottle and poured them each another glass. She sat with her legs crossed and looked up with her eyes round and friendly.

6

"It's fun to find somebody to act silly with."

"We live in a silly time. Morality has lost all meaning, thank God . . . I learned that during the war. Ever heard of Dada?"

She pulled in her lips and shook her light curls.

"Well that was how my summer began . . ." He was started on his story: he was talking his head off and she loved it . . . He had been sitting in Paris gloomy as hell at a sidewalk café. Homesick; missed June, even if she was a peasant; missed his little daughter Mae. It wasn't that he didn't love his wife and daughter, see? He was just one of those people who ought to be a Mohammedan. His father was a Baha'ist, that was the nearest thing to it. He must tell her about J.E. He'd been converted to Baha'ism by Jed's godfather Laughlin Davidson, a famous old Scot, the *Manchester Guardian* correspondent, no she wouldn't know. Anyway, he was J.E.'s best friend. That was how the D. got into Jed's name . . . Well there he was sitting in Paris in the spring when the horsechestnuts were in bloom and the streets all smelt of lingerie. Homesick, needed a woman, he was sitting there feeling absolutely horrible, see? when who should come walking down the Champs Elysées but Bob Dunlap, funniest man in the world, carrying a gilt birdcage in his hand with an artificial bird in it. It wasn't artificial. It was stuffed. It had real feathers. Naturally Bob Dunlap sat down and had a drink and Bob Dunlap wound the bird up so it sang and all the people at the café thought that was great. Bob Dunlap could get fun out of a funeral. Well, it turned out Bob had a date with a poet, a French poet, but he didn't know any French. Couldn't even read the address. Jed didn't know much French either, couldn't even talk English good on account of being brought up in Noo York, see, but when the spirit was in him, cognac

7

or good scotch whisky, Jed could make himself understood to beat hell, like the apostles after Pentecost.

"How do you know about Pentecost?" she asked abruptly. He could see she was trying to find out whether he was Jewish.

"My mother was an Episcopalian," he heard himself say in a triumphant tone that immediately jarred on his ears. "It was only after Mother died that J.E. went whoring after strange gods." But she mustn't get him wrong, he hastened to add, J.E. was a saint, see? He'd tell her about J.E. . . . Anyway that night they drank le squotche when they got to this other café and there they found all these poets, fat poets and thin poets, tall poets and small poets, all very formally dressed and serious as hell. It was une manifestation Dada. "I tell you they were serious about being silly." Bob made a great hit with his artificial bird, but Bob and Jed they kind of got in wrong because they got to laughing so. What was the use of getting drunk if things didn't get funny? Except the little guy who was the head of them, he thought they were funny just because they were Americans. "He's all set to marry a rich American girl."

"Another rich bitch," she said in an acid tone.

"Who said that?"

"That's what you were thinking. Didn't you know I was psychic?"

"I wasn't thinking it meanly. A man has to make his classifications."

. . . Well anyway they had gone around to various bars and nightclubs and a maison publique; she knew the Parisian tour, it was always the same, and Bob and Jed had to pay all the bills. She knew the way the French were . . . Jed's voice had become ingratiating even to his own ears . . . Of course Bob couldn't understand a word anybody said as he'd never

8

been in Paris before so he thought everything was funny as a crutch. But Lord they were tired by two A.M.

The last thing they did was to parade through a Turkish bath. It had started to rain like it always did in Paris and Bob had bought a lot of umbrellas from a hatcheck girl at a nightclub. He'd paid through the nose for them but Bob was flush, see, he'd just published a very funny book and of course the exchange was wonderful; so the last thing they did . . . they had a lot of hangers-on by that time, des individus louches, like they say in the French papers . . . Well they'd opened up all of Bob's umbrellas and Bob led the way with this artificial bird and they paraded through the Turkish bath criticizing the physique of the bathers. Any place else they would have been in for a fight but she knew how the French were about a manifestation artistique. The whole thing began to take on a light flavor of pederasty that made Bob and Jed kind of sick so Bob and Jed, they crashed out of the joint with the artificial bird and a gigantic Russian, a big pale silent man just like a polar bear. All the French he seemed to know was "Moi peintre russe," but it worked. They thought hell this is France and they stopped to take a leak, see, in a back alley and first thing you know the gendarmes were leading them off to the hoosegow— des pisseurs—and Bob wanted to put up a fight, but this Russian he held Bob's arms with a bearlike hug and he kept saying "Moi peintre russe" and made such a speech in Russian . . . He said afterwards it was a poem by Pushkin about a mechanical bird, Jed guessed it was something like "The Emperor's Nightingale"; but anyway he distributed around a few more of Bob's hundred franc notes . . . And Jed wound up the bird and the gendarmes listened appreciatively and said, "Que voulez-vous?" and let them go. Well the peintre russe said they had to show Vera the bird so they

9

walked more miles in the rain. Their feet were wet and the bird was wet. Bob was so tired he got to hobbling on two umbrellas like a cripple. Then they took a cab.

They walked up about a thousand stairs and there was a big scrawny Russian woman in a dirty blouse painting on an enormous canvas by candlelight and Bob wound up the bird and it sang and she clapped her hands like a child and made them take their wet shoes off and made tea and pancakes for them and Bob went to sleep on the couch and Vera turned out to be just the nicest woman you ever saw; she knew French and a little English. Jed had a long talk with her over Bob's sleeping form about the theatre and the threedimensional stage. Cut out the proscenium arch, bring the drama into the middle of the audience, see? That's what Jed had always wanted to do. Of course in Germany and Russia they'd been doing it for years. "What do you suppose Vera was doing? She was painting scenery for the Ballet Russe . . . That began the greatest educational period in my life."

"That was the ballet that caused such a riot."

"Sure people rioted because it was real. It was drama. It moved them . . . Say how about a little more of that high grade gigglewater?"

Marlowe was stretched out behind him on the couch with her head on her hand. The sleeve fell away from her brown arm as she reached for the bell above her head.

"And cast discretion to the winds," she said.

Jed caught a flash in her eyes. He leaned over and kissed her. She pushed him away but not too hard.

When the steward came Jed couldn't help the triumphant sweep to his arm as he pulled open the door. The steward was a sallow browneyed little man about Jed's own height. He brought in with him a greasy pantry smell. "A votre service, 'sieur . . . madame." He must wonder, thought

Jed, but the steward didn't seem the slightest bit interested. Marlowe in crisp French ordered another bottle of the same. "Et bien frappé, n'est-ce pas mon vieux," added Jed fussily with a brotherly smile. Something made him want to explain to the steward that he was really traveling steerage, that he was a dramatist, an artist, a working man himself, and that he had crashed the first class bar and picked up a rich bitch. It was adventure on the high seas and he was planning to go to bed with her. The steward had already padded softly out carrying off the whitemetal bucket with the bottle upside down in it. "My poor friend, your accent," she let out a wail.

"It's Berlitz's best," he answered cheerfully. He felt that she'd weakened. He was on top of the world.

This time she let him sit down close to her on the couch. She wore a delightful light expensive-smelling perfume, something like morocco leather, a tanned, seabeach perfume, he told himself. "After all we can't be compromised, we're both of us half divorced," he said with his lips close to her ear. "My golden girl," he whispered as he kissed her under the ear. "How did you come to speak French so prettily?"

"Parents put me in a convent. Don't rake that up." The muscles of her neck hardened under his lips. She got to her feet. "Go on with the story. I don't believe a word of it."

"I helped 'em paint the scenery. For three weeks I was one of 'em."

"Weren't they all bolsheviks at heart?" she asked with a yawn. No he wished they had been but they were white Russians, all very religious. He'd been brought up religious, so he could understand that sort of thing. If they'd been red Russians it would have been even more interesting.

"Why?" she asked.

At that moment the steward knocked again. Jed had been imagining himself creeping out of bed when the steward came back and going to the door with his shirt unbuttoned and his hair all rumpled and getting a knowing fraternal look as he took the bucket from him through the crack. But it was too soon. There wasn't any reason yet for not letting the little man come in and with two grubby thumbs push the cork pop off the bottle and swaddle the bottle in a napkin and pour the champagne into the glasses. "Des sandwiches," Jed heard himself saying. "In a little while we are going to need des sandwiches." Marlowe nodded gravely from her seat on the couch. "Bon," said the steward.

"They do dance well," she was saying as the door closed, cradling her glass in her two slender hands.

"You saw 'em?"

She nodded over her glass looking at him with narrow teasing eyes. He found himself launched on a speech. He was talking too much but he couldn't help it. He was trying to tell her how the music stripped the dress suits and conventions and the evening gowns and the prejudices and the rouge and the tawdry jewelry off the middleaged capitalists and their women folk sitting broadbottomed in plush seats and snatched out of their bourgeois lives something basic and primeval and set it to stepping to an ageless dance of the change of the seasons and the fertilizing of the soil and the planting of the seed down in the deep womb of the earth and the thawing waters of spring and sex bursting all maidenheads. Jed could hardly believe his own ears he was so eloquent.

Her eyes really were wide open now.

"It's a goddam revolution," he shouted. That was what Bob Dunlap said when Jed met him pitching down the red-carpeted stairs in a silk hat after the first act among the excited people rushing out of the theatre as if the place were on fire.

12

"That's what the halfvirgins of the fashionable world can't understand," he added in a tremulous voice. "We are living a revolution that destroys and renovates all the forms of man's life on earth. It's not a matter of statistics or economics or better wages here or less profits there. You are either on the side of life breaking out of the cocoon of a dead society or else you are on the side of sterile exploitation and paralysis and death."

"Rum romanism and rebellion," she said, ineptly he thought. "Hurray!"

"It's like birth. New societies are born in blood and misery and revolution!"

The little steward was back holding up a large platter of sandwiches. From something in his eye, Jed knew he had caught the last word. Jed walked over to the little man—he wasn't quite as tall as Jed was—and took the platter of sandwiches out of his hand. "Merci camarade," he said, trying to give the word the gruff throaty sound he'd heard years ago when he was working for the Red Cross and had been penned in a doorway in some industrial section of Paris with a group of angry working men by a charge of the garde républicaine during the Mayday riots.

There was no change in the steward's dead pan. "Any udder leetle ting?" he asked, in mangled English. Jed stuffed a blue banknote into his hand. Jed wanted him to understand that he too was one of the proletariat. Jed fancied the little man's eyelashes quivered in a trace of a wink as he backed out of the room. He turned toward Marlowe with a sandwich in his hand; easy does it, an admonishing voice was saying inside his head.

"Close the window," she said. They were suddenly both quite tense.

Outside the wind had freshened. The roar of displaced

13

air was muffled when he slid the heavy glass to. He closed the inner shutter and stood looking at her. Under his feet he could feel an occasional disconcerting movement as the liner pitched ever so slightly in the rising sea. No, he wasn't going to be seasick, the movement just made everything a little giddy.

Marlowe sat there looking remarkably selfpossessed. She'd pulled her feet under her on the couch. Her jaws moved as she took little bites on a sandwich. She motioned to a place beside her. He didn't lose any time gulping his sandwich and sitting down. The fingers of her free hand moved just for a second through his hair. Now he was glad it was curly.

"You've got nice hair," she said. "I was afraid it would be greasy." He couldn't help the start; she noticed it. "Up there in the bar, you know," she added almost gently, "we said we'd be absolutely frank."

He burst out laughing. "To be absolutely frank," he said, "you are the most adorable rich bitch."

"Tell me Jed," she started to stroke his head again, "how on earth did you get tangled up with Adolph Baum? I've met Adolph Baum."

"All I know is that he's elderly rich and philanthropic . . . Must be Eli Soltair got him interested in my plays. He's my best friend. He signed the cable. You know he wrote *Hobo*. He's a very promising young playwright."

"So are you?"

She pulled his face toward hers. He kissed her.

"That was nice," she said. "Tell me Jed where did you go to college?" His arm had been round her waist for some time now. His hand was under her armpit. His fingers were stretching toward her breast.

"I was voted the most likely to succeed," he said. "J.E. wanted me to go to a country college. He is a great believer in the wholesome influence of the country, see? He believed in country life because he'd never had any. After my mother died we always lived in hotels. There was just J.E. and me. J.E. always said it was from my mother I inherited my love for the theatre . . . I'll have to admit that from an early age my love of the theatre was chiefly directed toward the musical comedy chorus."

When she laughed he could feel her ribs move against his. She was laughing with him.

"How old were you then?"

"Oh about sixteen. At school I was considered precocious. I discovered early that it wasn't impossible to introduce young ladies into New York hotel bedrooms. A little blonde in one of the early Ziegfeld shows put me through my freshman course. My she was a nice girl. She really was good, treated me like a kid brother, except in certain particulars."

"When I was in that dumb convent I used to dream of running away and going on the stage," murmured Marlowe.

"Let's," said Jed putting his mouth to hers. Already they were stretched out on the couch. His leg was between her legs.

When she finally looked at her tiny platinum wristwatch she cried out, "Oh it's four A.M. . . . Jed you'd better go back to your stateroom wherever it is." Her voice was sleepy.

"It's in the third class. I told you. Or do you think I'm a stowaway?"

"One never knows what to believe." She yawned.

"Anyway we've got three more days," he said in a practical tone as he sat on the edge of the couch tieing his shoelaces.

"You won't like me when you get to know me." She yawned again. "Maybe you'd better not come back."

"You haven't heard my Tangier story yet . . . I'll meet you in the bar at twelve noon."

"Suppose we make it the third class bar."

"All right if you want to go slumming."

"I love slumming," she murmured with her eyes closed. "Now I am sleepy."

"It won't do you any good to stand me up. I'll be up here after you, see?" He leant over to kiss her again. He felt quite lightheaded. "You smell so wholesome," he whispered, his lips so close they brushed hers. "That's why J.E. wanted me to go to a country college."

"I am an outdoor girl. How's your doubles?"

"As a tennis player I'm some playwright."

The minute the door closed behind him, the click of the bolt gave him the feeling of being locked out. He stood there in the paneled passageway dazedly feeling for a match in the pocket of the flannel blazer he'd bought in that expensive English shop in Cannes. He didn't know when he'd put the cigarette in his mouth. Damn he'd forgotten his necktie. She must be awful rich. He was still giddy from that morocco leather perfume. His nostrils were full of her. His lips still tasted her. The word doubles had stuck in his head. Maybe Marlowe was the girl he ought to marry.

When he lit the cigarette it had a rank taste from the smell of the ship and the seadrenched air. All keyed up, try- ing to remember how he had come, he strode down rubber- tiled corridors, through empty salons, down broad mahogany companionways. He didn't dare take the elevator for fear the operator would ask him where he was going. He was con- fused. His ears were full of the hollow hum of the huge hull pushing through dark and wind and haycock seas. They must

16

be running into a gale. He didn't know whether he was walking forward or aft. In a hot passage that shook with machinery hissing and banging behind the partitions he tripped over the high sill of a compartment door and fell headlong into a steward who started to grumble that it was forbidden for passengers to unclass themselves. He was rapidly mollified by a blue banknote, and led Jed off through passages that shook with the pounding of the propellers, until with a gruff voilà he left him at the end of the airless vestibule that led to his cubicle.

Amid the snores and groans and the stale breath of his cabinmates Jed tore off his clothes and climbed into his narrow bunk that smelt of closed-up laundry baskets. He was luxuriously tired. This was his favorite role, he told himself happily: the slum child who wins the golden girl. He lay with his eyes closed. "When I love 'em they stay loved," he was saying happily to himself. He was in a hurry to go to sleep so that he would wake up and it would be tomorrow.

When Jed woke up the cubicle smelt of puke. The learned little Lithuanian rabbi he had been planning to get to know must have thrown up again. His cabinmates had all gone out. It was past eleven. Too late for breakfast. He picked out his best checked sport shirt and ran his finger down the press of his gunmetal gray flannels. He shaved very carefully, and examined his brown eyes and his thick brows in the mirror as he lathered his chin, where a few dark bristles persisted, for the third time.

An honest face, somebody had told him: except for the eyes. They popped out too much. He got a little crosseyed when he was excited. Felicia used to tell him he had the eyes of a mad monk.

Oh Lord Felicia. For a second he had the illusion that Felicia tall blonde and amused stood beside him looking into the mirror over his shoulder. He pushed the picture out of sight and tried to fill his memory with Marlowe.

Marlowe had changed everything. He'd have to put off the conversations with other third class passengers he'd planned the way a tourist plans excursions to various places in the environs for sightseeing. The Scandinavian girl with braided hair, the tawny little wop in purple corduroys who had lost three fingers from one hand. The English couple with starched faces who must be a parlormaid and butler. The East of Europe characters with too large eyes and too expressive lips. He'd have to put it all off now. Some other trip. Marlowe was the attraction now.

He washed his face and hurried to the bar. The place smelt of spilt beer. Every seat was taken. My what a lot of dead cats. He'd been planning to have himself a time telling stories about them to Marlowe, but now that he looked at them he thought he'd never seen such stuffy-looking people in his life. Marlowe would find it all too boring. She'd come hoping for bandits and bootleggers and international spies.

The clock said a quarter to twelve. Already the passengers were making their dreary way to the dining saloon. Jed sat down at a warm seat at a freshly emptied table. Among the stale beer glasses, somebody had left a pack of cards. He shuffled them drearily. Of course she would be late. She was that kind. With his eyes on the clock above the bar, Jed sat drinking sour coffee. He forgot himself rehearsing the Tangier story. Suddenly he found himself noticing the clock's blank face. It was twelve twentyfive and Marlowe hadn't come. The barman was closing the door of the closet where he kept his liquor. Wouldn't open till two. Well serve her right.

It wasn't till ten minutes past one that Jed admitted to himself that she wasn't going to come. He got to his feet and

18

walked up and down the vestibule glancing from time to time in through the glass doors at the passengers hunched sordidly over their fodder at the long tables. Oh the hell with this, he told himself. He still had three hundred dollars in his wallet he'd been keeping for his expenses during rehearsals in New York.

He went straight to the purser's office. On a fluke it was open. He wanted to unclass himself, he explained in slow discordant French. Were there any first class accommodations left? The waxyfaced assistant purser had a mouth moulded into a perpetual sneer. He answered in insultingly bad English. Jed found himself explaining volubly in Berlitz's best that he was a man of letters, a playwright, that he'd taken the third class passage merely for the experience. Now he needed a room to himself so that he could work up his impressions.

The assistant purser shrugged. He did consent to call the first class office. When he came back to the wicket he was rubbing his thumb and forefinger together. Monsieur would have to pay the full extra fare from the port of departure, he announced triumphantly. He looked disappointed when Jed brought out his roll of green and orange bills.

A half an hour later Jed had packed his bag and shot up in the elevator to a large inside room in the first class. In his hand he had a first class passenger list. Mrs. Jane M. Tompkins, that must be the name. He remembered the initials from an alligator traincase that fell off the end of the couch. Tompkins . . . there was somebody very rich named Tompkins.

Even before tipping the steward for bringing up his bags he'd called over the white enameled telephone to her suite. No answer. He ranged wildly round the decks looking into the faces of women in deckchairs. He walked through the salons and writing rooms. He gave a quick glance round the library. He walked through the gymnasium and looked down from the gallery into the empty swimmingpool. As he passed he craned his neck to see into the ladies' hairdressing parlor.

Several times he knocked on the door of Suite A. He even tried the knob but it was locked. You damn fool she's eating lunch. He looked into the main restaurant and the children's dining room. Plenty goodlooking women: blonde women, dark women, curly women, smooth women but no Marlowe. She's eating lunch with somebody, in some man's suite. The jealous pains were like a jabbing toothache.

At last when he had given up hope, there she was wearing a little pâtisserie hat all alone in the Ritz restaurant at a table for two. She looked bored and lonesome, thank God. Jed slipped around the coattails of an officious headwaiter.

"Mind if I sit here?" he asked. "There don't seem to be room anywhere else." He pointed to the ranks of empty tables.

"Doesn't is preferable," she said, showing her little sharp opinionated teeth; but she did give him a smile. "How did you ever get up here again?"

It was a tiny straw hat like an apricot tart, pitched forward a little. She'd put it on for him.

"Rubbed the magic lamp," said Jed all glowing.

"Do you know what I did? I went down to the cabin class bar. I never dreamed there were even lower depths. I thought I'd never get back. I expected they would send me to a home for wayward girls."

"Marlowe," said Jed, brandishing the bill of fare, "you are lunching with me. What do you think of hors d'oeuvres, Chateaubriand with soufflé potatoes and some champagne cocktails while they ice up a bottle of the Widow?"

"But I've ordered sole."

"Women alone always order sole. It means something. Countermand the sole. Look the sun's come out. I decided I'd spend that Adolph Baum money before it turned out to be an optical illusion."

He leaned back in his chair, looking at the golden girl with the little hat like an apricot tart so jaunty on her camomile gold curls and the restaurant with its starched cloths and glinting silver and the rolling tables ranked with hors d'oeuvres waiters were pushing toward them; and outside the broad plateglass windows the blue oceanic sky and the great piled puffed cumulus clouds casting purple shadows on green-blue foamstreamed seas.

She sat looking at him from under her little hat with her thin lips parted over rows of such small pearly teeth, waiting for him to entertain her, waiting for him to carry her away. "I know all about Adolph Baum," she was saying, "but you never did get around to telling me about Tangier."

"We were busy." He was trying to brim his eyes with unspoken ecstasies. "Last night." He tried to pack the words with meaning, but there was no answering expression of complicity on her face. He felt that the waiters must have noticed the helpless ogle of his eyes, the too eager bulge of his lips. He made a big play of picking out some hors d'oeuvres for her. He heaped up his own plate and settled down to eat.

"Did we get to Nice?" he asked with his mouth full.

She shook her head. "Well . . ." he drank off his cocktail and wiped his mouth . . . The ballet season only lasted two weeks. And Vera and Oleg, that was the polar bear, the peintre russe, they said Jed must drive down to Nice with them. Their friend Anna Glazunova had a car, but nobody knew how to drive it so that was how Jed fitted in. My those Russians loved Nice. It reminded them of the Crimea. Jed was already headed for Morocco. He had gone in to see Ted Kendrick in Paris, who was European representative for *Macaulay's Magazine*—he was an old friend of J.E.'s; J.E. knew all the newspaper crowd in his time—and he'd said why didn't Jed go to Morocco and do a story on Abd-el-Krim.

The war in the Rif, Jed began to explain patiently, was interesting from several angles, but mostly because it was one of those revolts of colonial people that were typical of the present stage of revolutionary events. First the revolution in an industrial country; then it spread in colonial revolts. History's iron law. Of course he didn't explain it that way to Ted because Ted represented the interests. Ted fixed him up with a letter to Mr. Corliss.

"Who is he?" Marlowe asked. She seemed to be a girl who clutched at names.

"He's the fabulous Englishman. From a beautiful house full of rare bricabrac he plays on Morocco like a piano. Officially he's only British consul general at Tangier but he's a great deal more."

"Oh," she said as if she'd known it all along.

He made a grand character for a play, Jed hurried to add, because he represented all the pathos of the dying British empire. He was a very old man and a very clever operator. When he went, there wouldn't be any more like him . . . "Just like when J.E. goes there won't be any more idealistic American journalists. Want me to prove it to you?"

She was looking at him with that puzzled look, probably she was thinking he oughtn't to be talking with his mouth full. Felicia was always complaining about his talking with his mouth full.

"In his house in Tangier quick as a flash I felt out in the main stream of history."

The main stream of history, Jed went on to explain, was

what his writing needed. Shakespeare wouldn't have been any good if he'd stayed in Stratford. He had to go to London to be bathed in the full current of the Renaissance. Nowadays it was different; you could live in New York all your life and not know you were alive while somebody in the next apartment would be acting his part in the great drama. Now J.E. always did know about history, though he misunderstood it because he hadn't read enough Marx and Engels J.E. believed in the good, the beautiful and the true, if she got what he meant. He had thought it was his duty to bring up his family in a backwater. "Until my mother died we lived in Plainfield, New Jersey. Now that's a backwater . . . So's Santa Barbara."

"Let's leave Santa Barbara out of it," Marlowe said huffily.

"Now don't be like that. Look at the nice steak I'm buying you."

"Only a small slice," she told the waiter who was showing off a great parsley-sprinkled porterhouse in a silver dish.

"If a woman goes around with me she needs to eat up strong," Jed expostulated.

"I really believe," she said letting her eyes narrow again and sitting up very straight in her chair, "I'd be capable of slapping your face."

Jed laughed; but she did look quite capable of slapping his face. "Wait till you've heard me out," he giggled nervously.

. . . There he was driving a carload of Russians down the valley of the Rhone. The Renault was a little thing like a miniature taxicab and there were those two enormous painters in back. They had to sit with their suitcases on their knees. It wouldn't have been so bad if Anna Glazunova hadn't turned out to have a husband . . . It was the damnedest thing the

23

way women had husbands. In this case that part didn't matter. Russians were too big to be jealous, at least not in that particular way, but this husband, they said he was a general, an oldfashioned czarist general. He wasn't tall but he was excessively broad. He took up all the front seat. Anna Glazunova had to sit on Jed's lap. She sort of took it for granted she sat on the chauffeur's lap. She was a tiny little thing but it wasn't easy to drive with Anna Glazunova sitting on your lap.

"It wasn't the Grand Duke Cyril?" interrupted Marlowe. "I've met the Grand Duke Cyril."

Jed shook his head impatiently. "It was General Zukiepof, the one who disappeared. I was with him when he disappeared."

"What do you mean disappeared?"

"He disappeared in Tangier of course. Everything happened in Tangier, but I haven't gotten to Nice yet." He made a gesture with the palms of his hands over the table as if to quiet an auditorium full of people.

. . . The trip took days. The damn Renault was always breaking down and they would stop for the night in these picturesque inns, see, and the general he would get himself a bottle of vodka from somewhere and sit in a corner drinking it out of a little silver cup he carried in his pocket. Vera, she said that's how you could tell he was ancien régime, the Reds they just drank it out of the bottle. While the rest of them would be eating supper the general would just pass out cold right where he sat and nobody ever troubled to move him. And quick as a flash Anna Glazunova would be sitting on Jed's lap again. She was a tiny little woman but she was remarkably passionate. That's the way it went all the time he was with the Russians. Jed began to laugh. "You know I have the reputation of being somewhat indiscreet."

24

"You don't say," said Marlowe arching her eyebrows. She was having a good time, he could see that.

Well they'd just treated him as this dumb American who made a convenient chauffeur and could always find a mechanic to fix the Renault when it broke down, and pay him, too; and when the headwaiter would bring out the bill in those picturesque inns nobody ever seemed to be there but Jed. As soon as he got to Nice he'd had to cable J.E. for a loan. J.E. was wonderful about things like that. Well one evening just to make conversation he'd said he was going au Maroc to try to interview Abd-el-Krim and that he had a letter to Josiah Corliss in Tangier. It was after supper in a hell of a picturesque inn up on a mountain back of Nice, sitting on a terrace with an enormous view all blue hills and twinkling lights. Jed knew right away he'd been indiscreet, because the general, who'd passed out cold over his bottle of vodka as usual hours before, suddenly opened his little pig eyes and looked straight at him. The eyes were damn bright and didn't look drunk at all. It was startling, like having a cow suddenly say, "How do you do?" with an Oxford accent. The general didn't say anything. He just closed his eyes and was drunk again. Quick as a flash Vera said la politique didn't regard her: the artist like the religious should ignore la politique. She began to talk to Oleg like a blue streak in Russian; and she and Oleg didn't seem to want to have much to do with Jed after that; but the Zukiepofs, they began to call him cher ami.

As soon as the money came from J.E. Jed went off to Marseilles to take the boat. Well when he got on the boat for Oran the first thing he saw, when he went into the bar after a good look at the Château d'If, was General Zukiepof passed out as usual in a corner with his blue pint bottle of vodka on the table in front of him. Jed had slipped out of there in a hurry; but that night he'd hardly laid down in his bunk when the cabin door opened and quick as a flash in came Anna Glazunova with that fever in her eyes.

"You seem to have trouble with women on boats," Marlowe said drily.

"Well I didn't want to get tangled up with a lot of mysterious white Russians. I was going to Morocco on business. I wanted to get my story and get the hell out of there. I'd met somebody very delightful at Nice. I wanted to get back there for some restful beach life in the sun."

"Oh who was she, Jed?"

"She wasn't half as cute as you are . . ." He looked hard into her eyes. "How about some dessert? Meringue glacée?" She shook her little hat. "Cheese?" She shook her little hat again. "Coffee?" She nodded smiling. She really was adorable.

Well it got to be a problem in Oran. Those damn Russians never left his side. The general was with him all day and he couldn't even lie down for a nap after lunch—it was hot down there—without having Anna crawl into bed with him. Well one morning he made a supreme effort to shake them. He'd packed his bag and paid his hotel bill the night before and when Anna left him to go back to see that the general got his tea he just rushed out of the hotel and jumped into a cab and quick as a flash he was on the train for Figuig.

It was on that train he found his windfall, a literary French lady who knew all about Morocco. Of course she wasn't as young as she had been but she was highly susceptible. "I haven't got any bourgeois morals, no more than any proletarian," said Jed, looking deep in Marlowe's eyes, again.

"I'll say you don't."

She took to looking at herself in the little mirror in her handbag. She had her lipstick out. She reminded him of a cat washing up after a meal. Lunch was over. He'd have to talk fast.

"When you know me better you'll find I'm crowded with morals, a different kind of morals," he said.

When she looked up at him a glaze of boredom covered her eyes. Jed hurried on with the story: Well anyway the train took hours and hours and the landscape got all gray from driving dust under the sun and the femme de lettres talked and Jed pulled out a pad and frankly took notes and that pleased hell out of her and by the time they got to Figuig, which turned out to be nothing in the world but a few mud huts and dusty palmtrees at the edge of the Sahara desert, they had decided to hire some mules and set off together across the high Atlas toward forbidden Fez. Of course Fez wasn't forbidden any more but she liked to call it that. She knew Arabic and Berber and she knew the Béni Amour. That was an Arab tribe, but there was something profoundly libidinous about the way she said the name. She even knew some Touareg. She knew everything.

And they all knew her. Right away the hotel proprietor got an old man out of the souk to cook her special couscous— couscous avec des truffes du désert. It was just cracked wheat, but the way she said couscous, it was like having your back rubbed. Well the next afternoon after an amorous siesta in a dategarden beside a creaking waterwheel . . . the fleas may have been bad at that hotel but the mosquitoes in the date- garden were worse . . . Jed and the femme de lettres sat on a rug in a back room in the ksour talking to three jokers from the Béni Amour; the way they had their eyes made up with mascara made everything very stagey. Half the time Jed thought he was acting in one of those lousy movies. "Imagine me playing sheik," Jed shouted popping his eyes.

Marlowe was laughing now. Marlowe was laughing her head off.

They decided to start across the mountains in three days at dawn. The femme de lettres had it all settled with the French commandant of the Foreign Legion for escorts and safe conducts and God knows what. That gal had a drag everywhere. Her old man was a general. "I tell you she was God's gift to a free lance writer."

Jed let out a hoot. Marlowe had tears in her eyes she was laughing so hard. Jed spluttered he felt he was old Benny Amour himself on the way back to the hotel for their apéritif, when who did she suppose they found in the lobby? General Zukiepof and Anna Glazunova. Was that a dash of cold water? That night quick as a flash Anna was in bed with him. There wasn't any time to pass the word to the femme de lettres and when she came in through the window off the flat roof in the moonlight whispering about les grandes chaleurs there certainly was a nasty scene.

And that was that. Jed caught the morning train back to Oran before anybody was up and started off right away on the other line to Tlemcen. He stopped off a couple of days in Tlemcen just to throw the Russians off the scent. There wasn't any question any more in his mind but that they were some kind of spies and that there was something they wanted to get out of him, but he didn't know what; nobody knew less about Morocco than he did. In Tlemcen he decided there was only one place he could get away from Anna Glazunova so he went to an oldfashioned disorderly house. Of course they were the most orderly places in the world but that was how he found out that Spanish girls used camomile on their hair. Well from Tlemcen he took the bus to Tangier.

Now he really began to notice the war. There were foreign legionnaires posted all along the road and every time the bus stopped at a village the French police came through to check on the passports and all kinds of people were taken off the bus and didn't come back. Nobody was shooting anybody but the French were just detaining suspicious characters so Jed was congratulating himself that those damn Russians wouldn't get through. But when the bus arrived in Tangier who did she suppose was waiting to meet him? Anna Glazunova and General Zukiepof.

The general had on a white linen suit and she carried a palm leaf fan. It was cher ami this and cher ami that and they had a room all ready for him at a hotel. That settled it for him. They must be Deuxième Bureau, that was the French secret service, see? They stuck to him like flypaper. Every morning when Anna left his room she would say: "Today we go to see Meester Corliss, non?" He'd say he was trop fatigué. Why he'd been a week at that hotel spending money hand over fist before he was alone long enough to find him a cab driver that spoke French so that he could explain he wanted to drive out to the Villa Corliss by a roundabout way.

It was out near Cape Spartel. They got there without being followed and there was Mr. Corliss, a small grayhaired man in an oldfashioned straw hat with a wide brim walking up and down among his roses. He was nice as he could be. He knew all about everything, see? He had an amused drowsy manner and kind of let the lids drop over his eyes when he talked like a wise old lizard. Of course Jed told him all about General Zukiepof and Anna and he said right away the general was working for the Russian bolsheviks. Jed said how could that be because he always talked so anti-bolshevik and old regime and Mr. Corliss said that was why he was useful to them. He must be working for the Deuxième Bureau too, Mr. Corliss agreed, or they would never have let him into French Morocco. His little plan must be to establish a contact with Abd-el-Krim. Tired of starving in Paris, probably, so he was trying to ingratiate himself with the Gay-Pay-Oo. He thought that with Abd-el-Krim as a peace offering he could go home and get a nice job in the army. The Bolshies saw everything in their own image so they thought the Rifi were staging a social revolution. All power to the soviets and all that crap. That wasn't just how Mr. Corliss put it.

"But I thought you were a Red." She took a pair of apricot colored gloves out of her handbag and started putting them on. She was ready to ditch him.

Aghast Jed looked up from the bill. It was staggering. He piled the greenbacks on the plate.

"You haven't seen my new room," he whispered to hide his confusion. "Come on down. We'll have some brandy and I'll prove to you that there's a great difference between a bolshevik and a social revolutionary of the left."

There was so little expression of consent on her face, he thought she wasn't coming; but she came. The door had hardly closed behind them before she was in his arms. She pushed him away breathless and sat down on the couch opposite his berth. "I've never been in an inside cabin before," she said. "Why it's quite airy."

"It better be," he said grimly. "It's costing me my future sustenance."

He'd had the forethought to order a bottle of Bisquit Debouché and two glasses before lunch, so he didn't have to ring for the steward. She sipped hers appreciatively. "You made me eat too much lunch," she said with an accusing angular look on her face.

"First I'll finish my story," said Jed . . . After Mr. Corliss had explained why Jed's Russians were cottoning up to him he invited him to stay to supper in the rose garden with a young Moroccan Wahabi in a white robe and a French professor who turned out to be a Mohammedan. He had something to do with an Arab university at Rabat.

That supper in Mr. Corliss' garden, Jed explained hurriedly, would open the first act of the play. The different scenes took place behind a transparency, see?

He mustn't let her get bored.

Of course what he really wanted, he went on explaining, was to have the dinner table right down in the middle of the audience . . . Abolish the proscenium arch.

She didn't seem a damn bit interested in the proscenium arch.

"The whole supper was pure drama," he cried out waving his arms. "Before we even sat down, the Wahabi, who turned out to be agent for Abd-el-Krim, sent off an old red-bearded messenger into the Rif to start arranging for my trip. He was a Berber in a striped tunic and he put his hand to his heart and his forehead and bowed and set off at a jog trot right from Mr. Corliss' garden gate."

. . . They all three pounded it into Jed that nobody ought to know a thing about his trip. Especially not his Russian friends. They would want to go along. There was no better camouflage than a naïve American. Unfortunate accidents had happened to people on their way to the Rif. He must be very careful . . .

"There we were," went on Jed in a low resonant voice, "four men sitting at a table in a garden waited on by soft-footed attendants and beyond the mountains, behind the green curtain of leaves spies lurked, detachments of bandits, terrible events. Snipers lie behind rocks in the mountains, villages are being pillaged, women raped. Spanish sentries are having their throats cut. Generals poring over maps. Little dramatic scenes are happening that in the end will change the course of history."

"Why didn't you go?" interrupted Marlowe. She really was interested. The story had drama.

"I'm coming to that."

Jed was spending the evenings with Mr. Corliss learning about Morocco—the raw material of his story—and the rest of the time he was putting it all into this play . . . "I'll read you the first act if we get a chance."

A few days later they were all invited to dine with that French professor, the one who was a Mohammedan convert. He was kind of a mangylooking little man with a motheaten beard. Jed never did discover what he proved. It turned out he had two wives. One of them was white and received the guests in the drawingroom and one of them was distinctly colored and stayed in the kitchen doing the cooking. A convenient solution for the servant problem.

"You think women are dirt," Marlowe piped up.

"I do not," said Jed. "Want me to prove it to you?"

He had done everything he could to keep Anna from knowing where he was going that night. In fact he had explained frankly to Anna that he had to write this article and that he couldn't be seen around with people who might be taken for subversive agents and Anna had flared up and said they were just poor exiles living from hand to mouth on a foreign shore and this was their petite vacance. Then of course she had to cry.

It was in his room. From the balcony where he usually ate his breakfast he and Anna were watching a little gray tramp steamer come snubnosed into the bay. The morning was so still they could hear the jingling sound from the steamer as the anchor chain payed out and the rumble of exhausting steam. To cheer Anna up he'd asked her if she could make out what the flag was. Looked red to him. Anna had remarkably good eyesight. She never said a word. He was so busy trying to make out what the flag was he didn't hear Anna go. When he looked up she just wasn't with him any more.

It wasn't till Jed got dressed and went down to the lobby that he found out from the manager, who was an elderly Maltese and quite indignant that a Soviet ship should be allowed to anchor in Tangier Roads, that the flag really was the hammer and sickle. Jed was excited, because it was the first time he'd seen it. He decided he'd try to go on board next day to see what the ship was like. Only it turned out it wasn't there next day.

Jed had drifted around like he usually did that afternoon to Mr. Corliss' villa to get the latest news of the Rif. The fighting was kind of at a standstill at that moment but no word had come out yet about Jed's expedition. "Your Russian friends are planning to go with you," Mr. Corliss said with his lizard's smile. "We must try to circumvent them."

Then he'd left Jed with the Moroccan. That young Moroccan was a terrific Wahabi, that meant a puritan, very careful about the Mohammedan rules, like orthodox Jewish, see? but when there was nobody looking except the family he'd drink Mr. Corliss' scotch like a fish. He didn't mind Jed. They all treated Jed just like a member of the family. Mr. Corliss would kind of encourage the Wahabi to drink, though he never drank a drop himself. Jed thought that was peculiar at the time. Mr. Corliss' relations with that young Moroccan were altogether peculiar.

Anyway that night Mr. Corliss took them around to the professor's in his limousine, and they all went in together. It was a little white mud house with a courtyard and of course, sitting at a Turkish table in the courtyard under a palm with the lightcolored Mrs. Professor—the dark one was in the kitchen cooking up the couscous—there they were waiting for him, Anna Glazunova and the general. Anna had on a new silver evening gown and really looked handsome in a skinny sort of way with her bruised looking dark eyes. When Mr. Corliss saw them, that drowsy amused reptile expression came over his face.

All evening Anna tried to talk about the Rif and Mr. Corliss he just didn't seem to know where the place was any more, but his expression got more and more amused. Well the general went into his usual act with the vodka bottle and after he'd passed out Anna was quite apologetic and explained that her husband was tres fatigué and that they mustn't wait for him to eat. So they all went in to the diningroom where they were served European style only the food was all Moroccan. Darn good too. After dinner they went back out into the courtyard for their coffee and quick as a flash Jed noticed that the general wasn't there. Something had happened, see? . . . but from the diningroom they had never heard a sound. The vodka bottle lay broken on the tiled floor beside his chair and the little silver cup full of vodka was still standing on the table. It struck Jed as suspicious right away that there was any vodka left in that cup.

When Anna saw it she looked like her eyes would start out of her head. She gave a screech and rushed up to Mr. Corliss: Would he please have her driven to the hotel? Mr. Corliss was very fatherly and kind, and drove her around himself, at least he sat in the back of his limousine with her while his Sudanese chauffeur drove them. When he came back he sure did look jaunty.

As the custom was in Morocco the professor was passing around a pipe of kif, that was a kind of hashish, after the

34

coffee. Jed took a puff for politeness, just tasted like stale tobacco, but the Wahabi and Mr. Corliss they seemed to enjoy the drags they took.

The professor had been talking endlessly all evening about the Berber dialects in the mountains. But when Mr. Corliss came back from the hotel he shut up suddenly like he was waiting to hear what Mr. Corliss had to say. Mrs. Professor Number One never did have anything to say, no more than Mrs. Professor Number Two, they just flapped about like bats in their Arab clothes, so they all sat there without opening their faces while Mr. Corliss took a long drag on his pipe. He sure looked like a drowsy reptile with his eyes closed. Then that amused look came on his face and he murmured that Russian women would be attractive if they weren't so intense. But he never said anything about the general.

"When Mr. Corliss dropped me at the hotel he put his hand on my arm and whispered gently that he was sure I was too much the man of the world to need a warning against designing females. 'A woman alone,' he added, 'unlatches the heartstrings . . . As for the general,' he said, 'we have no cause for alarm. His mission has not been an unqualified success . . .'" Jed was too sleepy to puzzle over what that meant. He was in a hurry to go to bed and go to sleep. My he was relieved that he didn't hear that imperious little scratch scratch of Anna Glazunova's fingernails on the door. He fell asleep instantly.

It was morning before he saw her. He'd just moved out on the balcony in his pajamas to drink his hot goat's milk and coffee out in the early sun, when there she was standing behind him. She still had her eveningdress on. She looked like death itself. "Cher ami," she said, "it is finished." With a crooked forefinger she pointed out into the bay. The blunt-nosed freighter they had been looking at the day before was

35

headed round Cape Spartel, leaving a little dark trail on the water behind it. In the calm and the blue and the haze she looked like a child's toy boat with her tiny speck of red in the stern.

Anna gripped Jed's shoulder with her steely fingers and pulled him inside and closed the french windows and double-locked the door. Then she hissed in a frightful whisper in his ear that he was being taken off to be tortured and killed. "Who?" "Mon mari, mon père, mon frère, mon tout. Zukie-pof you fool." All he had wanted was to help his fatherland but on account of his class origins they were suspicious.

"But who?" Jed had asked again.

He knew very well who ruled; she looked as if she were going to spit in his face.

Then she dropped on the bed and began to sob. Some-body had informed on Zukiepof. After she had been crying a long while into the pillow she looked up at Jed suddenly with such hatred it made his teeth chatter. "Vous?"

Jed shook his head.

After that she was just a tiny pathetic little weak woman blubbering into her pillow that she was alone in the world and couldn't pay her hotel bill. "Of course I gave her all the money I had. That's the way those things always end."

Jed and Marlowe were sitting side by side on the couch. Marlowe was running her fingers up his arm under the shirt-sleeve. "But what really did happen?" she was asking in a little astonished childish voice.

"The only thing I know is there's a play in it. That same day the cable came forwarded from Paris that Adolph Baum was starting this theatre and was I glad to get the hell out. Of course Josiah Corliss said it was just an agent being re-called home. The freighter had stopped to pick him up. Still if he hadn't been snatched I think he would have drunk that

36

vodka. He wasn't a man to leave an unfinished drink. That was all, but Mr. Corliss sure did seem pleased with himself.

"If you remember there was quite a stink in the European papers, letters to the *Times* about the poor security in Tangier and all that. Anna insisted that two men had come in the courtyard and put a bag over Zukiepof's head and chloroformed him. I did smell a whiff of something when we went out in the courtyard but I thought it was just the kif . . . It sure was a relief to get the hell out on that mail plane even if it was open to all the breezes."

"Cold kind of a fish aren't you?"

"Not with you," he whispered as their mouths met.

When they were getting back into their clothes to take a turn round the deck, he asked her suddenly: "Suppose we took a chance and got married?"

She didn't answer. She was doing her face in front of the mirror over the washbasin.

"In that convent you used to dream of going on the stage," he added haltingly while he tied his necktie. He knew he'd spoken too soon. "God knows the theatre is silly enough, but if you like things that way . . ." His voice broke like a schoolboy's. He was standing behind her to brush his hair.

When she turned to look at him her face was full of little straining edges. She didn't look pretty at all.

"We promised we'd be perfectly frank . . ." She spoke the words carefully as if she had been rehearsing the speech for some time. "You are big enough—I know that much about you—for me to give it to you straight from the shoulder. Honesty is our fetish, isn't it? I'd be perfectly miserable. It's not that it would be embarrassing to go home and tell Mother I'd

37

married somebody who was Jewish, you know Santa Barbara and all that . . ."

Jed's hands were getting cold. His knees were weakening. She went on and on in a low halting voice as if she were reading the words out of the book. "I know I'm not much good. Tommy, that's my ex, Tommy always said I had a screw loose. Maybe he was right, but honesty is my fetish. That's why it's been fun with you, being perfectly frank . . . It's not that, not what I just said. It's something else . . . Anyway it just wouldn't be practical." She took him by the shoulders and shook him. "Now don't be so glum . . . It's just made my crossing, hasn't it yours?"

His mouth was dry. He couldn't answer.

Nothing was fun any more as they walked around the deck in the gloaming, not her narrow shoulders and small breasts, not the rosy west or the gulls or the dressed up passengers, flushed and chattering from the five o'clock excitement all round them. He couldn't stand the sight of the groups in evening dress hurrying into the bar for cocktails before dinner. All at once he said he'd have to go do some work on his play and left her. Here he'd rented this expensive stateroom so he sure would have to do some work on it. And wasn't that a waste of money, he told himself, as the door closed behind him.

When they met next morning outside the elevator in the lobby, Marlowe's face still had an angular and metallic look. She had on a tailored coat of a disagreeably sharp green and an ugly spiky hat, not a bit becoming. Her eyes had lost the violet glint. Just a rich bitch, he said almost aloud. He wanted to hate her. They talked about the weather like chance shipboard acquaintances. As he turned away she gave him a quick little uneasy smile, but he couldn't make his face smile back.

THEATRE

Jed's entrance into New York was magnificent. He came swooping down out of the noisy sunlight. His ears were full of the hoot of tugs and the crying of gulls. His eyes were dazzled with the tall buildings that rose, sparkling with windows like mica, to meet him as the liner nosed into the harbor. Walking down the first class gangplank, briefcase under his arm, he squinted through the glare to try to make out the faces scattered like spilled peas in the shadow of the pier below him. A little face . . . no . . . yes it was Mae's . . . in a little pink poke bonnet. Snub nose tilted up like her mother's. And June's face, bigger and coarser, above it. Already he could make out that patient putupon expression. And the broad grinning Fausts alongside. And behind them, tall in tweeds, Felicia Hardestie standing aloof against a post.

Blinking he grinned into the greeting faces. He waved his felt hat and shouted hurray. Quick as a flash he snatched up Mae from across the barrier. He'd been afraid she'd cry but she cooed "Daddy, Daddy, Daddy," while, calling out scraps of adventures across people's shoulders at June and

Felicia and Maisie and Sam and the silent fashionplate in a tan fall coat who turned out to be George Pastor with a new mustache, he hurried her through the crowd toward the letter M.

". . . It was the wildest summer. I came back first class with a lady tennis player from Santa Barbara just to study the decadent bourgeoisie. I engaged in a Dada manifestation and helped put on a Stravinski ballet. I interviewed Abd-el-Krim in Morocco and wrote a play called *Shall Be the Human Race* but there's nothing worth seeing in Europe except the Ballet Russe and the révolution mondiale."

He went on talking across the inquisitive visor of the customsofficer's cap. When he opened the steamer trunk, there on top was the big Parisian doll, asleep with her eyes closed, just like he'd planned, for Mae. The little girl's eyes got big. When Jed lifted the doll out, with apologies to the customsofficer, the doll opened her eyes and said "Ma Ma" and Mae chanted, "Dolly, dolly, dollbaby" and the customsofficer showed a wide smiling Irish face and immediately put the stamp on Jed's bags.

"What no liquor?" roared Sam Faust, as they all started to follow the porter down through the crowded halflight of the pier.

"Didn't have time Sam. I was involved in international intrigue. In Tangier I saw a man vanish right before my eyes. Like the hindoo rope trick. In fact I may have been the cause of his vanishment. Crossing the Mediterranean I was pursued by a little Russian spy with eyes like the headlights on a Chrysler. In the Sahara I became involved with a frenzied female anthropologist who spoke only French and obscure Arab dialects. She was an anthropologist all right. Anthropos means man, don't it George?"

He was walking blindly through the crowd with Mae on

42

one shoulder, talking to his friends over the other as he walked. Mae had mashed his hat over his eyes and had planted the French doll firmly on his head. Beside him Felicia was carrying the briefcase with his manuscripts. June walked on the other side steadying Mae with one hand, so it seemed the easiest thing for Jed to slip an arm round her waist and the other around Felicia's. In front of the line of cabs he unloaded Mae onto the sunscorched pavement and stood mopping his brow and straightening his hair with a damp handkerchief while they waited for the Fausts whom he could see moving majestically through the hubbub in the wake of his baggage.

"Everybody's coming to lunch at my house," panted Maisie Faust. "I've cooked a paprika chicken."

"With knishes." Sam waddled up bandylegged and pulled out a monogrammed handkerchief to wipe the sweat off his forehead. Both he and Maisie had put on weight since Jed had seen them. There was a new prosperous gloss about their clothes.

"Where's Eli?" asked Jed.

Sam looked out of the top of his bifocals into Jed's face with the familiar green glint in his eye and the special curl to the corners of his thick lips which his friends agreed he'd patterned after Judge Wolman's expression on the bench in the days when he had served as that famous jurist's private secretary. "You know Eli," he said scornfully. "He thinks the sun rises at two P.M. A fine proletarian."

Sam was taking charge. "We'll send Jed ahead with the girls and George and I will follow with the baggage."

"As your honor pleases," said Jed.

Sam smiled indulgently. Being called Judge Faust was an old joke Sam always enjoyed. Jed started groping in his pocket for change. "No Jed I'll attend to the tips." Sam

43

closed the taxicab door on him firmly. "Jed I'd better break it to you quick that we've gone ahead faster than you think. You, for instance, have been appointed a director of The Craftsman's Theatre at the princely salary of twentyfive dollars a week. And you might as well know that we are opening your charming dramatization of *The Man Who Was Thursday* this very night at eight thirty sharp."

"I thought you were going to do my new play," Jed cried out. Instead of answering Sam gave the address and motioned to the driver to start. Jed was so disappointed his eyes watered. He found himself bellowing helplessly into the noises of the street as the cab swerved round into Tenth Avenue. "I worked my head off trying to get it finished."

"The boys decided," Maisie was explaining in her soothing contralto, "that they needed the Chesterton name for a sendoff . . . Kenneth Magill is duplicating the production he did at Cambridge with that amateur group. You remember what notices you got."

"It might be a whole lot worse," drawled Felicia in her precise New England voice. "Eli designed a constructivist set that looks like a roller coaster. The dress rehearsal was quite a circus."

"It just happened that they could get this old theatre up in the west fifties for almost no rent," went on Maisie. "Sam fixed that up with Rodney Acres."

"I'd think after *Flight from the Sun* you would never want to see him again," June was muttering over Mae's head.

In spite of everything her voice hadn't lost its possessive note, thought Jed. All at once he felt he was going to stifle alone with all these women in the cab. He remembered the free happy days with Marlowe on the boat. Why did things always go so sour? To get the look of dismay off his face he started to tell tall stories of his trip.

He'd hardly begun explaining what it was like working with the Russians out at their studio near the Place des Batailles, the "place of battles"—golly the French had a sense of history, and the beer in goldfishbowls and torrents of Russian among gluepots—when the cab drew up in front of the old New York house on St. Luke's Place where the Fausts had the ground floor apartment.

Jed went on talking and talking as they piled out of the cab. He was afraid he'd get left alone with June. It was a relief to see Lew Golton, back from Mexico at last, standing just inside the doorway, his arms folded across his chest, looking more like a Mexican than the Mexicans, with his olive skin and broad cheekbones and low forehead thatched with shiny black hair.

"Arriving first class on a luxury liner, eh? You goddam bourgeois." Lew spat the words out of the corner of his mouth.

"Smile damn you when you say that," said Jed.

He picked up Mae and they all poured into the tall dingy hallway, everybody tugging on the steamer trunk in a clumsy scrimmage.

A big fist poked into Jed's ribs as he staggered into the house weighed down by Mae and a suitcase. It was Eli Soltair lurking in the dark hall. "Attaboy Jed, just under the line," he roared; his wide pockmarked face shook with welcoming laughter.

"Eli you need a haircut," said Jed affectionately.

Eli ran a hand through his bush of crinkly hair, a little prematurely gray round the edges. "I'm waiting for Delilah," he said. Jed thought it was the funniest thing he'd ever heard in his life. They both roared with laughter. Eli had already snatched up a suitcase. With his free hand he grabbed Mae out of Jed's arms. "Snooks come to Grandpa."

Mae looked thoroughly pleased. Eli was the sort of

45

baboonlike character children loved, thought Jed indulgently. Eli dropped the suitcase in the rosy halflight of the Fausts' overstuffed front room and started shooting Mae up toward the ceiling with his big hands under her armpits.

"We just went ahead and jumped in with our clothes on," he roared. "Kenneth and I designed the set ourselves. We had to hire a lousy scenic artist but we told him what to do. The set's wonderful. The play's wonderful. Kenneth's production is wonderful. The stagehands are crazy about it. That's all I care about. Greatest farce since Officer 666. It's crazy as a junebug. We've changed our name to The Crazy Man's Theatre."

"Rodney Acres," interrupted Felicia, "promises to move it to the Martin Hayes in three weeks."

"That is," shrilled June butting excitedly into the conversation with her snub nose in the air, "if it catches on."

Jed suddenly felt so tense he was afraid he was going to burst into tears. He looked June hard in the face. "What business is it of yours?" he whispered gruffly. He was dismayed at the sour sound of his own voice in his ears when he said it.

June winced as if he'd slapped her and gathered little Mae up defensively into her arms. "Time she took a nap," she said. Mae's eyes went from Jed's face to her mother's. Her mouth began to pucker. She was going to cry. "I'll take the child in the other room and give her some food," went on June in a businesslike way. "Then maybe she'll sleep a little."

Mae let go the French doll and began to wail in her mother's arms. Jed caught the doll dexterously so that it didn't drop to the floor and break, and feeling hangdog and ashamed followed June across the hall with it. He laid the doll carefully on the bed and turned away without looking at either of them.

46

In the front room he found Sam was sitting in an arm-chair and tapping on his knee with an imaginary gavel. "Will the meeting of the directors of The Craftsman's Theatre please come to order?"

Maisie had disappeared. From behind a Japanese screen stewing peppery smells crept through the close air. Felicia, wearing the absentminded air she always assumed when she did housework, had started setting the big center table for lunch.

Sam began by making a longwinded speech about how his position in this organization was merely that of a teaser, now that the stallions were all collected it was up to them to serve the mares. Various ribald remarks were passed and Sam got red in the face and dropped the metaphor. "Lay off will you? . . . I'm only a lawyer and I promise you I'm one lawyer who hasn't got a play in his desk drawer."

"Write us a play Sam," shouted Eli. "Write it on legal paper and we'll perform it in a courtroom. We'll call it the foolscap drama, especially for dunces."

"Children," murmured George Pastor stroking his little wisp of mustache, "should be seen and not heard."

On his lap Sam was coddling a sheaf of long typewritten sheets clipped into a blue jacket. For quite a while he studied the first sheet through his bifocals. He cleared his throat from time to time when he began to read the constitution and by-laws. Maisie, in a ruffled apron, an expression of dim religious light on her face, started to pass around a tray of little glasses brimmed with some sweetish wine. The directors silently sipped while Sam read.

Forgetting everything else in a giddy kind of elation, Jed listened. For the first time he admitted to himself that the theatre was real. He was the director of a real experimental theatre. He was associated with some of the brightest young

47

men in New York. There was twentyfive thousand dollars in the bank. He was one of five men elected to spend it. Sitting with his legs stuck out in front of him in an overstuffed chair in the filtered flushed light that came through the flowered draperies, and listening to Sam Faust's ponderous periods, he had the feeling that the armchair was beginning to soar. This was success.

Sam talked on and on, elaborating the ifs and the buts, but the minute a proposal was put to a vote the directors acclaimed it unanimously. They were all too delighted to argue. Jed was elected chairman because his was the bestknown name and George Pastor secretary-treasurer because he knew accounting. The minute Maisie brought in the paprika chicken they adjourned the meeting.

Jed felt ravenously hungry. Now he was enjoying being home. They all set to, heaping up their plates with chicken and potatocakes and cole slaw. Even Sam Faust was quiet. Eli wiped a stream of gravy off his chin. There was no sound but munching and an occasional smacking of lips over Sam's sweet sacramental wine. They had hardly finished the chocolate cake and scalding coffee, before it was time to start uptown. There was the theatre to visit and the set to see. They had an appointment with Adolph Baum in his Fifth Avenue mansion at five. Jed went spiraling off into the busiest afternoon of his life.

It was two A.M. and his knees were knocking together with fatigue by the time he got back downtown for a moment with Felicia. He felt weak as a cat as he stumbled up the stairs of the house on Barrow Street. He could barely make it up the four creaking flights. There was a little streak of light under the door. He tapped with the tips of his fingers.

"Come in feller," she said as she opened the door. She grabbed him by the ears and held his face steady and kissed it. It always surprised him how different Felicia's private manner was from her public personality.

"Well I don't know how it went. Only a few of the critics were there. The audience was crazy about it. There were about twenty curtain calls, cries of author etcetera . . . I made a speech. I never would have thought I could do it. Did you hear it?"

"Feller, I got so excited I had to leave. I was getting the screaming jeebies."

"Well you missed a damn good speech. May I take off my coat and stay a while? . . . Make me a sandwich, I'm starving."

"I saved a bottle of scotch."

"Felicia, you're the one, the one and only," he snatched for her hands, "that's what I told that rich bitch on the boat when she asked me to marry her. 'Engaged,' I said, 'irrevocably engaged.'" He pulled off his coat and necktie, let himself drop in a heap on the bed, and lay there watching her move around the room in her slim silk dressing gown that was the faded straw color of her hair. "Well that opening cost us eight thousand dollars," he yawned. "Seventeen thousand left."

She brought out some ryebread and sliced ham from the delicatessen and poured two deep shots of scotch.

"Got any mustard?" he looked up with his mouth full. "Thanks . . . You oughta see Adolph Baum. He's the cutest little man you ever saw, a cross between the Easter Rabbit and Foxy Grandpa . . . But what is he getting out of it? Answer me that. The funny thing is the one he likes best is Eli Soltair. You know Eli claims to have Negro blood. He thinks he looks like Pushkin, the big bum. He absolutely fascinates Adolph Baum, a banker and a banker's son, brought up in that rich cultured bankers' world of Frankfort-on-Main. It fits in with some daydream he must have had as a boy, the tousleheaded poet of the slums sleeping in doorways and vestibules. He fell for Lew Golton too, fresh back from the Mexican revolution, where he slept with the wives of the lousy peons while the lousy peons were out in the hills fighting their landlords. Eli and Lew; they are competing for the job of the American Gorky. Mr. Baum seemed to like that gunman look Lew has. He didn't pay the slightest attention to any of the rest of us . . . Felicia sit down and stop pacing. Don't you like this lousy old peon a little bit?"

"So much I have to pace to keep from screaming." She was staring at him with thin lips and narrowed eyes. "What about this girl on the boat?"

"Marlowe?" Jed yawned with his mouth full: "An episode, feller, you know how I am. Sometimes I think I make love to women just to cover my embarrassment, instead of small talk, see? Never did have any small talk. She threw herself at my head, see? Is it my fault if I have a generous nature? What can a man do if a girl follows him down into the third class bar? Steamboats are floating bordellos they used to say in Rome. Anyway to hell with her. You are the only one I can be really honest with. You're the one and only, Felicia." He pulled her down beside him on the couch and kissed her. Felicia's face was suddenly all curves. Her pupils spread. "If they give us a break I'll have the money to fix up June and let her get her ridiculous Reno divorce. She's got her heart set on going to Reno. It's idiotic . . . And then you and me we'll get married right away."

"Marriage doesn't mean anything to me; you know that," Felicia said tartly.

Jed paid no attention. "I wish you'd seen him," he was saying in a retrospective drawl.

"Who?"

She was pressing her face against his. Her lips were half open. She wasn't listening any more.

"Adolph Baum. He's such a nice neat little man, with a toy mustache. Feller, we live in a farcical world!" Jed let out one of his great guffaws. "Eli, the proletarian poet, isn't any more a proletarian than a rabbit. It's funny how little you know about your best friends. Eli, the old wobbly, the original stumblebum, turns out to be the favorite son on the left hand of the polished Dr. Magnes, you know the Zionist. You could have knocked me down with a feather. This theatre business all started as Dr. Magnes' idea of how to give his boy a boost. Anybody can see that Eli's as full of talent as a dog is with fleas. Dr. Magnes played up to Adolph Baum's Medici complex . . . You ought to see Adolph Baum's library. It looks like a room in the Bargello. Everything in the house is Florentine. It wasn't too hard for him to convince Adolph Baum that he'd be doing a real Lorenzo the Magnificent if he gave some money to an experimental theatre . . . The fact that it's a theatre dedicated to overthrowing the Adolph Baums of this world don't worry him in the least. That's the real Medici touch, see? A revolutionary play that runs a hundred nights on Broadway is no longer a revolutionary play. It's a goddam hit. So in giving us the means to become successful Broadway playwrights he's paying the insurance for the international house of Baum Brothers."

Jed jumped up and poured himself another shot of whisky. With his glass in his hand he started striding up and down the narrow room. "Of course he's wrong. Ideas can't be bought with money." He gulped down the rest of his drink.

"The idea of a just society where we all share alike from the product of our work: justice, that's too strong for him."

He shook his finger threateningly under Felicia's nose. She began to laugh. "Was that in your speech, feller?"

He nodded with an abashed grin. Then he set his empty glass on the windowsill, dropped down on the couch beside her and began to stroke her hair.

"You and me, Felicia," he whispered, his lips very close to her pretty waxen ear . . . Suppose it all worked out the way Adolph Baum had planned it, after all Adolph Baum was a man accustomed to making his plans come true. Jed was talking very low and dreamy and stroking her hair as he talked. It would be funny as a crutch if the two of them went to live in a penthouse and Lew and Eli took up their abode at the Ritz where money talked whether people's ancestors had come over on the Mayflower or not. He could just see Lew being soaped up by a headwaiter in tails. He would tear up his Party card in a minute . . . It wouldn't matter anyway in the long run. Other proletarians would come along with other revolutionary plays. The ideas would go marching on. The revolution would come just the same. "Me, that sort of thing don't affect me. I'd be as good a revolutionist on Park Avenue as in the ghetto."

Felicia droned drowsily that she could certainly use a studio on top of a tall building with one of those views that made New York look like the Garden of the Gods. She yawned. She couldn't stop yawning. "Say feller don't you ever get sleepy?" She pulled him down on the couch beside her.

Sure, he said, they had better go to sleep so that they could wake up early to read the notices. He'd only seen one and that was lousy. The afternoon papers would be better; maybe the Sunday sections would give them a break, but for real understanding they'd have to wait for the liberal weeklies.

52

The capitalist critics would be a firing squad: but the people who bought tickets and came to see the show, they didn't pay too much attention to the critics, now did they?

Felicia was stretched out beside him already fast asleep. He grabbed her by the shoulders and shook her. "This is the great opportunity of my life, don't you understand?" he shouted in a rasping voice into her ear. The sockets of his eyes were dry; his skin itched; he would never get to sleep. He felt like hitting her.

"What is?" she was murmuring without opening her eyes.

As he snuggled closer to her the irritation seeped out of him. She was just too sleepy. It made him sleepy to look at her. "The opportunity to hug and kiss Felicia," he whispered tenderly. He forgot everything else in a fit of drowsy affection. He put his mouth over her mouth and began to squirm out of his clothes.

The newspapers next morning were worse than Jed had imagined they could be. None of the critics had ever heard of expressionism. John Taylor Briggs ended his short notice by saying that the kindest thing to do was to treat the whole thing as a boyish prank.

"A boyish prank," the phrase rankled in Jed's head all week. He kept imagining it printed in bold letters across the tiny advertisements of The Craftsman's Theatre that cost so much to run on the theatrical pages. The Sunday theatrical sections were full of it as he thumbed through them sleepily on the stale train out to Asbury Park Sunday morning. Every critic repeated the phrase in some form or other. Most of them added something about bad taste.

Jed was too tired to care. He and Kenneth Magill had been up with the cast until five in the morning rehearsing changes in the script after the Saturday night performance. Kenneth had talent Jed had to admit, but he'd never liked him. They'd been classmates in college, together in all the local theatricals. Red hair and mushroom white skin, something too soft about the touch of his hand. He was quite masculine though when he was directing. And patient, my God. That performance had been a mess. Empty seats. Saturday night of all nights for Sylvia Levy to go up on her lines. Jed had a lousy headache and he felt tireder than he ever had in his life but he just had to go out to see J.E. He'd planned to sleep on the train but he couldn't close his eyes.

As he stepped off the coach into the fuzzy glare and the salt seabreeze, he almost walked past a small man with dark glasses. A hand pulled at his sleeve.

"Emmanuel dear, you didn't recognize me. Can I have aged so in a few short months?" His father pulled off his dark glasses and was kissing him on the cheek. As he looked into J.E.'s face Jed felt with a pang how much like his own face it was, only so yellow and shriveled. The wrinkled skin round the eyes had a trodden look. The closecropped hair was still as dark as his own. Less wave to it perhaps; after all J.E. was seventyfour. It was like looking at his own face in some stained reducing mirror.

"Your train was late," J.E. was saying querulously. "You know it plays hob with my digestion to be late to my meals. I've ordered a shore dinner for you. You always used to like a shore dinner. Emmanuel, you're looking thin."

"The girls complain that I'm getting a potbelly." Jed broke through the strain of meeting with a burst of laughter. "I can't please everybody, now can I, J.E.?"

"We must hurry or it will all be cold."

They had reached the curb on the street side of the station. J.E. was slipping the dark spectacles back over his eyes.

54

"My eyes can't stand the glare any more, dear. They are not as strong as they were," he explained. "I must save them for my work."

Jed tenderly took his father's arm. As he steered him through the cars and taxicabs backing and filling in front of the station he explained that he would have caught an earlier train only that he'd overslept. In this theatre business a man could never get to bed.

"You mustn't wear yourself out . . . Even as a cub reporter I was careful about my sleep . . . Here it is, the Olympic."

When they ducked in out of the hot September sunlight the shut in smell of cold grease and laundered napkins almost made Jed retch. If I could only have a drink or a swim, he was thinking. The place was empty and airless. On the back wall the hands of a clock were joined at twelve sharp.

"We're not late after all," said J.E. happily. "There's my table all ready for us."

They settled themselves at a table already set in a dark corner. A pimplyfaced waiter who needed a shave advanced smiling.

"This is my boy, Nick," said J.E. pulling off his glasses and blinking up at the waiter. "Back from across the herring pond . . . We'll start with the steamed clams. Drink the broth first, dear. Nick you know I only take the broth. Nothing more settling to the stomach than clam broth. Sometimes I eat nothing else all day, a cup of clam broth and a hard biscuit." He sat drinking his broth out of its thick cup with little noisy sips. "Emmanuel." He looked hard in Jed's face when he had finished. "How close are you to Adolph Baum?"

"I only met him once. Everybody else was so busy playing up to him I couldn't get a word in edgewise."

"Did he ask for me?" asked J.E. frowning. Jed shook his

55

head. "I fear no good will come of your relationship with that man . . . Eat the clams, dear, they are delicious." He wiped his mouth with his napkin.

"Emmanuel," he added suddenly, "I am going to tell you a story . . . Years ago when I was in my salad days," he smiled. "Even I had my salad days, dear . . . I wrote a column called "The Money Market" in the *Financial Times*. It had a certain fame in its day as any surviving old timer on Wall Street will tell you. There are not many left. I have attended most of their funerals. Well in the course of working up one of my columns, I think I was collecting opinions on the freesilver fallacy, I had an appointment to interview old Jerome Samuels in his office. I was a little flustered because he was not an easy man to interview. A great man on the Street in his day. A proud overbearing man. Suddenly I became aware that on the edge of his desk sat the most beautiful creature I had ever seen in my life. It was his daughter Judith, who became after so much heartbreak and trouble your darling mother. She had run into the office to get a check cashed. Some day, dear, I may be able to tell you about our secret courtship but today it is still too near. You were six years old and such a pretty little boy when she passed away. Sometimes it seems as if I had died with her . . . Only seven short years of happiness. But in those days I was full of fire . . . not so wild as you've been, dear, but a gay young blade at that. Until I met your darling mother . . . From the first she felt about me, as she told me afterwards, just as I felt about her. Jerome Samuels disinherited her. He never forgave her, or me. He treated her with heartless brutality. He never relented. Newspaper men were not considered respectable in those days, at least not respectable enough to marry bankers' daughters. Samuels' junior partner was Jules Baum, Adolph Baum's father. They were both creatures of old J.P.'s. When I incurred

56

their enmity I incurred the enmity of the most powerful men in the world. That enmity pursued me relentlessly throughout my career. The Morgan interests . . ."

Jed had been trying to think of some way of breaking in. The tense glitter in his father's eyes frightened him.

"Then there's a sort of poetic justice," he said laughing, "in Adolph Baum's giving me the break of my life." He threw back his head but his laugh sounded forced to his own ears. "I'll tell him that when I see him."

"Tell him nothing . . . Avoid him, Emmanuel . . . Deal with him through intermediaries."

"But he's such a nice little man."

"As nice as a rattlesnake. When your darling mother lay ill in the hospital he refused to transmit a message to her old father. He may even have helped bring about her death. There have been such torturing suspicions."

"J.E., how could Adolph Baum have had anything to do with it?" Jed found his own voice unnecessarily peevish.

A group of men in their shirtsleeves had lumbered into the restaurant. "Quiet. We may be overheard," said J.E. sharply. He went on silently picking the bones out of a piece of boiled scrod.

Meanwhile Jed chewed desperately on the bluefish and the lobster and the blueberry pie his father had ordered for him. Each bite seemed harder to swallow than the last. He knew J.E. had been planning the meal for days. He had to stuff it down. He could feel the tense dark eyes so full of concern, searching his face for every passing thought.

At last the meal was over and he was walking beside his father along the gray gritty street toward the beach, feeling again the stuffed constraint of all the Sundays when he was a small boy, the tedium of inspirational sermons at the Ethical Culture Society, the dreary dark men in turbans or round black silk caps his father and old Mr. Davidson took him to hear in outoftheway lecture halls, the dreadful slow meals squirming on the hard chairs of restaurants, while his father and godfather talked about the reign of peace and brother-hood that would come to all creeds and conditions when man-kind took heed of the words spoken in the East. As if he had been following Jed's thought his father said, stopping at a corner to look into Jed's face: "Emmanuel I pray for you daily to the allwise Father of all men."

Jed had a tantalizing glimpse of the beach, tanned girls in bathsuits running along the edge of the scalloped spume who brought up a stinging memory of Marlowe's sunbrowned body and of the sweet morocco leather seabeach smell that lingered in Suite A, as, still the little obedient schoolboy who'd won all the prizes, his father's pride, always at the head of his class, he turned his back to the shore drive to follow J.E. into the gloom of the rooming house. It was with the pain remembered from boyhood, the feeling of being cramped into his father's dingy life, that he followed his father up the grimy-carpeted stairs of the big old shingled mansion, bristling with turrets and baywindows, built by some rich man in the sev-enties.

J.E. unlocked his door and flattened himself against the wall, almost as a servant would, to let his son go in first. The smell of bayrum and shavingsoap and newsprint was so familiar Jed almost burst into tears.

"Always lock your door," J.E. was saying as he made sure the latch of the yale lock was set to close. "You never know who may have an interest in ransacking your papers."

"J.E. do you know what I'm going to do?" Jed mumbled through a yawn. "I'm going to lay down on your bed and take a nap."

It made his father happy to have his boy take a nap on his bed; Jed could see that through the blur of drowsiness.

"Meanwhile," J.E. was saying, "I'll sit up in the morris-chair and read the Sunday papers. I save every clipping . . . We both, Jed," he added in a voice that quavered with the fear of giving offense, "know too much about how the theatrical page is set up to let ourselves be worried by what the critics say, now don't we? They are ignorant poor devils most of them. We must always remember, dear, there is no evil for those who believe in divine love."

He went on and on, as he'd been going on all these years; Jed didn't listen. He'd heard it before. Still he got a childish pleasure out of his father's soothing voice. He pulled off his jacket and necktie and crawled up on the old brass bed that jingled when he moved. In a moment he was asleep.

When he awoke the sky he saw through the baywindow was full of amberedged afternoon clouds. In a panic he reached for his watch. It was four o'clock. Time to catch the train. He sat up carefully on the edge of the bed so as not to jingle the springs.

His father had fallen into a doze in his morrischair with newspapers piled on his knees. As he sat fastening his shoe-laces on the edge of the bed, Jed looked into J.E.'s tired old face with its green waxy skin so dark in the creases. His chin was sunk on his chest. J.E. was snoring very lightly. With his narrow head and lusterless dark hair he looked like a hand-some old Indian. Thoughts of the loneliness and womanless-ness of old age rushed through Jed's head, thoughts that made him feel ashamed, sinful somehow, like the sons of Noah who looked on their father's nakedness. When he got to his feet a board creaked on the floor and J.E. woke.

With an amused twinkle J.E.'s black eyes were looking

into Jed's. "I know what you are going to say. You have to hurry back to the city on the four fortyseven. I was going to wake you because it's the only train. These theatrical managers lead busy lives . . . I'm going back to the city myself next week. I don't like leaving my files alone at the hotel. Of course they are quite reliable at the Great Western. They have known me so long but sometimes—you'll laugh at your poor old father—I think that man's operatives are trailing me. Just a mental aberration, that's what you'll say, the aberrations of old age. God keep you safe, dear."

When Jed found himself alone and out in the Atlantic air walking fast toward the station everything looked amusing again. The people on the street were funnypaper characters. He felt like a funnypaper character himself.

He walked fast with his hat in his hand. The salty seabreeze was cool in his hair. He felt rested from his nap. Having done his duty to J.E. had left a feeling of lightness in him.

Jed loved J.E. better than anybody in the world, he was telling himself, but being with him put him back into the straitjacket of childhood. Thank God he'd gotten over being a child. He was a man, he told himself as he looked out at the graygreen salt marshes sliding past the window of the train. He was a man grown, with wives and concubines and a little daughter; with his way to make; and plays to write and a theatre to run.

He must get all that into the play. The bursting of that straitjacket, the mastery of the environment. The man who thought the great thoughts imposing them on all the rest. He got out his notebook and started to cover page after page with his rapid scrawl. By the time the train had slid through the tunnel into the Penn Station he had a new ending for the first act of *The Man Who Was Thursday*. He rushed into a phone booth in the station and called the theatre.

Nobody there yet.

He called Kenneth Magill's apartment. A marcelled dramatic school voice answered. Was Kenneth there? "Oh dear he's in his bath." It was Hugh Atwood. The broad "a" irritated Jed so that he almost snapped at the mouthpiece. "Shall I make him come all wet and drippy?"

"I got to speak to him. I've got a new finale to the first act."

When Kenneth came to the phone panting and apologetic, Jed talked his ear off about the new finale. At first Kenneth sounded doubtful. Jed explained it again, in words of one syllable, he thought to himself; then suddenly Kenneth caught on. "Marvelous," he cried, "marvelous." His high jaunty voice jangled the receiver. "Shoot it into me, Jed old top. I'll call a rehearsal. We'll climax it by letting him drop out of sight through a trapdoor. We must be visual, you know. We'll make it . . . er . . . vibrate."

When Jed slipped late into the first directors' meeting after they had to close *The Man Who Was Thursday* nobody looked up to greet him. "You're late, Jed," said Sam Faust, his downcast eyes lost behind his bifocals. His lips outlined the words with a snarling smile. His face had a pale suety look: a turtle's face, the mock-turtle, Jed told himself trying to make it seem funny. "You don't say," Jed jeered. The rest of them kept their eyes fixed on the typewritten sheets of figures scattered round the table. "Here's your copy of the bad news," George muttered through his cigarette and held a sheet up over his shoulder for Jed to take. Although Jed was chairman

61

nobody had made room for him. He dragged a chair over from the corner of the room and edged it into a place beside Sam at the round table under the pinkfringed lamp.

"Now you can't blame me," said Jed looking huffily from face to face. "I never would have chosen that play to open with. I wasn't even consulted."

"Kenneth Magill sold us the idea," grumbled Lew Golton, "because he was in love with his own production . . . Damn little fairy."

"No more of a fairy than the next man. That's a lousy reactionary way of putting it," Eli blurted out.

"What we blame you for Jed," snarled Lew, "is writing such a damn fool play. You're supposed to be the voice of the new theatre in America. Ideologically it was a betrayal of the working class."

"A man's private morals are his own private business," Eli went on.

"It's a dramatization, merely a college boy exercise," Jed said lighting a cigarette and leaning defiantly back in his chair. "Chesterton's story is surely well enough known not to need apologizing for. Meyerhold made a great thing of it . . . And please don't forget that I didn't advise you to do it."

"We should worry," roared Eli cheerfully. "No use crying after the vodka's spilled. The damage amounts to about eightyfive hundred dollars. My lovely sets are on the way to Cain's."

"And we were supposed to limit each production to six thousand dollars," said Lew savagely. "That would give us one tryout each. Somebody's going to get gypped in this deal . . . It's up to you to explain that, George."

"You better ask Magill that question . . . I had no control over the production. After this everything will be budgeted in advance."

"No more bourgeois experimentalism," Lew grumbled on. "We got to keep close to the masses. Strikes are broken by the police. Breadwinners are clubbed down into jails. Their children go hungry. Here we have a windfall from a crazy millionaire and we waste it on the stale mishmash of a fat old clerical fascist."

"Hear hear!" shouted Eli laughing and pounding with his big fist on the table. "Down with the fat men, this is the thin man's theatre . . . Who's got a play ready?"

Lew let the black lashes droop over his eyes.

"The man's blushing. Let's call up the newspapers." Eli upset his chair as he jumped to his feet. "The revolutionary dramatist can still blush." He strode to the phone and pretended to call a number.

"Cut the comedy Eli, for crissake," growled Lew. "I don't care if you never do the damn play."

"Jed," said Sam yawning, "we'll have to buy you a gavel to keep these clowns in order."

Looking pleased with himself, Eli plunked back in his seat. "Well, I can tell you frankly I shan't have *The Eternal* finished for three months. That's the play that will really get us out of the hole." He let out his belly-shaking laugh.

"Well," Lew was actually stammering, "it's a simple proletarian story. It's a simple story of the peons' revolt. Every sweatshop worker in New York will feel they are his brothers."

"It's so simple it's silly," shouted Eli.

Jed found himself talking above the battle in measured tones. After all he was chairman, or wasn't he? It was time the meeting came to order. "Now let's not make any hasty decision. We've got all night. Let's talk all around the subject. Lew and Eli are both wrong."

"You said it," hissed George.

63

"We've got to do both things." Jed kept his eyes fixed on the columns of figures in front of him but he felt himself growing eloquent. "We've got to express the strivings of a new society struggling to break through the shell of the old."

"Attaboy," shouted Eli, "that's the way my wobblies talk."

"To do that we've got to sweep the stage clean of the dead conventions. Human society is suffering and drying up for lack of a creed. The churches are played out. For young people growing up, rejecting the husks of their fathers' castoff phrases, the theatre will take the place of the church. The theatre is the ritual of the revolution. That's what I learned working with the Russians last summer. We've got to go further than they went. Abolish the proscenium arch."

"Can't you damn liberals understand that those Russians Jed thought so hotsytotsy last summer are all clerical fascists, the dregs of czarism the workers swept out of Leningrad?" Lew's eyes glittered. He used his voice like a whip. "Why can't you guys get wise to yourselves for crissake?"

"Why can't you get wise to yourself Lew?" Eli roared. "You're too narrow. You can't do anything unless you look it up in the rulebook first. That may be all right in political life, but the theatre's an art. We got to make poetry out of the struggle. Shakespeare wrote the plays and the critics came along and made the rules. It's enough for us crafties that we're all for the underdog."

"Crafties," Sam's oily laugh rolled out easily, "that's a good one."

"Eli said a mouthful Sam." Jed leaned forward eagerly across the table, talking into Sam's jowly judicial face. "We've got to be crafty . . . Craft means skill, we've got to dramatize the underdog in terms that are boxoffice and also great art. Shakespeare was boxoffice."

64

Jed caught a glimpse of a pitying smile on Lew's face. It was reflected on Sam's. Sam shrugged and put on a mock pained expression. "But my dear boy," he droned, "you must know that Shakespeare was a fascist."

"Exactly," shouted Jed. "It's plain as mud if you read the damn plays. He was first and foremost a political dramatist. The plays are all about the problems of leadership: the rise of monarchy in a disintegrating feudal world. We face the same problem at a different stage in the historical process . . . Read your Marx and Engels, Sam. Socialism, democracy, and working class leadership in a disintegrating capitalist world. We can learn a lot from Shakespeare."

"How about *Romeo and Juliet?*" There was a puckish expression on Eli's big mouth.

"Of course that's about sex."

"Hurray for sex," shouted Eli. "Sex will still be with us even after the revolution. As an artist I appreciate sex."

"But does sex appreciate you?" asked George looking pokerfaced across the table with his fingers to his little mustache.

"That would be telling." Eli shook with laughter until the tears came to his eyes. "I never tell tales out of school."

"Sex in the modern world," said Sam unctuously, "is an economic problem."

"I'm glad Maisie isn't here to hear you say that," shouted Eli suddenly angry. "She'd give you an earful."

Sam's face froze. Jed caught the look of spite on his face.

"Gentlemen, gentlemen," Jed had to shout to be heard. "Aren't we getting off the point?"

"You flatter us," said Eli quietly. "Sam old boy, no offense. You know how much I love Maisie . . . so much you ought to get a gun and shoot me . . . But I'm safe to have in the home because I love 'em all; love 'em and leave 'em, you know that. Not as many as Jed does, maybe . . ."

Jed leaned back in his chair red in the face and comfortably laughing. "Hadn't the meeting better come to order? . . . What I'm trying to get into your thick heads, if you'll pardon the expression, is that this theatre has got to be in the mainstream of history"—he was talking up toward the ceiling— "political; economic, sexual. Once we abolish the proscenium arch we take the theatre right into the middle of people's lives. The Greek theatre was in the middle of life, the Elizabethan theatre was. Now we've got twentyfive thousand dollars to spend on setting the theatre right in the middle of American life."

"Sixteen thousand five hundred," George sharply clicked off the figures.

Jed felt the eloquence seep out of him. "You guys know all this better than I do . . . All we need is one great play, one real hit . . . that will express the enormous . . . the gigantic . . ." he was groping for words. Inside his head he was telling himself: only enough money for two more productions.

"You'll tell us all that in your next play," said Sam waving a pale soothing flipper in front of him. "I make a motion we do Lew Golton's play next. Anybody second it?"

Jed sat limp in his chair. The cigarettesmoke, crinkling in dense folds under the pinkfringed lamp, choked him. His mouth was full of the taste of burned paper. As if somebody had pulled a stopper in his head all the fine phrases he'd thought up drained away. When he tried to speak he found himself dully dragging each word out like lifting a heavy stone out of the mud. Lew sat across from him with his black hair over his eyes and half a grin on his face, every inch the mischievous schoolboy hauled up before the principal. Sam

66

and George argued precisely and coldly back and forth. George was fencing for a postponement but Sam couldn't get him to say whether his own play was ready or not. Sam's turtle's face glistened with little drops of sweat. Jed couldn't catch hold of the things they were saying. He'd long ago lost track of the argument. All he knew was that they all were saying the things they had said before over and over again. Nobody would listen to what anybody else had to say.

It was past midnight when Eli suddenly put his arm round Lew's shoulder and shouted that he'd thought Lew had written a wonderful play all along. He'd fill it with guitar music: "Dawn over Mexico, and the lone voice of a heartbroken whore singing in a cribhouse."

"Hey you can't do that," cried Jed coming to suddenly. "That's in my play."

"We'll make it an old blind marijuana merchant," Eli roared, in his deep rattling voice. "We're bighearted boys."

They all burst out laughing and voted Lew's play unanimously. Everybody started talking at once. Right away Jed got to his feet. "Motion made and seconded. Meeting adjourned," he called out into the din, "and I'm headed for a hamburger."

"Night, night, fellow crafties," intoned Eli and tagged along after him.

"The trouble with this business is a man never gets any sleep," Jed began to grumble as they walked in step into a damp northeast wind. He didn't want to talk to Eli Soltair now. Right now he needed Felicia; he'd have to make Eli go home.

"Sam and Lew they always stick together, that's because they are Party members," Eli was saying in a ruminating tone as if talking to himself. "Now George I'm not sure about. I can't help admiring them for having made up their minds. If they ever get power God help us . . . They'll ride us worse than the bankers and loansharks . . . The guys on our side they always get theirs: Sacco and Vanzetti, the sailors at Kronstadt."

"Preposterous," said Jed. "Sam, that rising attorney, he can't be a commie; he's too prosperous."

"Maybe that's why," Eli hissed into his ear. "Jed you're a babe in the woods."

Jed suddenly felt the gooseflesh climbing his back. For an instant, like in a nightmare, out of the corner of his eye he seemed to see the street and the fronts of the buildings folding to engulf him. He took a deep breath of the wet gusty air. "I hate that place of Sam's," he shouted shrilly at Eli. "After this let's have our meetings at the theatre."

"Sure thing," drawled Eli cheerfully in his purring bass. "But first we've got to find ourselves a theatre at a reasonable rent. There's an old movie palace on Second Avenue I've got my eye on. Then we've got to work up a proper repertory company. Atwood and Sylvia Levy, and Kenneth for a director. At least we've got the beginnings."

Jed liked Eli in this practical vein. Everything seemed suddenly solid and real and congenial again, the taxicabs rolling up the broad avenue under the low scudding clouds rosy with reflected light, and the flickering electric bulbs round the sign on the lunchroom. Looking in through the plateglass he felt that the people inside wore a friendly runofthemill look amid the tile walls and the metal fittings. The pleasantfaced young man in the shortsleeved shirt behind the counter was looking expectantly into Jed's eyes while he waited for the order.

"I hope you got some dough," Eli rumbled laughing as he settled himself to lean comfortably against the counter. "I'm hungry for a steak."

Jed looked in his wallet. "By gum I haven't . . . I can feed us a hamburger each. I'll call Felicia. She's a regular bank."

The pleasantfaced youth behind the counter showed even white teeth. "There's a guy's got a dame where he wants her."

Jed couldn't help the swagger of his hips as he bustled into the phone booth. Thank God she was in. Felicia laughed gruffly and said she'd be right over to bail out the theatre's two white hopes.

When she walked, slim in her slicker, into the lunchroom they both already had their faces full of steak. She slipped Jed two dollar bills. The guy behind the counter popped his eyes. Jed could almost read his lips exclaiming "Class!"

When they were ready to leave they found rain driving in gusts over the empty pavements. It turned out Eli had no place to sleep. Jed handed him the key to his hotel room. "No floosies, Eli," he warned him teasingly. "I shan't have time to look for another room . . . By the time Lew's play flops mine has got to be ready."

"It ain't agoin' to flop," Eli called back as he jerked up his coatcollar. "It's idiotic enough to succeed." He bent his matted head into the driving rain.

"Poor Eli," Felicia was saying as she let Jed in to her house with a latchkey, "he looked so lonely walking off into the rain."

"Eli's nothing but talk," said Jed coldly. "I shouldn't wonder if he was a virgin."

"I like Eli," said Felicia quietly.

"You can have him . . . I'm sick of the whole gang of 'em . . . I got to get to work on this play," Jed was muttering in a low voice as he followed her up the steep familiarly creaking stairs. "I thought it was finished but of course it isn't. It's got to be ready when Lew's play flops. I need a month in the country."

"Suppose we went to Hingham and stayed with the Hardesties?" Felicia had the funniest way, Jed was thinking, of speaking impersonally of the Hardesties as if she hardly knew them. "They might be out on the Cape. It's lovely there in the fall. You'll be shocked at the Hardesties, but I can't help it."

Jed's cheeks burned he hardly knew why. "Wouldn't they prefer to see me after the ceremony?"

"You're so conventional feller," Felicia answered with her silvery laugh. "Mother was a famous suffragette and Scho, that's Father, he's a philosophical anarchist . . . I don't know whether they ever really got married themselves. Mother always calls herself Agatha Hicks. She's a charter member of the Lucy Stone League. They are still in revolt against Queen Victoria. It all seems kind of dated to me."

"You've got a brother, haven't you?" asked Jed hesitantly.

"Yeats? Oxford and Harvard. He doesn't count."

"If they are your people they must be a little like you." Jed had hardly spoken the words before they sounded phony in his ears, like a line he would have had to cut out of his dialogue in a play. "I'll have to like them," he added lamely.

"I guess you're all just about cuckoo enough to suit each other," she said looking him up and down. "I don't know why people have to have families."

As they undressed, he kept following her round the room, asking questions about what her father did for a living, what kind of poetry her mother wrote, what courses her brother taught at Harvard, until she stopped it with "Feller, you ask

70

more questions than a small boy of six. It just sounds too awful when I tell about it."

"I tell you all about J.E."

"I love to hear about J.E.," she answered yawning. "He's my favorite person."

The next night when, ravenous with hunger because they hadn't had time for lunch, they had finally made the Fall River boat after a wild ride in a taxi just as the winches started jingling to haul up the gangway, and were settling down breathless in the dining saloon for an early supper, Jed began questioning her about the Hardesties again. He couldn't seem to get off the subject. A playwright had to know these things. Was her father faithful to her mother? He was aghast when all at once he discovered she was crying.

"You'll just have to find out for yourself when you meet them," she blubbered dabbing at her eyes with a handkerchief. Quick as a flash she was gone from the table.

He'd never seen her cry before. He had an impulse to run after her, but he was too hungry; so he sat there glumly gobbling his food. He'd hardly had time to clean his plate before she was back, tall and crisp and cool again, complaining that he'd been a big pig and eaten all the supper. "I guess I got too hungry, that's all," she said. "I didn't know I could be so emotional."

"It's this damn theatre's getting us down." Jed leaned across the table and patted her hand. She looked gratefully into his face. A warm sweet almost tearful tenderness welled up in Jed when he thought how much she loved him. For once he couldn't find anything to say. When they left the table she took his arm and held on to him tight as they walked silently back and forth on the deck.

71

They walked aft and stood close watching the wake of the broad sidewheeler fade in foaming ripples into the night. The deck underfoot shook with the beat of the paddlewheels and the distant revolving rhythm of the engines. The night lay still over the water. The steamboat's decks were empty. Jed had never felt so alone with Felicia as in this wide wan darkness of the Sound, watching the dim lights along the shore, a buoy that slid by, a lighthouse's faraway flash. He thought how together they were, listening to the crunch of churned water, feeling the moist air like a cool hand on their foreheads. He kissed her quickly in the corner of the mouth as they turned to walk up into the breeze of the steamboat's speed. "My this is a happy night," he said. "Happy," she echoed his words.

When they woke up in the morning everything was quiet. The boat was tied up at the wharf in the stagnant dank reek of Fall River. They dressed in a scramble to catch the train. Felicia was announcing they'd have to stop over in Middleboro so that she could call up the Hardesties. She was explaining she hadn't been able to raise them from New York. No use going to Hingham if they were out on the Cape. "There'll be plenty of time for Hingham. We may be married some years," she said.

In the restaurant across from the station she settled him at a table to eat breakfast while she went into the booth to phone. She kept coming out of the booth for more nickels and quarters. "I'm on their trail," was all she'd answer to his enquiring glances. "They aren't in Hingham," she announced at last when she sat down at the place opposite him where her fried eggs were getting scummy and cold.

The coffee was wretched. The eggs weren't fresh. Felicia wore a mysterious air. Jed was telling himself he liked her better in New York. Why didn't they go take a couple of rooms at some boarding house, he suggested. He didn't want to lose any time getting to work on his play. His voice had a peevish quaver in it . . . "Because we haven't got the money," Felicia answered in a bossy practical voice. Jed began to complain that he wouldn't have come if she hadn't told him everything was all set. Why was everything so vague? She answered ominously that the Hardesties were always vague.

The clanging of a locomotive bell interrupted their little tiff. A lovers' quarrel Jed was thinking tenderly as he paid for breakfast in a hurry. They ran over to the station with their suitcases. A train was waiting at the platform. "Buzzard's Bay" intoned the conductor. "That's right," Felicia chirped, "we'll go to Buzzard's Bay." She climbed into the day coach just as if that was what she'd been planning to do all along.

"It's a relief," he began, all of a sudden cheerful again, "to get out of New York, and away from those damn theatrical people . . . I want to see an entirely different class of people. Maybe we'll never go back."

The train lingered interminably in the station. Jed took his manuscript out of his briefcase and started making pencil marks on it. Going through the motions of working made him feel easier. At least he wasn't losing time. The train slid out of the station and started to wind through slender woodlands all russet with fall and green patches of pine. Felicia kept interrupting him to show him a yellow fern or a clump of purple sumac or a crimson square of cranberries. There were stops at groups of small frame houses; salt marshes, a dory drawn up on a lawn by the front door of a cottage. She cried out at the first sand dune. The train was crossing a trestle. There were streaks of blue water. She was tugging at the suitcases. "Buzzard's Bay," intoned the conductor and they were stepping out into a breeze that smelled of the sea.

73

At the end of the empty platform Jed caught sight of a weedy lighthaired young man in a tweed suit. His thin face was lost under a very large pair of blond tortoiseshell spectacles. Felicia strolled ın a haphazard sort of way toward the young man while Jed followed lugging the suitcases that had begun to cut into his hands and the briefcase that kept slipping out from under his arm. The young man turned toward them without a sign of recognition: "We've lost the Cape train," he drawled in an accusing voice.

"Where are Mother and Scho?"

"I haven't the least idea."

"Have you got a key to the Rambler?"

"I thought you probably had it."

Jed found them both looking at him. Now he could see how much they resembled each other, the same build, the same eyes, the same strawy coloring, only everything that was crisp and collected about Felicia seemed vague and scrambled in her brother. "Oh," Felicia said, as if she'd only just then remembered him; "Yeats this is Jed."

"Oh," said Yeats. He had an odd way of working his big adamsapple up and down before he spoke.

Yeats Hardestie turned out to be the most difficult man to talk to Jed had ever met. Whenever Jed tried to liven things up with a crack of some kind, he would answer with a condescending look and say "Oh." He went on explaining to his sister, as if Jed weren't there at all, that he had come down from Cambridge to spend the weekend at Hingham. Of course the house was locked and he'd missed the right train and of course he'd forgotten to bring any money. "We can afford to feed Yeats some clams, can't we feller?" chirped Felicia.

Jed was answering that he supposed they'd have to when Yeats suddenly looked him in the face in a musing sort of way

74

and asked him: "Can you remember what it was like in your mother's womb?"

Jed opened his mouth but no words came.

"Sometimes I think I can. But after we were weaned," Yeats hurried on, "we effected a transference to the Mater's alligator skin handbag, didn't we Felicia? Like little kangaroos. That's why I can't ever remember to bring any money. The Mater always had it in her pouch. Of course being female Felicia grew up more independent. The male," he intoned, while behind the spectacles the colorless lashes blinked over the pale gray eyes, "is a mere accident of nature."

They left their suitcases with the stationagent and Felicia led the way down toward a landing where she said there was an old man who rented boats. She just had to get out on the water, she was explaining. Thoroughly confused Jed trotted along beside her holding on to her arm. Yeats rambled distractedly after them, every now and then stopping to jot something down in a little notebook he carried in his hand.

"You row," she said to Jed when they had climbed into the lurching dory. The old man with a nutcracker jaw who was holding the gunwale against the weathered boards with a boathook gave Jed a suspicious look. "Keep out of the canal." He talked through his nose in a crackling voice. "The tide'll be running too strong for you there."

"We're old capecodders," said Felicia.

"Humph," said the old man as Yeats almost tipped the dory over scrambling into the bow with his notebook held under his eyes. "We're not going anywhere," Yeats explained.

"I'd be surprised if you wuz," said the old man in a sharp and nasal tone.

It was years since Jed had rowed a boat and then just as a small boy in the still Shaftsbury river. A little sharp chilly breeze nibbled his knuckles. Whichever way he tried to go the tide seemed to be against him. It wasn't long before he felt blisters puffing on the palms of his hands. The day had been a pearly pale blue when they started out. Now white wisps of fog began to crowd in upon them. Invisible gulls cried above their heads.

"The friendly fog," chanted Felicia. "We won't need any suits to go in swimming . . . I know where there's a hidden beach. Keep pulling on your starboard oar feller . . . there's an ancient mariner," she crooned encouragingly.

Behind him in the bow as he tussled with the heavy oars, catching crabs at every other stroke, Jed could hear Yeats murmuring over and over again: "Wanderers, wild, wan, weird, wingéd."

Jed couldn't stop rowing long enough to turn his head. He yanked on his oars to the right and left as Felicia directed him. His arms felt pulled out of their sockets by this time. The bow grated on the sand.

"Haul us up Yeats," Felicia ordered from the stern.

"Assonance and alliteration," cried Yeats and jumped smartly into the water "are the soul of English prosody."

"I didn't tell you to get your shoes wet, silly," Felicia scolded from the stern. They climbed out of the dory and found themselves hemmed in by fog on a small beach of clean sand under a high bank.

"We got to hurry before the fog clears," said Felicia as she stepped out of her dress, "or we'll be in full view of the town."

Jed, feeling thoroughly embarrassed, started glumly tugging at the laces of his shoes.

"Don't mind me," said Yeats as he wriggled out of his trousers, "I'm quite sexless."

"That's what they teach them at Oxford," Felicia shouted

back. She was already in the water, tall, pinkywhite, the blob of her breasts plopping into the crinkled waves. She didn't seem to mind getting her hair wet.

Jed was down to his underdrawers. The fog wrapped round his legs like a damp cloth. He couldn't make up his mind to take the underdrawers off so he plunged in with them on.

Neither Felicia nor her brother paid the slightest attention to him while he floundered around in the chill clear brine near the shore. They swam out fast in different directions until their heads were out of sight in the fog.

Oh God suppose they drown, he was thinking. He took the opportunity to scramble back ashore, wring out his underdrawers and scrub a little of the water off his shivering limbs. He hurried into his shirt and trousers and by the time their wan wet skinny frames reappeared each at a different end of the beach, he was pulling his socks over his sandy feet. While they were dressing he backed off into the underbrush holding the rolledup wet underdrawers behind him and shoved them in a hole in the bank. Felicia looking rosy and fresh, shaking the water off her short hair that lay dark and spiky on her forehead, was announcing that now she really felt they were on the Cape. Yeats chirruped that he hoped Felicia had plenty of money. "Hunger," he added, "is one of the least interesting sensations."

Either they had taken longer than they intended or they had the timetable wrong, but they'd hardly gotten the dory back to the landing and were paying the old man, who was cackling facetiously that he'd expected he'd have to send the Coast Guard after them, when they heard the engine whistle. They had to run for it and just managed to swing aboard the coach as it moved along the platform. "Oh well," cried Felicia breathless, "we'll have a big meal tonight

77

when we break into the Rambler . . . I'm afraid feller," she whispered tc Jed in afterthought, "you'll find the Hardesties a little vague about their meals."

"Vague is one of the really lovely words," intoned Yeats, "vague," he repeated dragging the word out into a moan.

The train rattled and jiggled through the fog. Felicia sat by the window and at each station penciled in her sketchbook outlines of the gray frame houses looming out of the fog, outlines that she never had time to finish before the train started rolling with much clanking and jerking toward the next stop. Yeats was reading a book of verse. He batted his pale eyelashes when he found Jed was looking to see who the author was.

"Being named for him has ruined my life," Yeats explained. "The Mater thought he was her affinity in the early days though I don't really believe they ever met. At Oxford I was a laughing stock."

Jed had hauled the latest draft of his play out of his briefcase and was going through the motions of correcting the third act. "I can't abide the theatre," Yeats added after he'd scanned a couple of lines over Jed's shoulder. "Not even the Irish Players . . . An American theatre? Oh, no, positively not."

Jed was worn to a frazzle and hungry enough to cry before, late that evening, they tumbled off the train at a small empty station. The foggy twilight had wiped every shape and color off the landscape. From the wet sting of the wind Jed guessed they were near the ocean. Felicia jumped out first leaving the men to bring the bags. She came back from a lively interchange with a stubby old dark man with a lantern. "Mr. Francis says the Hardesties are in residence . . . Agatha bought a steak at Mrs. Francis' store this morning so we'll have something to eat, but he doesn't know whether the Ford's

78

running or not. Scho's probably got it stuck in the sand some-place so I guess we'll have to walk."

Felicia led the way across the trestle with Jed's brief-case. Jed followed with two suitcases, planting one foot after another unhappily on the ties. He was sure his foot would slip. There was dark water below. He felt easier when stones and then sand gritted under his feet. Yeats tagged along be-hind carrying only his book and kept complaining that Felicia had taken the wrong path. Jed was too tired to look to the right or left. It was all he could do to drag his feet through the damp sand. The fog was too thick to see anything anyway.

"Are you sure you know the way?" he panted. Finally he lost his temper and stopped in the path and bellowed back to Yeats, "Hey, suppose you carry a suitcase. My hands are sore."

"Ah yes," said Yeats meekly, "I was merely holding my-self in reserve."

It was growing darker by the minute. At last lights loomed dimly above them. Felicia called back to cheer up, it was the next cottage. Now they were climbing up a dune. Jed's shoes and the cuffs of his trousers were filling with sand. They stumbled puffing onto a shaky wooden porch.

Through a torn screen door, Jed caught sight of an elderly woman with scrawny gray hair writing at a board on her knees under an oil lamp. In spite of the noise they made she didn't look up. Yeats was whining that he had dropped the suitcase at the foot of the hill, so Jed had to go back and grope around after it.

When he managed to clamber back on the porch again a voice addressed him through the screen. It was a voice like Felicia's but brassbound with authority. "Better take your shoes off . . . I don't like sand in the house." When he stum-bled in with his shoes in his hand, Felicia's eyes looked out at

79

him from under the elderly woman's gray hair. Obviously the Hardesties all looked very much alike. "Well here you are at last," the elderly woman was saying. It was Felicia's mouth. "Thank God Felicia can cook . . . Go back in the kitchen and don't make too much noise . . . I'm writing."

In the dim back room he found his own Felicia frying a piece of steak over a smoky kerosene burner. What looked like tomato soup was heating over the other burner of the rusty stove. At the oilcloth-covered table Yeats sat munching bread and butter, his pale eyes fixed on the tiny autumnal midges that hovered over the unshaded lamp.

"Is that all there is?" Jed asked miserably. Felicia nodded. Jed cut himself a slice of bread and managed to snatch a sliver of cheese Yeats was already reaching for. "Cheer up," Felicia was saying, "we'll provision the fort in the morning."

Jed stuffed down all the bread and burned his mouth on the soup. The little piece of steak she put on his plate just made him hungrier. He was reaching for the T bone left on the platter when he found a big dirty brown hand covered with black hairs had pounced ahead of his.

"Pardon," said a fluty tenor voice.

When Jed looked up he saw a very tall bronzed young man in a leather jacket standing on bare feet planted far apart in the middle of the kitchen. He had lustrous black hair and lustrous black eyes. "Thanks Felicia darling," the young man was saying. Felicia said Jed this was Ivan and the young man's white teeth gave Jed a confidential smile from behind the steak bone. "I was sent over for Agatha but she won't go. You better all come. We're drinking Belgian alcohol."

"Where?" Jed groaned.

"You walked the poor guy from the station. Felicia how could you?" Ivan seemed to be feeling very good. Jed was wondering whether it was natural high spirits or the Belgian alcohol. "I wouldn't blame him if he walked out on you."

"Any more cheese?" asked Jed. Felicia shook her head.

"Felicia turned me down, oh hundreds of times." Ivan looked Jed in the eyes smiling confidentially. "I escaped a fate worse than death . . . but don't worry Jed, they've got grub over at the Godwins'," he added flashing his toothy smile. "Scho and Dr. Godwin are in wonderful form. They've already taken the universe to pieces and put it together three times."

As Jed got shakily to his feet Ivan put his arm round his shoulder. Jed pulled back a little from the sour alcoholic breath. "You won't have to walk, Jed old boy, I've got the Ford. Better put your shoes on. Toes get stepped on. Mine are tough." He held one of his big dusty bare feet up, and admired it in the lamplight.

"You children go along," commanded Agatha's voice from the front room, "then I'll have some peace and quiet."

Climbing after her into the rumbleseat of the roadster, Jed reached for Felicia's hand, but she pulled away from him. "I'm back in another world," she whispered in a little tremulous voice, "I'll come to you later, feller."

Just as Ivan started the motor, Yeats, who had been awkwardly adjusting his long legs in the front seat, started to clamber out again. "I've changed my mind," he chanted in his most Oxonian tones. "The Mater won't mind me . . . ta ta." Felicia and Ivan burst out laughing at the same moment.

"Always in character," said Ivan.

"Yeats always changes his mind," Felicia explained to Jed. "Yeats suffers from abulia."

The Godwins' house was large, square, whitepainted, set under dripping trees. Electric light glared from out the win-

81

dows. As soon as Ivan stalled his motor with a screech of gears on the lawn, Jed heard the muffled babble of voices. Following hard on Felicia's heels in through the front door he caught sight of a granite hewn square face under a massive bald head plastered with swatches of hair streaked gray and yellow. A pair of opaque blue eyes far apart glowed dully behind a tumbler of whitishlooking liquid. That must be Scho.

"Without the intense purification of the sensual," Scho was saying in a rumbling expository tone, "man cannot free himself from his own libido." He was addressing himself to a neatly dressed man across the table from him who wore a trimmed square black beard above a bow tie and a starched white shirt. Jed groped his way toward the table stepping over the legs of a number of shaggylooking couples propped on their elbows on the floor. "Behavioristically speaking . . ." The man in the beard tried to break in, but Scho went on talking. "It is only through his senses, through his vices" —Scho lifted his glass—"see, I'm willing to admit it . . . that a man is able to escape from the principled barbarism of today." He let out an oddly rasping dry laugh. "This doomed intellectualism aims to inhibit life . . . Life flows."

The man with the beard had a cast in one of his brown eyes that gave him a leering expression so that everything he said seemed to have some faintly smutty connotation. "But how are you going to reduce life's flow to practice Scho? All behavior is essentially formal."

Waiting with "How do you do" frozen on his lips Jed stood shifting his weight from one foot to the other. Scho was looking down into his glass with the expression of an actor trying to remember his lines.

"In a misguided effort to free themselves from this formalism," the words poured out in a sudden rush from Scho's wide mouth, "people throw themselves into revolutionary movements, religion, psychoanalysis, anything to forget the ego. But the id remains."

"Scho," the man in the beard was asking impudently, "have you ever thought of getting yourself psychoanalyzed?"

"I don't need to, my whole life is a confession. I confess my shortcomings to Agatha, to my daughter, to my son, to the first stranger I meet in a speakeasy . . ." Scho's blue eyes were focusing on Jed's face with an expression of mild surprise at finding it unfamiliar, "Perhaps, young man, you can tell us how you anesthetize your ego?"

"If we could produce a decent social system," cried Jed jumping into the argument, "we wouldn't have to worry about our egos."

"The cart before the horse," cried the man with the beard.

"My Lord," Scho suddenly cried out, "nobody's given the young man a drink." Scho closed his mouth over his square jaw and looked Jed over ruminatively. "You are undoubtedly the longawaited Jeff Morris. Jeff meet the doctor. Everybody calls me Scho." He laughed his rasping selfdeprecatory laugh. "Where has Felicia gone? Felicia, can't you get your friend Jeff a drink?"

Somebody had pushed a chair into the back of Jed's legs. "I'm Martia Godwin," said a cosy looking little redfaced woman. "You mustn't mind me."

"People usually call me by my initials, J E D," said Jed firmly.

"Quod est demonstrandum . . . Just what I was saying," said Scho.

Feeling thoroughly nonplused Jed sat sipping the tumbler somebody had placed in his hand. Not as bad as he'd expected, tasted of lemon. A phonograph in the back room had started up "*I'm just wild about Harry.*" Out of a corner of an eye Jed saw Felicia and Ivan flit dancing past the doorway. *"And Harry's just wild about me."* The shaggy couples were dancing.

Jed made a move to get up from his chair, but Scho's amused blue eyes held him down. "Of course," he was saying, "you are impatient to lead us into the promised land. What you'll have to learn, Jeff, is that the promised land is within . . . The light within . . . Debs understood that when he said that if he led the American working class into the promised land somebody else would be there waiting to lead them out again. We Hardesties came to this country on the Speedwell, not on the Mayflower like Agatha's people. But we all came seeking the promised land. The first Schofield Hardestie was a disillusioned man. In every generation there was a Hardestie ready to protest that whatever arrangements the local authorities made weren't good enough to be the promised land. My father and grandfather made money in the Colorado mines. Their smouldering disillusionment with the materialism of capitalism flamed up in my generation in a new search for the light within."

Jed drank his drink down. "But Mr. Hardestie how can people working for ten hours a day in a shirtfactory find time to seek the light within?"

"Answer him Scho," said the doctor leering over his beard as he refilled the glasses from a pitcher.

Jed tried to get to his feet.

"No. You've started something. We must argue this through." Scho leaned over and put his hand on his shoulder and made a gesture of showing him off to the doctor as if he were some zoological specimen. "The unrestrained violence of the idealist," he exclaimed in almost an admiring tone. "The trouble with the revolutionary movement is that it's as materialistic as capitalism. He would have us all be paid full

84

wages for marching in columns of four . . . Onward Christian Soldiers and nobody must walk on the grass."

"But that's what the revolution is for," Jed found himself shouting. "We want to produce enough grass for everybody to walk on. Belief in individual liberty is my profoundest conviction, but first you've got to have economic justice."

"Have you faced the fact that every man is alone in the universe?" asked Scho, his eyes flaming an alcohol blue. "It is through the gentle arts, drinking and dancing and music and singing, that we can foment that progressive getting together of all elements of the community that makes the essential development of civilization. Politics makes men brutes. Only art melts the hard outlines of the ego. The theatre now—"

"The theatre"—Jed snatched at the word—"that's where I live."

Right away they were all three of them on their feet and shaking hands. Scho was pouring what was left in the pitcher into their glasses. Scho's face had become very red.

"I should have been an actor, Jeff," he was whispering confidentially into Jed's ear. "An opera singer, maybe a dancer . . . A girl in Havana told me I should take a job as a professional rhumba dancer." He gave his potbelly a sudden jiggle under the checked flannel shirt. "With practice, she said." His short laugh rasped into Jed's ear. "Life has taken on a new wonderful beauty since I learned to cultivate my abdomen. We should all cultivate our abdomens. The rhumba takes practice." He sighed. "I've been too busy living to practice much of anything . . ." He was looking sourly into the bottom of his tumbler. "Ted, it can't be that the medicine's run out."

The doctor slapped them each heartily on the back. "We can remedy that. Martia," he called. Nobody answered. His voice couldn't be heard above the racket of the dancing couples singing *"I'm just wild about Harry."* The doctor poked his beard toward Jed's ear. "Makings are in the kitchen," he whispered hoarsely.

The room lurched when Jed took his first step to follow them. What on earth was that tune? His ears hummed. Asking himself dully why the hell wasn't he dancing, he wove his way after them among the couples spinning to the lurching tune. Then he stood looking preternaturally wise while, slowly, with exaggerated care, Scho poured the colorless fluid into a pitcher out of a shining tin can, and added drops out of some little bottles. After each step in the operation Jed and the doctor nodded wisely, as if they were taking part in an arduous scientific experiment. Scho added a squeeze of lemon, stirred some ice into the pitcher and triumphantly poured the liquid into the tumblers.

"Delicious," said the doctor. "Delicious," echoed Jed.

"I'm just wild about Harry." Jed felt very wise when he remembered what the tune was. They'd been playing it since time began. *"And Harry's just wild about me."* He had to hold tight to his tumbler to keep the room from spinning with the disk on the phonograph. Faces, faces, no Felicia. Whirling faces, no Ivan. He began to roam through the house, opening doors, squinting at figures passed out on beds.

At the foot of the stairs he met a curlyhaired tweedy man in plus fours and a striped necktie. "Bathroom's right at the head of the stairs," he announced. "Put it in myself, I ought to know." He inspected Jed carefully. "Now I suppose you are a visiting artist."

Jed pulled himself together. "Playwright," he growled.

"My, my, I never met a playwright . . . A real Broadway playwright?"

Jed nodded huffily.

"My name's Nickerson." The tweedy man was holding

out his hand. "I furnish the refreshments. I don't drink myself, but I find the conversation educational. Had to leave school early, you understand."

Jed grasped his hand. "Mine's Morris, J. E. D. Morris," he said threateningly. "Where's Felicia?"

"The Hardestie girl? Very artistic. It all broadens a man's horizon."

"I'm not jealous," Jed was insisting, "jealousy is a petty bourgeois emotion."

"You understand Mr. Morris," the tweedy man was answering with an air of exaggerated tact, "these folks are very freespoken but they know where to draw the line, the girls particularly. I found that out right away. I respect them for it. A man who wants to improve his mind needs to meet people he can respect, intellectually, you understand . . . Not many intellects a man can respect in my business. Rum row and that sort of thing . . . Here I find the conversation educational. These folks read books."

Jed felt very thirsty. He was painfully climbing the stairs to the bathroom. There was a huddled couple on a cot in the dark upper hall. The light was too bright in the bathroom. Jed couldn't find a glass so he drank from the tap. Hope he doesn't drink too much, he was telling himself sagely. "Alone in the universe," he could still hear Scho's voice and that horrible tune. On the way back downstairs he slipped and slid. Horrible racket. Horrible argument. The bootlegger had gone so he stood in the hall alone in the universe rubbing the calf of his leg where he'd skinned it. Where the hell was Felicia?

All the doors were closed. Eeny meeny miney mo he opened the wrong one and stumbled out on a back porch. He stood with his legs wide apart looking down into a hollow filled with a hunched confusion of appletrees silvered over from a moon that rode over tattered blurs of fog. "Felicia!"

His voice echoed back off an old barn on the hill behind the appletrees.

"Where you been feller?" Her voice came from under his feet so loud it startled him. "Give me a hand . . . No, other hand." Her face appeared suddenly above the porch floor at his feet. She scrambled over the rail and they both stood swaying in the moonlight. "Time to go home now," she said thickly. "Moon's in his last quarter and a lil' squiffy, but we mushn't tell Agatha . . . Agatha won't like Felicia lil' squiffy."

"Where's Ivan?"

"Fell off the porch," she giggled and made jabbing motions downward with her forefinger. "Down among the deadmen."

"Let him lay," snarled Jed.

She looked up at him with muzzy surprise. "Musn't worry about Ivan, feller. He's just a pet puppy . . . Known him all my life."

"I'm not jealous, you understand. Jealousy is a petty bourgeois emotion." Hadn't he heard himself say that somewhere before? "It's a damn lie that we're alone in the universe," he shouted at Felicia.

"All alone," she chanted. "I know the way home. Time to go home feller." Before he understood what was happening she was leading him down a sandy road. "All alone," they chanted together. Jed was so tired he could barely put one foot in front of the other. He never would have made it without Felicia. It was all muzzy mist and moonlight. He held on to her hand and let her tow him up the last sandy hill. He let go Felicia's hand and dropped. She'd vanished up into the muzzy moonlit house. But he was too tired. He had a bright idea to stop and rest a minute inside a little house. Cutest little shingled house. He leaned against a door. Cleverly he worked the latch, just to rest a minute and lay down on the straw.

When he awoke he reached out for Felicia. An agitated cackle startled him. He sat up with a start and hit his head against some sort of shelf. A white hen was cocking one shining eye at him from out of the darkness above. His head ached horribly. How in hell had he ever gotten into a henhouse? His nose was full of the acid reek of chickendroppings. Better get out of there before he puked.

It took him a while to find a way out. When he crawled out of the bottom part of the door blinking into bright sunlight he ran head on into a woman's skirts. "I beg your pardon." When he looked up he saw it was Agatha, tall and angular in an oldfashioned poke bonnet with a basket on her arm. She yelped with laughter. "What a plight for a soninlaw," she shouted. "This makes my day."

Jed straightened himself up huffily and began to brush straw and chickendroppings off his suit.

"Come along," she said with unexpected kindness, "I'll give you some hot coffee. I'm certainly going to give Scho a piece of my mind. Sometimes I think he arranges things like this on purpose."

Jed shambled sheepishly after her into the kitchen.

"Mrs. Hardestie," Jed stammered through the towel after he'd washed his face in a basin of cold water at the kitchen pump. "I came up here to work."

"That's what they all say. The trouble with Scho is he's never had to do a lick. Had plenty of money all his life. If he had to work he wouldn't drink. His selfindulgence is monumental . . . Sit down at the table. While the coffee's heating I want to talk to you."

Jed sat with his eyes on the rose and trellis pattern of the worn oilcloth tacked unevenly on the table and stiffened himself for a lecture. He could hear the older woman's short decided steps as she moved round the stove. He felt that he was balancing a huge weight of headache on the brittle stem of his neck.

"I'm worried about Felicia," Agatha was saying.

"Felicia's one of the best adjusted people I ever met," he answered, making an effort to turn his face up toward her with his boyish smile. "Maybe that's why I'm so attracted to her. She's so competent. My first wife was thoroughly incompetent."

"Men don't know anything about women," Agatha said sharply as she set a cup of coffee down in front of him.

"But she's a successful illustrator."

"Scho and Yeats complain that she's commercializing her art, but I say, rats!" snapped Agatha.

"She gets well paid for her work," Jed answered eagerly. "Coming out of this environment . . ." his voice trailed off.

Agatha stood across the table from him with her bony hands clasped across her stomach. "You don't like it?" she asked.

He shook his head. She smiled appreciatively.

"You remember this and never forget it." Her eyes glinted sharp as a hen's from under the poke bonnet. "Women seem collected, but actually we are often near the breaking point . . . Making your own living isn't any trick. Thousands of women make their own livings. I made my own living till I met up with Scho Hardestie. I could right now if I had to . . . Ever since she was a little thing Felicia's been on the ragged edge. Be careful of her drinking, Jed Morris. Of course she has talent. I don't know why I had such high-strung children. It's a wonder I didn't wring their little necks."

"Of course," said Jed, "it's hard for anybody to adjust to the cockeyed society we live in."

Agatha was looking him hard in the eyes. Jed fancied her thin lips drew together as if she didn't like what she saw. She must have noticed he was ever so slightly crosseyed. "I hope you won't let her down," she added in a tired voice, "she's the only daughter I've got. That's all for now." She turned her back and walked out of the room.

Jed sat slumped at the table, taking little sips of the hot bitter coffee. His skull ached. His stomach was sour. He couldn't remember having said anything sensible all evening. His head felt puffed up like a balloon with last night's dismembered phrases. Lord he wished he was back in that quiet room at the Hudson Hotel with his typewriter and the New York *Times*.

When Felicia came in looking fresh and brisk as usual he caught himself giving her a searching look to see if she was sober. "Feller I feel awful" he mumbled into his coffee cup.

She put her hand on his forehead. "A man has to be a capecodder to drink that stuff," she said soothingly.

"You feel all right?"

She nodded cheerfully. "Felicia's never had a hangover in her life."

"I don't know that country life suits me," he grumbled. "There isn't any place to work . . . I've got to finish this damn play."

"We'll go up on a hill, in the hogcranberry," Felicia was saying dreamily. He followed her in a daze. He really did love her. He needed her selfpossession he was telling himself. It turned out to be a beautiful azure autumn day. On Felicia's hilltop they sat in the bronzy hogcranberry looking out at a river meandering through salt marshes and the bay and the white churches that lay like ships at anchor on the swelling hills around them. Felicia unpacked her things and started to paint a watercolor.

In spite of the hot steel rims on his eyes Jed lay beside her trying to convince himself that the corrections he was scribbling on the margins of his typescript made sense and taking a numb sort of pleasure in the view and the high air and the humming solitude until all at once he fell asleep.

The tenor voice woke him saying "Don't you think hangovers are charming?" How the hell did Ivan find his way up there? Jed lay on his back without opening his eyes. Ivan was talking to Felicia. Jed didn't hear what Felicia said. "The feeling of being outside of it all, the feeling that time is suspended," warbled Ivan. "Do you suppose we drink for the hangover? Just not to have anything to do next day?" Jed felt his muscles stiffening with irritation as he lay in the hogcranberry listening to their voices going on and on. How did they find so much to say to each other?

Suddenly he opened his eyes and sat up and faced them. "What I'm going to do," he announced to Felicia, "is go down to the cottage and get your mother to find me a bed where I can get a good night's sleep."

Felicia smiled at Ivan the same funny little smile she'd smiled at Yeats, the little smile that made Jed feel a hundred miles away. Ivan smiled back fawningly. "Already," her voice sounded amused, "he's siding with Agatha."

Jed jerked to his feet and walked away from them down the hill.

When he woke up rain was driving against the window next his head. From the bluish light that filtered through the streaked panes he couldn't tell whether it was evening or morning. His watch had stopped. He stretched himself and felt his forehead carefully with his fingertips. No headache. His mouth felt clean. He felt cheerfully hungry. Felicia tall in her wet slicker stood smiling affectionately at him from the foot of the bed. "You slept round the clock, feller. You must have been dead tired. Everybody says that was why the alky hit you the way it did."

"You know how I hate to get drunk," groaned Jed.

"Agatha thinks you're the nicest guest she ever had," Felicia giggled a little. "Let sleeping guests lie, that's her motto. Look feller, a northeaster's blown up. It may rain for a week. That racket you hear is the mobilization of the Hardesties. We're all catching the morning train to Hingham. Ivan drove Yeats up the Cape last night. Yeats said to tell you 'Cheery O.' Isn't he awful?"

Jed jumped out of bed. He actually had his pajamas on. He grabbed Felicia and kissed her skillfully all over her face. "I feel like a fighting cock," he said. "I'll have my bag packed as quick as a flash."

He shaved in cold water in the basin with a picture of the old mill on the bottom. As he scraped his face with a dull blade he caught himself singing. *"I'm just wild about Harry."* Where in the dickens did he pick up that tune? Lord that bootlegger. He burst out laughing. He would have to get him into a play. Clear as magiclantern slides, scenes for *Shall Be the Human Race* started skimming through his head. He found himself a clean shirt and snapped his bag to. "I'm going to have to work on the train," he proclaimed as he slid in between a chair and the oilcloth, facing Scho, whose big shoulders were crouched over a plate of fried eggs on the opposite side of the table. Scho smiled vaguely. "We accept the universe," he said.

While they ate their breakfast they sat looking at each other in mild appraisal. Agatha and Felicia made bustling

93

thumping noises as they dragged suitcases around in the front room. "The squaws of the tribe break camp," Scho murmured, "while the old chief and the young brave sit at the council-fire."

"I'll have to work all the way down on the train," Jed said to nobody in particular.

"The optimism of youth," Scho rumbled.

"This has all been . . . very restful," Jed was beginning in a polite embarrassed tone when Felicia interrupted. "You men have exactly eight minutes left to eat." She plunked a plate down in front of him.

Still chewing a mouthful of toast, with the feeling that he had egg on his chin, he slipped into somebody's oilskins, grasped two suitcases, and followed at the end of the procession down the sandhill into the driving rain. Whichever way they walked the rain drove into their faces all the way to the station. They had to cross that wretched trestle again and Jed had a vision of the engine ripping into them from behind. His feet were soaked and there was a cold trickle down his neck by the time they got into the shelter of the station. He was sure he was catching a cold. Jed got to the ticket window ahead of anybody. "Two to Hingham," he told the ticket agent. He gritted his teeth. "And two on the Fall River boat to New York."

He barely had money enough to pay for the tickets.

"But what'll we do when we get there?" whispered Felicia.

"You can do what you like," Jed thrust out his jaw. "I'm going to shut myself up in the Hudson Hotel."

All the way up the Cape he sat huffily in a seat by himself scratching away on the margins of his typescript. As a part

94

of the background racket of the train he could hear Scho's voice rumbling on in the front part of the car. By the time the train pulled into Middleboro he'd accomplished enough to be in a boisterously cheerful mood. He made himself charming when he said goodbye to the older Hardesties, so charming that Scho pressed both his hands and quoted: "The youth who bore 'mid snow and ice, a banner with the strange device: Excelsior." He even got a farewell smile out of Agatha'a bleak lips.

When the train pulled out leaving them alone on the platform waiting for the Fall River local, Jed grabbed Felicia's hands and spun her around. "Alone at last, feller," he shouted.

"All alone," she mocked. "I told you the Hardesties were embarrassing," she went on gaily. "Introducing one's loved ones is always an ordeal."

"At least there's a play in them," shouted Jed.

Felicia frowned. Jed had to spin her around some more to get the frown off her face. They were chirpy as crickets waiting for the Fall River local. "We've got the whole afternoon to ourselves," he kept exclaiming. "And then a lovely dinner on the boat and the quiet Sound. The trouble with the country is it's too crowded."

They loved it in Fall River. The rain fell in sheets. They sat through a flickering Western in a smelly little motion picture house and cheered the villain and giggled and clapped. They bought comic postcards and hurried on board the boat to write them to their friends. At first they had the decks to themselves. They felt like highschool kids on a holiday. Hand in hand they ran up and down the companionways and nudged each other and made uncomplimentary remarks about the passengers that poured on board from the Boston train while the phlegmy whistle shook the air. "If we only had a drink,"

Felicia was murmuring under the din, "just to wet our whistles before dinner."

Jed looked up into her face. She was smiling at someone. Ivan was shambling toward them through the crowd. He needed a shave. He still wore the leather jacket, but at least he had sneakers on his feet.

"Bless you my children," he said smiling his fawning smile.

"Alky?" asked Felicia.

"Yea verily," he said and put a hand on each of their shoulders.

"Where on earth are you going?" asked Jed in a not at all cordial voice.

"To prostitute myself in the public market," Ivan answered laughing. "To New York to get a job. You plutocrats must have a stateroom."

Felicia led the way. Ivan produced a bottle out of the pocket of his leather jacket and mixed the drink with a ceremonious air that set Jed's teeth on edge. There was only one glass so they called it a loving cup. Felicia and Ivan drank most of it. Felicia counted the money in her handbag and announced she could feed them all supper.

"Be sure you save out taxifare," Jed heard himself say in a stuffy husband's voice. "I can't lose any time in the morning."

Dinner dragged. Jed heard all about Ivan's uncle who edited a pulp magazine and always had a job for Ivan when he needed it. "Doing what?" asked Jed. "Writing crap," said Ivan triumphantly.

As soon as he'd finished his coffee Jed left them chattering over glasses of gingerale Ivan kept spiking from his bottle. Muttering how do they find so much to talk about he undressed and climbed into the lower berth with a volume of

96

Shaw's plays. Not to copy but for the stimulus, he told him-self. He couldn't keep his mind on the lines. How do they find so much to talk about? he kept asking himself. He locked the stateroom door. Then he unlocked it. "Well if she don't come we're through," he said aloud. "That will be that."

When she came he had already dozed off. He looked up at her blinking. "Poor Ivan," she was tittering, "Mother would say he hasn't found himself."

"He found us all right," shouted Jed sitting up. "He spoiled my evening."

She ran to him and kissed him hard on the mouth. "You," she said. She was quite tight. He jumped up and pulled her clothes off and dragged her brutally into the bunk.

Next morning he hustled her off as soon as the boat docked for fear of running into Ivan. It was a drizzly November dawn. Pricked out with dim lights in the mist the sky-scrapers roared and hummed about them. He slammed their bags into a cab and shouted to the driver: "The Hudson Hotel on 10th Street, please . . . He can take you around to your place afterwards, feller," he added soothingly. Already he saw himself stepping into the narrow hotel lobby, picking up the New York *Times* off the pile on the corner of the elevator and settling himself over a cup of coffee at his typewriter in the quiet of his hotel room.

He didn't call up anybody from The Craftsman's Theatre until he'd finished his final draft and taken it to Felicia to type. He left the top copy for Sam Faust at his office. A couple of days later the phone rang while he was shaving. "Why Jed you mysterious fellow we thought you were still out of town," Sam's voice oiled his ear. "Your play is something of a masterpiece. Lew and I have both read it. Only a few mini-

97

mal details to iron out. Order us breakfast and I'll stop by your hotel before I go to the office. Has Eli seen it yet?"

"No, I haven't seen hide or hair of him . . . I've been saving him a carbon."

"Just as well," Sam's enunciation grew scornfully precise. "He claims to have his dramatic masterpiece finished too. I'll get Lew out of bed and we'll be right up."

They arrived at Jed's door at the same time as the waiter with the breakfast, Sam wide and spruce in a pink shirt and a doublebreasted brown suit and a cashmere overcoat and Lew grubby and unshaven as if he'd been dragged out of a Bowery dosshouse. Sam did all the talking. Looking everywhere except in Jed's face, he talked and talked. *Shall Be the Human Race* was a great human document, it had all the possibilities of a smashing success both commercially and artistically. It was timely, it was significant, but there were loose ends that needed to be tied up. It was a question of a more disciplined distribution of ideas.

Lew, his swatch of black hair over his eyes, had been stuffing on the scrambled eggs and bacon. Glowering over his coffee cup he hissed at Jed: "Social-fascist implications . . . We want a play that the movement will stand squarely behind."

Jed's cheeks began to burn. "It damn well ought to stand behind it. It's the first time the revolution has been put on the stage . . . I mean in this country, of course," he added lamely.

Exactly. Sam made motions with his pudgy pale hands as if he were stroking velvet. That was why they wanted to smooth the kinks out. He had a friend who was thoroughly disciplined in Leninism, a man high up in the movement, a Marxist scholar. He'd consented to read it. Jed should consider it a privilege to have him read it. In spite of a crushing load

98

of duties he was reading it today. Sam had arranged a little dinner at his house that night. His voice dropped to an awed whisper, like a man talking in church. "V. F. Calvert has consented to come."

"They are talking about us on 12th Street," Lew chimed in solemnly. Their tone made Jed uncomfortable. He had a second's vision of himself pushing chocolate cream pies into their solemn faces, like the tramp in burlesque. He began noisily to insist he'd rather have Rodney Acres or Mark Sugar's opinion, at least they knew what was boxoffice.

"They don't know from nothing," snarled Lew. "Get wise to yourself, Jed. The workers don't know you're alive. Now they'll come to see my play . . . for personal reasons. They know I'm one of 'em. But they don't know who you are, just some damned social-fascist Broadway highbinder." Jed couldn't help wincing at the sting in his voice. "If V. F. Calvert"—Lew's voice dropped to a whisper when he pronounced the name—"likes your play he can line up real working class support."

"If we can get the backing of the real working class organization"—Sam looked Jed warily in the eye—"your play would be the logical production to follow *Dawn over Mexico*."

"Oughtn't we to decide that at a directors' meeting?" Jed was stammering.

"We've got a majority right here." Jed's eyes followed the curious cruel curl of Sam's lips. He suddenly found himself sweating.

"By gum we have." Jed could feel his heart beating inside his shirt. He had a feeling of being clamped in a straitjacket. "All right Judge Faust," he made an effort to drag a laugh out of his throat. "Bring on your attorney for the prosecution. I'll certainly listen to what he has to say."

Sam cleared his throat, reached for his hat and looked Jed in the face out of green eyes lusterless behind his glasses. "Six fortyfive exactly," he said. "Our . . . er . . . friend," his voice stumbled over the word, "has a tight schedule."

"Get wise, guy." Lew dribbled the words out of the corner of his mouth as he filed out of the door after Sam Faust.

Jed was too jittery to stay in his hotel room. The green-papered walls were closing in on him. Where had he read that green walls drove people mad? He hurried over to Felicia's. She had on her blue smock and was leaning over her drawing board with an abstracted air with a cigarette in the corner of her mouth. When he put his arms round her to kiss her she wriggled away from him. They had just called up she explained. Illustrations for a magazine article. Rush order. Since she couldn't have a vacation, she might as well make some money. She tossed her light curls off her forehead and went back to her drawing board.

Jed picked up an evening paper of four days ago he found on a chair and stretched out on the unmade bed. He read column after column without understanding a word. Words and phrases raced through his head. He wanted to tell Felicia. He was used to spilling everything to Felicia. He wanted to tell Felicia but he couldn't find the right words. He jumped to his feet. "I've got the heebiejeebies feller, I'll go to a burlesque show."

"Too early," said Felicia without looking up.

"Hell, it'll have to be a movie."

"How about supper?"

"I have an engagement . . ." Jed heard his own voice drop into the conspiratorial whisper that had so jarred on his ears in Sam and Lew that morning. "Theatre business."

"After?"

"Sure thing feller."

When he got out on the street he felt intolerably lonely. He fought off an impulse to go back up to Felicia's warm room. It was a too bright day of steel sunshine that stung the eyes and of lashing northwest wind. His mouth was full of grit by the time he'd battled along the cold pavements as far as 14th Street. He ducked into the first motion picture show and sat through two reels without paying attention to what he was seeing. He couldn't even remember what he'd been thinking when he came to with a start and pulled out his watch. It was after twelve. He snatched up his coat and hat and walked out.

He had hardly stepped blinking into the glare and bustle of 14th Street when he was being pummeled by a grinning ape with a windblown frizzly head. "Just who I wanted to see," Eli was roaring. "The crafty playwright, hooray."

"I got to go to a burlesque show," stammered Jed.

"To study the art of the theatre. The old craftie! Of course it's the only real tradition, that and the circus. Dates back to Roman times .   . But first we'll eat lunch . . . An apocalyptic lunch. I got plenty money. Floos, dinero, mazuma, denguee. I've finished *The Eternal*. Let's go on a binge. I know a place we can get real beer. Come along."

Jed was carried away on a torrent of talk. As he followed him east through the hustling crowd, just to keep his end up, Jed began in a high strained voice to tell tall stories of life in an artists' colony, redhaired girls on studio couches, nude bathing on foggy beaches. "I had to come away . . . I couldn't get involved . . . on account of Felicia," he confided as they ducked down some steps into a little restaurant off Second Avenue.

Eli wanted to order everything on the menu. Jed finally

got him to settle for beer and wiener schnitzels à la Holstein, with liverpaste to begin with.

"Seen any crafties since you got back?" Eli asked with his mouth full of ryebread and liverpaste.

"Why no," said Jed. He felt the muscles of his face stiffen. His hands were cold. There was a quaking in his chest. "Been working on my play."

"Damn good thing." Eli took a swig of beer and wiped the foam off his thick lips with the back of his hand. "A couple of our fellow craftsmen have been sucking around after me to get me to join the Party. The Party it seems is taking an interest in the arts. They'll be after you too. Give 'em a straight arm, Jed. What do you think of this goddam Communist Party anyway? I think they are worse than the capitalists. I agree with the poor old wobblies."

"That's ancient history." Jed suddenly felt cool and collected again.

"So's burlesque, so's the circus, so's Jesus Christ and every good thing in this cockeyed world."

"I haven't made up my mind yet," said Jed coldly. The redhaired waiter with blue sacks under his eyes had brought the schnitzel. Jed kept himself busy cutting and chewing the succulent veal while Eli talked Yiddish to the waiter. The waiter's sagging face came gradually to life and he was beaming fraternally on them when he brought them two fresh glasses of beer.

"Who's this guy named Calvert?" asked Jed cautiously when the waiter had moved away.

"V. F. Calvert?" Eli waved his arms and roared. "Don't you know what the V.F. stands for? Very foolish, if you ask me. Of course I know the sonofabitch. He's a kind of unfrocked rabbi who's taken to Marx instead of the Talmud. You have to be Jewish to understand these doctrinaire bolsheviks . . . Ask Moishe here. He's waited on 'em all. Trotsky still owes him two dollars."

"Well?" Jed flushed huffily. "Aren't I . . . ?" he couldn't quite say the word.

"Jed it's not the same thing." Eli smiled in a fatherly sort of way into his face and leaned across the table to pat him on the shoulder with a big paw. "You are a native born American citizen, God bless you. You've had an American education. The trouble with you Americans is you're so damned ignorant. Look at me . . . I've had a piece of a German gymnasium, a scrap of Russian, a little cheder, two years in an American college . . . I'm the most educated man in the world. It's all in my play. Educate the little yids out of the ghetto and they become human beings. That's the proudest title in the world . . . Isn't it Moishe?"

The conversation was drowned in gargling Yiddish.

"But we ought to learn about Marxism," insisted Jed when the waiter had moved off to another table, "to know what's going on in the world."

"All right," Eli pounded with his fist till the plates danced, "if you're game we'll do it, Jed, you and me. We'll go to the Soviet Union as soon as we've produced your play and my play. That damn bookkeeper Pastor, let him produce his own play. I don't trust bookkeepers. We'll go on the bum there just like I've done in the States . . . Learn from the underdog. Ass side up, that's the only way to see a society . . . I know just how to do it. Won't cost you a cent."

Eli was talking loud, making wide gestures, screwing his lips up. Everybody in the place was looking at him.

"An uncle of mine, a courtesy uncle by one of my old man's offhand marriages . . . He's in New York right now buying *mushrats* for the Soviet government."

Eli made his face small and showed his front teeth so that for an instant he almost looked like a muskrat.

"Sure. They are going to teach 'em to be little Marxists and breed fine furs to warm the slats of the commissars. We'll go to see him this afternoon. No kidding. Even on the way to the worker's paradise *mushrats* have to eat. We feed 'em *mushrat* food every evening and get a free passage on the boat. It'll be a circus. You'll have to hold their fuzzy little heads if they get seasick."

Eli was laughing so hard tears spurted out of his eyes. Jed couldn't help laughing with him at the thought of sailing out of New York with a shipload of muskrats. Then his face froze. A chill climbed up his spine as he remembered Tangier and the bluntnosed freighter with a speck of red in the stern headed around Cape Spartel and Anna Glazunova sobbing on the bed in the hotel room.

"Seriously," Eli smoothed all the grinning wrinkles off his face and looked at Jed with an exaggeratedly school-teacherish expression ". . . we begin our Marxist education on the boat . . . We cross on a Soviet freighter."

"There's little Mae to think of." Jed's voice trailed off.

The waiter was leaning over the table, talking fast into Eli's face

"Moishe says I'm crazy. He says we better stay in America till we get sense enough to know where we're well off. He says we'll land in Siberia. Why not? I've never been in Siberia."

"This is all fools' talk," the waiter exploded into very tolerable English. "When you talk like men instead of greenhorns I'll sit down and talk to you." Huffily he piled up their soiled plates on his arm, gave the crumbs on the tablecloth a contemptuous flip with his napkin and stalked off into the back of the restaurant.

Eli wanted to go to find his uncle but Jed insisted they take in the burlesque show at the end of Second Avenue. Eli forgot everything. He laughed and stamped at every joke. After that Jed pointed out that it was too late to call on Eli's uncle. Eli was demanding that they get hold of Felicia and go dancing uptown. To get rid of Eli Jed had to make up a story about a date with another woman. It was so late he had to call a cab. Eli made a big show of trying to come along. Jed told the driver Hotel Hudson. It was only after Eli was out of sight in the early evening crowds that Jed tapped on the glass and called out the St. Luke's Place address instead.

At that he was ten minutes late at the Fausts'. Maisie was just setting a dish of her famous paprika chicken on the table. She smiled her cozy smile. There was a preoccupied look on her face. She had on her hat and had evidently been told to go right out. The table was only set for four. From under the fringed shade three faces looked up at him with the same prosecuting attorney's expression.

"We were beginning to think," said Sam with an angry curl to his lip, "that our Broadway friend had stood us up . . . If you want to eat, eat quick . . . V. F. Calvert has a meeting at eight." Jed looked around to smile hello to Maisie, but she had already vanished. "Just a moment," he said as he piled up his plate.

V. F. Calvert was a thin man with a small black beard. Everything was yellow about him, his skin, his teeth, his tobaccostained fingers, his eyeballs, except the black irritated peering pupils of his eyes. He ate his food in small quick bites and kept his mouth puckered all the while as if he were tasting something sour. As soon as Sam took away the plates V. F. Calvert whipped out Jed's typed script and opened a small looseleaf notebook in which Jed saw numbered sentences written in a clear microscopic hand.

105

"Now Meester Morris, pay attention please . . . Number vun," he began with a slightly Germanic accent.

It was like going over a paper with one of the more old-fashioned professors at college. V. F. Calvert went through the play page by page. Jed nodded and smiled; small details mostly, he told himself. If he could get the great scenes intact on the stage what would the small details matter? he told himself.

V. F. Calvert had only gotten through two acts when at a quarter of eight he rose abruptly to his feet. "His meeting," Sam whispered reverently to Lew. V. F. Calvert tore his notes out of the book and laid them carefully on the typed script. "If you have understood thus far you vill understand the rest," he said in a not unkind voice. He snatched up a shabby greenish colored overcoat and was gone.

Jed couldn't stand the idea of talking any more to Sam and Lew. He closed the script on the notes and shoved them into his overcoat pocket. "I'll try to meet his objections," he told them. "He's convincing." He felt his cheeks getting red. He hurried out the door.

Jed couldn't wait to get to Felicia's. She always gave him the feeling of being far away. The minute he saw her the strain started to relax. She was waiting for him, tall, coolly smiling. On the table was a bottle of whisky and some liver-wurst sandwiches.

"I wouldn't open it till you came feller." She snuggled up against him.

"Greater love hath no woman than that," he whispered affectionately. "But haven't I laid down my wife for my friend?"

When he'd eaten the sandwiches and drunk a little whisky he began to talk. This life was killing him. He wished he'd never come back from the Cape. He'd been trying to think why he'd acted like such a dope on the Cape. He'd been too impatient to enjoy the seashore, worried about his work. In the theatre if you stepped out for a minute there was always somebody waiting to cut your throat. Everybody was intriguing to see who could get his play done next. All they thought about was themselves. They had been in his hair all day. He'd hardly opened his eyes before Sam was after him to make changes in his play and then Eli had gotten hold of him and wasted the whole afternoon with an idiotic scheme to sail for the Soviet Union with a shipload of muskrats. Grandiose but impractical. He couldn't help laughing when Felicia started to laugh. And now he'd spent all evening wrangling with Sam and Lew about little insignificant details. Why couldn't they save their bright ideas for their own plays? They'd brought in a kind of a Marxist sea lawyer to advise him. But he'd ended by convincing them all and they'd decided unanimously to propose at the next directors' meeting to produce *The Human Race* right after Lew's play. "Feller we've got to have a hit. We've got to have a smash hit to put this theatre over . . . Then we'll have plenty of money to do the other guys' plays." He yawned. "Let's go to bed. Have you got a kiss left on your face, feller?"

They opened *Dawn over Mexico* in a little box called the Miniature Theatre Eli had found in a brick sidestreet in the Village. By a lavish use of paper George managed to keep the house moderately full for four weeks, but they were losing money. No choice but to close. As usual in The Craftsman's Theatre the crisis occurred long after midnight. The argument over whether or not to close Lew Golton's play had already been going on for four hours and they were all half dead with sleep when Lew suddenly jumped to his feet, pulled his hat down over his eyes and said God damn it, they could close the damn play whenever they wanted to, he was going to butt out of this damn theatre. With his hand on the knob of the office door he turned and mumbled out of the corner of his mouth that there would have been plenty of money to keep the play going if funds hadn't been misappropriated.

"What was that?" shouted George so shrilly that his voice broke.

Jed slid his chair back to the wall to get out of the way.

"I don't mean you George." Lew stepped back into the room and squared his shoulders. "You just write the checks. You're not the guy who spends the money."

Kenneth Magill, whom they'd asked to sit in on the meeting, and who had sat there all evening wanly smiling without saying a word, dragged himself shaking to his feet. His thin white face was wet.

"Just exactly what do you mean by that Mr. Golton?"

When Kenneth got up from the table Jed noticed he had clenched his pallid fingers over his thumbs. "I have accounted for every cent." He was shaking so he looked as if he might break in two.

"Will the meeting please come to order," intoned Jed.

"Ain't you ever heard of cutbacks?" Lew asked in a jeering tone.

Right away Kenneth jumped on Lew with his fists swinging in all directions. Before anybody else could move Eli had picked the little man up and was carrying him kicking and screeching like a baby in a tantrum out of the room.

"It surprised me to hear Lew use such a formal expression," Jed said laughing when he began to tell Felicia about it over a cup of coffee next day. It all seemed funny and far away from Felicia's quiet room. He'd waked up in her bed about three o'clock in the afternoon feeling as if he'd been on a horrible drunk though he hadn't touched a drop all night. The situation had been too tense for drinking, he had told her. He went on to explain that of course Lew was sore because they'd decided to close his play. What else could they do? They had sold seats to every furworker they could drive past the boxoffice with a switch and to several garmentworkers' locals. The workers complained that Lew had made his Mexicans too sordid. Anyway they had used the sordidness for an excuse to cut the price so the theatre was losing three hundred a week with every seat filled. What the hell, Lew was trying to do a *Lower Depths* in pajama suits.

"I've done my best to like it but it's absolutely childish, feller, and I swear the plot is lifted out of *Flight from the Sun* . . . Of course Lew don't know that. You know Lew's too lazy to read a book. He went to see *Flight*—I saw him there myself—so now he thinks he made it all up. He wrote down the first thing that came into his head and got V. F. Calvert to class-angle it for him. It's just like a play written by a six year old child but we just had to do it because Lew is God's gift to the furworkers."

"Well that's two strikes," said Felicia with a smile that Jed found completely uncomprehending as she brought him another cup of coffee from the bathroom where she did her cooking, "Batter up. It's up to you, feller."

"I don't see how you can kid about it." His lips were pouting. "It means as much to you as it does to me."

He disentangled himself from the bedclothes and started to pace up and down the floor in his bare feet. "This time we've got to have a smash hit."

He'd lost all the buttons off his pajamas and had to hold the top together with one hand as he paced. "You got to have discipline to get along in life . . . In this damn theatre we keep riding off in all directions at once . . . I'm learning a lot feller from these talks V. F. Calvert is arranging for me to give to workers' study groups. Get 'em interested, see? so they'll come to see the show. These workers, they know what they are talking about, feller. They've been very much impressed with what I've been saying You'd think it would be over their heads but they get it the way I put it to them. V. F. Calvert says that I have a knack with the proletarian audience . . . After we open *The Human Race,* if I ever catch up on my sleep . . ." Jed swallowed the last of the coffee and let himself fall back yawning and stretching on the bed, "I'm going to get up a course of lectures."

There was a hurried knock on the door. When Felicia opened the door a crack Jed heard Kenneth Magill's high tense voice outside: "I'm awful sorry honest, I know it's horrible to intrude but I've just got to talk to Jed. Felicia darling, forgive me."

To hide his ragged pajamas Jed ran into the bathroom and climbed into a wadded robe of Felicia's. Draped in that he arranged himself crosslegged on the bed.

When Felicia opened the door Kenneth groped his way into the room like a man walking in his sleep. There were sharp blue shadows under his eyes. The skin of his face was like crumpled bluish tissue paper under his wispy red hair.

"Jed I haven't been to bed all night. I knew you knew Lew Golton was lying. I know everybody knew he was lying but what tortures me is I may have spent too much money. I know that charro suit was expensive but Hugh insisted he had to have it and he does look stunning in it, and when Hugh had the charro suit, Sylvia had to be the china poblana to go with it. Honest I thought it would be the hit of the show. I thought people would come downtown just to see them dance the jarabe. And we had to pay union rates to the guitar player."

As he talked he walked up and down the room with small hasty steps. Jed watched with disgust the flicker of the pointed toes of his highly polished shoes. "You know they were threatening to make us take on a full Mexican orchestra," Kenneth was looking pleadingly from Jed's face to Felicia's. "We wouldn't have been able to open the show if I hadn't gotten round the walking delegate. But it cost money . . . It's all my fault."

"Kenneth," said Felicia, "you need a cup of coffee."

She went into the bathroom.

"It's the goddam critics' fault and the Broadway managers'," Jed began to say in a soothing tone. "They are all banded together to keep anything new and progressive out of the theatre . . . but look here Kenneth, I don't want you to resign. I want you to direct *The Human Race*. Even Mark Sugar—he's boxoffice down to the marrow of his bones—he says you ought to direct it. In fact your direction has been the outstanding success of The Craftsman's Theatre."

"I'm such a softie," said Kenneth staring into the cup Felicia had brought him while big tears ran down each side of his nose. "I just don't know how to say no to anybody."

"We tabled your resignation, Kenneth. We told Lew to go home and sleep it off."

"I'll tell you what I'll do." Kenneth was brightening. Jed could see he was enjoying having Felicia wait on him. "I'll direct your play if you want me to, Jed. I've got the production all planned. I'd hate to give it up now. Eli will help with scenery and props. He'll have to handle the music too. I've got a thousand dollars in the bank I was saving for a trip abroad . . . If I put that in the kitty it will help pay for all those extra trimmings on Lew's play. He and George'll say I'm restoring stolen funds . . . I don't care what they say. I'm never going to speak to either of them again but I want to see your play a success." He gave his head a toss. The curl in the red hair over his forehead seemed crisper. "Though I want to tell you right to your face I don't care one way or the other about all this talk about the labor movement. All I see is people. People moving among lights. I think the play is magnificently theatrical . . . Felicia, forgive me for intruding . . . Thank you, darling, for everything . . . I'll go now."

"He sure played us his big scene," said Jed as they listened to Kenneth's steps creaking down the stairs. "That guy's boxoffice if we handle him right."

"First Lew's big scene, then Kenneth's," said Felicia. "You boys would be a hit if you just put yourselves on the stage."

Jed found himself staring peevishly into the face of Felicia's alarmclock. "Great cats feller," he cried, "I've got a speaking date . . . it's a featherworkers' local . . . girls who trim hats, I think. But it's way up on the upper East Side."

He rushed into the bathroom to shave.

The brilliant blue of a December morning made Jed's eyes blink as he dodged past the great grinding trucks on Seventh Avenue on his way to Felicia's place after the first desperate all night run through of *Shall Be the Human Race*. He could barely drag himself up the last flight. When Felicia opened the door he pitched into the room and fell on her unmade bed. "I'm almost dead, feller."

Felicia, wearing a fresh new crisp white blouse, had been

eating breakfast at the table by the window seat. She stood over him with her coffee cup in her hand. "Do you need food, or do you want shuteye?"

"Fry me some bacon and eggs." His voice was a croak. "Please," he added like a small boy remembering his manners.

Felicia slipped on an apron and went in to light the gas stove in the bathroom.

Though Jed was too tired to move he had to keep talking: "You know it's a remarkable thing about Kenneth . . . He's really the boss when he's directing. Outside of the theatre he seems such a sissy, but you ought to see him handle those actors. Talk about discipline and solidarity being the watchwords of the working class. He sure does get team work out of them. Cracks the whip. Sylvia Levy broke down and cried three times . . . I had to love her up a bit to keep her going. I knew you wouldn't mind feller. The theatre's like that."

Felicia said "Humph" in a way that reminded Jed of her mother.

"Kenneth told me that his mother used to make him wear girls' clothes when he was little," she went on in her cool voice as she bustled about the room. "He played girls' parts in all the school plays . . . The lad confides in Felicia," she added sarcastically.

"If we could just get him interested in Marxism I think he would pull himself together. You can cure homosexuality. He needs a philosophy of life."

"Do you reckon it's pulled me together?" asked Felicia harshly.

"It's your petty bourgeois intellectual upbringing . . . I fought it too at first. Now I just can't stop talking about it when I get started." He yawned. "You'll be the last to learn, but you will."

113

Jed forgot what he intended to say in a frenzy of yawning. He closed his eyes. The light was red through his eyelids. He fell into a second's ruddy sleep. When he woke up Felicia had his head propped up with her hand while he lay on his back on the unmade bed and was feeding him little sips of coffee out of a cup. "Now sit up and eat your eggs before they get cold," she was crooning gently.

Jed sat groggily in his shirtsleeves on the edge of the bed. Felicia carried the table over from the window and set it in front of him. He drank off a fresh cup of coffee at a gulp.

"My, feller, it's cozy at your house. I don't know how you do it. Maisie Faust does it. She's the only other woman I know who makes a house cozy. June made every place feel like a barn, that's because she's such a peasant." Jed pulled at Felicia's sleeve and tried to kiss her. She held herself stiffly away from him. "Don't muss up my new blouse. I'm on my way uptown to see my publishers."

"I hope they owe you money . . . June keeps calling up about the house in Nyack. You know I gave it to her. At least she took it while I was in Europe. Every time I slipped back to the hotel to get a wink of sleep she wakes me up with a phone call. There's amortization and interest due on the mortgage and the bank's threatening to foreclose . . . It's been a lovely week."

"How much do you need, Jed?"

"One thousand and fortyfour dollars and fifty cents on Tuesday next . . . I just can't borrow any more from J.E."

"I might do another children's book. The illustrations usually net about a grand."

"But they wouldn't pay in advance, would they?"

"Could be, if I told Gresham I was going to have a baby."

Jed gave a start. Felicia seemed to have forgotten about

114

her blouse. She sat down beside Jed and began to play with his free hand that lay on the table edge as he piled the bacon and eggs into his mouth with his fork.

"And besides, it's true."

Jed stopped chewing. He swallowed everything he had in his mouth and almost choked.

"I'm two months overdue. You know how regular I am. I've decided I'll have him anyway."

"But Felicia, the first few weeks it's so simple." He hated the whine in his voice.

"No, it's my baby and I want him."

"But there couldn't be a more inconvenient time, feller. It's not fair to me," he couldn't help whining. "It's putting me on the spot." A feeling of panic had hold of him. His hands were cold; he began to talk big. "This winter I have to give all my time and thought to the theatre. I'll be lecturing all the time. We've got to put it over. It's our one big chance . . . *The Human Race* is a sure thing, feller. It's revolutionary. That'll bring in Lew's theatre parties, see? And study circles. Then it's idealistic. On top of that it's boxoffice, see? Mark Sugar says so himself . . . But it all takes work." He put his arm round her shoulders and began to talk with his mouth close to her ear. "You have to convince people . . . That's why this isn't just the time for another baby. There's little Mae to think of . . . All these events." He was sitting with his elbows on the table and his face buried in his hands. "Oh God and never any sleep. We'll find a doctor and fix it up . . ." He had risen to his feet. He looked up at her pleadingly. "Don't you worry, feller!"

"Who said I was worried?" Felicia's lips were thin over her taut jaw. She picked up his plate and carried it back to the bathroom. "I guess I must be an immoral woman," she called back to him cheerily.

115

"You knew Sam Faust was resigning," said Jed just to change the subject for a moment when she came back with another pair of eggs. "He's got some mysterious job out on the Pacific coast. I bet it's with the Hayes office. Wouldn't that be a scream?"

"Who'll take his place?" asked Felicia.

"That's the big question. I'd like to have Kenneth, but Lew and Sam can't see it . . . In any case we have got to put over *The Human Race*." Jed jumped to his feet with his mouth full. The words came racing out of his mouth. "These theatre parties will turn the tide . . . We figure—you know George is a wizard with figures—that if we sell the theatre out to working class organizations three times a week and keep our payroll low enough we'll make expenses. Lew's play was the tryout for the new system. We lost money; that was because it was such a flop . . . Eli's play isn't really ready." He'd told her all this before but he couldn't stop talking. "Eli's ideas are just too damned undisciplined. He's a hopeless romanticist . . . Of course Kenneth Magill is worse. If he'd only study history. Kenneth is the typical outoftown intellectual. He don't know the difference between *Progress and Poverty* and *The Wealth of Nations*. He thinks Marx was a partner of Schaffner and Hart."

Jed let out a braying laugh. All the time he was thinking: she can't do this to me, no, no woman can ever do this to me again.

"We've all got to straighten out our thinking feller," he added in a firm voice. "Here's one thing . . . You have an influence with Kenneth . . . Couldn't you get him to go to a psychoanalyst? We need the guy's talent. Repertory, see? We've got to build up our permanent audience. We got to teach these members of the lumpenbourgeoisie like Kenneth

116

and Eli that they have to talk the language of the working class."

"Jed," interrupted Felicia in the clear tinkling voice she used when she hadn't been listening, "I don't want to be late. I've got to get started uptown. Now's the time to see if I can raise that thousand dollars."

Jed strode over to Felicia and grabbed her by the shoulders: "But not a word about the . . ."

Her eyes in his were cold and harsh like her mother's. "Maybe I was just kidding," she said as she pulled away from him. "I don't want to be late," she added from the mirror where she was straightening her hat.

"But what'll I do?" he called after her when she reached the door.

"Lie down on my bed and take a nap."

"I'm too nervous to sleep."

"Read a book, feller, why don't you?"

"Got a *Das Kapital?* I gotta read up."

Felicia walked with brisk steps back into the room, found the book for him in the bookcase, fluffed up his pillow and gave him a lot of little kisses round the edges of his face while he went on chattering: "You gotta meet V. F. Calvert. He'll really explain things so you can understand them. It's a face like in those pictures of Spanish monks . . . I can't remember the painter's name. I saw them in some damned gallery in Europe . . . Feller if *The Human Race* succeeds let's you and me go to Europe together. Then we'll get married and have a big family . . . I could make some money," he added yawning, "if I could ever catch up on my sleep."

"All we got money for right now is the Staten Island ferry," said Felicia. Again her voice sounded like her mother's. She laughed her mother's short laugh. "If you get rested while I go uptown, I'll set you up to a trip."

Felicia walked out of the room with her firm silent step. Jed tried to calm his nerves reading Marx but the pages blurred and he fell asleep.

"No woman can ever do this to me again." The words were on his lips when he woke up. The room was purple with twilight. It's not the expense, he wanted to explain to her, but Felicia hadn't come home yet. Of course Agatha would come across with the expenses. He went into the bathroom and shaved with a shaking hand. She's the type that would. The Hardesties were probably filthy with dough. It's not that, he told himself, as he scraped the razor round the little point of his chin, it's that I'll be emotionally involved. He looked himself pityingly in the eyes. There was always that bit of a squint when he was upset. It would be too upsetting. It would take his mind off his work. Damn her he wouldn't let her upset him. "The revolutionist," V. F. Calvert had said, "is not affected by personal problems. He is a soldier of the working class." She hasn't any right to upset me emotionally this way. He looked pityingly into the liquid brown of his eyes in the mirror.

While he was rinsing his face off in cold water he remembered a speaking engagement. He turned on the light in Felicia's room to find his coat and groped in the pocket for his little black notebook. Oh Lord it was way up in the Bronx, December 22nd; five o'clock. He'd be late. He went down the stairs on the run. All the way up in the subway, instead of trying to think of what he was going to say to the Uptown Shavians Discussion Circle he kept repeating to himself over and over: No woman can ever do this to me again. That's what had happened with June and look at the emotional involvement and the trouble and the expense. This

118

damn mortgage, and Mae's playschool, and the doctor's bills. Never again. No never again. The working class was bigger than personal problems.

The Uptown Shavians turned out to be a reading circle made up of comfortable looking middleaged women, lawyers' and doctors' and dentists' wives. The room was all decorated for Christmas and smelled of coffee and cakes and Christmas wreaths when Jed arrived half an hour late. After the hurried walk up the Grand Concourse from the subway station he felt he looked very young and rosy and bright in the eyes.

Mrs. Segal, the president, started to scold him for being late but half way through Jed could see she was weakening. "Why Mr. Morris, when you came in," she smiled pudgily into his face, "I thought you were a highschool boy. I thought the speaker had sent his son to explain."

"I'll get older, Mrs. Segal . . . I promise you that," said Jed. "I get older every day."

After that everything was very cozy. The tiredlooking woman who introduced him he'd certainly seen somewhere. Of course she was Sylvia Levy's mother. When he turned to her, as he spoke of the splendid group of hard working young people The Craftsman's Theatre had managed to gather around it, he could see the tears come into her eyes.

He was among friends. He felt lifted quite off his feet. He seemed to be pulling words out of the air. He remembered something Kenneth had said about people moving among lights. When he spoke about abolishing the proscenium arch he made them feel it was a wicked weight that he would lift off their lives. He would sweep away the cramping threats of tradition and they would see their lovely lives moving beautifully among lights. He was carrying them with him. Men and women, plain men and women like us, moving among lights.

119

Having abolished the proscenium arch the theatre would deal with real life instead of the wornout puppets of Broadway.

"People moving among lights." Every time he used the phrase he found himself looking hard into a pair of china blue eyes in the back of the room. It was a big strapping woman, must be Scandinavian. She was standing against the wall. "People moving among lights," he said again for emphasis. The broad face responded with a rapt kind of a smile. While he talked he was thinking; after the show. She seemed to know what he was thinking. His words seemed to affect her like a secret code.

When he stopped talking the women really clapped. They loved him.

Blue eyes didn't clap, she just smiled at him across the heads of the clapping women.

Afterwards Mrs. Levy brought him a cup of coffee and a piece of cake. Jed tried to listen to what she was saying but he was looking over his shoulder trying to find the blue eyes again in the crowd. Mrs. Levy was talking on and on about how worried she and her husband were about Sylvia's future. They didn't believe in loose living. They had tried to bring her up strict and decent and it had almost broken their hearts when she had insisted on going to that dramatic school, so expensive too, and they'd been so worried when she joined what they felt was a radical bohemian group; they were afraid it would damage her reputation not only morally, but professionally; but now that she'd heard Mr. Morris speak she knew he was sincere. Didn't he believe that everything came out all right if people were only sincere?

As several ladies gathered round him, Jed broke out his story about the girl who wanted to go on the stage in the worst way, so somebody told her to try out for The Craftsman's Theatre. The ladies giggled contentedly.

Before he left they held a business meeting and decided to take the entire theatre for a Saturday matinee and, quick as a flash, Jed had George Pastor on the phone to nail down the proposition. It would be their Christmas party they explained. At least that would fill the theatre for one performance.

When he got through talking to George he began to look for the blue eyes in earnest.

He looked into face after face. They were all smiling at him. He didn't feel too discouraged when he couldn't find the blue eyes. All his worries had left him. This would be a funny adventure to tell when he got back to the theatre. No matter if he was a little late for rehearsal he'd be bringing home the bacon. That woman would be waiting. He managed to dodge several invitations and to slip out of the apartment by himself. When he stepped out of the elevator into the marble lobby downstairs there she was. She was certainly a formidable looking woman. The ample fur coat, no it couldn't be real sable, made her look even larger.

Her voice came from her boots, almost a baritone: "If you are as good playwriter," she said in an accent he decided was Swedish, "as you speak, you are the new Ibsen, perhaps."

With the firm blunt fingers of one large hand she seized the lapel of his overcoat. The blue eyes had a pleading schoolgirl look. "In my country in this season it is the time we make glug, so . . . In my office just one glass for good success." She tossed her head of short blond hair in the direction of one of the apartment doors that opened off the hall. "So."

For some reason he was blushing furiously. She had a latchkey out. As he followed the broad expanse of fur through the groundglass door he caught sight of the lettering over the bell: Dr. Olga Swenson, Chiropractic. This was too good a story: already he was hearing his own voice telling it down at the theatre. Even Felicia would have to laugh. The woman switched on the lights down the narrow corridor and turned to him smiling as she pulled off the fur coat and hung it on a hook on the wall. "Yes I am masseuse, it is our national art," she whispered with a roll of her eyes that made him blush till his ears burned. "What a bashful," she said, "please." She pointed to a leather couch. He sat down.

The room looked like a doctor's office. Outside of the couch the only furniture was a high hospital bed with a sheet over it, and some sort of electrical fixture on a whitemetal stand, also draped with a sheet. She brought the drink out of a highly antiseptic looking little closet with a sink under glass shelves lined with medicine bottles. The glug was sweet and fiery.

She sat down close beside him on the couch. She taught him how to drink her health . . . so . . . looking her hard in the eyes . . . skol . . . and skol again. The blue eyes looked a little blurred now that he was so close to them. They drank out of little gilt glasses that had an enameled rose in the bottom. To see the rose you had to drink the drink. That became a great joke between them. One glug led to another and before long the glug led to massage; Olga was a masseuse, wasn't she? The massage became mutual. Once it started her hands were all over him.

When he remembered it was late—oh God that rehearsal —he got his clothes on helter skelter. He blew her a kiss from the door. "Good night, Doctor Glug."

They rehearsed all Christmas Day. Eli's skyblue back-drop which he'd shaded to look like a cyclorama because it had turned out much too expensive to build a real cyclorama, was up for the first time. The transparency that represented the consul's garden would hang crooked on its roller so they had to ditch it for the time being, but some of the spotlights had been placed and Eli had his kettledrums and a set of tiny bagpipes that quavered a few opening notes in the darkened theatre. As the spots came on there was the table on a platform among the first three rows of seats and the white cloth and three men in their streetclothes sitting at it. Hugh Atwood was properly plausible and inquisitive as the young newspaper man. George Pastor was perfectly adequate as the British consul general. The Wahabi would be all right when he got his burnoose. Sitting in the aisle seat in the dark empty theatre, the smoke of his cigarette curling blue in the beams of dense white light from the baby spots in the balcony overhead, Jed fell into a sort of rapture as he heard his own words coming from the actors' mouths. At last they were perfect in their lines. They were building up suspense. It was the way he'd imagined it last summer in Mr. Corliss' garden.

Kenneth moved back and forth up the aisle orchestrating their voices like a conductor. He even had a little stick he used like a baton. The little guy did know his business, Jed thought to himself. When the lights dimmed and Eli started rumbling on his kettledrums and the wailing started from the Arab village, even though the actors were all in their streetclothes and some of the girls wore fur coats because the theatre was so cold, the scene had illusion. The lines had rhythm. Jed sat listening in such a rapture that they were half through the first act before he pulled himself together enough to take notes.

Sylvia Levy was lovely as the Russian girl. George seemed quite skillful in letting the villainy of the agent of international capitalism become gradually apparent through the mask of the kindly old archaeologist. When Hugh Atwood, just as he was going to start off for the war in the Rif, grabbed Sylvia's hand and said the last lines of the act: "There are things nobody has ever told me. These are the things I must find out for myself," Jed couldn't help clapping.

Jed felt quite miffed when he saw Kenneth with contorted face throw his arms up in the air to call for house lights, and advance threateningly on the huddle of actors round the table screeching, "Your rhythm, ladies and gentlemen, the rhythm you had yesterday, where has it gone? Your mystery? Miss Levy you're just about as mysterious as a hatcheck girl." He was pumping up and down in the air with his fists. "Where is the danger, the terror that lurks behind the transparency? . . . You seem to have forgotten that this is all false, the learned scholar, the suave cultured chatter at the dinner table among the roses . . ." He pointed a trembling finger at George Pastor's jaunty bow tie. His voice rose to a shriek: "This man is a murderer . . . Let's go back to the beginning."

In the middle of the afternoon they knocked off for a half hour so that the actors could have coffee and sandwiches sent around from a lunchroom. Sam Faust, who had turned up in a new doublebreasted brown suit smoking a cigar and wearing on his face the sleek sated expression of a man who has just eaten a good Christmas dinner and now asks only to be amused, suggested that they take the opportunity to hold a directors' meeting. They left Maisie, sitting in her fur coat under a spangly hat that looked as if it had come off a Christmas tree in the middle of the empty auditorium, watching Eli and the two boys from the settlement house who were acting as volunteer scene shifters, drag out into the light the heavy canvas planes which were supposed to indicate the mountains of the Rif, and crowded into the windowless office. The minute Jed sat down at the table piled with packs of throw-aways that had just come from the printers, he felt that Sam and Lew and George had already decided something. They all had the same look on their faces. Right away Jed had a chilling feeling of having been left out. George must be one too.

It took them some time to get Eli off the stage. When he finally came shambling in all smeared and sweaty in his soiled shirtsleeves, his big hands black from handling the dusty scenery, Sam had already started on a speech.

Since he was retiring, though certainly he hadn't been much help, though perhaps, he added with a smirk, he might console himself with the thought that his legalistic mind had acted as a practical corrective amid all this artistic enthusiasm, well he wanted to say first what a stimulating experience it had been and what an inspiration to discover how much real hard work went into making a theatre; well now the notion had come to him that perhaps it would be proper to have the actors represented on the board of directors . . . the democratic way of doing things . . . Eli, who had stepped out of the door to yell something to his assistants about setting that flat six inches forward, stuck his head back into the room. "George is an actor," he said in a businesslike tone. "He's turning out a damn good one." He pulled the door to behind him.

"No I meant one of the permanent acting company." Sam smiled condescendingly as he would at a child. "George who would you suggest?"

"I nominate Kenneth Magill," shouted Eli. "He knows more theatre than the whole gang of us."

"Suppose we moderate our voices. It's not my impression that nominations are in order yet," said Sam. "Mr. Chairman?"

"Anybody second Mr. Soltair's motion?" asked Jed.

Nobody said a word.

"If you don't stop mistering me," roared Eli, "I'll rub your head on the floor . . . All right Lew," he jeered, "speak up for your little girl friend. I know you're sleeping with her."

"None of your damned business," growled Lew with a selfsatisfied grin on his face.

"All right," shouted Eli, "let's have her. I nominate Sylvia Levy . . . If the Party wants to run the theatre let it. Maybe you can make a go of it. I'm just a goddam stage hand and don't forget I'm a stage hand because I like it. You guys had this all stacked. What a bunch of mushfaced hypocrites." He slammed the door after him as he left the room.

When the rest of the directors filed out of the office after making Miss Levy's election unanimous and regretfully accepting Sam Faust's resignation the theatre was already dark and Eli was pounding away at his kettledrums and Kenneth, standing in the aisle, his red hair curling crisply off his thin bluishwhite face, was swinging up his arms in a wide winglike sweep to bring up the lights for the opening of the second act.

"Feller, it turned out a goddam fraction meeting," Jed told Felicia when, his head spinning from having smoked too many cigarettes, he climbed groggily up the creaking stairs and burst in the door of her room. Felicia, who must have fallen asleep with the light on, sat up in bed blinking. "Fraction? What fraction?"

"A Party fraction. Of course the joke really is on Adolph Baum. They control the board of directors three to two. And now they are all in a stew because V. F. Calvert said my second act is ideologically immature. We got into such an argument it almost broke up the rehearsal. They want me to cut out the scene with the Ouled-Naïls. They say it's not sufficiently explained that prostitution is the result of capitalist exploitation of the toiling masses . . . I went over all that with Mark Sugar. He says the scene's boxoffice and I say it's poetry . . . There are things more ageless than economics."

"Want some fodder, feller?" Felicia asked in a wobbly voice. She got up yawning and went into the bathroom. She came back wearing her strawcolored bathrobe and carrying a plate of turkey. "The Hardesties are established for Christmas in a suite at the Brevoort," she said. "Scho was tight as a drum but amusing. Agatha's in a pet. I hardly drank a thing. Doctor's orders. I didn't forget to bring home a leg for the playwright . . . By the way," she added when she had settled him at the table to eat, "June called up . . . She's selling the house. She wants you to sign the deed. She's going to take the money and start for Reno."

"That's wonderful, feller."

"She sounded sour as a pickle, feller." Felicia hovered over him sleepily pushing the hair off her forehead. "She was mad because you wouldn't let her try out for any of the good parts."

"Damn tootin' I wouldn't. She's much too fat. I told her if she'd settle down and get a New York state divorce right away—you can get one for a hundred dollars; I could have let her have all the evidence—then I'd let her play an Ouled-Naïl."

"You can be kinda tactless, feller." Felicia laughed her dry laugh. "Some day some woman's going to beat your brains out with a rolling pin." She seemed to find the idea amusing.

"There's nothing the matter with being a character actress," he said chewing on his turkey leg. "She'd be lucky to get the chance . . . It isn't as if I wasn't paying for little Mae . . . And now you're adding new burdens."

In the bathroom he put on the new bluestriped pajamas Felicia had bought him for a Christmas present. "Feller, these are wonderful," he said. When he came out he sat down on the edge of her bed and made her a speech: "If it wasn't for the capitalist conventions we wouldn't have all this misery and expense. June and I could go just to the registry office like they do in the Soviet Union and say we're sorry, gentlemen, it didn't work, but we both promise to do the best we can with the baby. And you and I would say: 'Gentlemen, it does work; we're lovers until something goes wrong.' Feller if I was perfectly free, I think I'd get over, you know, hellin' around. It's the need to revolt against bourgeois conventions makes me do it . . . Though theoretically I believe in perfect promiscuity. Now just the other day, there was this woman . . ."

Felicia lay in the bed yawning and stretching. "Not now," she said sharply, "I've already had all the confessions I can stand from Scho. This is our Christmas, feller," she said and all the hard lines in her face dissolved into curves.

Jed opened the window a crack and was chased back by the cold air. It was warm and cozy in Felicia's bed; he reached up to turn out the light over their heads. "Don't mean a thing," he said yawning confidentially. "If it worries you feller," Jed mumbled between yawns, as he snuggled down under the covers beside her, "tell yourself it don't mean a thing."

Lying with his face against her pale hair a small boy feeling of repentance came over him. He had to tell her. "Felicia," he began. She didn't answer. He cleared his throat just a tiny bit to see if she were still awake; from her breathing he could tell she was asleep.

Next afternoon the argument about Jed's second act started all over again in the stuffy little office without any windows where the directors met. They began to make so much noise George Pastor was afraid members of the cast, rehearsing the war scenes in the dim theatre under the single electric light bulb that dangled over the stage, would hear; and suggested they slip over to his room on Eighth Avenue. It would be an hour before they would need him for the next scene in the garden. Over at George's place the argument turned into a yelling match. The trucks rattled and roared so on the crowded street outside that they had to yell to be heard, anyway. Once they started yelling they could not seem to stop.

Eli and Lew Golton sat scowling at each other with Sylvia on the couch between them crying quietly into a handkerchief rolled into a little damp ball. She was blubbering that she knew the artist should be untrammeled, but V. F. Calvert must know best. George, who took the lead in everything now that Sam was gone, kept suggesting new scenes that would, so he put it, do the same thing in another way.

"Are you with us?" Lew stuck his face close to Jed's. "Now is the time to show your face."

That was when Eli got to his feet and shouted that if they didn't all shut up he was going uptown to tell Adolph Baum the comrades were taking over his theatre. Adolph Baum was giving his money for artistic experimentation, not for political propaganda. He added that he had work to do. He was an artist not a political propagandist. He had to rehearse the girls for the Arabian dance. He walked out. Those days nobody connected with The Craftsman's Theatre ever walked out of a door without slamming it.

Eli slammed the door so hard an enlarged snapshot of some relative of George's in some East of Europe military uniform that looked like a costume out of the *Prince of Pilsen* fell off the wall. While George was picking up the broken glass, with puckered lips, Sylvia staged a scene of her own. Her pretty little face was dead white. Her dark eyes swelled between their heavy lids. She jumped to her feet, tossed her black hair off her forehead, shook a trembling forefinger toward the door, and hissed out "Stoolpigeon."

"Feller . . . I had to calm her down. You know how hysterical she is. Eli says she's crazy about Lew, but it can't be true. I was the one she ran to. That guy never washes his neck," Jed explained to Felicia as he lay on her bed while she cooked supper for him between rehearsals that night. "If some old cat brings the glad tidings that I'm petting the leading lady think nothing of it. In the theatre it don't mean a thing . . . I can't have her taking a fit before opening night. She's going to be the hit of the show . . . But what burns me up is that Lew don't take a damn bit of interest in the production any more. He always was a lazy hound, but now he's on an ideological strike; and George, when he's not rehearsing—he's all right when he's rehearsing—sits there in the boxoffice stroking his damn little mustache with a face that would sour a pickle. Sabotage I call it. In spite of them there's a very considerable advance sale. We can do without their damn theatre parties. Mark Sugar says this is a play for the wider audience."

"There's a broken heart for every light on Broadway," hummed Felicia from the bathroom where she was cooking supper. "That's what they used to say back home in Hingham."

Jed had just sat down to eat the steak Felicia had cooked

in a frying pan over the gasburner when the phone rang. Groaning Jed got up to answer.

It was Eli in high spirits. "Wake up bright eyes, things are looking up," Eli roared until the receiver jangled in Jed's ear. "Adolph Baum is going to give a champagne party for the cast after the show opening night. His secretary just called me up to ask if it would be suitable if he came incognito. I told her I'd make him a mask and he could come dressed as Harun-al-Rashid but she said no he'd just wear a tuxedo not to embarrass anybody . . . Isn't he the cute little duck? Come the revolution we'll get him stuffed and put in a glass case at the Museum of Natural History . . . him and Kenneth, the daffy director, they'll symbolize the drama in the last days of the bourgeoisie." He hung up with his idiot cackle.

"That was Eli," grumbled Jed. "Say feller, you don't suppose Kenneth is going to crack up before opening night do you?"

"Could be," said Felicia. "He was mighty near off his trolley the other night. You were at one of your protracted meetings. He came around here dead sober and asked me to marry him."

"What did you tell him?"

"The same thing you told the lady tennis player: I was otherwise engaged . . . He insisted so I told him about Peter." Jed winced. "I thought that would shut him up. He said it would be just his act to father another man's child. He said I'd be saving a human life. This way he was only half a man anyway. All these pansies were driving him crazy. He wasn't really like that, only when he was drunk . . . You know I'm quite fond of Kenneth, only I couldn't bear to touch him."

"Hugh Atwood is two timing him with some guy who

131

calls for him with a Mercedes roadster every night after rehearsal," said Jed with a mouthful of steak. "Mother fixation," he added in a soothing tone, "an only son, an inhibited childhood. Mother really wanted a girl all the time. It's the typical story of the bourgeois intellectual . . . I ought to write a play about it . . . Oh Lord I ought to be at the theatre right now. They are rehearsing the new scene. The war correspondent who's been captured by the Bedouins tells them the story of the revolution and instead of carving him up with pocketknives they follow him into battle to liberate the Rif. That ought to satisfy the doctrinaire boys. You wouldn't believe it but Hugh Atwood's wonderful in it. Mark Sugar says we won't have him in the cast two weeks after opening night. Some uptown manager will give him a contract. He's headed for pictures, that egg is."

"What does old sourpuss think of the play?"

"Mark? He don't understand historical materialism."

"Neither do I, feller," said Felicia.

"Sure you do, feller." He kissed her and ran down the creaking stairs. "Now I can lick my weight in wildcats," he shouted back up over his shoulder as he ran.

When he got back to Felicia's place at four in the morning after an argument in an allnight lunchroom on Sheridan Square with George and Lew that started after the actors had gone home to bed, the first thing he noticed was the smell of whisky. When he switched on the light he found Felicia still dressed sitting on the edge of the bed. Her eyes stared at him without blinking. Her pupils were so dilated her pale gray eyes looked dark. She sat swaying back and forth bigeyed as an owl on the edge of the bed.

"Tried to shave some whishky for you, feller," she was

mumbling thickly. "Kenneth. He wanted to talk my head off. Why din you get back sooner?"

"I was trying to straighten out Lew and George. V F. Calvert's all wrong about that play. Actually it anticipates the popular front. The Party in America, I was telling 'em, is so behind the times they can't recognize a pure piece of Marxist-Leninist art when they see it. V. F. Calvert has consented to come to the dress rehearsal . . . We argued on and on . . . It's worse than hooch when I get arguing about Marxism. I just can't stop . . . We're not too far apart. They just parrot what V. F. Calvert says, but I reach my views independently."

"Makes me nervous. Kenneth makes me nervous. Kenneth was drinking so hard telling me about his love life I had to drink up too. Afraid he'd pash out." She sat looking at him blinking with her lips frozen in a smile. "Kenneth said it would make everything all right if I'd sleep with him. Couldn't do it. Isn't that awful?"

"He's sober at rehearsals and that's about all. Well his work will be done in three more days. For once feller, I'm not too nervous about opening night. Everybody who's seen rehearsals has been so impressed. The fact that Adolph Baum is giving us a party means he's heard things that have impressed him."

"Not to save my life I couldn't," Felicia said staring across the room.

"Feller, you're squiffy," said Jed soothingly.

"Squiffier'n hell, feller." Giggling she pressed her mouth against his.

About midnight after the dress rehearsal Jed came running up the stairs two steps at a time and burst into the room:

"Feller, where are you? I thought you were going to meet me at the theatre. I've got a taxi waiting outside."

Felicia was lying on her bed passed out cold. There was a burnt out cigarette in the corner of her mouth and a little grime of tobacco across her lips. Lord she might have set herself on fire.

"Felicia . . ." He shook her by the shoulder. Her body was limp. Her face was paperwhite. Jed felt frightened, the way the sight of a drunken person used to frighten him as a child. "Come on feller, wake up," he heard himself pleading. "I promised to go up to the Levys'. They are giving a party for Sylvia. I've got to go act the cultured European gentleman to prove to them we aren't a lot of longhaired bohemians. Come on, feller, I need you. I don't want to go up there all by myself."

His voice had risen to a childish whine. He lifted her by the shoulders and shook her so hard her head wobbled.

"All right damn you." Tears of vexation spouted into his eyes. "Don't blame me if Sylvia expects me to lay her."

The sound of his voice shouting brutally into the empty room smote his ears. He closed his mouth and walked downstairs and stepped stiffly back into the cab.

The next days were a race with each hour. Jed gave up trying to get any sleep. His eyes stared out of hard red rims. One rehearsal had no sooner finished than another began. Kenneth was taut as a guitar string but he wouldn't give up. He kept asking Jed to rewrite small scenes. Then he would explain them to the actors, as patiently as a nurse telling stories to children. Jed had to be there all the time they were rehearsing to keep Kenneth from snapping.

Jed kept telling himself his head would be clearer if he

could only get some sleep, but there was no time. Every minute there were conferences, in the office, in the corner of the stage, in the men's room, in the speakeasy down the block; conferences with Kenneth, shaking and haggard, about what to do about the old character actress who would go up on her lines; with sullen Eli about the drummer who got sick at the last moment; with George Pastor, more snappish than ever, about where the money was coming from for four new baby spots; with leery Mark Sugar about the dead place in the second act.

The conferences were always interrupted by something else before anything was decided. If there were only time everything could be straightened out. The hours ticked by like minutes.

And all the while in the back of this head Jed carried on a dialogue with himself about Felicia. He really loved her, but she oughtn't to have tried to do that to him. She'd stop this drinking if only she'd let him give her a philosophy of life, he kept telling himself. One noon he was standing out on the pavement outside the tiny theatre entrance talking to Mark Sugar and Rodney Acres, redfaced and fat as a Chinese prosperity idol in a checkered suit, about the terms of a possible contract for a Broadway production, if the show did happen to turn out a hit, when he caught sight of Felicia walking past on the other side of the street. She always had that cool wellbred fashionable look so that he didn't mind a bit having the two men see him break away from them and run after her.

He was out of breath when he caught up with her. "Feller, you mustn't drink like that," he panted. "Like the other night. It's bad for little Peter. You wouldn't want little Peter born with a hangover? You go to Dr. Whately and get her to give you a sedative . . . I know it's all the excitement about the play . . . Dr. Whately's a very understanding woman. You go tell her the whole story . . . And please don't drink anything tonight . . . I want you to be sober for Adolph Baum's party . . . You always give things that air of refinement, feller, that Brahmin note . . . That'll be just the thing for Adolph Baum."

"So that's what you like about me," began Felicia with a curdling laugh. As they turned the corner of the street he snuggled his face into her neck and kissed her as persuasively as he could: "Be a good little girl, feller: you're the one and only."

There wasn't time to talk to Felicia properly. He had to go back to pick up Mark Sugar for lunch, so that they could be seen at Sardi's lunching with a man from the Shubert office, just to let Rodney Acres know they had other oars in their boat. When he left her at the grimy brownstone steps of her house he was thinking: As soon as I get time I've got to straighten out Felicia. Women take so much loving to keep 'em straightened out . . . From now till opening night there wouldn't be a minute.

By the time the curtain rose opening night, only there wasn't a curtain; just the spotlights glowed, and the light came up with the music, on time for a wonder, to illuminate the scene he'd rewritten so often he didn't understand the words any more—three men suavely dining at a table in a garden against Eli Soltair's beautiful green transparency that cost too much money—Jed had an odd hysterical feeling of standing outside himself.

It was a cold sweating little figure with popeyes and drenched curly hair that stood gripping the rail in the back of the theatre. It couldn't get its breath. Better take himself for a walk around the block. Why suffer? There was nothing he could do now.

Walking jerkily like a marionette, careful not to jar his joints for fear he would come apart, he walked over to Seventh Avenue and up to Sheridan Square.

Out in the street he began to feel less broken in two. Nobody knew who he was. He was just a tired young man strolling among the weary couples on a winter evening of light flurrying snow.

Passing a florist he sniffed a tiny scent of flowers that mingled with the gasoline smell of the traffic. Ought to send Felicia some flowers. Ought to send Sylvia Levy some flowers, ought to send all the girls flowers, but he didn't have the jack.

Crowds, he noticed, gaylooking crowds were pouring into the Greenwich Village Theatre. They looked better dressed than his audience at the Miniature. They looked richer, the girls looked prettier. A speakeasy crowd laughing and giggling as they shoved toward the boxoffice to buy their seats. *Village Frolics.* A damn fool musical show . . . People pouring into a girl and music show instead of going to see something that would make them understand. A doomed society marching to the scaffold. "You've got to understand that, damn you."

He stood with his back to the curb, just as if he had a seat himself for *Village Frolics* and was taking a breath of air before going in to see the show. Looking through the crowd he began to feel angry. The speakeasy crowd. They were the ones who were marching to the scaffold. Goddam stupid bourgeois playboys necking the dregs of the Junior League. He could feel his face stiffening with hatred as he stared at them. His fists were clenched in the pockets of his jacket. Suddenly he caught a glimpse of himself from outside

137

and began to snigger: "Nice story. Playwright assaults play-goer . . . in front of rival theatre."

He could feel the little fortifying core of hatred hard-ening inside him as he hurried back toward the Miniature all in a sweat for fear he'd miss the first act curtain . . . Felicia. Now that was the trouble with Felicia, she was like them: the dregs of the Junior League. How horrible if she turned out a lush. The thought of Felicia made him run down the stone steps into the little basement blind tiger next door to the Miniature Theatre.

There she was sitting up very straight with a highball before her opposite Kenneth who was slopped all over the tablecloth. As soon as the waiter let him in Jed had heard Kenneth's voice in thin falsetto. "And, dearie, they want it to fail . . . They're doing everything they can to make it fail . . . Because they hate me and because Jed wouldn't re-write his second act to suit their ideas. He tried to please them and he fell between two stools. What do we care about ideas? We are artists, Felicia!"

The grayhaired Italian waiter, whose name Jed remem-bered was Giovanni, started to reach for a third chair to set at their table. "No, I'll be back in a minute," whispered Jed.

"You bring big crowd, Mr. Morris," Giovanni said smil-ing. "Wish you luck, Mr. Morris. Much good luck."

Jed found himself enthusiastically shaking hands with Giovanni. The working people were on his side. Kenneth didn't make any sense, just a bourgeois lush, the dregs of the Junior League. Feeling suddenly lighthearted, Jed ran up the steps and slipped back to the theatre. The girl who took tick-ets was smiling. The house was full of applause. The lights were dimming on the first act.

After that Jed was the smiling master of ceremonies. In the lobby he teamed up with Mark Sugar whose gray moonface smiled portentously above full evening dress for the occasion. When Mark smiled Jed smiled, when Mark said thank you Jed said thank you. Jed began to wish he had on evening dress too. The anesthesia of conformity, he whispered to himself, more effective than drink.

Now he was almost enjoying the play. It sure had sweep. Only in the middle of the second act he felt a jab of pain, like when a dentist's drill hits a nerve, at the ripple of coughing that went through the audience. He could hear feet moving. That damn love scene. The rewriting was lousy.

Everything was happening too fast for him to pay attention. There were introductions. Congratulations, a little speech to make, a tribute to all his fellow workers whose ceaseless efforts had made The Craftsman's Theatre possible, the actors' hands to shake, so many smiles to smile.

Rodney Acres pounded him on the back with a pudgy hand. "It moved me by God . . . If you can move me, you can move . . . er . . . mountains."

The man was being funny. His fat cheeks were quivering. He was beaming at Jed. The show must be a hit, or he wouldn't be so good natured, Jed noted hurriedly to himself; then he noticed that Rodney Acres was beaming not at him but at a group of people who were making their way down the aisle as the last stragglers of the audience filed out. It was Adolph Baum and his friends.

Jed rushed forward to help the little man up the steps from the aisle. Mr. Baum hopped lightly on the stage and stood beside Jed, casting his twinkling smile round the awed circle of actors and backstage workers.

"Well how does it feel Mr. Morris, to have cast your throw? Nothing you can do now, is there?" he said in his dry rustling slightly breathless voice, "except wait the turn of fortune's wheel." There was a trace of an accent. A very distinguished accent. "It always seemed to me that the first night of a play furnished, for the spectator at least, the same interesting suspense he enjoys watching the roulette at Monte Carlo . . . Faites vos jeux messieurs mesdames, rien ne va plus."

Jed didn't like the way he said the French. It gave Jed the feeling that Mr. Baum wasn't going to put any more money into The Craftsman's Theatre. He felt an awkward grin appearing on his face.

"I say spectator advisedly, Mr. Morris," added Mr. Baum, "I understand that for the gambler the operation is fraught with considerable pain. I never gamble."

Jed didn't have time to worry about what Mr. Baum meant. He went to work to introduce the cast.

When the time came to open the champagne Mr. Baum stood rubbing the palms of his hands together ever so slightly beside the long table stacked with glasses and salads and sandwiches which had appeared magically in the middle of the stage. Mr. Baum had the air of an unusually welldressed magician who has just performed an unusually difficult trick. His white hair and mustache were trimmed so that every bristle was in place. His starched shirtfront and cuffs, like the damask tablecloth beside him, were of an intense glossy white.

By contrast the theatre people all looked as if they needed a bath. George Pastor was wearing a tuxedo but it had the air of being hired for the occasion. Eli as usual was a mess; he'd been helping move scenery in spite of the union rules and had gotten his gollywog head full of cobwebs. Lew Golton's shirt was clean for once but he'd managed to get cigarette ash on his nose. Even Sylvia, usually so neat and pretty, had a tired lackluster look. She'd done a smudgy job making up her face after the greasepaint; her black dress had hung too long at Klein's. The rest of them might have been hustled in off the benches on Union Square. What a bunch of bums. Jed looked desperately around for Felicia and Kenneth Magill. At least they would have given the uptown touch.

"I must tell you all," Adolph smiled and nodded toward the actors as he began his little speech in his low dry penetrating voice: "I must tell you all that it has been a privilege to assist you in what small measure I have been able in the launching of this little theatre so full of youthful ardor . . . I consider some of your protest mistaken, but I bow to the generous ardor of youth. Youth is a disease that time will surely cure. The ship is launched, my young friends. May you have a long and prosperous journey . . . It is time for an old landlubber like me to go ashore and wish you bon voyage . . . In your eager young faces I seem to read the cry: All ashore that are going ashore."

He took a sip out of his glass and set it on the table and started moving toward the edge of the stage. A couple of glumlooking men in gray business suits who seemed to be in his party followed close on his heels. Jed wondered if they were bodyguards. He wanted to follow, to bow him out the door at least, but like in a nightmare he found his feet glued to the floor.

As Adolph Baum had turned to go down the steps he had whispered something to Sylvia and to Hugh Atwood that seemed to please them mightily. The little man waited for them to walk ahead of him and, with the flatfeet bringing up the rear, they all moved slowly up the aisle.

Lord, thought Jed, he must find Felicia. As he hurried out of the entrance he got a glimpse of Hugh's and Sylvia's delighted faces in the midst of flowers and evening clothes in Adolph Baum's glistening automobile. The light inside went off and the long limousine moved gently away from the curb.

Jed ran down the steps to the speakeasy to find Felicia. No, Giovanni said, they'd both left an hour ago. Jed walked as fast as he could round to Felicia's place.

She was standing beside the telephone wearing the plain silk dress that matched her hair. She seemed sober. She nodded to him with a preoccupied frown. She was trying to get a number that didn't answer.

"Feller honest I meant to come . . . I got all dressed up, but I couldn't. I'd have been carried off kicking and screaming. They'd have had to fetch me in the hurryup wagon. What do we do now?"

"Nothing to do till we get the notices. Adolph Baum filled the theatre with gigglewater and lobster sandwiches. Want to come around to have a bite?"

"One minute, feller. I just want to call Kenneth. He's acting so strangely. He said he'd go home and go to bed."

"He probably went out and got drunk."

"I'll call again later. I'm worried about him . . ." She set her firm hands on Jed's shoulders and looked with pale anxious eyes into his eyes. "How did it go?"

"I may be crazy feller, but I think it's a hit . . . I oughtn't to have said it . . . I know it's bad luck."

"Let's go someplace uptown. All by ourselves."

They got a cab and went to the Basque's. It was like going to a foreign country. There wasn't a single familiar face. There was accordion music. Everybody was dancing. "Let's dance," Felicia said, "my it's a relief to be uptown." Jed tried to dance but he was too tired. When they went back to their table they couldn't find anything to say to each other. Jed drank several shots of some poisonoustasting scotch but it didn't cut into his dense apathy. He was just too tired. Finally he paid the bill.

"Let's go home and go to bed, feller," he mumbled. "I can sleep now. Don't let me buy any papers. We'll get 'em in the morning. Kenneth always has them all. I've got to have some sleep before I read the papers."

They had to take the subway because neither of them had any money left for a cab. Felicia held on tight to his arm without looking at him. Felicia was very quiet all the way downtown. When they got out at Sheridan Square, Felicia said: "Feller let's go by Kenneth's place, just so I won't worry."

It was odd that there was a policeman in the lobby of the small walkup apartment house. Up the three flights, outside Kenneth's door there was another. Already they could smell gas.

Felicia tried to push past the cop through the narrow corridor. He thrust a blue uniformed arm in front of her. "You don't want to go in there, sister," he said.

"What's the trouble, officer?" asked Jed in his most crisp official tone. "I'm from the theatre where he works."

"Suicide," said the officer wearily. "Stuck his head in the gas oven. They do it all the time. Lucky he didn't blow up the joint."

Already two men with a stretcher were pushing them out of the way.

"They got a pulmotor but it ain't no use. I been on the force long enough to know when a guy's dead."

The little hall was suddenly full of people. Tamely Jed and Felicia let themselves be pushed down the stairs with the rest of them, down into the lobby and out into the street. They waited in the crowd till the men in white coats came out of the apartment house with the stretcher. The body was covered all over with a blanket. The sweet sickening smell of gas filled the street. Jed marveled at Felicia. She stood quiet beside him, with tight lips and narrow eyes. She didn't cry. Together they followed the ambulance around to the hospital to see if they could keep the body from being taken to the morgue.

PICTURES

J ed walked slowly down the hall from the old hotel elevator which still had the faint flavor of castor oil that used to gag him so when he was a boy. In the cramped passage that led to J.E.'s two rooms he stopped. He didn't have the courage to lift his hand. In the draft from under the door he could taste the dry close bookish air of all his father's rooms. He stood on the worn place on the carpet his feet had helped wear, waiting so many other times to get up his courage to knock—in those days, each time, he had been ready with a new success at the tip of his tongue: a scholarship won, the award of a debating prize, the Phi Beta Kappa key, the final Latin parchment engrossed with *magna cum laude* from his college commencement. Jed felt a bitter laugh curdling inside him when he remembered that. Damn little praise he'd had for the plays that were the work of his life. And it was getting worse instead of better. His early plays might have flopped, sure, but they'd closed as John Taylor Briggs, the leading critic, put it, in the aroma of promise. This time he'd fallen flat. Flat on his face. Twentyfive thousand dollars gone. It would be the hardest thing he'd ever done in his life to explain to J.E. how The Craftsman's Theatre had come to fail.

Minutes went by before he could raise his knuckles to the door. Then he stood with thumping heart listening to the familiar light squeak when the chair was pushed back, the sound of his father's slippered feet shuffling over the carpet, the furtive click of the bolt, the light clank of the chain undone. The door opened slowly. "I thought I knew your knock," J.E. said in his quavering voice as all the wrinkles in his face twisted into the so familiar loving smile. "I couldn't be sure. I hear it so rarely these days . . . Come in, dear."

J.E. stood against the wall with his hand on the doorknob to let his son walk in. Jed walked across the dark red oriental rug, glanced round the bookcases and filing cabinets that packed the walls, and looked for a painful instant at the cabinet photograph in sepia of the handsome eager woman in a feather boa who had been his mother. The photograph in its silver frame stood always in the same place with a bunch of red roses in front of it on the corner desk.

Jed had a momentary impulse to rush to the window and throw himself out. Instead he let himself drop into the red morocco chair beside the desk. Not knowing what to do with his hands he lit a cigarette. J.E. was pushing the bolt to and replacing the chain on the door.

"Coffin nails," he murmured in a tone of gentle reproach as he settled into his place across the desk from Jed. "I wish you wouldn't."

"J.E. we laid an egg," Jed blurted out.

"I knew it would fail, Emmanuel," his father said quietly. "I didn't want to discourage you. I knew the interests wouldn't let it succeed."

"Adolph Baum is through."

J.E. shrugged his small shoulders. "What did you expect? They could not let a son of mine succeed. For twenty-five years I have been working to expose them."

"From a Marxist point of view," said Jed, trying to laugh his old boisterous laugh, "that's quite true but I still don't think the House of Morgan actually sat up nights keeping people from buying seats to The Craftsman's Theatre . . . People just weren't ready for it. It's the decadent bourgeoisie. Afraid of the new and the bold. My play was too straight from the shoulder."

J.E. shook his head slowly. "Emmanuel, first you must learn to know the truth."

Jed didn't answer. He sat looking out the window watching the sunset flooding the building on the corner of the avenue with rosy light while the crowded street below went blue with dusk. New York was his city. Now he had to leave it . . . "But just stay two years," Mark Sugar had drawled in his singsong voice from behind the manuscripts in blue and yellow jackets piled in front of him. "Figure it out for yourself. Say you work a hundred weeks at five hundred bucks a week. It costs you six thousand a year to live. That's ample even for a genius. The arithmetic's simple."

"Me write a part for Mary Pickford?" Jed remembered himself shouting as he pitched back in his chair.

"Boy you'd be lucky if you got the chance." The blue lips at the bottom of Mark Sugar's pale moonface wore a fishy pout. "Get wise to yourself, Jed . . . You come home with thirtyeight thousand dollars. That ain't hay, Jed. You buy a little house in Connecticut Jed, and settle down to write the plays that will wow them . . ."

"J.E.," Jed said aloud, his eyes still following the peo-

ple walking along the sidewalks, lighting on girls in spring
hats on the tops of buses. "I've signed a contract to write for
the pictures."

"Indeed, dear?" J.E.'s voice shook with sudden emotion.
"Perhaps we can see in these things . . . a divine hand. All
things work together for good, you know what St. Paul said
. . . for them that love God. That is the gist of the teaching
of the Bab and the Bahai." He paused. He seemed to be finding it as hard as Jed did to find words. "My account at the
Fifth Avenue Bank, Emmanuel, stands at seven hundred dollars and ninetyeight cents. That is all I have left in the
world."

Jed turned suddenly to look at his father. The long
creases of J.E.'s face were absolutely still, the eyes were almost closed. Jed rose to his feet. As he moved, the turned-
down corners of the old mouth wrinkled into a distant,
detached unamused smile. In the cold reflection from the twilight sky the smiling face looked waxen and green; it was a
dead man's face. Jed's voice rose hysterically shrill in the silent room: "But J.E. I owe you three or four thousand at
least . . . I'll send you so much a week from the Coast."

"I've never told you, dear," said J.E. while the smile
deepened the lines round his mouth, and his voice became
quaveringly brisk, "about the little pellets I have in my medicine cabinet. Your godfather Laughlin Davidson procured
them for himself when he found he had cancer. His end was
peaceful. He was a noble soul. He contracted pneumonia
before he needed to use them. I found them among the papers
he had bequeathed to me in his will. As you know we were
the closest friends. When you went overseas I determined to
use them if I heard bad news, dear. Why should I live on if I
had no one to live for? If it weren't that I felt I ought to complete my exposé of the financial conspiracy that is destroying

our civilization like the cancer that destroyed poor Laughlin"
—his narrow mouth made a curious w as he grinned into
Jed's face—"I would feel that now was the time."

Jed began walking up and down in front of J.E.'s carved
ebony desk. He couldn't help waving his arms. "But J.E.
you've supported me all these years . . . It's about time I
did something. What's happened?"

"If you followed the financial page, dear, you would
have read of the failure of Burnie and Wilk, the Liverpool
cotton brokers . . . Something very strange is happening in
the world . . . Laughlin and I both considered that house
firm as the Rock of Gibraltar. As an old financial reporter I
have been uneasy about the frenzied rise of values on the
New York market. I sold out my holdings at a very high figure
and bought Burnie and Wilk until I was the largest minority
stockholder . . . I thought I was doing the best for you dear
. . . Emmanuel, I can truthfully say the loss has occasioned
me no ripple of pain except the knowledge that it would
cause my boy concern. I'd always thought of it as Emmanuel's little fortune." He folded his old greenveined hands in
front of him on the desk. "I need so little."

"But J.E. everything will go on exactly the same . . .
Unless you would like to come out and live with us on the
Coast." Jed's hands were cold. He was talking too fast. He
began to stammer a little. "As soon as I've settled this divorce
business with June, and Felicia and I have gotten a house and
settled down. I know you'll like Felicia. June was a peasant.
You'll love little Mae."

"By the way," dropped J.E., "I wonder if the child
would like your old puppet-shows. I've kept them all. The
Davidson girls helped me pack them in mothballs."

"Felicia's crazy about her. She'll love her granddaddy."
The words hurried out of Jed's mouth: "She'll spend lots of

time with us. She'll have a lot of little brothers and sisters. We'll be a quaint oldfashioned family." As fast as he spoke them the words jangled false in his ears.

J.E. shook his head. "My place is here . . . among my records. It would be dangerous to try to move them. The weeks I was at Long Branch last summer I was sleepless for fear my papers would be ransacked." He waved his hand in the direction of the row of locked greenpainted metal cabinets. "In this room, Emmanuel, is the evidence—the correspondence, the clippings, the financial statements, the obscure monographs—the evidence which will convict the House of Morgan before the bar of history."

Jed felt he was strangling for lack of air. The cold sweat was trickling down under his collar. It was the feeling he'd had as a child sometimes when he'd stayed on in the closed-up library at the Central Park West apartment to read on a fine afternoon and found himself staring at the book with stinging eyes when the light failed, strangling for lack of air. Old Mr. Davidson's daughters Aunt Edith and Aunt Agnes, so sweet to him but they weren't his mother, used to find him there blinking and dazed and scold him for ruining his eyes and bundle him up and hustle him out into their car that Wesley their colored chauffeur drove so slowly round the drives everlastingly curving in on themselves through the trampled greensward, through the breathedout boredom of the park in the fading light. He was strangling for lack of air.

"J.E.," Jed heard himself gasping in a shaky voice. "A business engagement." He was on his feet. Between his fingers he was crumbling an unlit cigarette.

He felt his father's cold lips on his cheek. J.E. seemed to take forever to undo the chain on the door. When he'd clicked the bolt he pulled the door open and stood back against the wall with that gesture of deference that so troubled Jed, as if he were a favorite client instead of his son.

"J.E., I'll call up," Jed said breathless.

"Better leave a message at the desk, dear," his father whispered, giving a suspicious scared birdlike glance past Jed into the hall. "I have reasons to believe it unwise to talk over the phone."

As soon as the door closed Jed heard the bolt thrust to behind it.

He walked fast to the subway. He had to see Felicia. The platform was crowded. Something had held up the downtown local trains. Why hadn't he made Felicia come uptown with him and wait for him in the lobby while he went up to see J.E.? She was so understanding about things like that. He kept snapping his fingers from nervousness while express after express thundered by. He ought to have known seeing J.E. would upset him. He had too much to do to let all this upset him. He was just about to start up the stairs again to catch a cab on Columbus Circle when a local eased into the platform. It was a relief, after the aching solitude of his father's room tucked away in the silent shell of the old hotel, to find himself moving, packed in among the jiggling six o'clock crowd, with strange people's elbows in his ribs, somebody's breath on his neck, a little dark girl's buttocks against his thigh, a whiff of black hair and sachet powder in his nostrils. At Times Square the crowd thinned. Jed was too nervous to sit down. Cursing himself for not having changed to the express he paced about the halfempty local till finally the train crawled into Sheridan Square. It was dark when he got to Felicia's. Thank God she hadn't gone out. She was waiting for him.

"Feller," he announced as he flung open the door. "You thought you were marrying a prince. Well, you're going to marry a pauper."

Felicia didn't even seem interested when Jed told her J.E. was cleaned out. She just stood there smiling her tight little thinlipped smile. For just a second her face looked haggard, as if she were very very tired. "Why you wouldn't think," she started in a puzzled tone, "anything like that . . ." She put one hand on Jed's shoulder and pushed his hair off his forehead with the other and looked him enquiringly in the face like a mother inspecting an excited small boy. "What a little silly. With that salary we'll live like Newport millionaires." She kissed him on the eyebrow. His heart jumped in his chest. For the first time it occurred to him that now he was going to be rich.

The trip out to the Coast was fun. "Wonderful sensation," Jed murmured sleepily when the slow rumble of the wheels began under the green plush seat of their drawing-room as the train started to move out of the station. His head was full of drinks and farewell faces. His ears echoed with goodbyes and last admonitions of friends, kidding, scolding, jeering. His finger hurt where he had pinched it closing a trunk. He was dead tired. The hangover from last night's party weighed in his head like a stone.

"The West's where I belong," Felicia was chirping. She was still a little squiffy from the champagne puffing old Rodney Acres had bought them in a fatherly way at lunch in a salmon colored speakeasy. "Colorado's the Hardesties' real home."

Jed burrowed his head into her shoulder. Her hair smelt

of brandy and cigarette smoke, like a bar, like a very nice bar, he told himself happily.

He went on talking drowsily with his eyes closed. "The trouble I had, feller, getting that last grand out of Mark Sugar, you'd have thought I was carrying off a piece of his liver. Gosh he's a sordid guy. We never could have gotten out of town without it."

"We'll wake up in Colorado," she yawned.

Jed got to his feet and lit a cigarette. "That's not according to the Southern Pacific timetable"; he stood up laughing with his hands in his pockets as he surveyed their new pigskin luggage, Felicia's new spring coat, her new broad brimmed straw hat with a green velvet band. "Well, at least it's a clean break."

He yawned. She fell to yawning in sympathy. They sat facing each other, sleepy as owls, jiggling faintly to the motion of the train, soothed by the fast shuttling noise of wheels over rails. They decided they were too sleepy to eat any dinner. They slept almost all the way to St. Louis.

"This is the first time I've crossed the Mississippi," he announced after they were settled on the western train. They spent a long time next morning at breakfast in the dining car. Felicia was trying to tell him over the sound of the wheels about what it had been like when she was a little girl in Colorado: Cripple Creek and the gaunt snowy mountains and trout streams and Pike's Peak on a mule and the red rocks of the Garden of the Gods. He couldn't manage to listen. "The sky's bigger," he kept insisting. "Men are smaller. The grain elevators are something out of H. G. Wells . . . Do you notice, feller, at every station there's just a grain elevator and a watertank? The grain elevator's the symbol of monopoly. This country's empty inside. Did you ever think, feller, that this country was a hollow shell? The false fronts of the big cities on the Atlantic and Pacific coasts, and three thousand miles of emptiness in between."

She looked at him with pale narrowed eyes over her trembling coffee cup. The harsh light off the plains streaming in through the glinting plateglass windows of the dining car seemed to wash all the color out of her face and hair. There were shadows under her eyes he'd never seen before—on account of the baby, he told himself—strained lines from her nose to the corner of her thin mouth. For the first time he found himself wondering how old she really was.

"It's this damn capitalist system," he exploded impatiently. "It's highly impractical for the majority of men . . . for everybody except the insiders, and nobody stays an insider long. Look at J.E. now. He knows more about the theory and practice of Wall Street than any man in New York, but just because he don't know the right people any more he finds himself wiped out, the savings of a lifetime. So now I gotta work twice as hard to support J.E., to say nothing of the heir apparent."

"He'll be apparent all right," said Felicia wryly and wrinkled up her nose as she ground out her cigarette in the ashtray. They sat silent a while looking at each other, listening to the hurrying steel rattle of the train.

"What do you say, feller," Jed said haltingly, "when we get to the Coast, suppose we stop smoking and drinking?" He'd been getting up his courage to say it all morning.

"I've thought of that," said Felicia vaguely, "but I get so nervous when I'm sober."

He didn't join in her little titter. "That's what ruined Kenneth . . ." he went on, leaning eagerly toward her across the shaking table. "He had family, a good education, artistic skill, imagination. If it hadn't been for his drinking he'd have learned to rise above the decadent bourgeoisie. Drinking finished him. He could have been as great a director as Stanislavsky, if he hadn't had that little rotten core, something weak and decadent that made him get drunk every time he had to make a decision . . . Feller, a man has to have a core of belief in him. Capitalism is dying of unbelief. That's why the bankers are climbing out of eighteenth story windows and poor Kenneth stuck his head in the gas oven. If he had believed in the future, if he'd believed in the working class he wouldn't have had to stick his head in that gas oven: a thoroughly antisocial act, by the way, because he might have killed a lot of innocent people, a psychopathic act." Jed drank off the cold coffee left at the bottom of his cup. "Capitalism drives people to psychopathic drinking."

"I'd be doing a little psychopathic drinking right now," said Felicia with her dry laugh, "if the mean old boy friend had brought anything along."

He couldn't help laughing with her; he leaned over and patted her hand on the tablecloth. "Wait till we get to Tucson, we'll spend our honeymoon in Tucson. That's why I borrowed that extra grand."

The morning they woke up and found themselves winding among the pale prone mountains of New Mexico Jed pulled Felicia to the window of their drawingroom in her nightgown. "It looks like Morocco feller," he shouted excitedly. "Why they've got everything in this man's country, everything except civilization. That'll be the business of the revolutionary class when it takes over."

When they climbed off the train onto the open platform at Tucson, their eyes blinking from the stunning light, he was talking into her ear as they followed their bags to a taxi: "The air's so dry it crackles. Look at the enormous sky . . . It's all too big to be exploited by a few lousy bankers."

157

In the cab he grabbed her hand, pulled it to his lips and carefully kissed each finger. "We register as Mr. and Mrs., see?"

"A living lie," said Felicia with her dry laugh.

The first thing he did when they got up to their room was call June long distance in Reno. The connection was terrible. June was grumpy over the phone and tortured him a little before she admitted she had gotten her decree that morning. "And a hundred and fifty dollars a month alimony, darling . . . And we can't remarry for three months," she added in a teasing voice.

"Nonsense," shouted Jed. "How's Mae?"

Mae was fine. She was crazy about the horses. Did he want to talk to her? "Please no," Jed whined, "I wouldn't know what to say right now." They exchanged unfamiliar addresses. Before she hung up June called out in a choking voice. "No hard feelings Jed. Now are they?"

"Let's celebrate feller," Jed shouted brassily as he turned away from the phone. "From now on we're married."

Right away he wished he hadn't said celebrate. It wasn't any fun drinking together any more he was telling himself because he was always worried for fear Felicia would drink too much. "I wouldn't know how to go about getting a drink in the state of Arizona," he added lamely.

"All we need to do is ask the bellboy," said Felicia in a nagging tone. "Scared cat."

"Seriously, feller," Jed took her hand, "we gotta lay off on account of the baby." He had to make her understand. He began to shout: "Pictures is a goldfish bowl. It's full of people counting on their fingers." She wasn't listening. He felt himself getting red in the face. "It isn't like the Village or Cape Cod. We gotta be circumspect," he was trying to keep his voice down.

"I don't suppose the Hays office will mind if I take a hot bath," Felicia said testily.

"Go ahead," he said. He was anxious to get out of the room. "I'll kind of ask around about restaurants."

He'd no sooner stepped out of the elevator into the pueblo-style lobby with yellow stucco walls festooned with artificial peppers and pumpkins when he saw a familiar face beaming at him from above a silk stock and a broad yellow vest with pearl buttons. Sam Faust had put on weight. His bulging cheeks were tanned. He looked like a dressed up pumpkin in riding breeches and a checked sports jacket.

"My how you've put on weight," Sam said as he seized Jed's hand.

"Well you don't exactly look as if your meals were disagreeing with you, Sam."

"It's the climate," said Sam.

"What are you doing in this dump, Sam? I didn't think they let you boys out of the office."

Sam tapped the flange of his nose with his forefinger and pressed his fat lips together. "None of your goddam business, Jed," he whispered and stifled a cough with a small fat hand.

The first thing Felicia wanted to know, when Jed got back to the room and told her he'd met Sam, was whether Maisie was with him. "I love Maisie, there's so much of her," she said giving Jed a smiling mischievous look. My, Felicia was a handsome girl. She looked so tall and fresh after her bath, Jed felt he was falling in love with her all over again.

"No, Sam's up to some monkey business." Jed began to talk fast and cheerfully. "Sam said Mark Sugar was slipping. Sam said he'd written me a lousy contract. Sam said with my reputation and my kind of dialogue I ought to make seven hundred and fifty to a thousand. Sam says dialogue is what they're buying. They got plenty plots. But they haven't gotten over the changeover from the silent films. Talking pictures put a premium on dialogue . . . Dialogue's my long suit, feller . . . He knows a company he thinks might take my contract over . . . He wants me to let him do some finagling. He says I mustn't mind if they try to boss me a little in those story conferences. It's just like the cloak and suit business, they think of dialogue as trimming and buy it at so much a yard . . . At that Sam says some of them are real liberalminded people. They sympathize with the movement at heart. Of course they can't show it too openly. Maybe we're going to like it out here." Jed went on talking from the bathroom washbasin while he washed his face.

There was a knock on the door.

"Open in the name of the law." It was Sam's voice. Sam Faust's protruding belly jiggled under the yellow vest as he pranced into the room with his arms wide. "It's Judge Faust come to kiss the bride . . . Wedded bliss becomes you my dear."

"I told Sam," said Jed coming in from the bathroom at the same time with his face in a towel.

"Told him what?" asked Felicia.

"That you and me were hitched, feller."

"That's a detail I'd almost forgotten," Felicia singsonged in a strained voice.

Jed slapped Sam on the back. "Your honor is the first one we've told. Did your honor bring us a drink?"

With pursed lips Sam turned to lock the door behind him. "Joking aside," he said, "we have to be careful. In some of these Western towns they can raid you for possession. Particularly if they think you are connected with Pictures. The yokels are always looking for a chance for a shakedown."

Sam inched a pint out of his back pocket and disappeared with it into the bathroom. He stood there over the washbasin pouring the drinks with a shaking hand and filling the glasses up from the icewater faucet. "Conspiratorial methods," he puffed as he came back with the three glasses. "It's safer when you can pour the evidence down the drain."

"Better give us a little more just in case," said Felicia holding up her empty glass.

Sam drank off his drink and backed off grinning toward the door. "Bless you, my children," he was saying. "I have an engagement. I'll leave you the pint." He paused with his hand on the doorknob. "Don't forget you never saw me in Tucson," he added. "Just a case of mistaken identity . . . Telegraph Maisie and we'll meet you at the Los Angeles station with the car." The door closed softly behind him.

"Still the same old mysterious Sam," said Jed.

"Why did you tell him we were married?"

"Well aren't we?"

"What you say goes, feller," she said and took a last deep gulp of her drink. "What's Sam up to?" she asked from the bathroom.

"Darned if I know. He asked me a lot of questions, searching questions."

"About the contract?" She came out and shook the empty pint bottle under Jed's nose.

"He's got that all fixed up, feller," Jed hurried on. "You know how Sam loves to play God . . . What he was asking me about was where we stood. About the movement, radicalism. I told him I was out here to make some money so I could go home and write some more radical plays. He said that was great but there might be ways of being useful to the movement right out here. Sam's a mighty good friend to have."

"He might at least have brought us a full pint," said Felicia wrinkling up her nose. "Here, feller, I owe you a dividend." She poured a little out of her glass into his. "That's all there is," she chanted. "There isn't any more."

"Sam knows the wheels within the wheels," Jed went on.

"I'll find out all about it when I get hold of Maisie," said Felicia. "Maisie tells all."

"I bet she don't."

"How about trying the bellboy?"

"Feller, we can't afford it. I'm up to my eyes in debt."

"But you said celebrate," she said defiantly.

"Let's not." He hardly knew how the words got out of his mouth. Felicia's face began to look thin and strained again. The fun had gone out of everything. The evening was spoiled he told himself, before it began.

When their train pulled into the Los Angeles station the first people they saw through the dusty double glass of the window were Sam and George Pastor strolling up the station platform. They wore genuine-looking panama hats and starchy linen suits. They both had the same prosperous sun-bathed look.

"Why George," Jed shouted laughing as they stood amid the swirling crowd in bright resortclothes on the platform, "you look as if you'd lived here all your life."

"Don't I wish I had," said George quietly.

George had brought Felicia an orchid corsage that just matched the print dress she'd bought at Best's. She looked cool and erect standing beside their new pigskin luggage while she pinned the flower to her waist. A bunch of young girls who were running in and out among the arriving passengers were pointing her out one to another as if they thought she might be a movie star.

Maisie Faust, her smiling bulk packed into pink piqué,

was waiting for them outside the station in Sam's limousine. The Negro chauffeur wore a uniform cap. He drove them out through the dazzle and the billboards and the dry back lots to the Fausts' Mexican style ranch house set in a grove of eucalyptus trees. Right away they had a swim in the pool and then sat drinking frozen daiquiris in wicker chairs under the palms on the green lawn.

"This is better than Greenwich Village, eh Jed?" said Sam, stretching his short hairy legs in the sun. "In the old days the only place we East Side kids saw the sky was Coney Island, or a table at the Café Royal."

"Nonsense," giggled Maisie. "Sam how you do go on."

Sam and Maisie had asked them to stay to dinner and to meet a few of their friends afterwards. While they were drinking their cocktails Sam was busy at the telephone. It was a white enameled French-style telephone of a type Jed had never seen before. The chauffeur, who acted also as butler, had brought it out deferentially from the house at the end of an extension line. Sam sat there in the late afternoon sunlight sprawled in a big wicker chair, kidding maids and social secretaries, calling everybody by his first name, calling people sweetheart and big boy and wet smack and schlemiel. Jed sat watching him as he twisted his face up and curled and uncurled his lips as he talked, noting with some admiration that he could hardly understand a word Sam said. "It's a different world," he whispered to Felicia.

"Sam sure does know the ropes," Jed summed the party up after midnight with his face against Felicia's as they sprawled together in the back of the cab on their way to the hotel. "I swear I never felt so out of place in my life." He kissed her under the ear. He was delighted with Felicia tonight. Sam's guests had all seemed so impressed by her Junior League manner.

163

"I like the way the place smells, like old dry baskets or something," Felicia was saying. "I always thought New York smelled terrible. The shadows are lovely, all violet."

"I wonder where Sam buys that real scotch." Jed yawned.

"I couldn't get a laugh out of anybody," she broke out all at once. "Nobody would talk about anything but money and contracts . . . They must have thought I was a dumb bunny."

"They thought you were wonderful," crooned Jed. "Now that fellow Weaver," he added. "I thought he made sense."

"It was like being in the middle of a lot of white suits and evening gowns walking around by themselves." Felicia let out the gruff laugh that sounded like her mother's. "I thought it was wonderful. Maybe I'm tired of being with people I like. Now and then I'd see some old hag looking my way as if to say: Look what the cat brought in . . . I didn't see you getting many laughs either, feller."

"Did you hear me start to tell Pierre Monceau's brother Gaston about how much I liked Ring Miller's *Multitude?* I haven't had such a feeling of doing the wrong thing since the time J.E. took me to see some orthodox Jewish friends on Passover and I forgot to keep my hat on."

In their airless room at the hotel, worn out with the day, they tore off their clothes. The tired boxsprings of the folding bed stuck into their backs but they were too drowsy to care. "At least I don't have to buck this all alone," Jed whispered into her ear as they clung together breathless under the sheet.

In the morning the telephone woke Jed. It was that agent named Weaver. Jed sat up all in a glow. At least people knew who he was in this town.

Mr. Weaver said he'd called Mark Sugar last night before he went to bed. He and Mark were just like that. He could say anything to Mark. Well he'd told Mark he didn't think Mr. Morris would be happy with that contract. Mark had been big about it. Mark was big anyway. He'd agreed to split the commission, if he, George Weaver, could so something better for Mr. Morris. He'd explain later. What he wanted to know right now was: if Metropolis was willing to take over the contract from Crystal at a somewhat better figure would it be agreeable to Mr. Morris?

Yes indeed. No. He better think about it. Jed added hastily he'd call him right back. With beating heart he called Sam: Was this guy Weaver on the up and up?

"Sure, don't you see my fine Italian hand?" Sam's sibilant whisper was so loud the phone whistled in Jed's ear. "Sign up quick before they change their minds."

The night Jed came home from his first story conference he was so tired he insisted on their having their supper sent up to the hotel room. Felicia was a little huffy about it because she wanted to go to a Mexican restaurant Maisie had told her about in downtown Los Angeles. She was crazy about the Mexicans; she was going to do a lot of drawings of Mexican children.

"But that's fifteen miles away, feller. I'm too doggone tired," whined Jed. "It would cost a fortune in taxifares."

"Even before I take you out to see the little Porto Rican style house with a gallery all covered with bougainvillea Maisie's found for us," said Felicia, while she studied the menu, "we've got to buy a car."

"I don't even know if I want to stay," Jed shouted as soon as the waiter had left with the order. "I've never bucked anything like this before. Nobody gives you an inch, see? In the theatre I've been up against some tough eggs. Rodney Acres ain't no lily. But feller, I've never been in a place where there's no give and take. This conference now. Nobody laughs at any gags. This guy Michelson, he sits up at his desk like a wooden image and it's yes Mr. Michelson, no Mr. Michelson right down the line. One of two of the highest paid men call him Milt but the way they say it sounds like a title, like duke or something the way they say it. And everybody's watching for an opportunity to cut everybody else's throat . . . It's like the court of the Sun King . . . And I'm damn tired of being told that the American public's got a twelve year old mind. I learned that in New York seeing them pour into the girl and music shows and stay away in droves from anything that's real. When I piped up and made a couple of suggestions they all looked at me like I couldn't talk English good. Who let that yokel in? was the way they looked at me. I'm not going to stand for it."

Jed was striding up and down the room when the waiter opened the door all of a sudden. Jed stopped talking in the middle of a sentence and let himself drop back into the overstuffed chair. He sat frowning and silent while the waiter pushed in the rolling table. The man took ages to set out the meal. Jed waited a good minute after the waiter had closed the door behind him before he began talking again.

"See? In this man's town you have to be careful what you say. You never know who's going to pass along the good word to who. At the cafeteria where I eat lunch I don't say a thing any more that I don't want carried right to Milt Michelson's private ear. But I don't know why they want to make a guy feel like the new boy in a boarding school. Sam says not to worry. Sam calls it the treatment. After all they invest a lot of money in a writer, they've got the right to give him the treatment, says Sam."

Jed started eating the soggy fried chicken.

"Well I'm getting the treatment all right and I'm goddam sick of it." He was talking with his mouth full; he didn't care. "They try to break a man's spirit just like the third degree. Sam says when you work in a mass production industry you got to have discipline. Sam's a great believer in discipline for everybody but himself. Discipline hell. Feller I'm going to stick it out just to fool 'em. Then when we've got a little nest egg I'll go back to New York and write a play that'll make 'em sit up. I'll take the pants off the damned industry. It isn't religion that's the opium of the people it's the goddam motion picture business . . . By gum, feller that's what I'll call it: *The Opium of the People*."

"Jed," said Felicia with a mischievous little smile when she had finished her last spoonful of icecream. "Suppose we look in on a picture for an hour." She ran her hand through his hair. "A woman in my condition, she needs the opium."

On the way home they decided they'd better buy that house rather than rent even if they weren't going to stay. George Pastor went along with them Saturday afternoon to shop for a car. Jed had wanted a Ford but George said people would notice it on the parking lot, if he had to be conservative he'd better drive a Buick. When the Buick dealer offered to take them out for a trial spin they went by the house Maisie had seen advertised for sale furnished. Right away Jed said it looked like the first act set for an oldfashioned musical comedy. Yellow stucco. Red roof. Green shutters. The Buick dealer said to him it looked like a buy. Hard times. Owners selling at a loss. Jed said they would name it Canary Cottage.

So there were payments on the house as well as on the car to take out of the weekly paycheck, and remittances to J.E. and amounts due on Mark Sugar's loans, and commissions and personal publicity expenses. The first four weeks they only banked twelve dollars.

Felicia seemed to be enjoying fixing up the house and spending money for baby things, but the only thing that pleased Jed was punching the timeclock. That made him feel like a real factory worker. The minute he shut the ground-glass door behind him and sat down at the goldenoak desk and started staring out across the typewriter at the unending sunshine scorching a bed of red geraniums bordered with blue lobelia in a piece of green lawn where nobody ever came but the tobaccocolored old Japanese gardener who mowed the grass every Thursday, Jed would feel unutterably alone. In solitary.

Lunchtime wasn't any relief. He'd start out across the lawn to the cafeteria with a cringing in the pit of his stomach he hadn't felt since he went reluctantly to his first dayschool. As his feet crunched along the gravel path he'd be nerving himself to meet the stares. The other men who ate at the cafeteria all looked through him as if they knew how little money he was making. He was so uncomfortable at lunch that he regularly got indigestion afterwards. The afternoons were horrible. He usually finished his stint in the morning but he wouldn't want to send it upstairs too soon for fear they'd think it came too easy, so he'd sit there, yawning and belching over his typewriter, eating soda and charcoal tablets, and waiting for five o'clock in an agony of boredom. He never did relish his lunch until the day he was assured of his first screen credit.

He'd been scared to death when the call came in from Milt Michelson's office, because that very day Jed had stood in line behind Milt's tailored shoulders at the cafeteria, and had fallen into such a stew trying to decide whether he ought to speak first that he'd ended by not speaking at all. As soon as he got home he took Felicia out for an airing in the still newsmelling Buick, to tell her about it.

"Naturally feller," he said when he got into a side road up a canyon where the traffic was light, "when Milt Michelson's secretary called me I thought I was going to get fired. He's a delicately made little man. He has one of those chiseled Greek faces with a small precise mouth. You can't ever tell what he's going to say before he says it. The first thing he did was to ask me why I was so goddam intense. He said he'd been intense too until his doctor told him it was bad for his arteries. He said I tried to get too much intensity into my dialogue. The studio wanted its money's worth, he said, but not a word more. He went on, like giving candy to a child, that I had integrity as an artist and that was what the pictures needed, artistic integrity. God was I scared? I thought he was leading up to not renewing my contract. Then quick as a flash he said he'd get me a screen credit on *Moonlight Bay*. You know feller there's something big about Milt."

Felicia didn't answer. When he stopped for a traffic light he turned to look at her She hadn't heard a word he'd been saying. She sat slumped on the seat beside him with her face all screwed up, crying like a child.

"Feller what's the matter?"

"I don't know," she whispered. "I feel like I was going to have a miscarriage."

"Are you bleeding?"

"No I think it's all imagination."

"Well quiet down, for cat's sake," he shouted. All at once he felt his nerves were going too.

He pulled the car into a filling station, strode angrily into the public phone and called up the patriarchal old Viennese gynecologist a friend of Maisie's had recommended. Dr. Schoenbrun wasn't at his office but Jed caught him at his residence. The old man's voice was very bland. His words were out of a play by Schnitzler. He said go right home he'd meet them presently. When the doctor came downstairs smiling through his white whiskers, after giving Felicia an examination on her bed, he was saying in his slow Viennese English: "Pheesically Meester Morris it is nutting. Everything as nature intended. The last month the first child. Ve must be careful . . . If you do not mind tomorrow I shall call Dr. Fine. He is a great specialist in the pseechologic. You must be soothing and calm, Meester Morris, but remember no cigarettes or alcoholic beverages."

"That's what you think," Jed growled to himself.

The Morrises had invited Sam and Maisie to dinner that night with George; and Spike Shapiro, the coming young director, was dropping in afterwards to play poker. It was their first attempt at a party. When Jed wanted to phone everybody and call it off Felicia burst out crying again.

"What I need's some company and a nice beaker of gin," she blubbered. Her face had gone white and haggard. She swore she would only drink one martini if he made up a shaker of cocktails. But the cocktail glasses turned out to be so small she had to have another; then when the Fausts came she had to have a couple more to keep them company. It was a buffet supper so they had let the Mexican maid go home early. When the time came to bring out the ham and the cold turkey and the potato salad, Jed had to ask Maisie to help him serve it because Felicia was already dropping things.

She paced in and out through the french windows with the look on her face of trying to remember a name she had forgotten. She dropped a whole tray of glasses trying to set them on the table under the palms in the patio.

Maisie was a great help. While Sam and George were

sweeping up the broken glass, she managed to get Felicia to go upstairs to show her the baby things. Jed was so edgy he kept lighting cigarettes and leaving them burning on the corners of the table.

When Maisie seemed to have quieted Felicia the men settled down to play poker. Sam hadn't finished dealing before Felicia was on the loose again, this time leaning out from the shaky little wooden balcony over their heads and screeching down at Jed in an unnatural shrewish tone "There's the old meanie." She was hysterical. "Look at him. Doesn't he think he's something? He won't let anybody drink because he's afraid they'll embarrass him." The voice didn't sound like Felicia's at all. "As if they weren't embarrassed enough . . . He won't look up. It's your own fault, everybody's saying. It's your own fault for taking up with him." Her voice dropped to a whining undertone, like the voice of a little girl talking in her sleep. "I knew what he was like when I took up with him. He doesn't care about anybody. All he ever thought of was himself." None of the men seemed to dare look up. Over his head Jed could hear Maisie, cosy and sensible: "Now dearie you help me put the things away."

Jed got to his feet and walked up and down the tiled floor running his hand through his hair. His head was soaked with sweat.

When Maisie finally came back saying quietly that she'd given Felicia a sleeping tablet and put her to bed, Jed took her by both hands and said, "Maisie, what is it? Is she losing her mind?"

"Don't worry Jed," Maisie answered in her deep comforting voice. "You'd be acting funny too if you were eight months gone with child. You can expect anything from a pregnant woman. You mustn't let her take anything to drink."

Jed was shaking so, Sam went into the house and found him a stiff drink of scotch. They never did get back to the poker game. They sat in a dismal huddle in the white drawingroom. The men began to shuffle about and clear their throats and to say they ought to go home. The party was a flop. Jed kept begging them to stay. He couldn't face being left alone with Felicia.

Sam Faust took charge. "Let's take our weight off our feet," he said settling himself comfortably on the zebraskin settee in the living room. "There's something I wanted to talk to you men about anyway," he went on letting his voice drop to a hissing whisper after he had looked each one in the face with his small smile. "Of course nothing we say will go out of this group." All at once he was talking about how it was winter, though here on the Coast they would never know it, and the miners were on strike up in the Kentucky mountains. It was cold up there, they needed warm clothes and soupkitchens. They'd just had a soupkitchen blowup. The mineowners were trying to beat them down with terror and starvation. It was up to the fortunate to help the unfortunate. He added he'd been going to suggest that whenever they played poker after this the winners should give a percentage of their winnings to a fund for the miners' defense.

Jed reached for his wallet with a shaking hand and brought out a twenty dollar bill. "Send that to your fund, Sam. You always were a public spirited old crook."

Spike Shapiro pulled out his check book and started to write a check. He was a darkbrowed squarejawed, silent young man. He had hardly said a word all evening.

Sam stopped him. "The way things are out here that's hardly prudent," he said. "Some bright little vigilante working in your bank might tip somebody off. Radicals in Pictures. What a stink that would raise."

172

"Terror and fascism in the coal fields," barked out Spike suddenly. "It's terror and fascism in the studios that worries me."

Jed pushed his wet curly hair off his forehead and started talking: "What we ought to do is take a leaf out of the miners' book. Organize in unions. Look what a mess the playwrights were in. Didn't get their royalties half the time till they organized their guild. We ought to set up a branch right here. Then we could call our souls our own."

"In the legal department," whispered Sam, "that would be considered high treason." He looked from face to face.

"Then you'd hear the thud of unrenewed contracts," Spike was saying, "like apples falling off a tree."

"Felicia and I could run a dandy soupkitchen," broke in Maisie.

"No more writers," shouted Jed. "No more pictures . . . When they put us out of our houses, we'll start a tent colony on one of the beaches. They'll give in after a while. They can't write the scripts themselves."

"Shush." Sam's voice was a whisper. "You know me, but you ought to be careful who you talk to . . . You must learn the science of organization. You must educate yourselves in the working class movement. Education . . . class consciousness," he added, his lips curling in his sly insiders' smile. "A union of the mass communication industries . . . It will come. It will come the day when the workers start to rise." He rose to his feet as if to illustrate what he was saying. "It's an enlivening notion to go home and savor in our beds. Of course as you all know my lips are sealed. Get a move on Maisie, we've got to get up in the morning."

Jed didn't dare get into bed with Felicia for fear of waking her. What's the use of having a wife, he thought

173

bitterly, if you can't sleep with her? He put a lot of pillows in the chaise longue and tried to sleep.

Felicia woke up early, the same puzzled look on her face. The pupils of her pale eyes were dilated. She couldn't remember a thing that had happened last night. At nine o'clock Jed called the studio and said he would be a little late on account of illness in the family. At ten they were in Dr. Fine's office.

Dr. Fine turned out to be a dreamylooking man with overlarge eyes and a grizzled goatee and a pale uneven nose he kept pulling and tweaking. Jed fidgeted for an hour in the reception room while Dr. Fine talked to Felicia. Then Dr. Fine came tiptoeing out. "My dear young man there's nothing to worry about. Nervously distraught. One theory is that in certain cases during the later stages of pregnancy the brain fails to receive its full quota of blood . . . So many young husbands nowadays don't quite manage to displace the father image." Jed blushed and opened his mouth to say something. "You see I'm an eclectic," the doctor interrupted with a horse titter. "To be on the safe side I think the dear lady should spend the remaining period under medical care. I have just reserved for her a room at my sanatorium at Ocean Heights. She's going to start her painting again. Dr. Schoenbrun has her reservation for the great event." Dr. Fine gave Jed a lopsided grin and pulled at his twisted nose. "You need have no further concern."

A few days later the Hardesties arrived. Jed didn't even know they were coming until he heard Scho's voice rumbling on his phone. He was sitting at his desk that morning all nerved up because he'd been called into conference with Milt Michelson in the afternoon. Though receiving visitors during working hours was distinctly frowned on he couldn't very well turn Scho away; he was already down in the lobby.

174

Scho walked in beaming. He looked exactly the same in California as he had on Cape Cod. He wore the same frayed gray suit and the same scuffed shoes.

"My boy," he said, shaking both Jed's hands, "we need have no further concern." Jed winced; it was the same phrase Dr. Fine had left in his own ears. "Agatha has the situation in hand . . . This Dr. Fine is a most interesting man. We had a long conversation on the subject of couvade . . . I mentioned the fact I'd had a few pains myself. He said it had been authenticated in the father many times, but was unusual in the grandfather. He said I must have an unusual gift of sympathy."

Scho sprawled in the chair across from Jed's desk while his big belly shook with internal laughter. When he was through laughing he began to suck his belly in and out from under his belt. Jed, who was busy wondering how the devil he would get him out of the office, couldn't help an enquiring glance.

"It's my abdominal exercises," Scho explained smiling. "They correct the situation. I notice you've put on a lot of weight, Jed. You have a short neck, Jed; it won't do. I'd advise you to take these exercises up immediately. I'll get you a copy of the book . . . If I had started them at your time of life I'd still be a veritable sylph . . . It's the principle of the Polynesian hula dance."

"Scho where are you staying?" Jed broke in. "There's plenty of room at the house. I'll call Agostina. That's the Mexican maid." Jed caught himself getting flustered. "Felicia would have a Mexican maid," Jed was stammering. He got to his feet. "Right now, you must excuse me. I have a tight schedule today."

"You shan't put yourself out for us in any way, my boy," said Scho. "We are staying at my old friend Charley

Collins's ranch out in one of these valleys full of orange trees. Did you ever notice that the scent of orangeblossoms was . . . er . . . aphrodisiac? Agatha can't understand it. How do you find . . . the moral atmosphere?" Scho settled back into his chair.

"Scho I really must get to work." Jed began to pace the floor between Scho and his desk.

"But I'm here on a matter of business, Jed." Laughing his internal laugh, Scho straightened the pillow behind him. "You know how much of the actor there is in me. It occurred to me that while I was here waiting for the grandchild you might arrange for me to take a small part in one of your pictures . . . It would keep me busy . . . You know Satan finds some mischief still, for idle hands to do." Scho's belly shook. He was grinning all over his face. "Salary's no object. Charley knows a lot of the top executives, but I thought it might be a feather in your cap, a young man working his way up from the bottom, to introduce a new actor. People have told me that I breathed the spirit of comedy."

"If you're serious," began Jed distractedly.

"I'm never serious," interrupted Scho, letting out a sudden chortle like a pot boiling over. "Still it would be a novel opportunity for some studio to introduce the man off the street, the medium sensual man." Scho looked inordinately pleased with himself. "Too bad you can't come out for a drink to talk about the possibilities . . . A slice of life say, a grandfather's reaction to the birth of his grandchild."

"After five"—Jed was spluttering with impatience—"at the hospital . . . Maybe I can find you an agent." It was a quarter to twelve before Jed managed to ease Scho out the door. To get his outline ready in time he would have to skip lunch and skipping lunch would give him a headache. He'd have to go to this important conference with a headache.

When Jed walked into Felicia's room at Dr. Fine's sanatorium that afternoon he found everything transformed. He felt he was back on the Cape. Agatha was sitting in the corner with her board on her knees. When she finally noticed that Jed was in the room, she merely tossed her head in the direction of the bed and grunted, "Nothing wrong with the girl," without lifting her eyes off the paper. Felicia was smiling up at him in a vaguely friendly way as if she hardly recognized him. She lay on top of her madeup bed in the old strawcolored dressing gown she used to wear in New York. In her hand she had a large volume of Freud's *Psychopathology of Everyday Life* . . . "It won't be long now, feller," she said cheerfully.

Jed had hardly exchanged two words with her when he heard Scho's heavy breathing in the hall. "I've felt some more pains," Scho was rumbling. "Jed don't you think we should call Dr. Fine? He might want to examine me. It's a matter of real scientific interest."

Agatha got to her feet and pressed her board full of papers against her flat chest. "Charley and Esther will be frantic," she said, "if we are so much as five minutes late to supper. Jed will drive us out to the ranch."

Jed started to stammer that he had an engagement but Scho put both hands on his shoulders. "We want you to know each other. Charley Collins was a warm friend of Eugene Debs. We'll have an interesting discussion. He knew Altgeld and Henry George."

"No drinking or smoking on his ranch. He has that much sense," interrupted Agatha. "Come along." She gave Felicia's pillow one decisive pat and strode off down the hall.

The road seemed endless out through the San Fernando Valley. Jed could hear Scho's voice rumbling on from the back seat about the sympathetic nervous system. The minute he turned the car into the drive past the fieldstone gateposts with wrought iron lanterns on them, it became obvious that the Collinses were very rich indeed. Just inside the gate there was a sign: CAUTION: Peacocks crossing road. An oldfashioned graveled carriageroad, circling round the edges of wide lawns where spinning sprinklers twinkled in the twilight, led to a long low stone house. A Filipino houseboy in a white coat met them at the door. "It will be cold cuts again, Mr. Hardestie," he said with an apologetic little bow. "They are already at table."

"Nothing better than cold roast beef," drawled Scho. "Especially with a glass of Guinness's stout."

The houseboy frowned and shook his head. "Mr. and Mrs. Collins will be nearly finished. They have one gentleman," he was explaining hurriedly over his shoulder as he led them almost at a run through a long livingroom where a fire of logs blazed under a gothic mantel crowned with the antlers of an enormous elk. The diningroom walls were all glass. Beyond them the colors of the flowergarden glowed in the last dusk. A tall stooped whitehaired man with bushy white eyebrows and a dumpy little whitehaired woman sat at either end of a long dark oak table lit by candles in very large silver candlesticks. In the expanse between them, lost under the high carved back of a Spanish chair, sat an inconspicuously small yellow man whom Jed was amazed to recognize.

"Late again. Sit down all of you," said Charley Collins impatiently, cutting short Scho's elaborate introduction of his soninlaw. "Glad to meet you, son . . . Scho, you'll have to make short work of your supper . . . We have engaged Mr. Calvert here to deliver us a talk on Russian Marxism, at seven fortyfive sharp. The people will start arriving at any minute. Come my dear." He rose to his feet.

When Mrs. Collins pulled herself out of her chair, she

178

gave her bobbed white head a shake. "Charley's so drastic," she said. She smiled a wandering little smile all round the table. For a minute she faced Jed. "I know all about you young man," she said. "I know you'll be interested. Of course we consider the dictatorship of the proletariat a little extreme, but we're not too old to keep an open mind . . . I've known little Felicia ever since she was a baby . . . I'm going to call you Jed." She gave him an extra nod and followed her husband out of the room.

Jed tried to get a look of recognition out of the yellow man but he was already walking stifflegged after the Collinses across the dark parquet floor.

While he ate his supper Jed was so busy wondering why V. F. Calvert hadn't spoken to him he couldn't pay attention to Scho's elaborate banter. Probably thought he'd sold out to the reactionary fascists of the motion picture industry. It wasn't like that at all, Jed told himself. How could he explain he was still a radical at heart? On their way back into the livingroom Scho was beginning to grumble that Marxism was a dry subject without a drink.

"Gives me a chance to see you sober for once," said Agatha, "sometimes I forget what it's like."

Ten or a dozen welldressed grayhaired men and women who all had the same easy look of people who lived on incomes in comfortable retirement, were sitting very far apart on hard redwood chairs facing Charley Collins who stood with his watch in his hand in front of the fireplace. As soon as the houseboy had escorted the Hardesties to their chairs Charley Collins briskly pocketed his watch and began to say in a casual querulous voice that they had all read about these new movements, Communism and Nazism and Fascism, in the newspapers and that he'd make up his mind to save himself the trouble of reading a lot of books, full of hard words you had to look up in the dictionary, by getting a leading exponent of each to come and explain his theory in words of one syllable. "All right Mr. Calvert go ahead . . . I don't expect to agree with you, but I shall defend very vigorously your right to tell us what you believe."

As Jed sat listening to V. F. Calvert's involved pedagogical sentences, saturated with the staleness of an oldfashioned German classroom, he kept telling himself how much better he could explain the same thing to these people. Use words out of their own experience. Make them feel the emotional lift. After the lecture he got up his nerve to stride up to the little man and to stick out his hand. "Of course I missed the beard," he said smiling brashly. "I didn't recognize you."

V. F. Calvert did not take his hand. "I am wondering," he said looking past Jed without a smile, "if your experience in the motion picture industry has rectified your ideas of the superstructure."

"I've done a lot of reading. I think I am ready now to base my work on scientific socialism. The emotion was there already. You remember *Shall Be the Human Race?*"

"What a headache. What ideological immaturity."

Jed started to laugh, but V. F. Calvert had already turned away to answer a lady's question about collective farms. Jed's laugh died on his lips. He swallowed his glass of fruit punch and made for the door. He'd made the wrong impression again. It was time he started for home. He had to get to bed to be fresh for work in the morning.

When Dr. Schoenbrun announced to Jed and the Hardesties sitting in a row on an uncomfortable settee under a potted palm in the hospital waitingroom that the baby would have to be delivered by Caesarean section, Agatha gave Jed a sharp angry look, as if she felt it was all his fault, and said gruffly, swallowing her words, that there had never been anything like that in the Hicks family. Scho laughed a wheezy laugh and said that the Hardesties bred naturally as rabbits. "Too naturally sometimes, eh Agatha?" he added patting Agatha's bony knee.

At that moment Dr. Fine came into the room. Jed couldn't imagine what he could be doing there except running up a bill. "Dear Dr. Schoenbrun and I asked the eminent obstetrical surgeon, Dr. Smathers, to fly down from San Francisco for the operation." My God, thought Jed, that's going to cost money. "We have a superb anesthetist. The young lady's physical condition is excellent. There is really no cause for alarm," he wagged his beard and smiled soothingly as he talked.

Before Dr. Fine could say another word Scho was on his feet and had him by the lapel. "But that will spoil my little experiment . . . Are you sure it's necessary Dr. Fine? I had been planning to time any pains I felt and see if they corresponded. Do you suppose I shall feel the incision?"

Agatha put on her nutcracker expression and made herself small in the corner of the settee. She reached for her writing board and started to pencil something on the paper. Jed was left fidgeting dismally on the couch beside her trying to read a medical book Scho had brought in which he had open on his knees. He couldn't make out the print much less understand the words. While Scho and Dr. Fine walked back and forth in the corridor outside talking in loud voices about the neuropathology of couvade, Jed watched the minute hand on the clock over their heads moving desperately slow round the dial. He was shaking so he could hardly hold his cigarette when at last Dr. Schoenbrun, smiling like Santa Claus behind his whiskers, appeared all out of breath in the waitingroom door.

"I hasten to put your minds at rest," he panted. "The dear vife is safe. It is a manchild. All is vell."

Jed could hardly help dropping to his knees. He almost bowled Dr. Schoenbrun over brushing past him on the way to the phone booth to send a telegram to J.E.

The pleasantest thing that happened to him in connection with little Peter's birth was the letter of congratulation he received from Milt Michelson. While Felicia was in the hospital he was keeping out of the house as much as possible on account of Agostina the maid. She was a plain woman with a pockmarked face, married he understood, but she had a roving black eye under her straight brows. Something about the way she moved her hips when she waited on him told him it wouldn't be too difficult. The last thing he wanted was to be caught messing with Agostina. This time she was nowhere to be seen when he opened the front door with his latchkey to slip up to his room for a rest and a shower after an exhausting conference over at the Administration Building. Felicia always kept a pot of heliotrope on the marble table in the front hall. He stood beside it for a moment, tired and sweaty, looking down at the day's pile of bills on the silver tray beside it.

The musky fragrance brought back little scraps of happy times with Felicia when they'd first arrived on the Coast and it had all seemed another adventurous funny story to tell his friends when he got back to New York. No more fun in it now, he was telling himself; Felicia had changed so and the baby had come and he could never get a word with her without the Hardesties butting in. He felt lonesome as a neglected child. Pay the bills, that was all he was good for. Among the bills his eyes lit on a blue envelope with a gold monogram on it. The minute Jed saw the monogram he slipped the envelope into the pocket of his sport shirt and tiptoed with beating heart up the stairs to his bedroom.

The afternoon was stifling hot. He stripped down to his underdrawers and lay down on the bed. It was some time before he could get up his nerve to tear open the envelope. Suppose it was just a polite note to tell him he was through? To read it he lay with his head on the pillow looking up at the small precise handwriting. In Milt's own hand. On his own personal stationery. "Congratulations on the birth of Peter Morris." He had the name right . . . "the happiest moment in a man's life" . . . How big of Milt to write it, busy as he was. "Personal good wishes." Milt was too busy a man to waste his time writing letters like that to just anybody Jed told himself. Milt must think a lot of him. Milt was a real person. Jed read the note over a dozen times before he fell quietly to sleep.

When Felicia and the baby came home from the hospital the Hardesties moved in too. They were so absorbed with buzzing about their grandchild you would have thought they had produced him themselves. There always seemed to be a crowd around the crib. Jed could hardly get a look at the baby. All he knew was that he had a big mouth and a few lank black hairs and vague blue eyes that Agatha, with an accusing look at Jed's eyes, said would soon turn brown. Mae, he remembered, had been such a pretty mild little baby. Peter had leather lungs and yelled night and day. They had tried breast feeding, but had to switch to the bottle when

Felicia didn't produce enough milk. Agatha insisted on mixing the formula herself. The house was either full of bustle and clamor or else everybody was being shushed because the baby was asleep. At the first squawk Agostina would come pattering up the stairs from the kitchen.

Agostina was living in now, and Felicia had taken on the husband, an elderly Mexican named José Maria, who wore a pair of philosophically drooping gray mustaches, to help with the garden and housework; but so far as Jed could make out all José Maria did was sit in the garage door and philosophically smoke his pipe in the shade. Canary Cottage looked like a slum; Jed gave up any idea of entertaining. Agostina kept the balcony over the patio festooned with drying diapers. When Jed got home in the evening he never could find a place to sit. Agatha had taken over his study and was always shut up in there with her writing. Scho, who kept explaining that he was investigating the native wines of California, spent his time making rings on the mahogany table in the diningroom and addressing long disputatious remarks to anybody who came within earshot As Jed couldn't get to sleep after the baby's feedings had waked him up, and he had to have his sleep to be fresh for his work, he took to sleeping alone in the little single bedroom down the hall. He was finding it harder and harder to get in a word with Felicia. To cap the climax he came home one evening to find Scho and Felicia and José Maria all sitting round a gallon jug of wine at the wroughtiron table in the patio listening to a stocky man with a gray gollywog head who of course had to be Eli Soltair.

Eli, dressed like a bindlestiff as usual, ran up to him and hugged him and breathed his winey breath in his face and cried, "Jed what a happy house. The baby's a fine big bozo . . . How's Mae by the way? Two children already, what a lucky bastard. Scho and I are old friends already and we got in José Maria to talk Mex. You didn't know I was half Mexican?"

Jed was twisting his face around trying to show some of the old cordial feeling for Eli. "What are you doing out here, you big bum," he shouted, "trying to horn in on Pictures like the other craftsmen?"

"Hell no, I got a grant from a foundation to study migratory labor. I'm just finishing up. I'll write a play about it. That's why I had to learn Spanish."

"Well that makes four of us on the Coast," said Jed. "There's only Lew left to come."

"He's already here," said Eli with a guffaw that sounded like the old days. "He's agitating hell out of the migrants in the name of the C.P. It's some of his boys who were planning to cut my throat. Lew's a big hombre in these parts."

Jed felt a cold chill down his spine. "The first I've heard of it," he said stiffly. "Eli you make yourself comfortable. I got to go upstairs to change my clothes. I got a dinner date."

"Felicia's fixed me up in her studio over the garage. Where are you going to eat Jed?"

Jed cleared his throat. "I'm dining with Sam Faust."

"Do you suppose I could go along? I'd love to see the old smoothie. I love Maisie."

"It's just a stag affair. Better call up," said Jed trying to give his voice a kidding sound. "Sam's particular about his guests."

"Sly old bastard, what's his number?"

When Jed came down, freshened up by a shower and a change into a white suit, Eli met him in the hall beside the pot of heliotrope. Eli was frowning. "What's the matter with the guy?" he was asking. "He sounded like we'd never been introduced."

Jed cleared his throat again. "Sam has a very responsi-

185

ble position out here," he said. "When he asks a man to dinner it's for some particular purpose. That's the way it's done out here."

While he was walking out to the garage to get his car Felicia ran after him and grabbed him by the shoulder. "Do you remember me?" she asked. "Haven't we met before some place?" Her breath was full of wine. "We'll have a better time than you will. José Maria's going to take us to a Mexican place with mariaches. Haven't you got a little kiss left in your pocket?"

He kissed her perfunctorily. "Do you think you ought to go out?"

"I feel absolutely wonderful . . . Eli will drive us all down in his jalopy. Agostina will stay with Peter. Suppose you told Sam to go to hell and came along with us. It would be like old times, feller."

"It isn't old times," said Jed. "I got to attend to business. Somebody's got to pay the household bills."

He got stiffly into the car, backed carefully out of the garage and drove to Sam Faust's place.

There was something impressively quiet about the men sipping cocktails in Sam Faust's study. These are men that count for something Jed started telling himself right away. Sam himself, in a white messjacket with brass buttons and a cummerbund, wore his air of a judge entertaining counsel in chambers. The first face Jed made out as he came into the room was that of John Taylor Briggs, recently arrived at Metropolis. He knew the features from the dramatic sections of the Sunday papers. Then there was Roy Monks, the mystery story writer, who in spite of all the money he was making still looked like a character actor out of work cadging drinks at the Lambs Club. Fred Walton and Gehring Weeks, two of the highest priced writers on the lot, sat side by side on an oak settee. George Pastor, very much on his mettle in such eminent company, sat in a corner stroking his little mustache over lips compressed with the determination not to say the wrong thing. Sam first introduced Jed to Mr. Briggs, who gave him a wan smile of recognition, and to Mr. Monks, and then motioned to Calhoun the house man, who looked unusually solemn that evening, to pour him a martini. "Drink up Jed," he said. "We are going to dine early tonight. Some of these gentlemen have other engagements."

Jed had hardly time to swallow his drink before they were being ushered into the diningroom. Talk at the table was slow, about the cold weather in the East, and the depression and the coming political campaign. None of it was amusing. Sam told a couple of smutty stories but they certainly did fall flat. Jed had a feeling he was making too much noise with his jaws while he ate his food.

They filed out back into the study for coffee afterwards. As soon as Calhoun had passed round a tray of varicolored liqueurs and brandies he retreated silently and Sam closed the door after him.

He stood leaning against the corner of his desk. "Gentlemen," he said looking blandly from face to face through his bifocals, "the time has come for a short discussion of the filmwriters' association, which as you all know is the burning question of the hour in the industry. Now you probably are all asking yourselves what business it is of mine, because I work in the office on the other side of the street. First I want to assure you that I am not speaking for management, that this little gathering has no official significance whatsoever. In fact it might do me a good deal of harm on the other side of the street if it were known that it had occurred. My future in this town is very likely in your hands. I know it is in the hands of honorable men and that nobody will breathe a word of what we say this evening." He spread out his short arms appealingly.

"Sam," enunciated Roy Monks dramatically, "it will be the silence of the grave."

"I am taking this risk, if you call it a risk, because I feel, as a liberalminded man and as a convinced antifascist, that a great deal depends on the success of some such organization of writers. It is up to you to keep this great mass medium out of the hands of the enemies of the human race. I don't need to tell you that there is no influence comparable to that of Pictures on the minds of the masses today. At a time when the liberalminded intellectuals and the downtrodden masses of the world are grouping themselves for a battle to the death with the brutal forces of reactionary totalitarian evil, exemplified by what is happening in Germany, personal considerations must be left out of the scheme of things. What I want to say is that if such an organization as a number of you gentlemen sitting in this room seem to contemplate really gets under way, I know enough of the men who steer the destinies of this industry to know that they too have hearts. Many of them have friends and relatives in the old country whose very lives and property are endangered by the monstrous forces of reaction building up—not only there but in this country, as you can judge by the savage repression of working class organizations we read of in every newspaper we pick up—and that if this association is properly steered there will be opposition to it, yes; but that opposition will be a token opposition because the hearts of the men who manage the industry will, in spite of their economic interests, be on our . . . I should say on your side." Sam's eyes glowered green through his glasses. Little beads of sweat stood out on his broad face. His head was thrust forward and moved from side to side with a

188

turtle-like motion; he wore the look of a man who was baring his innermost thoughts.

"In my legal work, gentlemen," he threw back his head as if shaking himself free of some malignant trance, and took a deep breath: "I have represented trade unions and corporations and business partnerships of various sorts and attended thousands of board meetings and committee meetings where policies were decided by a show of hands and I can tell you right now that nothing happens accidentally in these organizations." His voice took on a confiding practical tone. "The people who know what they want before they sit down at the table are the men who carry the day. I just want to suggest that it is up to you gentlemen who are leaders of your profession to see to it that such an organization, if it does start, is kept in responsible hands, in the hands of the kind of men who are sitting round this room tonight. If such an organization gets started under firm and liberal direction and manages to get behind it the wholesome fervor of antifascist feeling, I think I can promise you that in the end the studios will not only acquiesce, but will cooperate."

Jed caught himself beginning to clap. "Hear, hear," chanted Fred Walton who'd been a Rhodes scholar and cultivated English ways. "Of course, we are reasonable men . . ." began John Taylor Briggs in his small piping voice. "Pure gold . . . pure gold," Roy Monks kept saying. "That's the way to go about it," cried Gehring Weeks. Every man had crawled out of his shell. When Calhoun appeared in the room with a tray of glasses of scotch and soda they reached out for them as cheerfully as they would in a bar.

Jed wormed his way up to Sam through an animated discussion of ways and means and whispered that he was worn out with the baby and everything, and had to go home to bed.

"Wait a second," Sam hissed in his ear, "they'll all go . . . Pierre Monceau's party . . . we don't rate that yet." A tiny smile curled bitterly at the corners of his lips.

In a jiffy Jed and Sam and George were alone in the study. While Sam was undoing his bow tie and loosening his collar, George reported triumphantly, "The men round your dinner table, Sam, represented salaries amounting to eleven thousand six hundred dollars a week."

Sam laughed. "In this town, that's peanuts," he said. "George," he let his voice drop, "I hope I didn't say too much. It was bad Marxism, but it was as much as they were ready for."

"It's hush money really," Jed burst out. "We are paid to coat sugar over the exploitation of the masses."

Jed caught a sharp questioning look in Sam's face, as if he weren't quite sure he'd heard right.

"Don't be surprised," Sam went on blandly talking as he escorted them with a plump hand on each of their shoulders across the lawn under the moonlit palms to their cars, "if I return to private practice . . . It would be an interesting experience don't you think, to represent the writers' association."

When Jed drove his car into his own garage and walked back across the patio he noticed with relief that all the lights were out. The Hardesties had come home and gone to bed, thank God. Jed was about to turn the knob to open the door when two big hands were clapped over his eyes. He could feel Eli's burly giggling frame behind him. "Quit that," he said and squirmed to get loose. "Get your big dirty hands off me."

"If you'll promise to come up to my room and drink a little nightcap I'll let go."

"All right all right." Jed turned angrily on Eli's baboon grin. "I've got work to do in the morning . . . Eli I'd say it was about time you graduated from kindergarten."

"I've graduated from a lot more colleges than you have including the university of hard knocks . . . I want to talk to you Jed. That's why I stayed up. Had to drink to keep awake. Come on." Eli pushed Jed ahead of him up the stairs to the loft above the garage which Felicia had started to fix up for herself as a studio just before the baby came. The loft smelled cosily of linseed oil and turpentine. "I know you're just piling up the dough Jed," Eli was saying, "and I admire you for it. All I know to do with money is spend it."

He poured Jed a glass of wine and let himself drop on the couch. The springs creaked under his weight. Jed stood in the middle of the room looking sourly down into the glass in his hand. He was determined not to drink it, not after the scotch at Sam's.

"Here's the thing," Eli began. A yawn overtook him. "We missed you Jed," he rambled on running his fingers through his mop of hair. "We had a lovely evening. Felicia and Scho and Agatha—isn't Agatha an old witch? They are people after my own heart. I wish I could find a girl like yours to marry." Eli pulled himself together with a start and glared into Jed's face out of his dark eyes. "But anyway from what they said I gathered you were starting to be a real fellow traveler. Next thing you'll be joining the Party . . . It's your conscience bothering you for poisoning the public mind. But Jed that's not the cure. I can imagine a state of affairs in this country where all the Babbits start joining the Party." Eli's face had begun to sag again. He dragged himself yawning to his feet and shook a big finger under Jed's nose. "I just want to remind you that you are an artist."

Jed stood staring into the blank canvas on Felicia's easel.

"Party wouldn't have me," he said in a surly tone. "A man has to prove himself a devoted servant of the working class or they won't take him in."

"Words, words," declaimed Eli waving his arms. "You guys all believe in words. I believe in people. Words are either little levers in a machine or else they are poetry when people say them . . . You keep forgetting about people . . . Now look here, here you are living in the house with José Maria and his wife and I bet you don't know that he's a retired bandit, an old Zapatista . . . and he strums the guitar like a dream, and though he can't write his name he can play a very decent game of chess . . . Mexican culture is the culture of the cantina . . . Think what Chekhov would have done with a man like that. And you don't know he exists . . . That comes from classifying everybody according to St. Marx. A playwright ought to love people the way Felicia loves colors and shapes because words fresh out of people's mouths are his raw materials . . . the theatre is beautiful words, and the dance!" Eli tried to do a few crouching Russian dance steps, slipped, sat down with a thump on his big behind, and went on talking from the floor. "That's what a man gets drunk for, to be able to tell off his old friends."

"But Eli," Jed started in the patient tone of a teacher to a child, "the reason the Mexican revolution you are so crazy about never got anywhere . . ." Jed suddenly felt the old pleasure in argument. He was going to convince this damn fool Eli Soltair. "Political action without direction just gets to be opportunism and anarchy and ends in fascism and war. It's the men who know what they want before they go to a meeting or sit down at a table who have the direction of events in their hands. We know that the day is coming when the masses are going to be heard. There's nothing particularly sinister in wanting to direct those forces toward the highest good. That's what a disciplined organization of revolutionists is for."

Eli got unsteadily to his feet and poured himself another glass of wine. "Bosh," he shouted. "It was the bolsheviki who destroyed the beautiful October revolution of the soldiers and the peasants."

"Impractical balderdash . . . We have to meet steel with steel. A few bankers run the motion picture business. You know that as well as I do. We've got to turn the tables on them. It wasn't Lenin who invented the modern conspiratorial technique. It was J. P. Morgan. All Lenin did was use the method for the benefit of the working class, and a hell of a lot more efficiently."

"It's too damned efficient." Eli pushed his bloodshot eyes very close to Jud's face. He was so excited he spat a little when he talked. "It's all based on envy, hatred and malice. Robespierre was efficient . . . at cutting off people's heads."

"He established the bourgeois revolution. Did he or did he not?"

"Like hell he did," roared Eli. "He established Napoleon's dictatorship. Massacre, misery and war followed," he added in a dramatic whimper, "by apathy and reaction."

Jed began to yawn. "This argument isn't getting anywhere," he was gasping through his yawn.

"You mean you haven't cut my head off yet," said Eli slapping his knee. "If you can't convince 'em shoot 'em . . ." All the lines of his face were curving with laughter. "Well I'm pulling out in the morning," he added in a suddenly practical tone . . . "before you turn me in to the Gay-Pay-Oo." The idea seemed to amuse Eli a great deal.

"I wouldn't be talking like this to anybody but you, you

193

old bum, not in this town," Jed was saying in the friendliest tone he could muster. Now that Eli was leaving Jed felt fond of him all over again. "Why not stick around? With your talent and your connections you could land a very substantial contract." The words, as he said them, were unconvincing, even to his own ears.

"A fat chance," said Eli. "By gosh I think I'll take the Hardesties along. You've probably had enough of your in-laws."

"Honest? Could you?"

"Why not? Agatha won't let Scho drive a car any more . . . they are crazy to see Colorado again. I'll drive 'em as far as Chicago. I got to stop and talk to my foundation. I'm just a bighearted boy." He put his heavy hands on Jed's shoulders and talked earnestly into his face. "Jed you ought to travel around this damn country! Talk to people. Get all this hatred out of your system. This town's getting you. Pull out of the damn place and see the world. You used to be an adventurous guy. Let's you and me go to the Soviet Union. Uncle Yasha went off with his *mushrats*"—Jed couldn't help joining in Eli's reminiscent laughter—"but there'll be other ways."

"The real adventure," Jed found himself talking in a cold earnest voice he hardly recognized, "is right here . . . You blabbermouthed bohemians don't know it. The little theatre movement . . . all that's just make believe, kid stuff . . . Out here we play for keeps." Suddenly Jed had a chilly feeling of having said too much. He turned toward the stairs. "If I don't see you in the morning, bon voyage."

On his way to bed he stuck his head into Felicia's room. He could hear her heavy familiar breathing and the baby's light tiny breath. He missed her so in bed. He wanted to say goodnight, but mother and child were both fast asleep.

Peter was already toddling about and had even said a complete sentence when on arriving at the studio one Monday morning Jed got the surprise of his life. For months he'd been trying to get a real private smile out of the receptionist in the lobby. She was a handsome blonde with an icy profile and hair about the same color as Felicia's only much more carefully dressed. This morning she smiled right up into his face, a smile just for him. "Mr. Morris," she said in a tinkly voice that sounded a little like Felicia's when she was at her most Bostonian, "they've put you in new quarters. I do hope you'll like them." She rummaged in the drawer of her desk with rosy pointed fingernails and produced an envelope containing a key. "One flight up. We moved all your papers."

The first thing he saw was his name: J. E. D. Morris in gilt on the groundglass. The desk was mahogany. There was a toilet and washbasin adjoining, individual, just for him. Immediately he called up George Weaver. Sure George said in a purring voice, they are ready to sign a new contract at one thousand five hundred. "Jed, your success in this town has been, if you allow me to say so, phenomenal."

Jed was tempted to call up J.E. long distance, but he remembered how much his father hated talking over the telephone, so instead he wrote him a long letter describing how little Peter was talking and walking and how a new baby was on the way and all about what a great guy Milt Michelson was.

In the middle of the letter he decided he ought to have a better car. He laid down his pen and called up the Cadillac dealer and asked him about the turn-in value of his new Buick convertible. He'd just made an appointment to meet the dealer with his floor model at Canary Cottage when a New York call came in.

It was Mark Sugar's rapid lisping voice telling him J.E. had been taken ill at the hotel. He'd better arrange a leave of absence and catch a plane that night. Jed called up Felicia to ask her to pack his bag. Her voice was husky over the phone. Though she had never met him, she loved J.E. she said. She'd drive Jed to the airport.

Jed arrived in New York more dead than alive after his first long plane ride. At the Great Western he found the stately silverhaired manager Mr. Leamy talking distractedly with a pale bluejowled man with plastered black hair. "My boy," he said putting his two hands on Jed's shoulders, "the end has come . . . Most regrettable." He made a clucking with his lips. "I know your dear father would rather have had it happen in a hospital, but there was no chance to remove him. He was always so considerate. How regrettable, after so many years. Why I remember you in short pants, young man. Most regrettable. Something of this sort is awkward for the hotel . . . He suffered a light stroke three days ago. We immediately called your friend Dr. Wilton. Dr. Wilton wouldn't allow him to be moved. He passed away quietly in his sleep early this afternoon."

"I want to see him." Jed's voice broke.

"Meet Mr. Noonan from the funeral chapel . . . I'm sure you'll understand we had to call somebody. Mr. Noonan will remove him tonight."

The bluejowled man bowed his head. His lips moved silently as if in prayer. "If you will follow me please," he said aloud.

Jed had to suffer the familiar smell of the elevator, the bookish smell of the room, the faint whiff of bayrum; the filing cabinets; the dying sweetness of the roses wilted before his mother's picture. He kept his lips pressed together tight. Through dry eyes he saw J.E. stretched out in his dressing gown on the hotel counterpane as he had seen him so often taking his nap after lunch. The face was not distorted. In the

196

horizontal light from the window, again it seemed molded of green wax. The mouth still wore the remote unamused so distant smile. He wouldn't have known that J.E. wasn't asleep.

Jed was choking for air. He couldn't stay in that room.

"Everything the best," he mumbled to the bluejowled man, who insisted on communicating with him in dumb show as if he were a deaf mute. The bluejowled man took his arm to lead him from the room. Jed pulled himself free and hurried down the hall.

As soon as he stepped out of the elevator into the lobby Mark Sugar jumped up from a leather chair and walked up to Jed and grabbed both his hands. "Jed old man, I'm here," he said, his pale moonface all puckered with woe. Jed had always thought of Mark as a cold kind of a fish, but now he was amazed at his thoughtfulness. Mark explained he was up to his neck in engagements, because he was just about to leave for the Coast himself, "To make sure my dear friend George Weaver hasn't been cutting my throat too bad," he added with a smirk.

Mark stuck by him through the lawyer's office and the will and the disposition of the estate and of the effects of the deceased, and the service at the funeral chapel, and the long deadly ride out to the cemetery. Right after the funeral Mark insisted on Jed's going home with him to Westport. Everything was a blur on the train. As soon as he'd been shown to his room Jed locked the door and lay down on the bed and burst into tears like a child.

Next morning Mark made Jed ride into town with him amid the morning crowd of commuters. At his office he kept him busy reading scripts. Had to have Jed's opinion, Mark said. Jed felt better just doing everything Mark wanted. Mark had a drawingroom reserved to Chicago on the Twentieth Century, so Jed went along with him obediently although he

197

had his return ticket by plane. He just couldn't imagine going anywhere alone. Anyway it was snowing so hard no plane could fly. Mark gave Jed the feeling of being treated like a package of breakable china. All Jed could think of was how good it would be back with Felicia and Peter. Mark didn't drink, but he had let Jed buy himself a bottle of scotch in New York.

The whisky took away a little of the feeling Jed had of having no skin on his flesh. When he followed Mark's padded shoulders into the diner he discovered that the whisky had given him an appetite. After he'd ordered his meal he found himself looking past Mark's concerned face into a pair of black eyes with mascaraed lashes a few tables away. He knew that patent leather hair. It was Jade Haman. Quick as a flash he'd said excuse me to Mark and was standing over her looking down into her eyes like into a well. "How now sweet prince?" she said.

Her mouth was already shaped like a kiss by the lipstick. "Jed you must tell me about California," she said. "I'm on my way."

"In the club car."

She batted her heavy lidded eyes and nodded several times like a Chinese doll.

"Who was that?" asked Mark a little peevishly. "I didn't like to turn and stare."

"Jade Haman."

Mark let his breath out in a slow hiss. "A job in Pictures? They must be desperate out there."

It was long after midnight when Jed found his stumbling way back to Mark's drawingroom. Jed's drunk, he was telling himself. Mark, in the upper berth, was snoring with the light on. He had fastened a black silk bandage over his eyes. Jed tittered at the sight. He could still taste the lipstick, the rank blackhaired smell of her body. He got into his pajamas. He couldn't go to sleep. It was as if the woman were still in bed with him. He had to talk.

"Hey Mark," he called out, "I'm drunk."

Mark didn't stir.

"Mark," he called out again, "tell me why I do it, Mark. It never fails if I get on a train or a boat, or if I go to a strange hotel, quick as a flash I'm in bed with some bitch . . . I can't help it." He began to whimper a little.

Mark was awake. He'd slipped the bandage up onto his forehead and was looking at Jed cautiously from under it, through pallid halfopen eyes.

"Why do I do it? Damn it, Mark, tell me that. I love my wife. We are going to have a new baby."

"I have no experience of that sort. I guess I'd be afraid of venereal diseases," mumbled Mark yawning.

"You shouldn't say things like that, Mark," shouted Jed to make himself heard above the racket of the train. "Jade's a thoroughly nice girl, Mark. A brilliant girl, Mark. She just happened to feel in the mood. I'm always in the mood. Mark, I believe in complete freedom but why does it make me feel so horrible?" He shook his finger in Mark's prostrate face. "Mark, it's because my life is a vacuum, an absolute vacuum. When that ghoul from the undertaker's asked me what denomination the services ought to be, I had an impulse to say Jewish. You think I'm ashamed of being Jewish but I'm not. It just wouldn't be true, Mark. J.E. was a saint. His religion was the human race. Mother was an Episcopalian. I wasn't brought up Jewish. J.E. saw the good in all religions . . . That damned Catholic lowlife from the undertaker's, he looked at me like he thought I was dirt just because I didn't have a religion." He had to hold onto the edge of the upper berth to keep his feet when the train lurched. "Who am I, Mark?

Sooner or later every man has to ask himself that question. Who the hell am I?" He was outlining his words very clearly and distinctly to make himself understood over the rumble of the wheels.

Mark raised himself on his elbow: "Jed, suppose you lie down and get some rest. These aren't things to talk about when you are worn out and excited. Think of that nice baby. How about putting out the light?"

"I'm not excited. My mind's clear as a gem . . . He looked at him like he was dirt," Jed found himself screaming. "I ought to have buried him next to my mother. I couldn't even remember where she was buried . . . Under this goddam system we're all dirt."

To hide his sobs he switched out the light and swabbed his face off with water in the washbasin. He rolled into the lower berth and lay there with spinning head, listening to the trucks jolting over the rails as the train hurried west through driving snow. His head still ached when he woke up.

By Chicago the blizzard had stopped. Planes were flying. He suddenly felt worried about Felicia and Peter so he said goodbye to Mark, who merely made a fishface at the suggestion that he fly too, and drove to the airport.

The plane circled down out of the clouds into Salt Lake City in sunlight. There the passengers changed to a trimotor. They found the air bumpy over the mountains. The plane seethed shaking through great white cumulus clouds. Dazzling whiteness crowded against the windows. The plane became a crazy roller coaster. Jed was too dazed by the roar of the motors in his ears and too busy vomiting to think of anything at all.

At Los Angeles he stumbled off into the calm warm sunlight feeling like a crushed egg. He was through with New York, he was telling himself, now that J.E. was gone. Out here a man could live in the sun. This was the great adventure. That's what he'd have to explain to Felicia. It seemed that he'd been away so long he hardly remembered what Felicia looked like. Which was Felicia? Black spots danced before his eyes. Panic rose in him when he found that none of the greeting faces looking toward him in the sunlight was Felicia's. Instead there was Sam's house man Calhoun smiling with bright teeth behind the barrier.

"Is everything all right at home?" Jed asked breathless. Calhoun smiled and nodded. "Miz Faust tole me to meet you," he said. "Miz Morris was busy with the baby I guess."

When he reached the door of Canary Cottage Jed was in such a hurry he forgot to tip Calhoun. He snatched his bag and hurried into the front hall. The first thing he saw was the pot of heliotrope spilt on the white wool rug. Peter, his face all smudges, was happily scooping up the muck with the pieces of broken porcelain. "Daddy . . . all bake," he crooned. He'd cut one of his tiny fingers on the porcelain. When Jed picked him up he found his pants were wet.

Felicia advanced unsteadily from the end of the hall holding out a dustpan and broom. "I had to let Agostina off because it's José Maria's saint's day. They had to go to church," she hurried to explain. "Peter and I were playing puss in the corner." She kissed him with her wet loose mouth. "You're not mad feller? I'll get it up in a jiffy."

"Felicia you've been drinking again . . . The child's not been changed."

She was kneeling at his feet hurriedly brushing the earth and the mashed flowers and the broken porcelain into the dustpan. "I got so nervous . . . Decisions make me nervous."

Jed could still feel the pitching of the plane. The air sickness swooped inside him. What a homecoming. He had an impulse to kick her as she knelt there scrubbing at the rug at his feet.

All at once the strength drained out of him. Still holding Peter by his little wet bottom he let himself drop onto the settee. "A horrible trip." He was having trouble breathing. "Do you suppose it could have brought on a heart attack? I know I'm overweight." He could feel the weight of his belly against his belt. He sat there breathing hard feeling the wet from the little boy's pants penetrating his trouser leg.

"You need some gin, feller." Felicia grinned in his face and tottered off down the hall with her dustpan and broom. Peter proudly sitting on Jed's knee was making pleasurable noises. He seemed to be enjoying the scene. Jed sat jiggling him on his knee. When Felicia came back with two jelly glasses full of warm martini cocktail Jed didn't have the strength to refuse.

"This is my last," she mumbled nodding wisely over her glass as she sat down beside him on the settee. "Mustn't drink on account of my condition . . . Jed," her voice suddenly was quite sober, "let's go home and have the baby born at Hingham. Agatha's such a help. She can't come because of Scho. I want a baby born at Hingham and this is my last chance, so Dr Schoenbrun says." She paused for breath and then went on as if saying things she'd had on her mind for a long time. "Scho's not been strong since he had the pneumonia. You know they aren't either of them getting any younger and neither are we. Let's pull up our stakes. There's nothing for us out here. I've got a magnificent offer for the house. Thirty thou'."

"Felicia I cannot leave now." Jed pronounced his words very carefully so that she would be sure to understand. "I didn't get a chance to tell you in all the excitement. I've signed a new contract at fifteen hundred a week . . . Fifteen hundred a week," he repeated.

"Tell 'em it's all a mistake. Now that we don't have anybody except ourselves to support there's no sense to it . . . Dear J.E. It was mean of you never to take me to see him . . . I know I'd have loved him. I love him right now."

"It's impossible," said Jed getting to his feet. "Let's not argue. Let's not ever argue again," he added wearily. "I'm going to lie down a little . . . How about changing the child's pants? He'll be getting dermatitis."

Peter wrinkled his face up just as if he'd understood and opened his big pink mouth and began to cry. At that point Agostina, all frills and jingling with bracelets, wearing a flowered hat from her holiday churchgoing, came charging down the hall. She snatched up Peter off Jed's knee. As she brushed past him Jed felt the warm reek of her vigorous sweaty body and of the jasmine she'd pinned to her breast. "Pobrecito, pobrecito," she was crooning. Without looking at her, Jed pulled himself up the stairs to his room.

Next morning he left the house before Felicia was up. Sleeping it off, he told himself grimly. As he walked across the patio he could hear Peter's quavering treble and Agostina's low velvety voice from the kitchen. She was feeding him his breakfast. They were having themselves a time, he thought enviously. The new nilegreen Cadillac was waiting for him in the garage. As he slid his legs in under the wheel, something about the new leathery expensive showroom smell of the car made him think of that girl on the liner. What a long time ago that was. He couldn't remember how long. Marlowe . . . the Compagnie Générale Transatlantique. He'd been a fool not to follow that up. Greenwich Village, artists, what a dead end! He was through with drunks and bohemians and addleheaded liberals. With gritted teeth he pressed the starter.

The motor hummed so sweetly he could hardly hear it. Very carefully he backed out onto the gravel drive. The gears shifted with delicious smoothness. All the frustration and misery seemed to drop off him as he slipped the gearshift into high and drove away from Canary Cottage along the empty palmfringed street toward the studio. After he'd locked up the car in the vacant glare of the parking lot, he backed off from it enjoying the white walls of the tires, the gleam of the chromium, the contrast between the red morocco leather upholstery and the green finish. You couldn't tell the car wasn't custombuilt. A high executive's car. Everybody on the lot would notice it.

The tiled floor of the lobby wasn't dry yet from its early washing. The receptionist was standing over her desk. Her piled up curls looked crisp and cool. Her makeup was perfect. Her eyes were very sorry; she knew. She batted her lashes sympathetically and even reached out to give his sleeve a little pat as he walked past. He was glad now he had put on a black necktie, though he hadn't let Agostina sew on the black crepe band for his sleeve which she had brought out with a lot of bustle the night before. Feeling the solemnity of the sad look he couldn't help wearing on his face, he walked upstairs to his office. On his desk there was a pile of telegrams of condolence. Some of them were signed by big names.

Everybody was very kind. At lunch in the cafeteria men who had never spoken to him before came up to shake his hand and to say a few tactful words. Milt Michelson walked right up to him with short decisive steps and his eyes on the ground and, right in front of everybody, threw an arm round his shoulder. "That's what life is Jed," he muttered through gritted teeth. Then he added, with a flicker of a smile on his small mouth, that Herman D. Speyer, himself, wanted to see Jed, personally, at his office in the Administration Building at four.

Jed could feel the pulse quicken in his wrists when Mr. Speyer's secretary, a short woman in surprisingly plain school-teacherish clothes, came out to the waitingroom to fetch him in. The nap of the deep carpet felt very resilient under his feet as he walked after her into the great oval room which was furnished like a set for a picture about Madame du Barry. At a kidneyshaped table, with his back to the big window, with the light through the lace curtains like a halo behind him, sat a small man with sharp eyes set close together as a monkey's and closecropped hair part rusty and part gray that lay close to a knobby skull. Jed caught a quick sharp glance as he walked into the room and a hand in a white cuff with diamondflashing links waved to motion him to a chair. Mr. Speyer was talking on the phone.

"Don't ask me how to do it, Ring, get it done," he was saying. Jed picked a small gilt chair and sat down. His face fell naturally into the modest sad bereaved expression it had worn all day. Herman D. Speyer talked and talked, mostly in a voice so low Jed couldn't catch what he was saying. At last his voice rose to a waspish buzz. "You're on your own, Ring, remember that. I'm through being a nursemaid. It's the opportunity of a lifetime. There is a tide in the affairs of men . . ." He faltered. "What's the rest of it?" he whispered to Jed in a confidential aside that immediately made him feel at home. He had cupped his hand over the mouthpiece.

"Which taken at the flood leads on to fortune," Jed piped up like a small boy in class.

Herman D. Speyer gave him a grateful smile. "Which taken at the flood leads on to fortune," he concluded in a voice croaking with emphasis. He replaced the receiver and got to his feet. He was a slender man buttoned tightly into a double-breasted suit of very small gray checks. There was no side to him at all. "I need a scholar," he explained to Jed as if he were one of the family. Then suddenly there was condolence on his face. He had remembered Jed's father. "My boy," he stepped out with a sweet sad smile from behind his little desk and took Jed's hand. "Milt tells me you've had a bereavement. There, there . . . We must look for the silver lining. That has been the purpose of my life. They all come to me with every little cloud. How can I be a nursemaid to all the world? Ring's on location. He calls up from . . . Where is he, Milt?"

For the first time Jed noticed Milt Michelson crouched frowning over a wad of yellow typewritten sheets in an enormous padded chair with gilt cupids on the back.

"The Grand Canyon," said Milt without looking up from his reading.

"So much scenery you can't see their faces. Is it my fault? I didn't build it . . . Now you are a scholar, Mr. Morris. I have a little problem to discuss. I've just read a book."

Jed listened rapt while Herman D. Speyer talked and talked. He talked for an hour.

"He expects great things of me." Jed started to tell Felicia about it the way he was used to the minute he got home. He had found her playing with Peter in the sandbox in the patio. "The more I get to know my way around the lot . . ." He broke off. She wasn't listening.

"Hi feller." She looked up at him with a vague smile. She was kneeling beside Peter showing him how to shovel the sand into his bucket. "The more I get to know my way around the lot," Jed started again in a louder voice . . . "the more I get to know the men who've grown up in the business of making pictures, the more I realize that they have wisdom.

I've spent the whole afternoon with Milt. We started working together in Herman D. Speyer's own office . . . I never had a more interesting afternoon." She still didn't seem to be paying any attention to what Jed was saying.

"Are you sure we couldn't go home? A second Caesarean is a delicate matter. I don't like these doctors out here." She looked up at him with pleading eyes. "Agatha has arranged for a very good man at Massachusetts General."

"I've spent the entire afternoon with Milt," Jed ignored her question. He went on in a louder voice. "He takes me along now whenever he goes over for a conference with Herman D. in his own private office. They expect great things of me."

She turned the bucket upside down. The sand was too dry to make a mold. Peter's brown eyes looked disappointed. She made a little clucking noise with her tongue. "I meant to make a castle." She looked up in Jed's face. "Go on feller," she said.

"Public taste is changing," Jed declaimed. "The industry, so Herman D. put it, has been profoundly impressed by the election of Franklin D. Roosevelt and the measures he's taken to combat depression and all that. Of course he voted for Hoover; but these men are big, feller, they can see a trend. Of course I didn't tell 'em I thought Roosevelt was just a social-fascist. They expect great things of me. They think they see a demand for pictures about working people, real life, slums. Herman D. had just read a novel of Dickens his daughter gave him for his birthday because it had a pretty binding. It was *Oliver Twist*. He couldn't put it down. He ordered the research department to get him up summaries of all Dickens' books. He said the tears ran down his cheeks. He called Milt on the phone and said: 'Get me a writer who can write like Dickens' . . . 'Laughter and tears,' he kept saying, 'the

slums of New York, Chinatown, bums on the Bowery' . . .
Milt is going to produce it himself . . . Spike Shapiro is
directing it. Naturally he wants me to do the dialogue. It's
the opportunity of a lifetime. I'll be doing the sort of thing I
wanted to do back in New York, only with a great industry
behind me with its publicity, its advertising, its distribution."

"All right, maybe I'll have to stay," said Felicia. "I didn't
like that hospital. Agatha didn't either."

Jed couldn't stop talking about the project. "Spend a lot
of money. 'An epic,' said Herman D. Speyer. A *Birth of a
Nation*, only instead of appealing to intolerance and reaction,
we will appeal to the progressive element . . . The theme is
how we can eliminate poverty in this country. Those were
Herman D. Speyer's own words. He had tears in his eyes.
He's known poverty himself . . . Of course it's a damn lie,
I know that. Capitalist prosperity can only be a false prosperity . . . The film can't be radical but it can carry a message to the masses."

Felicia got to her feet. She moved slowly on account of
her pregnancy. Stooping to pick up Peter seemed hard for
her. "All right feller, you do your movie," she said. "It's time
for his supper. After the baby's born, we'll take her to Hingham to show her to her grandparents."

Jed felt his insides curdle at the thought. "Why are you
so sure it's going to be a girl?" he asked with a teasing grin.
"I kind of hope Peter has a little brother."

"If it's a boy let's call him Schofield," she drawled back
over her shoulder as she walked heavily with Peter on her
hip into the kitchen.

Agostina served them their dinner. They sat side by
side at the iron table in the patio, but when they'd finished
talking about Peter's new tricks for the day, they couldn't

seem to find anything more to say to each other. Felicia sat munching her food in a sort of stupor. It was her pregnancy, Jed was telling himself; Maisie said most women acted strange when they were pregnant; that was Dr. Fine's opinion too; at least she wasn't wacky like last time.

Right after he'd eaten, muttering that he had an engagement and that Felicia had better go to bed and get a good rest, Jed walked out to the garage past the old Mexican sitting in his chair and smoking his pipe. "Buenas noches, Señor Hed," said José Maria in a voice that flowed soft as the tobaccosmoke from his lips.

Jed eased the car carefully out of the garage and stopped in the drive before turning out into the street. Listening abstractedly to the gentle purring of the motor, he was trying to remember what hotel Jade Haman said she'd go to. As soon as the baby was born he'd get rid of those damn lazy Mexicans. Jade's train must be in by now. He wasn't too crazy to see her, but he had to talk to somebody. Funny he couldn't remember which hotel. Of course he'd been under a terrible strain. He was all wrought up from the excitement of that afternoon. He was so wrought up right now he couldn't even remember the names of the local hotels. To be doing something he drove round to the nearest drugstore and looked them up in the phonebook. At the Garden of Allah they said Miss Haman had just checked in.

She met him in the lobby. She looked fresh as a new penny. "Jed," she cried, "look what I picked up on the Chief." She pointed to the man beside her. "Imagine finding that on the Chief." Jed had seen Lew Golton as he came through the door, looking out of place in a new cheap tweed suit amid the welldressed crowd in the lobby.

"Howdy Jed," Lew said with an embarrassed laugh.

"They've got me on the plush horse circuit." He looked Jed up and down. "You sure have put on weight," he said. "You look as prosperous as a Delancey Street pimp."

"A bull in a china shop," Jade cried out and popped black eyes under her bang . . . "Let's go to the bar and drink a legal drink . . . before the novelty wears off."

While they were finding themselves a table she was carrying on about how she'd left New York to get away from Greenwich Village and here she'd brought it with her right on the same train. Wasn't that the dickens?

"I'm through with all that," growled Jed. "I brought it with me too. Great grief how through I am."

Jed and Jade ordered scotch. Lew morosely called for a beer. "Give me a decent proletarian drink," he said.

Right away Lew started asking Jed questions about the Collins Ranch. How did he know Charles R. Collins and his wife?

"They are friends of my wife's people."

"Good, good." Lew nodded his head over his glass.

"They're a funny pair of old dodos . . . Confused liberals and rich as coots."

"Could we go out there tonight?" asked Lew.

"They fold up the driveway at ten P.M. sharp." That struck Jade Haman as funny. She laughed and laughed. "They do everything by the clock. We couldn't get there in time."

Lew frowned. "Tomorrow at five," he said. There was no refusing Lew's doggedly set jaw.

"I might manage it . . . in the next few days . . ." Jed found himself stammering, "as soon as I can find the time."

"Scared of being compromised?" Lew grumbled disgustedly. "O.K.," he added out of the corner of his mouth. "I'll call you at the studio in the morning. I'll say it's Joe Smith calling. Don't forget now."

"Could I come too?" asked Jade in a pleading childish voice.

"They don't serve liquor and you can't even smoke," said Lew.

Jade made a face. "How do you know?"

"People tell me things." Lew grinned mysteriously down into his empty beerglass. "Let's get the hell out of this dump," he pulled down the corners of his mouth. "All these bourgeois bitches make me nervous."

When weeks later Jed finally got up his courage to tell Lew to meet him one afternoon at the Metropolis parking lot at five thirty, he hurried out to his car with his keys in his hand puffing with apprehension. Getting short of breath, shouldn't take risks he was telling himself. Lew was waiting for him with a derisive grin on his face. At least Lew looked as if he'd had a bath; he wore the same cheap tweed suit and a black felt hat pulled down over one eye. Lew seemed to know right away what Jed was thinking. "Nobody knows who I am at this end of town," he said. "Don't look so worried."

"Don't get me wrong, Lew . . ." Jed was still breathless. "I believe in what you're doing. I want to help."

"We judge a guy," said Lew, "by what he does."

"I can be a lot more help to the movement," Jed tried to explain, "inside one of the big studios, than sitting on a park bench, see?"

"Ain't it the truth?" said Lew and clamped his mouth shut for the rest of the drive.

Nothing had changed out at the Collins Ranch. Instead of laughing at the sign about the peacocks Lew only grunted: "Conspicuous waste." Jed thought he caught a trace of a sneer on the smooth oval of the houseboy's face at the cheapness of Lew's tweed suit, but, when they'd been escorted out to the balustraded terrace in the rosegarden, where Mr. and Mrs. Collins sat at a wicker table drinking their fruitjuices before supper, he was relieved to see the old people fall right away for Lew's East Side charm. Lew wore his boyish grin and began to talk about the tough lives the Mexican migrants led who picked lettuce and harvested fruit in Imperial Valley. It was exploitation to the limit. The spiky black hair fell over his forehead. He talked earnestly; he was modest; he was irresistible. It was the way he used to talk to Adolph Baum years ago. Esther Collins' face took on a horrified expression at his stories of starvation wages and crowded shacks without any windows; typhoid, and sick children sweating in the muck of the lettucefields. Old men beaten by vigilantes. Charley Collins was indignant. He said he'd call up his friends in Sacramento. He knew the lieutenant governor. He'd write letters to the Los Angeles papers. "A fat chance they'd have of being printed, Mr. Collins." Lew shouted with laughter. "Even over your respectable signature . . ." He summed the whole thing up with a solemn face: "This is the front line of the class war."

Jed raised his voice to be heard. "Profits against human lives . . . Anybody who comes out for the workers must expect to be vilified and ridiculed and abused . . . The best way people like us can help," he added confidentially, "is to help them set up a union . . . in a financial way."

Neither of the Collinses paid any attention to him. At dinner they had ears only for Lew. He told them about his boyhood on the New York East Side, how he used to go out with his mother who had come over from the old country too late to learn English, to gather mushrooms in Bronx Park, and about the public schools and the temptations of the city streets and the young gangsters he'd known as a boy. He might have gone that way himself and ended in Sing Sing, he added, if it hadn't been for a learned old European socialist who had helped him with his schooling. And the writers for the Yiddish press. Their belief in a decent world had given him something better to think about, even when he'd been a little kid selling newspapers, than the dog eat dog religion of the sidewalks of the slums. "I'll probably end in jail this way," he added grinning into their faces, "but at least it will be for a good cause." When he told about hearing Eugene V. Debs speak at Cooper Union, his eyes filled with tears.

Esther Collins sniffed and raised a corner of her handkerchief to her eyes and Charley Collins was heard to clear his throat repeatedly. When they rose from the table promptly at seven by Charley Collins' watch, and moved into the living-room, Jed began to fidget. He couldn't get a word in. As soon as he could manage it, he herded Lew toward the door, explaining that his wife would be going to the hospital any day now. He had to get home to see how she was.

"What hospital?" asked Esther Collins. "I'll go in to see her right away. Her mother can't come. Agatha writes that Scho is really failing . . . How dreadful that a man like that should ruin his magnificent intellect with drink."

"Scho," croaked Mr. Collins, "lacks the inner certainty. To make a success of life a man must have the inner certainty."

"Very well put, Mr. Collins," said Lew in a respectful tone.

When they had settled back into the front seat of the Cadillac, just as Jed was pressing the starter, Lew put his hand on Jed's sleeve in a friendly kind of way. "Suppose you drive me into downtown Los Angeles. There's a little meeting I want to get to . . . just social . . . I'll take you along if you like."

"I could call up the house," said Jed doubtfully, "to see if everything's all right."

Jed called from a filling station on the road. Agostina answered. Miz Morris had gone to bed. Conseedering her condition she felt good. Jed said he'd be a little late. "Ahah," said Agostina. From her tone he could tell she thought he was out with some woman.

"We can't take this car," Lew said when Jed came back from phoning. "Out here it's camouflage . . . Where I'm goin' to take you it would cause a riot."

"Damn class distinctions," cried Jed. "And I get so fed up with the liberal mind. The Collinses' liberalism is an upper class luxury like their peacocks or the Filipino houseboy."

Lew grunted. "Listen to him. A roaring radical on fifteen hundred a week. You better study Lenin's pamphlet on infantile leftism."

"I certainly shall read it," said Jed eagerly.

"Have a heart," said Lew. "Of course they don't know from nothing, but Mr. and Mrs. Collins are nice kind wellintentioned old people. They'll let the study group meet at their ranch . . ." A purring tone came into his voice. "I wouldn't wonder if they coughed up some dough."

Lew sat silent and glum beside him as Jed jockeyed his car through the thickening traffic of a long roaring thoroughfare rimmed with electriclightsigns into the city. The drive took longer than he expected. When at last he eased into a parking place on a sidestreet in downtown Los Angeles his Cadillac already looked out of place in a line of black Fords and beatenup chevies.

"We'll be able to use people like that . . . museum

directors . . . they can teach dietetics or landscape gardening," Lew was saying musingly as they climbed out of the car. Jed was closing his windows and setting the locks on his doors. Lew gave him a nudge to make him turn round. "Look here. Where I'm going to take you," he gestured with his thumb over his shoulder. "They'll be looking you over. Get that? Button up your mouth. Don't shoot your face too damn much." Grinning he shadowboxed with one fist in the direction of Jed's chin. "Damn you I don't want you to disgrace me."

They roamed along the dark street till they found a cruising taxi. Jed didn't hear the address Lew gave. Dark rattletrap houses, ill lit streets, factory sites, poolparlors, clothing stores flashed by; a cheap movie advertising pictures titled in Spanish. Jed paid the cabby and followed Lew up a gritty stairway beside a darkened grocery store.

"If we're raided"—Lew talked back over his shoulder as he climbed the narrow stairs—"it's every man for himself." Under the hanging bulb in the upper hall he turned to study Jed's face. "Meetings have been raided," he repeated teasingly.

Jed was still out of breath when Lew pushed him into a narrow livingroom. The air was streaky with tobaccosmoke. The settee and the couch and the chairs were all packed with men and women drinking beer out of mason jars. The first face Jed recognized was V. F. Calvert's poised sedately over an immense meerschaum pipe. When behind him Jed caught sight of the broad figures of Sam and Maisie Faust, he felt immediately at ease. He walked toward them grinning. They didn't smile back.

"Lew bring you?" Sam peered coldly into Jed's eyes through his bifocals.

Jed nodded.

"Well that's his lookout," said Sam. Maisie gave him a timid smile.

Lew had Jed by the arm and was pushing him round the room. He stopped him before a small man with a puffy pallid face and a bristling brown mustache who sat bolt upright in a straight chair, talking to a big blowsy woman across the table from him who was slicing salami on a piece of newspaper. Lew waited respectfully until the small man had finished what he was saying; then he said, without addressing him by name, "Comrade I thought you'd be interested in meeting a wageworker who makes fifteen hundred dollars a week."

The small man looked Jed over as contemptuously as if he were applying for the job of office boy. The blowsy woman stopped cutting the salami and glanced up inquisitively out of bleared blue eyes. Jed noticed that she had a pony of whisky beside her. With one breath the two of them let out a scornful "Whew."

"And no union dues to deduct," added Lew grinning.

"We'll have a union soon," Jed spoke up, "just like any other salaried workers."

"Jed Morris just took me out to the Collins Ranch," Lew continued in the tone a corporal would use reporting to a superior officer. "They are old people, filthy rich and they don't know they're alive. You know, the vegetarian type . . . They are crazy for a study circle."

"Take that up with Comrade Calvert," said the small man curtly. Then he gave Jed another glance, showed yellow teeth under his mustache, and held out a languid hand. "Curly," he said and nodded toward the blowsy woman. "Shake the hand that takes home fifteen hundred smackers. Give him a salami sandwich, the man's hungry." He looked up into Jed's face with a sneer. "I suppose even a man like you has heard of Curly Bryant."

Curly Bryant tossed her head of tangled reddish curls and looked hard in Jed's face. "The organizing I could do with fifteen hundred a week!" She sighed.

Deftly she buttered a piece of ryebread and folded a slice of salami into it.

"Here's a handout brother." All the wrinkles of her sagging face crinkled into the prettiest Irish smile. "Glad you came around, big boy . . . The workers need friends like you. Lew can't you find your boyfriend a beer?"

With a jar of beer in one hand and his sandwich in the other Jed worked his way back to Sam and Maisie. A cautious smile had appeared at the corner of Sam's mouth. His green eyes were twinkling behind his glasses. "For a long time now," he breathed into Jed's ear, "I've been waiting for this day . . . The movement needs men like you, Jed."

Jed made himself as inconspicuous as possible against the wall next to Sam, and began to look around the room. Shabby people mostly, not too different from some of the middleclass groups he'd lectured to in New York. Hungry eyes, thin lined faces. Not many of the girls were pretty.

Lew, the grin on his face getting wider every minute, was talking to a girl with black hair and an olive oval face who really was attractive. She was smiling and making little shrugs with her shoulders; she had eyes only for Lew. Jed managed to edge his way around till he was standing beside them. After a while Lew noticed him. "Comrade Rosita, meet Jed Morris," he said.

"Shake, comrade," she said. She gave him a quick enquiring glance and turned her face toward Lew's again. Lew started whispering to her in Spanish. She giggled and shrugged and made off toward the back of the room.

Lew nudged Jed's ribs. "We don't have to stay all night," he drawled out of the corner of his mouth. "Just wanted to introduce you." He made a sweep with his thumb toward the door.

Out in the hall he gave Jed another nudge. "You don't know what it's like till you've had it with these little Mexican party girls. Boy they're hot. Rosita's got a friend. Wanna come along?"

Jed took a quick breath. For a second his throat was too dry for him to speak. He nodded.

"Need it bad, eh?" Lew's smile was condescending. "That's one place where you don't have to accept the direction of the Central Committee. These little working class girls, they are always willing and able . . . They'll help a comrade out, you know the old gag, like giving a comrade a glass of water if he's thirsty. To hell with the scheming bitches of the bourgeoisie."

Rosita was standing beside them snuggling smilingly into a gray street coat with a squirrel collar. Without a word she followed them down the stairs. Fog had come in. Jed shivered a little in his thin suit. Rosita walked between them with her hands in her pockets. Her high heels made a light pecking sound on the pavement. The dark streets were so shrouded in fog, Jed couldn't see where they were going. After a block or two they turned into a cindered drive and walked round to the back of a little low frame house. A radio was going in the front room and there was a dim light in a window. They followed Rosita up some cranky board steps to a stoop. "Wait," she said, and slipped in through a screendoor. A neat little kitchen lit up as she passed and they heard a low rapid interchange of Spanish from the front part of the house, a lot of tittering and whispering, and another girl's voice saying "Cómo no?"

Rosita had taken off her coat when she came back into the kitchen. "Come." She beckoned through the screen. Jed and Lew shambled in awkwardly and stood beside the kitchen table waiting for the other girl to appear.

"Una cervecita Luis?"

"Sure," said Lew.

Rosita brought four bottles of beer out of the icebox and four chilled tumblers and set them on the gaudy oilcloth of the kitchen table. It was only after repeated calls of "Ven' Lola te esperen los muchachos" that the other girl slid bashfully into the room. She was dressed in black. She had a high-bridged Spanish nose and too much powder on her face, but she had lovely eyes and a big pouting mouth. She spoke only a few words of English.

The four of them sat giggling over their beer. Everything was very pleasant and easy. It was like the old days, Jed thought to himself happily. Nothing like this since the war, or that trip abroad. He remembered the Russians, Anna Glazunova . . . He felt like a boy again.

The men took off their coats and they all four sat at the table sipping their beer and quietly giggling. Rosita brought out some sweet crackers. The girls worked in a small garment factory. They told about their wages and how much the boss docked them for damaged goods, and accidents with the machinery and how the foreman tried to lay them in the lunch hour. Lew assured them nothing like that would happen when the workers owned the means of production. "Ojalá," said the girls. A few comradely kisses followed and some nudging with knees under the table.

Lew got to his feet and pulled Rosita by the hand out toward the front part of the house. After a minute he stuck his head out through the door and said: "Don't forget to pay for the beer, Jed. They're lucky if they make seventeen fifty a week."

Jed grabbed Lola and kissed her. Her body pressed eagerly against his. She put out the light and took his hand, and, walking tiptoe, led him into a little bedroom off the kitchen.

A rooster crowing under the window woke him with a start. It was morning. There was still fog against the windowpane. He lay there without having the least idea where he was. The rooster crowed again, louder. The motor of a starting truck roared nearby, backfired. In the distance dogs barked. Jed sat up in bed looking down smiling at the girl's sleeping head in its coil of black hair on the pillow beside him. Then suddenly he remembered Felicia, her condition, Dr. Schoenbrun, the room engaged at the hospital, an appointment with Milt at the studio. He pulled on his clothes helter skelter, snatched a five dollar bill out of his wallet, scribbled: Adios yo te amo—he'd already learned that much—on a slip of paper he found in his pocket, left them beside the girl's quiet face on the pillow and ran.

His watch had stopped. There was nobody stirring on the street. The pepper trees dripped. Everything was still blanketed in clammy fog. He walked blocks and blocks without knowing where he was going. At last he found a trolley line. It seemed hours before a car came. By the time he'd found the street where his Cadillac was parked the explanation was pat in his mind—if she asked for it—an organization meeting of the filmwriters' association. Lasted very late. Trouble with the car. A short nap in the house of a friend.

The first thing he noticed when he turned into the drive at Canary Cottage was Dr. Schoenbrun's antique Rolls Royce parked at the curb. The house was in such a bustle that there was no time for explanations. Agostina was running up and down stuffing things into a suitcase. Peter was screaming from his crib. Dr. Schoenbrun was helping Felicia down the stairs. There were blue rings under her eyes. She put her hand on Jed's arm: "Feller," she said. "Don't worry. I'm not scared a bit." She let her voice drop to a whisper until Dr. Schoenbrun, puffing like a locomotive through his whiskers, was out the door. "If I should pass out, don't raise Peter to be one of the horrid little radical children . . . I want to get him out of all this . . . I want him to be a plain warmhearted old Middlewestern business man like Scho's father was . . . So long feller." She made a funny little face: "We'll keep in touch."

This time Jed sat alone under the potted palms in the maternity wing of the Good Shepherd Hospital. The doctors put off the operation hour by hour. Jed was so nervous he couldn't stay with Felicia. He had to get out in the air "Damn them, they just do it to run up their bills," he muttered miserably to himself as he roamed among the beds of geraniums on the hospital lawn. When he went back up to the room he found that Sam Faust had telephoned from his office to hear how things were going.

At the end of the afternoon Sam appeared in person full of consoling unction. Maisie came along with roses and a basket of fruit and made a cheerful bustle round the bed. Felicia smiled wanly at her. "Hi Maisie," she said.

Then Dr. Schoenbrun stuck his head in the door and beckoned them out into the hall and whispered to Sam Faust through his whiskers that they had better take Jed home for some rest. They would operate at eight A.M. sharp. Jed could see that Maisie was trying to keep a look of alarm off her face. Something was wrong but he couldn't get Dr. Schoenbrun to say what. Sam and Maisie took charge. They couldn't have been nicer. They called off an important engagement to eat supper with him. They kidded Agostina who was taken with a fit of sobbing when she was bringing in the dishes and took to distractedly roaming about the house whispering a prayer over her rosary. They plied Jed with his own whisky and tried to distract him by talking about the writers' association. At last they induced him to take a sleeping tablet and to go to bed.

In the middle of the night the telephone woke him. Dr. Smathers speaking. In a singsong voice like a train announcer's he told Jed that the operation had been successfully concluded at two five A.M. His wife would live but the child was dead. Dear old Dr. Schoenbrun, the voice added scornfully, was too affected to speak over the phone. Sent heartfelt regrets. No it was no use his coming to the hospital now. It would be hours before she would come out from under the anesthetic.

Felicia came home weeks later. She never spoke of what had happened. If Jed referred to it, she didn't hear. She was busy all day with Peter. When Jed arrived in the evening he would find her stretched out on the chaise longue in the front bedroom wearing the old strawcolored dressing gown she used to wear in New York. She hardly looked at Jed when she spoke to him.

Dr. Fine was in daily attendance. He tried to get her to go back to her painting. He kept urging Jed to take her out somewhere to distract her; so one morning Jed called Montefiore's early so as to be sure to get a good table and not be tucked away in a corner, to make a reservation for that night. Jed was in his messjacket and Felicia consented to wear a new palegreen evening dress she'd bought before the baby had started. She was so thin the dress hung a little loose at the waist. She was haggard but she looked tall and erect and distinguished in the dress, a nordic femme fatale, Jed thought as they stopped to leave their wraps with the hatcheck girl in the restaurant lobby. But, lord, she looked old enough to be his mother.

They sat a long time at their table with the sign Reserved on it; each of them staring at the bill of fare by the pink light of the lamp without being able to make up their minds, while the waiter leaned over them with his little pad. At last the waiter broke in impatiently: "Cocktails of course."

"Of course, double martinis," Felicia chirped before Jed had time to say No; "and very dry please," she added. She smiled sweetly at Jed across the table. "Dr. Fine believes in moderate drinking."

The waiter was prodding her about her order. "You think of something," she said. When the waiter suggested vichyssoise and sanddabs and Kansas City steak and broccoli hollandaise and allumette potatoes and baked Alaska afterwards, Felicia nodded without listening and motioned him away.

Jed didn't feel much like eating either. Just before leaving the lot he'd heard the news that Milt Michelson had been taken to the Good Shepherd Hospital with a heart attack, at four thirty that afternoon, coronary thrombosis, somebody said.

"Too bad," Felicia murmured and went on sipping her martini. "I wonder if he'll get my old room."

"Too bad?" Jed blew up. "It's absolutely tragic. It's years out of my life. If he dies *Manhattan Jungle* will never be released. We'll all be back where we were when we first came out to the Coast . . . only worse. Screen credits make enemies. In Herman D.'s office they are already sharpening their knives. Herman D. respects Milt's integrity. He worships the ground he walks on. Milt has made more money for Metropolis in the last five years than any man on the lot. Only fortytwo. Only three years older than me . . . Imagine dying at fortytwo. And now they'll be laying for the big salaries."

"A good time to go back East," said Felicia. "That ought to be a lesson to us . . . Worked himself to death," she added drinking down her martini. "Overweight probably."

"Milt kept himself fit with handball from seven to eight every morning. He never smoked or drank. He was hard as nails."

"Maybe you ought to reduce, feller," said Felicia.

"You talk like a woman's magazine," Jed was yelling in her face when the waiter arrived with the soup.

"That's what I was thinking about," Felicia began to say, stirring her spoon round in the soup without tasting it. "I know I could get a job in the art department on a woman's magazine. A woman ought to lead her own life . . . Maybe Agatha's right."

"Of course, there's no earthly reason why you shouldn't . . . only it would mean cutting out the cocktails." There was a snarl in his voice. "And what about Peter and me?"

Felicia immediately ordered another double martini. Jed was clenching his fists under the tablecloth to keep his nerves under control. He leaned earnestly across the table. "I know that if you'd get interested in the movement . . . then your painting and illustrating would have a purpose, feller"— Jed was so much in earnest tears came to his eyes—"and everything would clear up." He made a vague gesture across his plate with his fork. "Remember poor Kenneth Magill. We don't want to end up like that, now do we? Suppose you start going to the Collinses' study circle?"

"I've had enough study circles right in my own home."

A drunken screech came into Felicia's voice. "When you and Sam and the rest of you get to going . . . and V. F. Calvert . . . my God. I've never been so bored since I first went to Sunday school."

Don't argue with her, Jed was telling himself. She was higher than a kite already. She wouldn't eat her fish. Even before the steak came she was beginning to kid the waiter about Communists infiltrating the restaurant workers' union. Then she got to walking round the tables of people she didn't know pretending to be a fortuneteller.

When Jed caught sight of George Pastor, just beginning to make a name for himself as a character actor in unpleasant Prussianlike parts, sitting at a table on the edge of the dance-floor with Paulette Stanwood, Jed called for the waiter in a hurry. George was on his way up: Paulette Stanwood was a big name. Fortunately Felicia hadn't seen them, or she'd be telling their fortunes, too. Jed paid the check, left the waiter an enormous tip and, slipping his arm through Felicia's began to draw her as gently as he could toward the door. It was the neck of the evening; the really important people were just arriving to take up their reservations. On their way up the crimson stairs to the street level, Jed found himself looking in a mirror at a short fat man with curly hair and discontented dark eyes with black rings under them, who was dragging behind him a scrawny struggling washedout blonde. Hair over her face; dress that didn't fit. What a jittery looking couple, he thought. It wasn't till he had her out in the air that it came to him who it was whom he'd seen in the mirror. "Oh God that's us," he said aloud. There was a taxi before the door. It was easier to bundle her into it than to get her out to the parking lot. He drove her home.

He got the taximan to wait. She let him help her up the stairs quietly enough, tottered in to take a look at Peter asleep in his crib, and then dropped down yawning on the chaise longue in her bedroom. Jed climbed back into the taxi. "Never again, never in public," he was whispering to himself.

His nerves had begun to quiet down a little by the time he got back to Montefiore's. He decided he'd say hello to old George before he picked his car up and drove home. It all began to seem like something that really hadn't happened at all when he sauntered to the music of the band down the steps again and walked slowly between tables of chattering diners toward George's long pale face with its whispy mustache. George looked up at him with the world-weary smile of a café diner in a motion picture. Must be having hard sledding with Paulette, Jed told himself.

"Long time no see," said George. "Have you dined?"

Jed rattled hurriedly that his wife had been taken ill and he'd had to drive her home. Nothing serious. They'd had the misfortune to lose a baby and this was the reaction. Nerves. The doctors had assured him she'd be quite recovered, but it would take time. Paulette Stanwood showed her long teeth in the smile he'd seen in a thousand closeups. "That's what I always say . . . We have to believe that everything is for the best, don't we Mr. Morris?"

"I have made up my mind," said Jed, "not to let things like this affect me. There are more important things in the world than our private lives."

"How true. How brave," said Paulette Stanwood.

They made a place for him at the table. He'd already sent back one dinner untasted, he explained, but he needed a drink to pull him together. While the drink was on the way he went out to the men's room to wash his face and comb his hair. He was through, he told his face in the mirror over the washbasin. Walking back through the restaurant he looked coolly from face to face. They couldn't high hat him now.

Dregs of the bourgeoisie. They lacked the inner certainty. Even if Milt died he was on the inside in this town. None of them counted. To hell with them. The only thing that counted was where a man stood in the class struggle.

When, after a couple of bourbons and a ravishing glance from Paulette, he got into his car to drive carefully home he was telling himself that even if he had put on weight he was still attractive to women. When he loved them they stayed loved. A man who had chosen his side in the class struggle had to look on women as a soldier does. Break ranks for an instant and then march on. Love 'em and leave 'em. It was an urge to be satisfied, like thirst. A glass of water from a comrade's hand.

When he went upstairs he found Agostina spreading a clean sheet in little Peter's crib. Naturally Felicia had passed out. Jed hadn't planned it that way, but before he knew what he was doing he was letting his leg brush lightly against Agostina's hip as he held the small warm sleepdrugged body while she pulled the wet pajamas off. Peter's eyes opened for a second, then the sleepy puffed lids closed contentedly and he settled smiling down to sleep again. Jed pulled the light blanket up under Peter's chin, kissed him gently on the forehead and followed Agostina as she tiptoed fast down the stairs. In the kitchen he caught up with her leaning over the laundry basket to drop in the wet bedclothes. He caught her big breasts from behind. "No no, it is bad." She giggled and struggled. She didn't struggle very hard. In the end she let him push her toward the couch in the study. He'd known all along it would be easy.

As soon as he heard that Milt Michelson was dead Jed called up Jade Haman. He had to talk. Jade was sympathetic. Come over quick, she said. She had a drawingroom at the hotel now. He found her alone. She walked toward him as soon as he opened the door. "I've heard . . ." she said. "Lord that'll upset a lot of applecarts." She shook the patent leather bang off her eyebrows.

"Beginning with yours truly," said Jed. "I know just what's going to happen. With Milt gone, there's nobody but Stan Slessinger to take over the picture. He'll bring in that old hack Roy Monks. He always does. It'll be straight boy meets girl . . . Herman D. is worried already. He sniffs a class angle. I won't even get my name on the screen."

"But you're vicepresident of the Filmwriters' Association, we're forgetting that." Jade smacked her forehead. "They can't afford to push you around."

"Roy Monks is president," said Jed.

"I better order up a drink . . . After all you don't know it's going to happen."

Jed let himself plump down heavily in a chair. "I been around this town long enough to know how it works . . . Anybody with any knowledge of dialectical materialism can figure these things out ahead."

"One of the other studios will roll out the red carpet," Jade cried out cheerfully. "Get a new contract . . . Anybody who's been associated with Milt Michelson will have the magic touch for a long time to come."

"Poor guy I really loved him." Jed let himself drop into a chair. "He never hesitated on a decision. He had a mind like a steel trap. He was big, Jade. He had wisdom, Jade. He understood the masses . . . I'd been hoping to get him interested in the movement."

There was a knock on the door. Jed closed his mouth tight. A waiter came in with ice and setups. When he had gone, Jade murmured, "You're not getting in too deep, are you Jed?" There was a concerned musing look on her face.

"Liberalism, sympathy with the underdog, that's all right . . . But," she added with her direct big sister's smile when she handed him a drink, "we don't want to lose our sense of humor, now do we?"

"I lost mine," said Jed, "a long time ago."

"You still pull some pretty funny cracks."

"Another war," Jed grumbled, "will knock this silly old system into a cocked hat."

"But who says there'll be another war?"

"A little guy in Germany with a Charlie Chaplin mustache."

Jed took a long drink.

"That damn fool Slessinger," he burst out, "called my dialogue little theatre. The tag's all over the lot. It follows me around like a stray dog . . . All he thinks about is copying the last hit picture, like telling a story to a child. You can't change a word. He makes up pictures like a druggist does prescriptions . . . Gosh I'm lousy company, Jade."

"There's none better." She gave him a tearful look through her jet lashes. "You've been getting an awful break lately, Jed . . . That's all that's wrong with you." She patted his hand. "You've taken enough punishment to put anybody on the ropes."

Jed jumped to his feet. "Mind if I use the phone?" He felt as if his collar were too tight for him. He guessed he'd had enough of Jade. "I better go round to see my agent at his home. Got to take action."

George Weaver made Jed wait a long time. When he did come downstairs he didn't look any too pleased to see him. "Keep your shirt on, man," he said. "It's not as bad as that. I wouldn't wonder if your position was improved over there . . . It's all up to you. Herman D. is going to need talent more than ever. Milt was an army in himself. My God what a man." He cast up his eyes. "Jed, we have known greatness."

He took a deep breath and brought his fingers up across his face as if to rub the wrinkles off his low forehead. "It's been a heavy day." His fingers furrowed the colorless wavy hair. "You'll have to excuse me, Jed," he added, running his words together in a hurry. "I got to get a shave and a rubdown and dress for dinner."

Walking out to his car Jed caught an odd expression on Weaver's face as he looked after him from the front door. "Thinks I'm a dead duck already," Jed told himself as he pressed the starter.

Jed drove home as fast as he could through the afternoon traffic. He wanted to be in time to play with Peter for a few minutes before he had to be carted off to bed. Peter was all that mattered now. Walking across the patio from the garage he saw Agostina's face all knotted with anguish looking out at him through the back screendoor of the kitchen. When she came running toward him, José Maria followed her, abstractedly tugging at his long mustache. He's got a knife, he's going to kill me, Jed told himself. With pounding heart he stood his ground. Agostina was brandishing an envelope. "Miz Morris," she croaked. The two Mexicans stood beside him, searching his face with black puzzled eyes while he read Felicia's scrawl:

> Feller, Agatha phoned. Scho's
> awful sick. I've taken Peter to see his
> grandpa. Don't worry. I'm a sober
> woman from now on. Write me at
> Hingham.

Right away he knew she would never come back.
He couldn't seem to catch his breath. He put on the

best face he could: "It's perfectly all right," he told the Mexicans. "Mrs. Morris's father has been asking to see little Peter. He's ill. They left on that noon train. I made their reservations. She'll spend a month with her people in the East."

Agostina translated what Jed said for her husband in a long string of words. Jed fancied he caught a proprietary glance in her eye as she looked in his face with a quick understanding smile. Then she turned with a shrug. Shaking his head José Maria followed her waggling hips through the screendoor into the kitchen. Jed walked back to his car. His hand was shaking so it took him a long time to fit his key into the ignition. This was a case for a lawyer. He could hardly see to drive. With the exaggerated caution of a drunken man he picked his way slowly through palmfringed twilit roads to Sam Faust's.

The Fausts were real people all right. They took him right in. Maisie hovered over him like a mother. "If a man didn't understand the allembracing nature of the struggle," said Sam blandly, "a thing like that could unhinge his reason. Don't worry, Jed, it'll take time. We'll get the boy back. Be careful what you write." He pulled off his bifocals and looked at Jed with blank tired eyes. "Something like that happened to me once," he began in a low singsong. "If that little East Side boy sweeping out the big lawyer's office really was me . . . running errands, stretching his big ears to pick up every word of law language the big lawyer said, if that little boy really was me . . . it seems so long ago . . ."

"Sam," Maisie interrupted sharply. Calhoun was ushering in Spike Shapiro and his wife. Cars were driving up.

After the dinner guests were gone Jed was too tired to talk. His mind was absolutely blank. He couldn't think of the words. He went up to bed, got into a pair of Sam's pajamas which were much too big for him, and slept like a dead man.

Next day Maisie took charge of Canary Cottage. Jed didn't have the strength to go back. He didn't want to face Agostina. Maisie went over there and saw to packing up his clothes, and closed the shutters and engaged a detective agency to protect the premises. She reported that when she paid off the Mexicans the woman broke down and cried. Jed had come back from the studio all shaking and sweaty. It made him feel better somehow to hear that Agostina had cried. Right away Maisie told him to take a swim in the pool.

She had a drink all ready for him when he came out. "Sam says you've got to stay with us for a few weeks." The curves of her face creased hospitably into little dimples. "Until you're feeling better . . You do what Sam says . . . Sam knows about these things," she said.

"I can't fight this alone," Jed answered dejectedly. "Slessinger's got me on the skids . . . I can feel it."

"Who says you're going to fight it alone?" said Sam. Treading softly in his bare feet he had walked up behind the beachchair where Jed lay sprawled. "You need the movement, Jed, more than the movement needs you. Then you'll feel behind you the power of all the oppressed peoples of the world . . . the irreversible progress of history. I don't often talk about things like this Jed even to my friends but tonight I'm going to talk about them. We got the evening to ourselves . . . What were you saying the other day about lacking the inner certainty? The movement will give you that. After all it took more than a little legal subtlety to get a selfeducated little East Side boy out of a back desk in a Tammany judge's office out here, to all this." For a moment he stood in front of Jed broad and bandylegged in his yellow trunks and with a sweep of a short hairy arm indicated the low vinecovered porch of the house, the terrace, the table with its silver icebucket and the serried glint of glasses and bottles, the palms

232

goldfringed by the setting sun, and the clean green pool. Then he walked out to the end of the springboard, squeezed his nose between thumb and forefinger and jumped in with a splash.

Sam and Maisie got Jed interested in all the great causes. There was the case of a young Italian who had been framed on the charge of exploding a bomb in a South Chicago waterfront strike. The case had been fought step by step through the courts. Only an appeal to the Supreme Court could save young Sabatini's life. Jed gave up his spare time to raising money. He induced Charley Collins to sponsor a California Committee for a Fair Trial to bring old man Sabatini to the Coast to speak. Sam had whispered with his curledup smile, that speaking as his lawyer he didn't think it wise for Jed to let his name be used on the committee's letterheads, especially since he was an officer of the Filmwriters' Association, but he did think it would be all right for Jed in that innocent, boyish way he had, to introduce old Sabatini at the meeting.

Between them they induced a redheaded little Scottish actress named Bonnie McClennan to sit on the platform. "Why not?" she said. She didn't understand a thing about American law but everybody she talked to thought it was so unfair. It would be risky. She tossed her head. "If they decide to deport me perhaps they'll pay my passage home."

Bonnie was a darling but she had a way of slipping over to the other side of the table when Jed gave her one of his warm personal looks. She did listen attentively when he told her about the poor Negro boys falsely convicted of rape in the South, and the Mexican labor organizer beaten to death by the ranchers in Imperial Valley. "Why do you Americans put up with it?" she asked, looking up into his face with parted

233

lips. "Fascism and reaction," hissed Jed, "that's why we need you on this committee to bring to bear the force of liberal British opinion."

At getting new contacts she was terrific. Such charm. It was Bonnie who persuaded Sir Herbert Watson, the famous English explorer who had the reputation of being so frightfully snobbish that everybody wanted to meet him, to let them hold the meeting in the reproduction of an old Spanish mission he occupied near Pasadena. Much easier to get people to come there than to a hall in Los Angeles. People who counted. They called the gathering a reception. No word of radicalism could be spoken because somebody said Mary Pickford had consented to be present. The minute people heard she might be there, they swarmed. In the end she didn't appear.

Old Mat Sabatini, however, made a fine impression. David Warfield couldn't have played the part better. Jed looking modest and boyish, he told himself, even if he had put on a lot of weight, in a new white serge messjacket, introduced him. The old man's speech was short and to the point. He stood up in a worn and shapeless old black suit and stretched out his arms to the crowd. "Good people save the life of my son."

There was a response from the audience. Several big names cried so hard they had to go right out to the powder room to do their eyelashes over, so Jade Haman told Jed afterwards with her malicious titter. She'd seen them. She had to go herself. Jed felt immensely exhilarated when, rising again to ask for contributions, he felt on him the admiring eyes of all these men and women in brilliant evening dress. The Craftsman's Theatre, Sam whispered as they stood side by side watching the guests stream into the chapel for refreshments, had really taught Jed how to speak to an audience.

They raised four thousand dollars in checks and cash that night.

Bonnie McClennan was so moved she ran up to him on the floodlighted terrace where they were waiting for their cars and gave him a big hug.

Jed was just suggesting that they ought to get to know each other better, and they were about to fall into a cosy conversation when Jed felt Sam's hand on his shoulder.

"Forgive me lovely lady," Sam was intoning, "if I interrupt our hero for a moment. There is someone I must introduce him to." He was smiling all over his face.

It was Pierre Monceau, tall and slender in tails, smiling under his black croupier's mustache, saying it had been a beautiful speech and asking Jed to his next party. Jed introduced Bonnie McClennan. The gloss on Pierre Monceau's mustache brightened. She was invited too. Pierre Monceau bowed and smiled again his famous mondain smile and walked away with Hedda Thomas on his arm. Bonnie couldn't contain herself. She jumped up and down beside Jed, giggling like a schoolgirl. "This, my friend," she bubbled, "as you Americans say, is it."

Pierre Monceau didn't forget. Hardly a week had gone by before a card appeared on Jed's desk with the invitation engraved under a crest in black of a mailed fist holding a pen. Immediately Jed called up Bonnie and asked her to go with him. When he called for her at her apartment she ran out to the car as excited as a highschool girl going to her first dance. What a pretty dress. A tartan in silk. Her cheeks were almost too rosy. No need for makeup. The crush outside Pierre Monceau's ranch house was terrific. Ranks of parked cars, floodlights, motorcycle cops holding back the crowd. They had managed to get through the row of private detectives in the entrance hall, and Jed was waiting for her outside the ladies' powder room, his imagination racing ahead to dancing, a night spot afterwards, the car parked in the dark on the way home, when Sam Faust, bulging suavely out of his dress suit, slipped up beside him and took hold of his lapel.

"Something has been arranged," he whispered. "It won't take long."

Feeling weak in the knees, Jed let Sam lead him out a side door to where Sam's long towncar was waiting in the Monceaus' private parking lot. "But Bonnie," Jed was expostulating.

"Maisie's gone into the powder room to get her. Maisie's an excellent chaperone, don't worry." Sam's lips curled. "She'll explain. Things here will go on just as well without us. These parties last forever. We'll be back before anybody knows we're gone. Get in."

Instead of Calhoun, Spike Shapiro was at the wheel. George Pastor sat beside him. Breathing hard, Sam lumbered in beside Jed in the back seat.

"Your work on that committee," he panted in Jed's ear as the car drove smoothly off, "has convinced certain people that you can accomplish any task the Party sets you . . . One thing only troubles them. Will you accept Party discipline?"

"Why not?" Jed mumbled.

In the dark he could feel that George had twisted around in the front seat to look him in the face. "No army can fight without discipline," George said in his tone of a Prussian officer. Spike was silent as a chauffeur at the wheel. "We are only a corporal's guard," Sam announced dramatically, "but tonight's invitation shows how far we can go in the struggle to liberate the class war prisoners. We have made liberalism fashionable in this town, but we must not forget that the confused liberals are social-fascists at heart."

236

Jed's hands were cold. His heart was so noisy he was afraid the others would hear it.

"It's hard for good natured people like us to learn that whoever isn't with us is against us," Sam was saying. His breathing was wheezy. He started to whisper. "There is something Jed for your ear alone." Sam's lips were so close they almost touched Jed's ear.

Sam paused. The men in the car were silent. Jed kept moistening his dry lips with his tongue.

Sam began to talk in a quick hissing whisper. "To explain why I understand your feelings since your wife went East . . . missing the boy . . . Maisie and I of course have had no children, but I had a little boy. I was married before while I was clerking in Judge Wolman's office and studying for my bar examination nights. It was a boy's love, the early love. She lived in the same cold water tenement as my people . . . Polish, Jewish of course. It was for fear of the war they'd sent her to her uncle in New York. When the war ended her father and mother were yearning to see her . . . He was a successful grain merchant, quite wealthy as things went in those days on the other side. The village was near Vilna. Naturally they were yearning to see the grandchild. They couldn't leave their business. As soon as the armistice was signed they sent her funds to come home. She was an American citizen; it seemed perfectly safe. I had to stay for my bar exam. Judge Wolman himself intervened with the passport authorities. She was to be gone three months. Meanwhile I was attending to redecorating a little apartment we had found in the Bronx. I was admitted to the bar with flying colors. Judge Wolman was very influential . . . When the news came I couldn't believe it. No details. Killed, that's all: Anna, her father and mother, little Sammy, all killed suddenly one night by Pilsudski's white guards. The house burned. How I lived I don't know but suddenly I understood that all this seeming pleasant friendly American world, where a little immigrant boy could get a free education and make money and be admitted to the bar with the help of one of the biggest lawyers in the city, was an illusion, a false appearance, something you must hate, a deceiving dream we had in our heads. The reality was over there: antisemitism and arson and murder. A little baby, imagine it. Our only hope was in the Soviets. Immediately I sought out the nearest revolutionary group in New York. There were two or three official parties in the confusion of those postwar days. I sought out the most militant. The police were hounding them. My connection with Judge Wolman was a protection. I was a hothead then. On a picket line in a strike in New Jersey I met a skinny little unemployed garment worker. That was Maisie. Judge Wolman disapproved of agitation, but he respected my sincerity . . . He convinced me that I would be more useful as a lawyer."

When Sam stopped talking, Jed couldn't find any words. He sat listening to Sam's heavy breathing beside him. "Sam, I never knew," was all he could say.

Spike was already parking the car outside a hotel in downtown Los Angeles. Sam was silent. All Jed's high spirits, all the pleasure of dressing up and driving round to fetch Bonnie to take her to the party had ebbed away. He needed a drink, but he did not like to mention it to Sam, whose face had settled into a solemnly devotional expression. Spike led the way through the hotel lobby and out the back door.

"Won't we be out of place," Jed began, "in evening clothes?"

"They are our work clothes out here," said Sam sharply. "Do you think I do this for pleasure?"

238

"The meeting is around another block," Spike explained.

The four men were walking abreast along a barely lit street of old frame houses set in weedy lawns. Dried up palms overhead.

"Bubonic plague," Sam spluttered all at once in his wet whisper. "The palms of Los Angeles are full of rats . . . A few infected fleas . . . The plague would start . . . I think of that sometimes." The idea seemed to please him.

"Shut up," said Spike in his low grumble. "This is the house. Sam goes in first . . . We walk around the block and go in one by one."

When it was Jed's turn to walk alone up the broken steps of the wooden porch he found Sam waiting for him just inside the front door. There was no light. Sam grabbed the muscle of Jed's arm so hard it hurt and pulled him to the end of the short hall. There he knocked. Immediately a slender bearded man with a professorial stoop opened a groundglass door. After he had closed the door behind them they stood blinking in a dimlit office that had no furniture in it. "Professor Silver," whispered Sam, "meet Jed Morris." Professor Silver gave Jed a watchful look and led the way toward another door.

"After V. F. Calvert he's the greatest Marxist-Leninist theoretician on the Pacific coast." Sam spluttered the words excitedly into Jed's ear as they followed the stooped back. "Of course V. F. Calvert is greater," he added.

They trooped after Professor Silver into a back livingroom lit by floor lamps with cutout figures of dancers on their yellow shades. People were sitting packed together on the chairs and couches. Young men and women sat on the floor. Jed had been afraid he'd be out of place but everybody turned out to be quite welldressed. Outside of the men he'd come with he saw nobody he knew. He let himself drop modestly down beside Spike in an empty space on the floor. Sam had walked up to shake hands with a tall stony man with sunken eyes who sat looking over papers at a table in the back of the room. "That's Comrade Carl Humphries," whispered Spike in his curt clipped tones. "Central Committee."

A woman behind shushed him because Comrade Humphries had started to speak:

"Comrades, it gives me great pleasure to address this organization meeting in the city of Los Angeles, which since the shameful McNamara case years ago and the failure of weak kneed liberal groups to free the class war prisoner, Tom Mooney, has become the very citadel of capitalist reaction. Where so many others have failed we Communists will not fail because in dialectical materialism we have the only effective weapon by which the class struggle can be brought to a satisfactory conclusion with the complete elimination of capitalism, and of some capitalists." With a kind of deathshead grin on his face, he looked slowly round the room.

Some of the younger comrades laughed. A few women said, "Hush! quiet please."

Carl Humphries' grin broadened. "Most of you are not workers with your hands, but workers with your heads and with your painfully acquired skills. In behalf of the Central Committee I want to say that you belong in the Communist Party just as much as the most exploited migratory farm worker. To each his own special task. Some will take over the farms and the factories, but the workers in motion pictures, in radio, in the press will take over the country's communications, which means the country's brains."

Jed wanted to jump up and cheer. This was big. This was the inner certainty. Carl Humphries was a real person.

240

When Sam, after the meeting was over, led him up to the table to make out his card, Jed's hands were shaking so— with exhilaration, this time, he told himself—he could hardly put down his name and address. Out on the street his hand still tingled from the handclasps of the comrades. He took Sam Faust's arm.

"We don't carry our cards . . . The safe deposit box is the best place," Sam was whispering in a matter of fact voice as he led the way back through the empty hotel lobby. "A comrade will be around to collect ten percent of your salary at the end of the month." He gave Jed a pat on the back. "You won't miss it," he said as he opened the door and waited for Jed to step back into the long towncar. "Now gentlemen," he added in his usual gentle tone of judicial sarcasm, "we can really enjoy Pierre Monceau's little affair."

THESIS AND ANTITHESIS

The buzzer was sounding. Jed sat with his chin in his hands, elbows on his littered desk. Across his typewriter lay the treatment on white sheets. On either side squirmed scraps of dialogue on yellow flimsy scribbled with notes from the last story conference. The buzzer had been sounding for some time. When he finally picked his phone up with puckered brow his secretary's voice was small and apologetic. "Mr. Morris I know I oughtn't to disturb you but this person won't take no for an answer. First I said you were out and then in conference and of course you were."

Jed felt the veins in his forehead harden with irritation. "It's a secretary's business to keep people undisturbed."

"I didn't know quite what to do," explained the secretary's voice.

"The name? What's the name?" Jed roared into the mouthpiece.

"She said just to say Marlowe."

Marlowe? The name made Jed's head spin like a squirrelcage. The Antibes tan, the enormous ocean, the little hat like an apricot tart sitting on the golden curls.

"Stella." He paused. He couldn't think what to say. "You were quite right . . . It might be important." Jed's voice choked. "Is she on the wire?"

"She's downstairs in the lobby. I told her you never received visitors at the studio. I told her she ought to see you like everybody else at the Filmwriters' Association between five and six. She just won't go away!"

Before he had his breath back she was standing in the doorway. At a glance he could see she hadn't changed, the tight figure, the warm even tan, the curls between platinum and gold. A few little wrinkles at the corners of the eyes. She wore her hair up now. Not an apricot tart but an improbable little pink hat like a valentine.

"No's not an answer, that's what my father used to say when he went out to sell bonds." She fixed her mouth in a smirk of mock dismay as her eyes took in the papers on his desk.

He didn't dare look her in the face; right away he knew he would be crazy about her again, crazier than ever. The same morocco leather perfume; he hardly dared breathe. He kept his eyes on the squirming lines of dialogue.

"If it had been any other time . . ." he started lamely. He couldn't help looking up at her. "You haven't changed. Not a bit."

She was looking him over with cool interested eyes. "I see you're trying for size," she grinned impishly. "Are we still going to be perfectly frank?" She settled herself in the armchair by the window, with her pink handbag on her knees, tapped a cigarette on her cigarettecase, lit it and took a deep drag. "If there's anything I hate it's bad manners."

When she looked at him, her teasing smile made his head swim with recollections.

"Don't you film kings ever get up when a lady comes into the room?"

"You never did like anything about me." He was tapping with a pencil on the edge of the desk. "What can I do for you? Is it still Mrs. Tompkins?"

"It happens that I want a job. I started to figure who was the most important man I knew. I decided it was my old friend the stowaway. You see I've been following your career from afar."

"You must have thousands of friends . . . Santa Barbara."

She gave her head an angry shake. "And then I was curious . . . A woman's always curious." She got to her feet and pressed out her cigarette in the brass ashtray on the windowledge. "Well?"

Jed got to his feet too. "I'm trying to think . . ." He was stammering. "We can't talk here. I'm on a rush job . . . Just a second." He plunked back into his chair and whispered into the phone. "Stella . . . What's on my pad for tonight? Yes. Well I'll have to go to the meeting . . . Golly I'd forgotten that speech. How far away's that? Meadowdale? Great cats . . . You call up Miss McClennan and tell her I can't come to her party . . . She'll understand."

"Stella's my personal secretary," he explained for no reason at all as he laid down the phone. "Marlowe," he added—for some reason it was terribly hard for him to pronounce the name—"could you stand hearing me speak? Just a few words before the League of Women Shoppers at the Meadowdale Community Center. Could you get out there somehow? The meeting starts at eight. I'll look for you right after I've spoken. I won't have to stay."

"I'll be sitting in an open Chrysler convertible," she said in a businesslike way. "A light gray convertible. California license. As near the entrance as they'll let me park. I'll drive you home . . . If you've got a home."

"You always could say the meanest things." He was smiling into her face with his old look of boyish admiration. "Marlowe." The name came easier this time. There were wrinkles under the tan.

Without saying anything, without putting out her hand, she was gone. The door had closed behind her.

Driving in from the studio to the Association office that afternoon after five he was trying so hard to remember just what she looked like, that cars, traffic lights, faces on the sidewalk kept blurring. Careful or he'd have an accident. All he could remember was the pink lace valentine of a hat; under it he kept seeing other faces: Jade Haman's big loose jaw gabbling under her bangs, Bonnie's red head, the inevitable little party girls. To hell with them, it was all too easy. A man got so he didn't care. But Marlowe . . . He must drive carefully. If he ran into something he'd never get to Meadowdale. How would he ever find her in that parking lot? There would be hundreds of cars. He'd never see her again. Please Marlowe come tonight. She needed him now. He'd be forgiving and kind. He'd be big.

Still trying out the big forgiving smile he threaded his way through the Association waitingroom crowded with familiar faces. A word, a smile, a hand on the shoulder, a poke in the ribs, "You old bastard you." These guys liked him.

A hand slapped his back. When he turned the smile faded off his face. It was Eli Soltair. The same large punch-drunk face only all creased up now. The mop of hair was grayer than ever. The blue shirt was frayed. Spots on the necktie. "How's tricks Eli?" Jed managed to croak.

"Hallelujah I'm a bum bum," Eli roared out of his baboon mouth. "I'm peddling an original. Greatest film idea since the Cruiser Potemkin. Want to take a chance? I might raffle it off."

Jed pumped the large hand. "Right now I've got a meeting Eli. We must get together. Long time no see," his voice trailed off as he hurried down the hall.

The door of the inner office closed satisfactorily behind him. The quiet humming of electric fans. The boardmembers were already seated. John Taylor Briggs, out of small lips drawn into a pucker at the bottom of a small meticulously lined face, was reading a set of mimeographed sheets. Next to him sat Roy Monks with his long hair and rambling eye. Fred Walton and Gehring Weeks lolled in their chairs and stared solemnly in front of them, their brows furrowed with the knowledge that they were the two highest paid writers on the lot. There were Watkins and Eberhard and Klein. Jed was the last to arrive. "Late as usual," said Weeks.

"I was reading the new minimum basic agreement paragraph by paragraph," John Taylor Briggs explained in his tremulous voice. "Shall I go back to the beginning?"

"I'm all too familiar with it, John," said Jed. "In fact I was with Sam when he wrote it."

After the reading and discussion had gone on for an hour, the Association's mousy little receptionist tiptoed into the room and whispered in Jed's ear that Mrs. Faust had called and said not to forget he was coming by her house for a cocktail before dinner. Jed frowned; he knew what that meant. There wouldn't be any cocktails. It would be a fraction meeting. At six thirty he managed to sneak out of the Association office. Briggs was still reading paragraph by paragraph. Walton and Weeks had already gone.

He parked on the edge of the drive and walked round to the door of the Fausts' rumpus room that opened on the patio back of the house. He hardly had his hand on the knob before he heard Lew Golton's suddenly expostulating voice.

Nobody greeted him when he walked into the room. Lew looked up frowning. Sam Faust was squatting in a wicker chair, his eyes invisible behind his glasses. Fred Walton was pottering about in the back of the room with a look of demure puzzlement on his face. Gehring Weeks leaned scowling against the billiard table. The men on the settee scowled too.

"What's the trouble, Lew?" asked Jed.

Lew cleared his throat. "If you've seen the capitalist press you'll know that the Soviet Union has signed an agreement with Germany." His words blurred as he drawled them out of the corner of his mouth. "It will have to be explained to the rank and file before the disrupters and deviationists put their dirty mouths to it. To tell the truth it caught me with my pants down." He looked around with a disarming grin. "My *Worker* column giving Hitler hell as usual had already gone to press."

"Who's the deviationist now?" muttered Weeks under his breath.

Sam was speaking slowly in his smoothest courtroom voice: "The Soviet Union has made this move to forestall the efforts of the running dogs of imperialism to spread a war which might well destroy civilization . . . A sacrifice for the cause of peace. The highest type of proletarian statesmanship." The little selfsatisfied curl appeared in the corners of his lips.

"They are already calling it the Hitler-Stalin pact," Lew insisted dolefully. "I'd started out here on my vacation when I got this message." His voice was full of selfpity. "They've handed me the job of explaining it to the guys."

"Vacation?" Weeks was sarcastic. "A real progressive doesn't take vacations."

"I always said Roosevelt was a social-fascist," Jed started glibly.

"Shut up Jed," said Lew.

"Anything else to come before the fraction meeting?" Jed asked. He got to his feet. He felt all their eyes going over him, as if searching for a deviation. "Party work," he said huffily. "I'm delivering an address in Meadowdale."

"Eli Soltair," Lew tapped with his knuckles on the rim of the billiard table. "Has he any right to become a member of the Association? You know and I know Eli's a goddam fascist."

"A Jewish fascist," said Sam. "The worst kind."

"If he tries to peddle his garbage around this town . . ." started Lew.

"I happen to know," interrupted Sam smoothly, "that he is sitting at this minute in the palatial home of Herman D. Speyer drinking a cocktail before going into dinner with Herman D. . . . and with Mrs. Speyer," he added with a significant shake of the head.

"Won't do him any good," said Lew.

"I don't see the advantage of trying to keep any man out," piped up freshfaced little Alec Marks who hardly ever said a word. "We need those dues."

"Hear, hear," said an Englishman named Townsend Fellowes from the seat beside him on the settee.

"In the debate over conflicting ideologies that lies ahead," Sam was beginning a speech in his mellow juridical voice.

251

Jed interrupted: "Eli's not so much of a clown as he looks. He's a disruptionist. I vote to keep him out. I got to go." He was already at the door.

"The father of a budding daughter. What a role for Casanova," sneered Sam parenthetically under his breath.

Jed lingered with his hand on the knob to hear what Sam was going to say.

"If you want my opinion . . ." Sam looked down at the manicured nails of his small fat hands . . . "This is a case for the coordinator's office. Soltair's association with unhealthy anarchist elements . . . His life is a pigpen. He's an uncontrollable. Why soil our hands? . . . But to continue . . . In the debate that lies ahead . . ."

The minute Jed had closed the door behind him, he felt a chill down his spine. What would they be saying about him? They all knew he and Eli had been friends in the old days. Close friends. Eli stayed in the house after Peter was born. Men had been expelled for less. Of course he always thought Eli's ideas were childish. Told him so in fact. Everybody knew that. What the hell Eli was a back number . . . A back number . . . He remembered Sam leaning back from his desk with green eyes halfclosed behind his glasses, his heavily jowled face pale with conviction, and saying "The driving force of the working class is terrible to contemplate . . . These silly intellectuals think they are independent. I tell you Jed, we think we are riding high, but at the slightest deviation the progressive forces can turn us into back numbers overnight!"

Jed drove up in front of Canary Cottage without remembering how he got there. For an instant he half expected Felicia, tall and coolly smiling, to come to the door. Never again, he told himself brutally; Felicia was back under her mother's thumb. Instead there was that dreary Mrs. Steiner, whom he hired to make a home for him during the months he took on Mae, asking him with anxious wrinkles on her face what car she was going to use to pick the child up after her dancing class. "I'm not using the Cadillac Mrs. Steiner."

The telephone was ringing.

"Please answer it Mrs. Steiner," said Jed.

"It's a Mr. Soltair."

"I've already left the house," said Jed. He clamped his mouth tight, and walked out the door.

A Mercury with a middleaged woman at the wheel was waiting at the curb. It was Mrs. Vaughan of the Women Shoppers who was going to drive him out to Meadowdale. No time for dinner. No time to think up a new speech. He could hear his voice repeating the old tag lines about a popular front of the liberal forces of democracy to stamp out war and fascism. And Mrs. Vaughan as she drove kept up an endless prattle about what a wonderful man Winston Churchill was.

When Jed got up on the platform and looked over the crowd of women in the hall he had a fit of stage fright for the first time in his life. Every phrase that came into his head sounded like a deviation. He hemmed and hawed like a debater at a highschool commencement. Those women must have thought he was the world's worst speaker. At last he got into a long rigmarole about how the forces of monopoly were squeezing the American consumer in a viselike grasp. The women coughed and rustled and moved their feet around on the floor. They weren't even interested when he attacked the chain stores. What a cesspool. Never again would he try to speak to that deadfromtheneckup middleclass audience. The sweat was still pouring off his face when he stumbled out of the hall.

Without a hat, only a brown band round her hair, right beside the No PARKING sign in front of the entrance, she sat slouched at ease over the wheel on the redleather seat of the open convertible. Her slim arms looked browner than ever under the glare of the floodlights that lit up the mission-style front of the building. She was talking over her shoulder to a handsome tanned young police officer with gold braid on his cap who stood smiling beside the car. Her small teeth flashed as she turned to Jed. "Come aboard professor . . . Well better luck with the spinnaker next time," she called back to the officer as she slipped the car into gear. "He's an old pal of Tommy's and mine," she explained to Jed. "He races a little sloop out of San Pedro."

Already the glare of the business district was fading into the trees. They were alone under a moon on the long straight road.

"Did you hear it?" asked Jed.

"What?"

"My speech . . . It's just as well you didn't, it was lousy. These damn middleclass housewives. You can't tell 'em anything. Might as well talk to the Ladies' Garden Club."

"Where do we go from here?"

"I didn't get my dinner. I was late as it was. Stop at the first roadside dump."

"We'll put nickels in the juke box."

"You always did like slumming."

She turned the car into a palmfringed parking lot under a red white and blue flashing sign: TEXAS BARBECUE. As he followed her in under the longhorn skull over the entrance Jed puffed his chest out and tried to pull his belly up under his ribs. To be with her made him feel proud again, the way he had felt proud walking with her round the deck of the French Line boat. Not so tall as Felicia; she was about his height. That look of belonging. And after years she'd come back. When I love 'em, he told himself, they stay loved.

She settled into a booth out back walled with growing bamboo.

"Pretty nice," she said.

"Marlowe where have you been all these years?" Jed heard his own voice asking. Banal. He must do better than that.

She answered in kind: "Hawaii, Tahiti, all kinds of places."

"If this is an act," Jed burst out laughing, "we ought to rehearse it. It's lousy."

She looked into his eyes with puckered brows. "But it's perfectly true." She'd aged plenty, Jed was thinking. The overhead light brought out the gaunt lines, the taut look of her neck. "I went back to Tommy, that was my husband Jeremy Tompkins, he won the Bermuda race three times running, you must have heard of him. We hit it off for a while. We had a little girl. Now we're divorced and Tommy's quietly drinking himself to death in Tahiti . . . on the beach I guess. We're both of us broke. A great yachtsman but an impossible husband . . . That's why I've got to get a job, a very well paying job."

"Felicia's a lush too . . ." Thank God they had that in common . . . His voice droned: "The boy's with his grandmother."

The waiter, gotten up as a cowhand in overalls and a red handkerchief, was standing over them with a bill of fare. "Bring me a steak and a double bourbon," said Jed without taking his eyes off her face.

"A plain bourbon, that's all since I'm driving," she said.

"Marlowe," cried Jed trying to carry her off with his laugh like he used to, "all these years I've been thinking of you as the original rich bitch."

Marlowe gave him an understanding grin. "Rich no more . . . A lot of stocks and bonds have gone under the bridge since we last met." Now they were both laughing.

The fake cowhand came back with the bourbon. "Here's how," said Jed. "Remember that steak up in the Ritz restaurant; that was the best steak I ever tasted in my life. The best everything."

"To the Compagnie Générale Transatlantique," she said and lifted her glass.

"But you must have enough to live on. You are the kind of girl people marry. Why on earth should you want a job?"

"You always talked about how you liked to be free and independent. Maybe I do too." She gave him a sudden stare and pursed her lips.

"Under capitalism nobody is free."

"Medical care certainly isn't," said Marlowe making a little pout with her lips. "The little girl, Nita, she's a spastic," she blurted out suddenly. "She has to have the very best medical care." Marlowe wasn't crying, but her face had broken into segments; every wrinkle showed. The tendons on her neck stood out. "That's why I have to talk to somebody."

Jed sat looking at her with sinking heart. It was going to be grim and he'd so wanted it to be all fun. He was sick of a miserable homelife. He couldn't think of what to say. He had to say something.

"When we have socialism," he began, vaguely waving his hand across the table, "medical science, free from the profit motive, will make gigantic strides. They'll find cures for things like that."

She was staring in his face. Her eyes were still dark blue but there wasn't the violet glint he remembered. Maybe it was the light. She wasn't understanding a word he was saying. Suddenly he grinned. "Want me to prove it to you?"

She managed to smile. "Tell me about yours," she said.

"They are healthy enough; Mae, my first wife's daughter, has had a very reactionary upbringing. She's with me now. Peter's nine."

The steak was in front of him. He started to eat. As he ate he talked. "June's married again. I'm trying to bring Mae up for the future, see? For years I've been trying to get Peter away from his grandmother. There's an old rich bitch for you."

She put her brown hand just a second on his. "Tell me about this Filmwriters' Association. Don't they need a secretary?"

Jed heaped his plate with fried potatoes. "I better begin at the beginning, see? Say wouldn't you eat some icecream or something?"

She shook her head. "You still talk with your mouth full." There had been tears in her eyes. They twinkled as she laughed into his face. "I guess I don't mind it as much as I used to. I guess it's a sign of individualism."

"It's all poppycock about individualism," Jed exploded. "We live in a period of organizations: corporations, labor unions to struggle for workers' rights . . . Consumers' organizations are a weak link, because the middle class has no solidarity . . . Employers' organizations trying to cut wages and rivet the old chains . . . The days of individualism when a man could talk to his fellow citizens face to face in town meeting and argue the point, those days are gone forever . . . And now there's another war brewing in Europe!"

As he talked he leaned over the table toward her. His

eyes followed the V of her dress down toward the curve of her breasts. Her tanned body would be as lovely as ever.

"The great period of history," he went on in his full lecturer's voice, "will be ushered in when the progressive forces of the working class . . . Of course the reactionaries try to label any liberal a Communist, you know: redbaiting, the Dies Committee, see?"

"In Santa Barbara . . ." Marlowe stifled a yawn, "they say Franklin Roosevelt's a Communist."

"They'll tell you we're just a bunch of Communists at the Filmwriters' Association. It's a damn lie . . . As the reactionaries feel the power of the working class growing, they become desperate see? Fascism and repression and war is their answer."

"Well Jed," she said pushing back her chair, "I don't see how all that's going to help me make some money."

"Give me a chance to think about it." He moved his stool over to her side of the table. "Don't go yet. I haven't got my wits about me this evening."

"The successful man invents his own jobs, Dad used to say." She was thoughtfully brushing up the crumbs beside her plate. She hesitated. "I was wondering if there would be any chance for a sort of consultant steering some of you bigshots around in a social way. Some of the stars maybe. Do you see what I mean?"

Jed ordered himself another bourbon and some cheese. "Marlowe just one more . . . I'll drive the car." He brought his lips close to her ear.

She shook her head smiling and edged her stool away from his a little. "Now Jed don't be . . . impetuous," she said with an indulgent smile. She was acting as if she had known him all her life.

"We better see each other a lot." Jed was talking fast. "And talk this thing out. We'll think up something."

"There's no time. I've got to do something right away." There was a tremor of fright in Marlowe's voice. "The bank's taken over Dad's ranch. That's all I had left . . . I've got to do something. The place Nita's in now isn't a bit satisfactory."

"You got to give me time to think. Suppose we go home to my house. Everybody'll be in bed."

She shook her head. "I'm staying with friends," she said. "At the beach. I'd like to get in ahead of the fog."

"I'll call you tomorrow."

She opened her bag and took out a pencil and a slip of paper and scribbled a phone number. Then she tore it up. "No I'll call you at the studio."

"If you don't I'll put detectives on your trail."

She was very silent as she drove him home. She had to drive slow with yellow foglights. When she let him out in front of Canary Cottage she wouldn't let him kiss her.

"I've got problems too," he whispered almost tearfully. "Your're leaving me all alone." His voice broke . . . "Full of bourbon and love."

She waved her hand and smiled and drove away.

Every familiar feature of the house rose up to sting him as he walked into the hall where the porcelain bowl used to stand with the heliotrope in it, up the stairs into his miserable bedroom that still had the saffron draperies he and Felicia had had such fun picking out together one happy afternoon. Precious little fun left in the world, he told himself.

Only one of the twin beds was turned down. He couldn't go to bed alone like this. He'd never get to sleep. He went

259

to the phone and called Jade Haman's number. No answer. Gone to a nightclub probably. He had started to look through his address book for phone numbers when he noticed by the marble clock on the mantel that it was three A.M. Too late to call anybody.

He pulled off his clothes and got into the shower. He ran the water hot then cold. He dried himself and lay down on the bed but still he didn't feel sleepy. He walked back and forth in his pajamas shivering in the chill white mist that blanketed the windows. In the bathroom cabinet he found a box of Felicia's old sleeping tablets. Six years old, they couldn't be any good. He swallowed one gloomily and lay down on the bed staring up at the ceiling papered with tiny silver stars. The tablet made him feel kind of sick but it didn't make him sleep.

He woke up late with his head aching. All morning at the studio he felt stupid. He couldn't get any work done. Every time the buzzer sounded his heart turned a somersault.

The morning dragged. Unnecessary phone calls. Once it was George Pastor's dry voice. Ever since George had made a name for himself playing Prussian officer parts in Fred Walton's pictures he'd taken to talking like a drill sergeant. "Fill me in Jed," he said clipping off his words. "This Stalin-Hitler pact . . . Don't like it. Don't see the necessity . . Pact with antisemitism and murder . . . A betrayal."

"It's not what it seems on the surface," Jed stammered. "I haven't quite thought the thing through yet . . . Let's talk about it later. I'm on a rush job. I haven't time now."

"Very well if that's how you feel about it," George's dry voice was barbed with pique. "You don't think it matters what an actor thinks . . . Well you may be right . . . I had confidence in your integrity. I wanted your opinion before I came to a decision."

The sweat was standing out on Jed's forehead. "George please suspend judgment . . . We must have confidence in the rightness—er—of the progressive forces."

"Nuts," said George and hung up. Damn these sentimental liberals, Jed was thinking. They don't understand history.

The morning dragged endlessly.

Finally at twelve thirty when he'd gone distractedly to his bathroom to wash his hands and face before going over to meet Merle Redmond for lunch, he heard the buzzer. With dripping face he rushed to the phone. Her voice was in his ear. "Some friends have lent me a cottage at 6745 Beach Drive." It was the crisp little businesslike tone. "Drive over this afternoon when you get through."

He'd intended to tantalize her a little, to talk about a pressing engagement, about consulting his secretary, but what he answered was "Sure thing." Before he hung up he gave the receiver a quick little kiss.

When he got back after lunch, feeling depressed as he always did after a talk with Merle, and bloated by the New England boiled dinner he'd been foolish enough to eat while Merle talked on and on in his lugubrious voice about this new vehicle for a starlet, he found Sam Faust sitting in the easy chair next his desk.

Sam had something on his mind. He sat there looking up at Jed inquisitively with the little curl of conceit in the corners of his lips.

"Don't ask me how I feel," Jed burst out. "You'd feel terrible too if you'd spent the morning writing down cute remarks for Linda Milton." He belched. "See? I had lunch with Merle Redmond . . ."

"You'll be getting ulcers," said Sam, stretching his legs out before him. "A man in your position has no choice but to remarry . . . You've done everything in the world for that poor woman . . . But that wasn't what I came to talk to you about." He dropped his voice very low. "Type while I talk to you. Go on make a racket."

Jed slipped a sheet of scratch paper into his typewriter and started to pound the keys: *Now is the time for all good men* . . . Sam pulled himself up out of the chair and stood behind him. "Never can tell who might have a dictaphone planted," he spluttered down on Jed's ear as he whispered. "Be at the Collins Ranch at six thirty tonight. There'll be a foreign comrade there who wants to have a little talk with you."

"Sam I can't tonight."

"Type damn you. You got to. It's Party work."

"Sam it's something I can't call off."

"Jed when are you going to grow up? Party work comes first."

"But this is special. There are some engagements a man can't break. It's no use my saying I'll be there when I can't."

"Nobody's going to ask you to do anything that might compromise you . . ."

"It's a business engagement."

"Who is she? Do I know her?" Sam hissed suddenly down the back of Jed's neck.

Now is the time for all good men to come to the aid of the party. Jed went on typing the phrase over and over, hitting the keys so hard they hurt his fingers.

Sam walked over to the window and stood looking out. "Not a bad sentiment when you come to think of it," he was saying in his ordinary musing tone when he came back toward the desk. "Well Jed I'll tell you what I'll do . . . I know you're lying . . . Don't think you're kidding me . . . You want to lay some dame and you just can't wait. I'll set the thing up for tomorrow night. If there's any backlash you better make a clean breast of it. Comrades have been expelled for less. You know that damn well."

Jed stopped typing and turned his face up toward Sam's. He managed to produce his old impudent grin. "You know I wouldn't miss a trip up the valley, not with the orangeblossoms in bloom."

"A naturelover," roared Sam, suddenly amused and relaxed. "I know what kind of naturelover you are."

"You go to hell."

Jed never knew how he got through the rest of the afternoon. He sat poring over the papers at his desk feeling like a firecracker with the fuse sputtering. At five sharp he jumped up from his chair. His was the first car out of the parking lot. The blood burned his veins. Like the old days, he thought, as he drove through the homeward-bound traffic to the beach and out the shore road north.

It was a cute little pink bungalow no bigger than a bath house with steps cut in the rock down to the beach. In the tiny garage he caught sight of the gray Chrysler convertible. She came to the door in a bathingsuit, tight, brown, almost the color of her skin. She still had her figure. "I'm going to take a dip," Marlowe said. "Want to come? The water's horribly cold. There are some men's bathingsuits in the bedroom."

While he took off his clothes, his hands already cold with anticipation, he could hear the pound and the long slow seethe of the surf on the beach below. Heavy, he thought. He hardly had time to be scared before he was following her into the roaring ocean, trying to make a proper dive through the wave, fighting the undertow. It was so cold he had no breath in his body. She came running out after him laughing, shaking her wet hair because the wave had torn off her bathing cap, running on narrow brown feet across the shining spume toward dry trampled sand and people placid under beach umbrellas and the steps to the bungalow. Jed had one ear full of seawater but otherwise couldn't find he had been hurt.

"Not too bad for a movie magnate," she was telling him consolingly. "It's a knack." He was still puffing when he followed her into the delicious privacy of the closed venetian blinds of the bungalow. She poured him a jigger of whisky. "It clears your head," she said. "I get so discouraged."

He threw his arms around her. Her body was wet and salty and firm. "How could you," he whispered, "ever be discouraged, you're too delicious to be discouraged."

They went into the bedroom with their arms around each other as if they had been living together for years.

It was night outside the venetian blinds before they put their clothes on. It didn't take her long to dress. Her hair was still wet so she tied a silk handkerchief around it. He sat at the redwood table on the porch sipping at a drink while she clattered pans in the kitchenette.

"Don't you want to go out someplace?" Jed had asked.

"Not tonight. You think I can't cook. A yachtsman's wife has to learn to cook . . . Not that that isn't all over and done with . . . You sit there and think up a way for me to make a lot of easy money quick. Could you stand another steak?" She stuck her head out of the door.

He nodded.

She pulled her head back into the kitchen. "My God," he said after a while, "it's pleasant to sit here after a dip in the ocean, drinking rye whisky and listening to a steak sizzling in the pan. It brings back the days when I thought I was going to be something in the world."

He got to his feet to kiss her when she brought in the

264

two plates with the knives and forks on them. She kissed him back.

"It's years since I've had a meal cooked for me by a woman I loved." As soon as she put the butter in front of him he said, starting in on a French roll, "Golly, I must have been an unlicked cub when we first met on that French Line boat."

"You were kind of a cute little bantam," she called back from the kitchenette. "Of course you were an awful four-flusher. I guess you still are."

"Ideologically immature, that's what my friends would say. I've learned a lot. I've learned the hard way." He could see her through the open door moving back and forth in front of the gas stove. "We have all had to learn that there are more important things than the individual. Of course a lot of people think that when a playwright comes out to the Coast he's just a goddam whore selling his talent to the highest bidder. That's all just on the surface. It takes a lot of study and thought to understand what goes on under the surface. Underneath out here there's a selfless dedication you don't find in many places in the world."

He was shouting at her through the door. He couldn't tell whether she was listening or not.

"What would you say," he went on in a low voice looking up in her face when she came back with the mustard, "if I told you that I had broken a most important engagement to come out here tonight? I can't tell you what it is but I may have jeopardized my entire career . . . It's worth it, Marlowe!" When she walked out from the kitchen with the steak swimming in gravy in its platter he jumped to his feet. "This isn't accidental. None of it is accidental. You turned me down cold when I asked you this before. When I get my divorce will you marry me?"

"That was where I came in." Marlowe leaned back in her chair and gave him a quick grin across the table. "I bet that speech is right out of a movie you're writing."

He answered bitterly: "There are times when a man can't help being sincere." He felt aggrieved.

She leaned across the table and gave him a light pat on the shoulder. "There there Jed old man . . . Only you mustn't address me like I was a Civic Center."

"All you ever did was make fun of me."

She was looking up and down with the sharp violet look in her eyes. "At that I might get some of that blubber off your bones . . . Didn't you say you played tennis?"

"No, I don't play tennis."

"Take it easy Jed."

When they'd finished eating he helped her stack the dishes in the lavendercolored kitchenette. When he took her by the shoulders to kiss her mouth her body folded into his. Later that evening when they were lying side by side on the glider on the small latticed porch, feeling all through them the measured pound and seethe of the rollers on the beach below, he whispered with his lips touching her ear. "A love nest. I never understood what it meant before. It's always the banal that's true."

"Like in popular songs," she said.

This time she consented to come to the house to meet Mae. It was late. She went ahead in her car. He followed in his. They found Mrs. Steiner sitting up in the livingroom sewing. "An old family friend just back from Honolulu," Jed explained. "She's never met Mae."

"Now please Mr. Morris don't keep her up," whined Mrs. Steiner. "She has to have her sleep or she gets behind in her studies."

Mae was awake in her own little room, lying on her bed

266

reading a book. She had her glasses on. "It's about a princess," she said. "A European princess in the naughty nineties." Mae was dark and had a turned up nose like June's. Her eyes were brown like Jed's. Her hair was in bobbypins.

"Mae, this is Marlowe," Jed began.

"Another of Dad's old flames." Mae giggled. "I can't keep them straight."

"We were very good friends for a very short time a long time ago," said Marlowe in a gentle tone. "I have a little girl. She's younger than you. She's not very well."

"Not polio," cried Mae. "I'm so scared of polio."

"Something very nearly as bad."

"Oh I'm so sorry." Mae dropped her book and sat up blinking with sympathy behind her glasses.

"How old are you, Mae?"

"I'm fifteen." She shook her bobbypins. "But I feel much older. It ages a girl to be the child of divorced parents . . . and Dad's old flames and that sort of thing. They make one feel quite sophisticated."

Jed kissed Mae on the forehead. "It's late little girl," he said. "If your light isn't out in ten minutes, I'll come up and play the heavy father." He let out a constrained titter when he left the room.

"You see," he whispered to Marlowe as he followed her down the stairs. "It's the hypocrisy of this capitalist social system . . . Between me and her mother the poor child's all confused."

"What does she do? Go to school here and spend her vacations with her mother?"

Jed nodded. "I wanted her to get a few progressive ideas."

Marlowe changed the subject with a shrug. "What about this fellow Weaver, Jed? You said he might have ideas."

Jed couldn't help the peevish whine: "I got to talk to him, to sound him out, see? My time's all taken up this week: meetings, speaking engagements. He's in New York this week anyway."

"But Jed if I had time, I wouldn't be nagging at you." Marlowe pulled in her upper lip to keep it from trembling. "I've got to get Nita into a better place. There's a very good one at Carmel, run more like a school . . . I know you'll do the best you can."

"Will you do the best you can?" Jed asked pressing his face against hers. "Come by the house tomorrow evening about eleven." He was happy in the firmness of his voice. Damn it, he was in the driver's seat now. "Not later than eleven. I'll get Mrs. Steiner out of the way. I'll be back from my other engagements."

Her face flushed and stiffened. Again he noticed the ugly tendons under the crinkling skin of her neck. She nodded and walked out with her lips drawn tight. From the open door he watched her step into the Chrysler and drive away. "You bitch," he felt like shouting after her.

When he got upstairs to his room the hatred was all gone. He found himself bumbling idiotically, "I love her. I love her. I love her," as he got undressed.

They were made for each other, he'd known that all along. She could fit the broken pieces of his life together. Mae would love her. She was so downright and direct, and that look of belonging . . . She'd be a wonderful mother for Peter. He'd make it up to her for her unhappy life. "A shambles, like mine," he whispered aloud. But she wouldn't like this Party work. Maybe this was his chance to make a break. A pact with Hitler. Didn't sound good. A betrayal, George had called it. To hell with Sam and his conspiratorial methods. George was making a break. A pact with antisemitism and murder was what George had called it. They'd be out gunning for George but they had better watch their step. The movement was going to be unpopular in this town. Old George had been mighty successful, now. Ridiculous to pay actors such salaries. Why George made more money than Jed did.

Sitting in his pajamas on the edge of the bed he found himself looking around the room in a fright. His hands and feet were cold. No sense in being scared of your own thoughts. Nobody could overhear his thoughts he told himself. He was an artist after all. An artist must be free. If they drove him to it he'd call up the newspapers, go to the F.B.I., join the American Legion: RADICALISM IN PICTURES. SUBVERSIVES MEET IN SECRET. FILM WRITER TELLS ALL.

He walked back and forth in front of his bed in his bare feet.

It would be a new life from now on, with Marlowe. Marlowe. She was throwing herself at his head. She needed him more than he needed her. He mustn't think of all these things, he must just think of Marlowe or he would never get to sleep. He rolled into bed, whispering "Goodnight Marlowe" into the pillow and closed his eyes. "The happy ending."

Next morning he woke up happy for the first time since he could remember. He enjoyed every bite of his breakfast and reached the studio early and fresh. At his desk he kept thinking how cute Mae had been when she was a little tot. Marlowe must have been cute too, a pert oldfashioned child. A pleasant family life, that was all a man needed in this world. A home with children. A teeny blonde tot. Lines for Linda Milton began to come easy. His typewriter chattered.

When he was interrupted by a call from Sam, "just to

remind you of your little nature walk," it was a while before Jed could remember what Sam was talking about. "The Audubon Society," insisted Sam.

"Sure, sure," Jed's voice rattled. "I haven't forgotten. The Audubon Society: that's good." He laughed vacantly.

There was no amusement in Sam's voice: "Six o'clock sharp at the Collins Ranch." His words made a hissing noise on the phone.

"Say Sam," added Jed shakily, "I want to talk to you . . . just us two . . ."

"What about?"

Jed's head spun. He couldn't find the words. "This divorce," he blurted out. After all he couldn't discuss Party matters over the phone.

There was a tone of relief in Sam's voice. "Want to pay some more alimony eh?" He chuckled. "All right. Come down and take me to lunch."

When Jed walked into Sam's office that noon his step was firm. He closed the door behind him and went straight to the point.

"George Pastor," he said. "He called me up the other day. He's unhappy about this pact."

Jed sat down facing the window. The shade was up. In the noontime glare all Jed could see above the desk in front of him was Sam's jowly face in shadow and the glint of light on his glasses. Jed kept blinking in the glare from the window.

Sam was doodling on a pad. "Ain't that too bad?" he said without looking up.

"A lot of people are uneasy in their minds, Sam."

Sam got to his feet and let down the venetian blind. "George better watch his step," he whispered over his shoulder. "He's played so many Prussian officer parts, people might begin to think he was a reactionary himself."

"That's just what I was thinking," Jed heard himself say "But Sam, we've known each other so long. We ought to be able to talk frankly, discuss the pros and cons. I'm ready to be convinced."

"In this office," Sam sat down with a plunk at his desk again, "I transact law business. What's on your mind?"

Jed couldn't find the words to get back to the subject of the pact. "This situation with Felicia," he burst out querulously. "You are supposed to be my lawyer and nothing happens . . ."

"I'm looking up California procedure on common law marriages. The cases are confusing." Sam was professionally bland. "You artists do the most damn fool things."

"You don't believe in bourgeois morality any more than I do."

"Even in the Soviet Union you have to buy a ticket before you get on the train. Who's the lovely lady?"

"None of your goddam business."

"Afraid I'll cut you out, eh?" Sam's lips curled teasingly. Jed got to his feet. "All right I'll go get a good lawyer."

Sam waved two small fat hands above his doodled pad. "Easy does it, Jed . . . Maybe a Mexican divorce. I'll have to look up some more cases."

Jed let himself drop back into the chair. After all Sam was his best friend in this town. "Sam," he began in a low trembling voice leaning toward him across the desk, "it means an awful lot. It's the only real chance for happiness I've had in my life. I met her years ago and she turned me down. Now she wants me. She's a real person even if she does come out of high society. Mae likes her. She's had a very tragic life."

"We've got two problems here," said Sam slowly, "the coordinator's office and California law. I don't want you to turn up a bigamist."

"That's what lawyers are for," said Jed. "I'd like to make some kind of cash settlement on Felicia and get the custody of Peter."

"What kind of lawyer has she got?"

"Agatha's the real problem. You met Felicia's mother when she was out here."

"It looks like you've gotten yourself properly hooked. Why the hell can't you take up with a girl like Jade Haman? She's a sympathizer with a heart as big as a church."

"Too many other guys sitting in the pews, I guess."

"A sentimentalist, eh?"

"I know it'll cost a lot of money," Jed was talking fast, "but Linda Milton's going to be a goldmine . . . Merle's mad about my babytalk."

"Let me tell you something, Jed Morris." Sam all of a sudden raised his voice and tapped with a stubby forefinger on the pad. "If this business is handled wrong, you'll be selling apples on Bughouse Square. A classconscious Party worker hasn't any right messing around."

Jed got to his feet. "All right, Sam, you handle it . . . I'll pay the bill. Now let's go eat . . . But I can tell you one thing. When I marry this person I'm telling you about, I'll be a hell of a lot more use to the movement than I ever was before . . . And I'll be right on time for the Audubon Society."

The sight of Marlowe's gloves and handbag on the hall table when he got home late that night made his head spin.

Marlowe to kid with. Marlowe to talk to. Before he knew it he was talking his head off.

"It was stimulating," he told her. "An interesting evening," he shouted. She looked up at him from a big white overstuffed chair with that haggard look of an aging woman he'd hated in Felicia; Marlowe was so much handsomer, though; the sort of looks that last; he didn't care; he was too busy trying to tell her about the evening at the Collins Ranch without giving away any Party secrets. "A socialist wienie roast. You wouldn't think that would be stimulating, now would you? There were old man Collins and his wife, old-fashioned bugeyed liberals who don't know whether they are standing on their head or their heels. A Filipino butler was solemnly toasting wienies at a rustic fireplace and pouring out fruit punch for all the cranks and cultists from La Jolla to Pasadena and the whole place smelling like a French whorehouse from the orangeblossoms, and there was Sam Faust and me looking like butter wouldn't melt in our mouths . . ."

"Sam Faust and I," interrupted Marlowe.

Jed paid no attention. "And right there in the middle of all this twaddle," his tongue rattled on, "we had the most interesting conversation I ever had in my life with a man I'd been specially invited to meet, a representative of an international organization directed by the really great minds of our time, see? for the purpose of putting an end to war and poverty and the exploitation that makes it possible for this rich trash to go on living on other people's labor."

"How about people living on unpaid bills?" put in Marlowe.

Jed's words gushed on. "I used to feel bad because I never got time to write plays, see? But now I'm living the only really great drama that's going on in our time. There are

273

forces that are bigger than we are. I suddenly understood that today. In this town people have to sacrifice their individualistic doubts. My doubts rolled away like clouds before the sun. A man has to make an instrument out of his life. Some day Marlowe, when you've gotten wise to the way things are a little more, I hope I'll be able to talk to you about it . . . like two comrades, see? We always said we'd be absolutely honest. But now I have to use the same kind of language talking to you we used right there in the middle of that crowd of reformist millionaires. If they'd known what we were really talking about they'd have run like turkeys calling 'Fire . . . Police.' This man I was invited to meet had a mind like a steel trap. He had high cheekbones and wore a tweed cap. I thought his eyes looked like Lenin's. He was working around all the time to see if I could be trusted. He had wisdom, see? He was putting me through a kind of examination to see if it was safe to let me in on the real workings. There are striking workers who have to be helped. If I live long enough to see the time when men are valued according to their real worth I could make it the first act of a chronicle play of the American Revolution."

"Mother was a daughter of the American Revolution," said Marlowe yawning.

Jed threw himself down on the settee laughing like he'd split. "Marlowe dear, that remark proves you haven't understood a word I've been saying." He slid into the big chair beside her and gave her ear a little bite and whispered against her neck, "Such a sweet little dumb bunny."

He was too excited to sit still. He jumped to his feet. The leathery perfume stayed in his head as he walked back and forth in front of her chair.

"Marlowe one of these days you'll be glad you took up

with somebody who chose the right side from the beginning,"
he said. Then he grabbed her by her two hands and pulled her
out of the chair. "Marlowe, I've just had an idea. This divorce is going to take some time . . . It's not my fault. It's
a complicated situation . . ."

"Your agent, George Weaver, has offered me a job of
receptionist," she interrupted, "but there's not enough in it."
She shook her head with pouting lips.

"Damn his impudence," shouted Jed, "but Marlowe, I've
thought of something . . . Suppose I pay off Mrs. Steiner,"
he began to whisper in her ear, "and you take her place. Mae
loves you already. Mrs. Steiner gives me the creeps, she's always so worried. Suppose you took the job."

She lit a cigarette and smoked a couple of puffs walking
back and forth over the white wool rug in front of the fireplace. She turned suddenly and looked in his face. "How
much does she make?"

"Five hundred a month."

"Found?" she grinned.

"And how."

Marlowe nodded with the cigarette in her mouth. "That
will just pay for Nita at Carmel."

"Wonderful!" shouted Jed. "Let's go out and eat an expensive supper. I'll reserve a table. I don't care who sees us."

Marlowe crushed out her cigarette, sat down and lit
another. "Let's be sensible Jed," she said after a while. "You
mustn't forget that I had a thoroughly conventional upbringing."

"I know. I know," said Jed.

"To a woman in my position"—she looked in his face
with her teasing smile—"a certain amount of deception
comes natural."

When Jed came back to his office from a conference late one afternoon a few days after Mrs. Steiner had packed her bags and gone, he found Sam sitting in the easy chair by the window. Sam's jowls had a waxen look. His skin looked greenish. He seemed to have lost all his tan.

"Jed," he began, frowning above his bifocals, "my car's in the shop . . . I thought maybe you'd drive me home and stop to have a drink with Maisie. She says she hasn't seen you for a month." Sam sounded very tired.

"What's the trouble, Sam? You don't look quite up to scratch."

"I'm all right. You are the one I'm worried about."

They stood looking at each other. Neither one seemed to find anything more to say. They walked heavily down the stairs in silence and out among the throng hurrying toward the parking lot.

Sam didn't open his mouth till Jed was weaving his way through the traffic on the avenue of palms that led to the Faust place. Then pronouncing each word with cold exactness he asked, "Jed, who is this woman? You haven't got your divorce yet. Isn't this a little premature?"

Fortunately Jed had to keep his eyes on his driving. He could feel his face getting red. "You mean the woman who's taken Mrs. Steiner's place?" he drawled. "How the hell did you know about that?" He took a deep breath. He began to talk fast. "She was very well recommended . . . I found that Mrs. Steiner was filling Mae's head with white chauvinism, so naturally I let her go."

"What's the new governess' name?"

"A Mrs. Tompkins, I believe."

"Humph," said Sam. He cleared his throat and went on severely. "Well, if you will get into messes I suppose it's your lawyer's business to get you out of them. Jed, I don't have to explain to you that you must be careful about who you take up with when you are engaged in Party work." He talked like a teacher lecturing a small boy. "California's full of British agents and some of them, I happen to know, have links with the F.B.I."

"Don't worry about Mrs. Tompkins," said Jed feeling his face go suddenly very red. "She's a needy gentlewoman."

"Jed," said Sam, "you know just as well as I do that Party members don't associate with reactionary individuals."

"Except for specific purposes," broke in Jed angrily. "You didn't hear what N. Roberts said . . . out at the Collins Ranch. When we were talking back of the outdoor fireplace . . . He said for me to drop Party ties, fraction meetings, all that crap . . . There are a few men, he said, whom the Party reserves for very special purposes, a subtle instrument . . . First a period of probation . . . merely a sleeper. Those were his exact words. You ask N. Roberts about it."

"You're talking too much right here and now," Sam burst out savagely. "You can't say you haven't been warned. In spite of all his connections Eli Soltair couldn't sell his original, went out of this town broke, don't forget that. Had to borrow money for his bus ticket."

"What the hell's that got to do with me?" Jed brought the car to a sudden stop at the edge of the drive behind Sam's house.

"I suppose you never heard of the Control Commission . . . Come on." Breathing hard Sam waddled off in front of him across the lawn toward the swimmingpool. "Don't ever remember names," he was saying quietly, when Jed caught up with him jiggling his keys in one hand. "I've already forgotten what you told me."

The arrangement worked. Month after month it got better. Marlowe was a splendid housekeeper. Living in a well run house for once did everything for Jed's writing. He'd never had a more successful year. The gross on the new Linda Milton picture was mounting up into seven figures. There was talk of an Oscar for Merle Redmond. "Combines clean entertainment and a wholesome respect for family life, with an artistic integrity new to this type of production," wrote one of the serious critics who really counted in the industry.

Marlowe—she was always Mrs. Tompkins when there was anyone else in the room—seemed to know exactly how to talk to Mae. Mae was doing better in school. No more fits of sobbing when she went to bed at night. Marlowe had gone to work to interest Mae in the housekeeping. She had her arranging flowers in the vases, coming out with her hair becomingly fixed to meet the guests when Jed entertained. Marlowe was encouraging Jed to give a few small parties which were duly reported in the trade journals. The highbrow set. Sir Herbert Watson. The Monceau brothers. The women who wrote the gossip columns began to refer to him as one of the film colony's literary bachelors. Eligible. They linked his name with stars. Mae began to clip out references to her father for her scrapbook. She took to collecting autographs. She was so happy that when school closed and the time came for her to go back to Omaha to spend her vacation with her mother, she broke down and cried. His family life was beautiful, Jed told himself.

Marlowe was a help about Peter too. She kept warning Jed against Sam Faust. "Don't get messed up with lawyers," she advised him one night. "Tommy and I went through the wringer with lawyers. That's one reason why we both ended up on the beach. We did what the lawyers said. Sam Faust may be a friend of yours but be leery of his advice. We were fool enough to get divorced and then we had to remarry, I told you about that on the Compagnie Générale Transatlantique . . . remember?"

It was in her housekeeper's sittingroom in the wing. These were Jed's happiest times when they were alone in the house, at night after the servants had gone. This night Jed had brought in a draft of a letter to Agatha for Marlowe to go over. He consulted her about everything now. Years ago he'd given up trying to get an answer from Felicia, he explained. Agatha wrote that Felicia just tore his letters up as soon as she found them in the mail.

"I can understand that," said Marlowe, looking at him with an indulgent kind of frown. "You're all right in bed Jed, but the rest of the time, my God!"

"Agatha always writes," Jed answered without paying any attention, "at length."

"I bet I'd like Agatha," Marlowe laughed. "Of course since her husband died she hasn't anything but the grandchild."

"She's a tartar . . . You're kind of a tartar too, do you know it?" Jed edged into Marlowe's chair behind the desk and managed to hoist her on his knees. "How do you like being my social secretary?"

She ran her fingers through his hair. "I must say that sending out a man's autographed photographs to movie fans is something I never did expect to do."

Jed felt happy enough to purr like a cat. He kissed her behind the ear. "This has been the best year of my life," he whispered. "I wonder why . . . If only I could get you to see my way . . . about the class struggle," he went on.

She pulled away from him, reached for a cigarette and walked up and down in front of the desk puffing on it. All the taut lines showed on her neck. "No use talking about that," she mumbled through her cigarette. "I guess you've never met a really loyal American before."

There was a whine in Jed's voice. "That's what you can't understand," he said, "that I am too . . . profoundly . . ."

She didn't listen. She was a thousand miles away.

Especially since Hitler's armored columns had started charging through Europe, whenever he tried to talk about world politics, she just seemed not to listen. Jed consoled himself with the thought that it was her early training in that Paris convent that made her sympathize so with the French. The plush horse circles she'd been brought up in were solid with the British ruling class. Winston Churchill, Lady Astor, they were gods in Santa Barbara. She couldn't see that Hitler's victories were all just part of capitalism's inevitable collapse.

He jumped to his feet and threw his arms around her. No use talking politics with women. His fingers were on her breasts. "All the women in my life have been pronounced reactionaries," he whispered in her ear. "I mean those I really loved." He grabbed her cigarette and dropped it in an ashtray and turned her around and kissed her. "We believe in different Americas," he went on whispering in her ear as they moved into the bedroom. "But love makes us one."

Whenever he got to thinking about it as he sat over his typewriter he would console himself with the notion that just by living together they would come to agree. Lovers grew together. Women had to get used to new ideas gradually. In the end she would be certain just because he was.

The June morning she called up at the studio to tell him she'd just heard over the radio that the armored columns of the Wehrmacht were attacking the Russian armies, he was too stunned to get mad at her. "And the Yanks are not coming," came her mocking voice.

"You can razz all you like," he answered weakly. "But don't forget Napoleon." The thought gave him courage. "Get out the encyclopedia and look up Napoleon," he added querulously. "Hitler will be swallowed up the same way . . . When I get home I'll prove it to you."

She had hung up before the thought came to him, all of a sudden: there was no barrier between them any more; now they were fighting the same war.

Right away Sam was on the wire. "Sam what do you think?" Jed asked excitedly. "What's going to happen?"

"Defense in depth." Sam's voice sounded impatient. "But that's not what I called you up about . . . There's a man named Evans in town, Larry Evans. He has an important story idea. Get it?"

"Sure," said Jed. His heart was beating so fast he could hardly speak. "Business connected with the Audubon Society." He was out of breath.

"He knows what you look like." Sam's voice had the precise metallic ring that always scared Jed. "He will wait for you this afternoon in front of the newsstand at the Los Angeles Biltmore . . . At six fifteen sharp . . . no dames this time."

"I'll be there," said Jed in a choking voice.

Jed had the fidgets so he could do no more work that day. He spent the afternoon reading the newspapers. When he couldn't follow the print any more he stood in the window smoking cigarettes and watching a stooped old Japanese gardener in faded blue denims that somehow had an otherworldly look pulling the weeds out of a bed of petunias. Jed was so nervous he couldn't wait for the office day to end. It was hardly six when he turned his car over to the doorman in front of the hotel to park.

It was a hot afternoon. His mouth was parched. He went into the bar and hurriedly drank down a glass of beer. He drank it too fast. The beer gave him the hiccups. He still had the hiccups when a little foxfaced man in a crumpled Palm Beach suit sidled up to him as he stood staring without seeing them at the headlines on the afternoon papers.

"Mr. Morris, I'm Larry Evans," the man said without looking in his face. Jed followed him out the door to the taxistand. The man opened the door of a cab for Jed in a deferential sort of way, gave the driver an address and stepped in after. All the man would talk about was baseball. Commercialism. Too much selling of players back and forth. The profit system was ruining the game. The Dodgers had gotten off to a bad start. The taxi drew up in front of a shabby storeblock out in Auburn Park. "You'll be meeting an old friend of yours," said Evans pleasantly. "Walk up the stairs. You'll see the name of a Japanese dentist on the first groundglass door to the right. Go in without knocking." He gave Jed another deferential smile. "This is as far as I go."

The stairs were steep. Jed was short of breath when he pushed open the door. The tall man standing with his watch in his hand beside the little table littered with dogeared magazines was N. Roberts. He put his watch in his pocket. The gray Slavic eyes set wide apart over high cheekbones glowed into Jed's face.

"All right." Roberts allowed himself to smile. "Please." With a motion of his hand he indicated an inner door. Jed bumped into the dentist's chair. "Do not worry," said Roberts showing a steel canine as he smiled. He was being pleasant.

He was putting Jed at his ease. "I will not pull your teeth. Dentist eess out . . . Please."

Roberts held out a package of Russian cigarettes. Jed clamped his teeth tight on the cardboard mouthpiece while Roberts held up his lighter. Jed was shaking so he had trouble getting the cigarette into the flame.

"Please sit." Jed avoided the dentist's chair and sat on the edge of the straight chair in the corner of the room. Smiling broadly Roberts made himself comfortable in the dentist's chair and swung it around till he faced Jed. Then he began to talk in his jerky English:

"Comrade Morris the task is now to find dollars. Until armies of Hitler are defeated everything is subordinate to patriotic war. Political agitation, trade union work, everything is subordinate. It is great opportunity to enlist leeberals in defense of Soviet Union. Even exploiting classes believe triumph of Hitler would be ruin of civilization, no? American millionaires are careless with money, no? Soviet Union must buy arms, medical supplies, food for devastated areas. We shall win war, make no mistake. Reaction cannot destroy Soviet Union, but we must have help against Hitler, like your president Roosevelt is giving Breetish. But more. We must have dollars. Your task Comrade Morris is to organize war relief in California."

Jed rose to his feet. His nervousness had left him. He bit his lips thoughtfully. "That is the sort of thing I can do," he said.

"You are not compromised by working class or poleetical connections. You are famous author of cinema of leetle children . . ." A sweet Santa Claus look came over Roberts' face. "Leetle Linda asks for help for Russian cheeldren. It will mean meellions, no?"

"The thing to do," said Jed in a firm deliberate voice, "is to start with Santa Barbara or Pasadena, maybe . . . any reactionary center. Labor, liberals, the intellectuals, they'll all come along. We must start with the multimillionaires."

"All right." Roberts reached out and gave Jed's hand a rough jerk and dropped it. "We will rely on you Comrade Morris. You will have much help from our organizations . . . please." With a stiff bow he indicated the door.

Jed walked down the street in a daze. He hailed a cab and picked up his car at the hotel garage. As he fought his way home through the traffic he kept repeating to himself again and again that this was how he could get Marlowe into the movement. She'd fall for war relief. No more criticism from Sam. A Mexican divorce. All the difficulties resolved at last. With her capitalist connections Marlowe would make a magnificent secretary for the Russian War Relief. The yachtsman's wife from Santa Barbara. Marlowe could make war relief fashionable. What more suitable than for the president of the statewide committee to marry the secretary? He began arranging the words he would use to address the first meeting.

When he hurried into Canary Cottage by the back door he was dismayed to find the table in the diningroom set for one. Didn't Marlowe always dine with him when they were alone? Distractedly he asked the maid where Mrs. Tompkins was. Carmel. Of course this had to be the day she drove up to Carmel to see her child. In his excitement he had forgotten. He usually arranged to be out for dinner that night. He'd often suggested she make it a weekend so that he could come along, but she'd always shaken her head with a closed look on her face. This night of all nights. He couldn't get started making plans without her. What would he do tomorrow? It would be late before she got back. Boiling with impatience,

Jed sat munching his lonely dinner. The food was tasteless without Marlowe. She always had a cutglass carafe of wine on the table. He poured himself a glass but forgot to drink it.

Like bile rising from a disturbed stomach, jealousy began to well up from some sour pit inside him. He'd never been so crazy about a woman in his life. He admitted it. He wasn't getting anywhere with her. It was years now and still he didn't know what she thought about really. He didn't really know whether she really cared for him. Did she really go to see the child? Who else did she see? Some damn tennis-player? Some seabitten millionaire yachtsman left over from her old life. In that rich sporting set they had no more morals than rabbits. In all the months she'd lived in his house she had never introduced him to one of her old friends. Who was it she wrote those long letters to he'd find her so absorbed with sometimes when he went to her room at night after the servants had left?

His thoughts disturbed him so he couldn't sit still. He startled the maid by pushing back his chair just as she was bringing in a meringue pie for dessert. "No dessert thanks," he said, "I'm late for an engagement."

He left the table and hurried up the stairs and down the hall to Marlowe's little sittingroom, bedroom and bath. The rooms were drenched with her light morocco leather perfume that always filled him with such tenderness. If he only had her there to put his arms around. Hardly breathing he began to go through her desk.

Odds and ends of jewelry. A few scraps of lace. A paper of needles. Letters from people he didn't know. He read scraps about sailing, incidents in Tahiti, Santa Catalina Island. Nothing personal. Snapshots dropped out of the letters. Not a familiar face. Men mostly. Outdoor men. A lanternjawed sunburned man with a tennis racket; that must be Jeremy

Tompkins. Sailboats. Shots of a schooner. Marlowe, young, smiling, happy, with the same man on a beach under a fringe of palms. Both of them in bathingsuits with their arms round each others' shoulders, playing chess at a table shaded by enormous leaves. The man rowing a dinghy, catching a fish, sitting at the wheel of a sailboat with a whitecrested wave behind him. In the back of the drawer Jed came on a little roll of tapa cloth fastened with elastic. With shaky fingers he unrolled it. More snapshots: baby pictures, a tiny girl with braces on her legs, a bigger girl in a wheelchair, the same girl propped up in a hospital bed, blonde curls round a small tortured face. What the devil am I doing here? Jed asked himself shuddering and tried clumsily to put everything back where he had found it.

Breathing hard he tiptoed down the hall to his own room. He couldn't stay there all alone. He snatched up the phone beside his bed and called Jade. Jade was home. Her voice spluttered with war news. Panzer divisions. Horror of Hitler. Confidence in the Russian steppes, General Mud next winter. She was crazy to talk to Jed. Hadn't seen him in a dog's age. He was neglecting his old friends. He must have inside dope. He must come right over, a few people coming in. Okey doke, Jed tried to kid. He hurried out to his car and drove away from the empty house.

Next evening he had to let Marlowe catch him waiting for her with an anxious look on his face outside the front door of Canary Cottage when her dusty old Chrysler turned into the drive. "We are setting up a committee for Russian War Relief," he shouted to make sure she wouldn't think he'd come out there just for her. He didn't give her a chance to take her hat off before he began outlining his plans. She nodded her head briskly. "Jed," she said in a serious voice, "thank God there's something we can agree on."

Right away after dinner she went to work, jotting down lists of names, calling up friends long distance. He was amazed at her efficiency. The response was immediate. All sorts and conditions rallied to the defense of the heroic Russian people.

After that they spent every weekend driving up and down the Coast to organize committees. Working with Marlowe was a joy. Jed had never been so happy in his life. Before six weeks were out he was delivering an address to an audience of bejeweled old ladies at the opening of the Russian Bazaar in Santa Barbara.

Their plane was delayed by fog the Sunday night after the opening of the bazaar, so that Monday morning he was late at the studio. The first thing he saw on his desk when he hurried in was a note asking him to call Herman D. Speyer's office. The note scared him; something must be wrong, but Herman D.'s secretary's voice positively chirruped when Jed repeated his name. Mr. Speyer was waiting for him. Could Mr. Morris come right over? Splendid. Mr. Speyer had a lot of people that morning, but she would sandwich him in. As it turned out Jed hardly had time to catch his breath in Herman D.'s outer office before he was ushered into the great oval room, where he found Herman D. talking over the telephone at the kidneyshaped desk in front of the tall radiant window in the midst of a huddle of stocky men in sports clothes. As soon as Herman D. caught sight of Jed he broke out through the group and came forward to meet him with both hands outstretched.

"Marvelous, you were marvelous, Jed," he chanted. "We heard it on the radio. Mrs. Speyer had tears in her eyes. What diction, what choice of the proper expletive. Let me congratulate you." Holding Jed by both hands Herman D. drew him across the room. "Gentlemen, meet a young man who has just made a speech worth a million dollars in public relations to the industry. In spite of their terrible government the Russians are a noble people . . . Relief for the villages, for the hungry children, for the freezing mothers . . . An appeal to America's great golden heart that never fails to respond to the cry of suffering from overseas. Too many men who earn their living in this industry spend their time selling the industry short. Divorces, nightclub brawls . . . the industry was getting a bad name . . . Jed has shown us how to change all that . . . I am about to make a little donation in four figures to the Russian War Relief . . . Joe tell the boys they can come in . . . Poor boys they've been waiting all morning . . . You were late in your office, Jed, we don't like that on this lot . . . but in what a noble cause." He spread his arms wide and ended up with a freckled hand on Jed's shoulder.

As reporters and camera men trooped in through a side door Herman D. Speyer stepped behind his desk and held up a check. "Gentlemen," he cleared his throat. "I want you all to meet Mr. Jed Morris. His name you know from his many screen credits as the author of the dialogue in Merle Redmond's Linda Milton pictures that have proved to the whole civilized world that nothing pays like wholesome family life . . . Mr. Morris' address a couple of nights ago was reported in all the newspapers. Magnificent. Many of you heard it among your own families, with your little children nestling on your knees. Mrs. Speyer and I were deeply touched. Tears were in our eyes. We asked ourselves what could we do to further this great cause. I am about to present to Mr. Morris a check in four figures, three thousand five hundred dollars to be exact"—he studied the blue slip in his hand—"as my personal contribution to start the ball rolling in this town for the relief of the poor people of Russia crucified by the horrors of Hitler."

Reporters scribbled on their pads. Photographers flashed their bulbs. They made Jed and Herman D. pose in front of the desk and behind the desk holding the check out between them. When he finally walked away across the deep carpets of the oval office with Herman D. Speyer's voice croaking excitedly after him "God bless you my boy," Jed's feet felt light as air.

The night of Pearl Harbor it wasn't until Jed got home to Canary Cottage that he heard the news. He'd driven his new custombuilt convertible way up into the San Bernardino mountains to pick up Mae who had been spending the weekend skiing with some school friends. As they came from the garage laden down with Mae's suitcases Marlowe met them in the patio. In the broken light from the ship's lantern over the door Jed noticed a taut look about her mouth. She hardly greeted him. She helped Mae in with her skis and her boots. He was surprised that she didn't have anything to say. Was she mad at him for some reason? It wasn't till Mae had gone upstairs to finish her homework, carrying a plate of sandwiches and a glass of milk on a tray, that Marlowe said to Jed, in a low accusing voice as if it were all his fault, "Japanese planes attacked Pearl Harbor this morning at dawn."

"That means we're in the war," Jed answered cheerfully. "We ought to have been in all along."

"They are not telling how many capital ships were sunk," said Marlowe. "The Philippines will be next."

Jed led the way into the kitchen. "How about making me a sandwich too?" he said. "I'm just as starved as Mae."

She brought the cold sliced turkey out of the icebox again and rapidly buttered some bread.

"It was inevitable," muttered Jed with his face in the sandwich. "As Herman D. Speyer is always saying, 'We must hitch our wagon to the silver lining.' We'll be allied to the Soviet Union . . . Fascism will be wiped out all over the world. It's the beginning of a great period of human history."

"Nobody," said Marlowe in an oddly gruff tone, "is going to have any more use for anybody who isn't a loyal American."

"All these Japs out here," cried Jed. "Half of them are probably spies."

"It's not only Japs," said Marlowe.

"You don't suppose they'll try to raid the Coast?" Jed had caught something ominously cold in the tone of her voice. "I was thinking of Mae," he added shakily.

"It's a mighty big old Pacific Ocean," Marlowe said. "You would know that if you'd ever sailed on it."

"That brings up something." Jed forced a laugh. "Something I was thinking about driving home from the mountains . . . What would you think of a nice big cruising boat for a wedding present? After the war naturally." Jed forced a laugh. "This war won't last forever . . . But it fits right in with the new Linda Milton picture. Merle and I sketched it out last week . . . Of course we were just thinking of preparedness. Joe takes the Army and Louy the Navy and little Malcolm, the one with the glasses, astonishes everybody by getting into the Marines . . . The boarder who pretended to be such a legionnaire, he turns out to be a Nazi spy . . . Of course little Linda turns him in. Maybe we can work in a Jap . . . You have to make things simple for the masses. If I can wangle a small cut of the gross this picture sure will get us into the upper brackets."

Marlowe wasn't looking at him. "I may go into war work," she said. Her voice was muffled as she leaned into the refrigerator to put back the plate of turkey. "I'm beating my brains out trying to decide."

"But what better war work than Russian Relief?"

She started to yawn. "I'm going to bed."

"There's no reason," said Jed haltingly, "why we shouldn't get married right away." He put his hand on her shoulder to turn her face toward his.

Marlowe brushed off his hand. "I want to be alone tonight," she said. "I haven't been sleeping well lately. I just can't seem to sleep." Before he could open his mouth she was gone.

Jed walked up and down the kitchen for a while, smoking a sourtasting cigarette with a frown on his forehead. Then he switched out the light and went upstairs to his bedroom where the covers were turned down on only one of the twin beds. God he hated to be alone. He did his setting up exercises. He took a shower. Still he couldn't sleep. Staring at the ceiling he lay wondering what Marlowe was thinking, sleepless too in her housekeeper's room at the end of the corridor.

At the studio everything was disrupted for the next few weeks. Draft calls. Enlistments. People taking their families to Arizona. Civil Defense. The lawn grew untended and turned brown under Jed's window since the Japanese gardeners had been removed from restricted areas. Weeds sprang up in the flower beds. Jed's career seemed suddenly to be standing still. Work dragged on the new Linda Milton picture. Merle Redmond who was of draft age spent most of his time in San Francisco trying to get into Navy public relations. Air raid precautions. Everybody was jumpy. After the Japanese submarine shelled Santa Barbara Herman D. Speyer took to keeping a car loaded with camping equipment in the parking lot ready to drive him up into the mountains at the first sound of an alert. Jed spent the days fidgeting at his typewriter writing and rewriting cute sayings for Linda. Crunched up scratch paper filled his wastebasket. It all seemed too silly.

It was a relief when he heard Sam's bland and friendly voice on the phone one afternoon. Sam was telling him that there was going to be a little gathering of a few friends of the Political Association out at the Collins Ranch. V. F. Calvert was living out there in solitary state while the Collinses were off on some damn fool wild goose chase investigating the civil liberties of the relocated Japs. They might as well use the facilities of the ranch. Sam and Maisie would pick Jed up at the lot that afternoon after five.

"You will be alone," said Sam. His words had a metallic edge. "Understand?"

When they turned off the highway onto the chattering gravel of the drive that wound between the orange grove and the lawn, Jed was surprised at the number of cars parked in front of the long stone house. There were towncars and sports models. A Mexican looking character was slumped asleep with his hat over his eyes in the seat of a dusty old Ford roadster. Next to it Jed recognized V. F. Calvert's out of date black coupé, a chevy iridescent with age.

V. F. Calvert himself came out to meet them under the heavy keystone over the front door. He looked thoroughly at home. He'd taken off his jacket. He wore a corduroy vest. Red sleeve garters held up his shirtsleeves. He greeted them almost jovially. There was an unexpectedly mischievous smile on the thin mouth that held the meerschaum pipe. "The mice have put the bell on the cat," he said. "Ve have sent away the Filipino. Come in."

Puffing portentously on his meerschaum V. F. Calvert led the way down the hall. Jed followed behind Sam's and Maisie's broad waddling forms. In the halflight of the huge livingroom he could see above people's heads ruddy reflections from the open fire flickering on the ceiling. There were so many people crowded together under the elkhorns that he couldn't see the fireplace. The room echoed with talk. The first face that turned toward him from the edge of the group was Bob Dunlap's. Jed hurried up to him with outstretched hand.

"Bob, I'll be damned."

"Fancy meeting you here," Bob answered, keeping his face straight. "In New York they're all saying you've sold out to the interests."

"Protective coloration," Jed stammered. "I hear you're making pretty big money yourself."

"They buy in from time to time . . ." Bob began to let the corners of his mouth curve up into a smile. "But a guy doesn't have to stay bought." Bob's bulging eyes were looking Jed up and down. "And to think when I knew you, Jed, you were a brighteyed curlyhaired lad."

"You still look like the thin man at the circus," said Jed pertly.

Bob's whole expression began to change. It was as if he were recognizing his old friend for the first time. He was really grinning now. "Still the same insulting old sonofabitch," he cried. They began slapping each other on the back. "To think that we should both end up on the same side of the fence . . . Why Jed when I first saw you come in I thought I'd gotten into the wrong church. You must meet the new missus."

He reached out a long arm and drew toward him a lankhaired woman in tweeds. Her hands were in the pockets of her norfolk jacket. She kicked out her feet and flung her shoulders about when she moved. As soon as she caught sight of Jed she threw her arms around him.

"J. E. D. Morris," she exclaimed in a twanging cockney accent. "You are the celebrity I've most wanted to meet . . . I'm thoroughly familiar with your magnificent war work . . . Allow me to introduce you to Colonel Buikov of the Russian Purchasing Commission."

She started poking at the elbow of a tall man in a khaki uniform with massive red and silver epaulettes. When the tall man turned Jed found himself looking into gray eyes set far apart above high cheekbones. The face looked startlingly like N. Roberts'.

Out of the corner of his eye Jed noticed that Sam Faust with his head tilted was watching him through the upper part of his bifocals.

"Glad to meet you Colonel." Jed managed to keep any look of recognition out of his face.

The colonel clicked his heels, gave half a bow and thrust out a large hand. "Meester Morris, eet is especially to breeng to you gratitude of heroic Russian people that I have come." When he smiled a steel tooth flashed in the firelight. There was no mistaking that tooth. It was N. Roberts.

Jed had begun to mumble something about not having gotten started yet, when he heard Curly Bryant's voice rise shrill out of the babble of voices in front of the fireplace: "This is the time we have waited for all our lives."

Colonel Buikov turned his broad back on her. "No improvisations." His voice was a bark. "Dollars, transport, muneetions."

"What was that?" With his hand cupped behind his ear Carl Humphries who had been leaning on a corner of the mantel thrust his bald skull into the conversation, "Communications. That is what we are organizing."

"Comrade Humphries," began Jed in an awed tone. Humphries gave Jed a suspicious sideways glance and stepped in between him and Colonel Buikov. As Jed let himself be nudged away from the group round the fireplace he could hear Carl Humphries' hard insistent voice: "Communications are the brains and nervous system of the country . . . That is the importance of our work out here. Mass communication. Motion pictures are the mind of the masses. Through the war effort we move into radio. We eliminate fascists from the newspaper workers' unions, we install progressives in the writers' organizations and the projected authors' authority. By the time this war is over we shall have captured the brains of the nation. For the first time we can see emerging the outlines of a Soviet America."

Colonel Buikov shrugged his epaulettes. "Nothing iss to interfere with the efficient production of munitions of war," he said harshly. "Please." He turned on his heel and tramped in his heavy boots toward the brilliant light in the diningroom door.

"He brought out a crew from the consulate with vodka and caviar," Lew Golton was whispering in Jed's ear. "It's a change from the old days." He grinned into Jed's face. The grin faded into a sneer. "But you wouldn't know about the old days. While guys like me were getting cracked on the head with the ordinary working stiffs out on the picket line you were always in the upper brackets Jed, sleeping with the millionaire dames . . ."

Jed tried to follow the crowd into the diningroom but Lew had a grip on his arm.

Lew was talking out of the corner of his mouth. "Come

over here you slippery bastard. I want to talk to you." He still had a smile on his face; it was just Lew acting tough, Jed told himself. Lew led him into the space between a bookcase and the mantel. "Some change from that dump over a downtown grocery store with the cops at our heels," Lew said glancing up and down the long room with its redwood furniture and its oriental rugs and the suits of armor flanking the door to the hall in the flickering firelight. He drew in the breath through his flat nostrils and pulled his mouth tight. "Jed I don't give a damn about this kinda stuff. Remember that clean little kitchen and the little Mexican girls? Rosita married a Mexican comrade . . . That's not the thesis now. Did you hear what Carl said about an authors' authority? Carl oughtn't to go off half cocked like that, but Carl's gotten so deaf you can't argue with him . . . Well we're suggesting your name to head it up, see? Got to have somebody whose skirts are clean. We got a good gang in journalism, we got the right guys working into the communications industry, telegraphists, radio technicians. If we can get that damn fool Roy Monks and his outfit out of the filmwriters we'll be sitting pretty there too . . . I know you want Roy Monks' job when we get him out, but you can't have it. You just remember this authors' authority may be bigger yet." Lew was looking searchingly into Jed's face. His eyes were narrow slits. He had his fists clenched as if he wanted to punch him in the jaw. "I've known you since you were a pup Jed and I've always been scared you'd rat on us . . . You watch your ps and qs and you'll go places."

Jed felt his cheeks going cold. His throat was dry. He moistened his lips with his tongue.

"Come on," shouted Lew, "let's try a spot of the Russian potato juice. Cheer up, you louse. Buikov's giving us the full treatment . . . just like we were a board of directors . . . And do they fall for it in Washington!"

Laughing over his shoulder he led the way into the diningroom. "Vodka and caviar have done more for the movement in six months than all our political and trade union work put together."

In the long diningroom the crystal chandeliers were blazing. Jed followed Lew's broad shoulders as he elbowed a path to the edge of the table. The Collinses' best china and glass and all their Peruvian silver dishes were laid out on a lace cloth. Everything was piled with caviar and cold fish and mayonnaise and cucumbers. A pair of flaxenhaired men with broad pale faces wearing illfitting gray business suits were hurrying about filling up the small glasses from long bluegreen bottles. At the head of the table flanked by Carl Humphries and Curly Bryant who, Jed noticed, had a fresh permanent wave and wore a new pale blue polkadot dress with frilly sleeves, Colonel Buikov was calling out toasts with military precision. At the foot of the table V. F. Calvert sat placidly smoking his meerschaum pipe with a glass of beer in front of him. Jed's eyes traveled over the rapt faces of Bob Dunlap and his wife across the table and Professor Silver's scraggly beard and Fred Walton's and Gehring Weeks' furrowed brows. Alec Marks looked thoroughly out of place. There were a number of men and women Jed didn't know.

"The Geroic Red Army!" shouted Buikov.

Everybody drank.

"The Patriotic War!" brayed Professor Silver in his goaty treble.

"Fordizatzia! American Assembly Line Urrah," shouted Colonel Buikov.

"Rifles for the Red Army!"

"Fighting Planes for the Soviets!"

"A Soviet America!" shouted Carl Humphries louder than anyone.

Colonel Buikov's eyes, flaring like alcohol flame, were on Jed's face. "Please," he lifted a spread hand for silence. He spoke in Russian to one of the flaxenhaired men, who immediately began to drag a bundle wrapped in burlap out of a corner of the room. While the attendants were unwrapping a large oriental rug, Colonel Buikov was making a pleasant speech about how the grateful workers of Soviet Armenia had woven this rug specially as a present for the genial chairman of Russian War Relief in California. "Meester Morris, workers, peasants, partisans, soldiers with arms in their hands to defend Soviet power against treacherous fascist invader all salute war relief in America and chairman, Meester Morris. Alaverdi. Prosit."

While everybody drank the toast the two attendants hoisted the rolledup rug and laid it across Jed's arms. "To a Soviet America," roared Carl Humphries from the end of the table.

Jed, still holding the rug and trying not to spill the vodka out of the glass in his hand, was just opening his mouth to say a few words of thanks when a scuffle broke out in a corner of the room. Jed dropped his rug, set down his glass, and followed Lew toward the noise.

Two men were dragging the Collinses' Filipino houseboy out from behind the screen that hid the kitchen door. One of Colonel Buikov's men brushed past Jed with an automatic in his hand. The Filipino's yellow face was beaded with sweat. His black hair was in his eyes. He was half out of his white jacket squirming in the grip of two Mexicans while the Russian poked his gun in his stomach. Lew Golton stood over him with his fists clenched.

"Pepe call Miguelito," Lew was talking through clenched teeth. "We can hold him. If he tries to run let him have it."

One of the Mexicans ran out softfooted through the door into the livingroom. "I got a guy out in the car will settle him."

"Easy does it Lew." Sam Faust sidled his way into the middle of the ring of faces. He had taken a little pad and a pencil out of his pocket and was taking charge of the proceedings with the air of a police magistrate. "Now, you, tell us what you are doing here."

The Filipino tried to smile. "Mr. Faust you know me. Serafino Sanchez, Mrs. Collins' houseboy. I serve you many times."

"It was understood you were going into L.A. for the night."

"Ascared, Mr. Faust, ascared they might pick me up for a Jap."

Colonel Buikov gave a command in Russian. The automatic vanished. The two flaxenhaired attendants went back to their work of circulating the vodka bottles. Smiling blandly Colonel Buikov turned his back and returned to the head of the table. The Filipino pulled a hand free and tried to brush the hair out of his eyes.

"No you don't," shouted Lew. Now he was giving orders to a sallow heavy shouldered individual in a straw hat. "Tie him up Miguelito . . . truss him up like a turkey." Pepe was bringing the cord and burlap off the oriental rug. "Sam," Lew whispered, "I better get this guy out of here. Miguelito can run him across the border. The comrades in Tia Juana will see he don't come back."

"And how about the United States Army?" Sam asked

scornfully. "You let me handle this. Serafino, I suppose you've got papers."

"I work for Mr. Collins five years. Before Mr. Smith in Pasadena. I have every reference," said the Filipino eagerly. "Always these days I carry all papers."

"Give me his papers," said Sam.

Miguelito frisked the Filipino in professional style and handed Sam a dogeared wad of documents out of the inside pocket of his white jacket.

"These might easily be forged." Sam looked up through the upper part of his bifocals. "The man is not an American citizen. He may well be a Japanese spy . . . Lew suppose you and your Mexican comrades run him into L.A. and turn him in to the G-men. They'll take care of him. It'll take him some time to talk his way out of Santa Anita."

The man was crying. "Mr. Collins," he sobbed.

"Mr. Collins," said Sam slowly and precisely, "will be very lucky if he stays out of jail himself, the way he's taking the side of the Japs . . . Lew, put this trash in the fire. He won't need it where he's going . . . There is no question in my mind that the man is a Japanese spy, eavesdropping for military information. He may well be working for the Nazis too."

"I am loyal Philippine national . . . I want to become American citizen," the man cried.

"Tell that to the F.B.I.," said Lew.

"A likely story," Jed heard Bob Dunlap's voice from the back of the room.

"The slant eyes," intoned his wife in her very English voice.

"The Mongolian fold," quavered Professor Silver. "Unmistakable."

300

"Gimme back," the Filipino started to screech. "Gimme!" One of the Mexicans clapped his hand over his mouth.

Whistling like a small boy Lew strolled into the living-room with the bundle of papers. Jed followed him and stood frozen in his tracks in the doorway while he watched Lew toss the bundle into the fire. Still whistling, Lew stood on the hearth and carefully stirred the curling blackening papers with the poker.

"Don't matter what he tells 'em now," said Lew out of the corner of his mouth as he gave the black ashes a last poke. "They won't believe it."

From behind him Jed could hear the hubbub of voices and Colonel Buikov's bark: "Please. The Geroic Defenders of Leningrad."

Out of the corner of his eye as Jed walked back shakily toward the table he saw the Mexicans carry the squirming houseboy trussed up like a carpet in cords and burlap out of the room.

"Friends and comrades," Carl Humphries was shouting from the end of the table, "this proves how vigilant we must be to defend the workers of America against the treacherous fascist foe. This war has brought about an alliance between the Soviet people and the American people which in the end will culminate through a union of the progressive forces of the world in a Soviet America . . . You will all join me," he added in a hollow solemn voice, "in singing the *International.*"

Not many of them knew the tune but they all sang:

Arise ye slaves who know starvation!
Shake off the curse that binds the earth!

Jed threw back his head and sang with the rest.

301

Jed's ears still rang with the workers' hymn when he drove his car into the garage at Canary Cottage. He looked anxiously for Marlowe's light. She was still up. Mae's light was out. The rest of the house was dark. Jed ran lightly up the back stairs and knocked on the door of the housekeeper's room. Marlowe slowly, as if reluctantly, opened the door. She wore her red dressing gown. She had a highball in her hand. "Dutch courage," she explained, with a deprecating smile. "The war news gets me down."

As Jed strode into the room, he gave one glance at the headlines on the afternoon papers piled on her desk, and fixed his eyes on hers. He felt his eyes were glowing. He felt on top of the world. Tonight he was going to carry her off her feet. "Marlowe," he said. "Look at me . . . Look at me like you used to sometimes . . . I've had a wonderful evening . . . I was presented with a testimonial by a member of the Russian Purchasing Commission for our work. I wish you'd been there. It makes you feel good to know your work is appreciated."

"What was it?" asked Marlowe.

"A magnificent oriental rug . . . By gum I forgot it in the excitement. It will be all right. It's out at the Collins Ranch." He threw himself down full length on the daybed in front of the window. "Golly I'm tired. Wouldn't you fix a poor guy a highball?"

Marlowe fished some icecubes out of the whitemetal bucket on the corner of her desk, fizzed some soda from the siphon into the whisky and brought him the drink.

"What was the excitement?" she asked.

Jed lifted himself on his elbow and took a gulp of whisky and soda. "Caught a Japanese spy," he said ". . . or at least a red hot suspect."

"Where did they take him?" asked Marlowe.

"Turned him over to the G-men in downtown L.A. I guess . . . Oh Marlowe," he sat up on the edge of the couch and drew her down beside him. "It's so wonderful . . . you and me working together. We were all at sixes and sevens for a while and now, we both want the same things."

"Maybe," she said. She sat gingerly on the edge of the couch. When he tried to draw her to him her muscles stiffened. She pulled herself away. "Jed," she began, "I've been wanting to talk to you for a long time. I can't help it. I've gotten kind of soft on you . . . But I've got to get into war work. Why don't you go into the Army or Navy or something? Lots of men older than you are getting in. I have friends who could help you if I was only sure. It would be a way of making a break from all the nonsense you've gotten mixed up with in this town."

"Sure of what?" asked Jed coldly.

All of a sudden she had her face in her hands. She sat beside him sobbing little dry hard sobs.

Jed sat beside her looking down at his feet. He never could have imagined Marlowe breaking down and crying. He didn't know what to say.

"I'm so sick of playing hide and seek all day," she whimpered.

This was the moment he'd been waiting for. Now she would really be his. Feeling warm and loving and masterful he pressed his face against her neck. "But Marlowe, don't you see. We've been in war work right along. We're all together to defeat war and fascism. Just this evening a man told me that the work I've been doing—the work we've been doing, you and me—was the equivalent of killing a million Germans . . . I lead a dedicated life. You know that. Relief. The Filmwriters. Now it has been suggested that I head up a new organization . . . organize all the authors in the country dedicated to destroying war and fascism . . . organize them for their own protection against the exploiting publishers . . . The reactionaries, the isolationists, the enemies of the working class can damn well keep their writings to themselves. The brains of the country will be with us . . . This work is a damn sight more important than getting into uniform and trying to shoot off a gun. I'm not a good shot. I wouldn't be good at it . . . When you organize the brains you can make the rest of the people do what you want."

"That's what I tell myself sometimes, suppose you were right. That's why I can't sleep sometimes, saying just suppose you were right." She was talking through her hands pressed over her face. "I've got to pull myself together." She sat up straight.

She was wiping her eyes with her handkerchief, dabbing her face with quick careful catlike gestures. She turned toward him smiling. "I'd rather be a nurse . . . I'm looking into that . . . There must be quick training courses somewhere."

"I need a nurse right now," he whispered. He kissed her. She kissed him back.

"The lad has big ideas," she said. Suddenly she was helplessly limp in his arms. Her mouth was meeting his mouth. "Marlowe, I love you," he was whispering. "I love you more than anybody I ever loved anywhere . . . anybody . . . anywhere."

She was still asleep when he got up. With her light wavy hair all over the pillow she looked like a little girl asleep. She must be about his age, how could she still look so young? Hardly breathing he leaned over and kissed her very gently

304

on the cheek. Then he draped her dressing gown around him, bundled up his clothes and hurried up the corridor to his bedroom. It was not seven yet; Mae never woke up early; the maid didn't come till seven thirty, but still he felt furtive. When he got to his master's bedroom he pulled up the venetian blinds on the front french windows to let in the sun. Standing there naked in the sunlight with the dressing gown drenched with her fragrance over his shoulders he felt the happiness of the night still glowing all over him.

He looked out of the window at the early light on the trees. Something sent a chill down his spine. Out past the giltedged palms he caught sight of a battered old black chevy parked against the curb at the corner. His heart started to beat fast. No it couldn't be. What the hell could V. F. Calvert be doing out there that early? As Jed stood in the window gnawing on his cheeks he began to remember long ago the french window in a hotel room. Looking out over the sea. Little fragments of memory began to group themselves into a picture. That horrid Anna Glazunova panting in his ear and pointing with a crooked finger at the snubnosed freighter with the tiny patch of red astern headed round Cape Spartel on the ruffled bay. "Cher ami it is finished." He couldn't remember just what had happened, only the terror and the Russian woman in her eveningdress lying sobbing on the bed. Silly, overwork. Pull yourself together, he told himself and went into the bathroom to shave.

His hand shook. Getting old. Can't take it, he kidded himself leering into his brown eyes in the mirror. He was in a hurry to get shaved. He nicked his chin with his safety razor. It took him the longest time to stop the bleeding. He couldn't find his septic stick. At last he managed to patch a small piece of toilet paper on the cut, hurried into his clothes

305

and out the front door. The black chevy was hidden by a bunch of bamboos. He'd just walk up to the corner to make sure it wasn't V. F. Calvert's car.

As he walked toward the car he noted with relief that there seemed to be nobody sitting in it. There were thousands of black chevies like that, he told himself. An electrician who did odd jobs round these houses had a black chevy. No sense letting yourself get jumpy. When he heard Sam Faust's voice right behind him he couldn't help jumping.

"All right, step in. We've got to have a talk."

V. F. Calvert's face was looking at him yellow and twisted through the stains on the windowglass.

"Early risers," Jed said. He was trying to get his breath. "Why don't you come in and get some breakfast?"

"Come along," Sam held the door open. V. F. Calvert's yellow teeth showed but he wasn't smiling. "This isn't friendly, this is Party work." Jed slid into the front seat. Sam closed the door after him. Jed could hear him puff a little as he climbed into the back and the jangling of broken springs as he settled himself on the ragged upholstery. V. F. Calvert drove off without opening his mouth. Taken for a ride. The thought galloped like vigilantes through Jed's head. They are going to kill me.

"How about cutting the comedy, Sam?" As Jed turned he found himself staring at V. F. Calvert's long profile against the bright morning light. The man wasn't smiling but the lower lip hung away from the gritted teeth. The man was scared. As scared as he was. Jed puffed out his chest. "This is my busy time," he said in the tone he used to his secretary at the studio. "I've got to go home and get my breakfast."

"Just any place V.F.," said Sam suavely from the back.

"Conspiratorial methods," Jed whispered sarcastically as V. F. Calvert drove through a dusty back road and out into an abandoned building lot. The car bumped to a stop in the long dry grass behind a tangle of fallen bougainvillea that still clung to the wreckage of the porch of a house that had been recently burned. The grass was littered with charred boards and broken brick. "You'll run over a nail and get a flat tire if you're not careful."

"This is a matter you've been warned about before." Sam sat bolt upright on the back seat and spluttered into Jed's ear. "In your case expulsion wouldn't mean too much I suppose . . . but I think you know enough about how this town works to know that your contract will not be renewed. You haven't seen George Pastor getting many jobs lately, now have you? We are not as strong as we're going to be, but we are strong enough to give quitters their comeuppance. Just exactly what are you planning to do for a living?"

"But there isn't any Party any more. We're just an association," stammered Jed. "A man has to live his own life . . . Look at all I've done for the movement."

V. F. Calvert had pulled a sheet of folded typewriter paper out of his pocket. "Read this," he said. In spite of himself Jed's eyes followed the smeary carbon:

> *Tompkins, Jane Marlowe, 43, divorced wife of Jeremy Tompkins, Santa Barbara sportsman and playboy reputed to have run through several millions left him by his father. Since her divorce, which coincided with Tompkins' reaching the end of his resources, this woman has been in extreme financial difficulties, but continues to be seen well dressed and evidently in funds in her old haunts. An occasional visitor at San Simeon in the company of notorious bundists and isolationists and reactionaries*

of every type, tireless in their opposition to the Soviet Union, such as Augustine Willis, R. S. Trammers, J. Schulz, etc., etc. Seen recently at a Monterey Hotel in the company of agent so-andso of the F.B.I. . . .

"The agent's name is blank. I suppose they don't know it yet. I read from the report of the Control Commission. Shall I read their report on you?"

"They've got the wrong party," said Jed. His throat fluttered so he could hardly get the words out. "Give me time and I'll prove it to you." He snatched the sheet out of V. F. Calvert's hand, crumpled it up and dropped it under his feet.

V. F. Calvert had to slide his thin cropped head round the wheel to reach for the crumpled paper. He picked the paper up and with his tongue between his jagged teeth smoothed it out carefully and respectfully on his knee.

"We have been empowered by the Control Commission to talk this matter over with you reasonably," Sam said. "This isn't playacting. This is for keeps. You know that."

"I know of no case," V. F. Calvert added in his schoolroom voice, "where the findings of the Control Commission have not been substantially correct. The F.B.I. is taking advantage of our cooperation in wartime matters to plant spies on us. The woman is a federal agent."

Jed's hands were trembling so he had to clasp them round his knees. "What does that matter? We are all fighting the same war," he mumbled in a weak voice.

"The statement is inaccurate," said V. F. Calvert.

Jed twisted to and fro in the seat. He looked wildly back into Sam's face. Sam was speaking gently, molding his words with his curling lips. "Now Jed . . . we know you're not the kind of man who blows his top over a broad. We all know you've got a bicycle. If you persist after a number of warnings in associating with agents of reaction it can mean only one thing."

"Treason to the workers," said V. F. Calvert staring at the speedometer in front of him.

"Give me time to talk to her."

"The suspicion ought to be enough for any classconscious Party worker. Hell. One dame's as good as another. You told me so yourself," said Sam.

"Give me two days to prove she's O.K." Jed's voice broke. "I haven't had my breakfast. I can't think what to do on an empty stomach like this." He was so hoarse he was croaking.

"Five minutes," said V. F. Calvert. From his frayed sleeve he stuck a gunmetal wristwatch out under Jed's chin. "Give him five minutes."

Jed's eyes were staring out through the grimy windshield at the dust that whitened the magenta mass of bougainvillea in front of him.

"The time comes to every man," Sam's voice hissed behind his ear, "when he has to prove whether he is with us or against us. The discarded instrument is thrown out on the trash pile. Nobody hears much about him any more."

Sam stopped talking. V. F. Calvert folded his thin hands under the wheel and sat with his eyes on his wristwatch. Jed could hear Sam's wheezy breathing from the back seat and the sound of cars on some distant thoroughfare.

When he couldn't stand the silence any more he asked in a low rasp, "What's today, Sam?"

"Friday."

Jed cleared his throat. "Do you suppose you and Maisie could drive Mae to the Springs for the weekend? You could pick her up at the school. That would ease the shock. Would Maisie take care of her?"

"Maisie'll do anything, you know that."

Jed cleared his throat again. "All right Sam. I only consider it a suspicion." Everything was blurred before his eyes. He was panting. He was drenched with cold sweat.

"A man of your importance to the movement," Sam began—his words were like warm oil—"must be above suspicion."

"You are my lawyer," Jed said. A feeling of importance swept over him. "You handle it. Go talk to her. Tell her I've been taken ill . . . I shan't be able to go to the studio . . . I might even have to go to a hospital . . . Explain to her that . . . that her employment is terminated. Be very tactful. If she cares she'll understand. What a thing to do to a man."

Jed felt Sam's small fat hands padding gently on his back. He felt himself slump over against V. F. Calvert's shoulder. He couldn't get his breath. "This might be a heart attack." His voice was a gasp. "Take me some place where I can lie down." He closed his eyes. His ears hummed.

"Drive around to our house, V.F." he heard Sam saying in a casual everyday tone as if nothing had happened at all. "Maisie'll have breakfast for us . . . Maisie don't know a thing." The words hissed through his lips. "Don't forget that."

When the time came to climb out of the car at the Fausts', Jed's knees couldn't seem to hold him up. Sam helped him to a seat under a beach umbrella beside the swimmingpool. The sunlight flashing off the water stabbed his eyes. Maisie came running out of the house all concerned.

"Need a checkup . . . Heart trouble," Jed murmured feebly. "Kind of a fainting fit. Better call a doctor."